John Harris was born in 1916 and grew up in South Yorkshire. He became a journalist and worked for the *Rotherham Advertiser* and the *Sheffield Telegraph*, joining the RAF as a corporal attached to the South African Air Force during the Second World War and returning to journalism when the war ended.

He became a full-time author after the success of his 1953 novel *The Sea Shall Not Have Them,* which was made into a film. He wrote more than eighty works of fiction and non-fiction, including books under pseudonyms Max Hennessy and Mark Hebden. As Hebden he created the crime series featuring Inspector Pel, which his daughter Juliet continued after his death in 1991.

John Harris
COVENANT
With
DEATH

sphere

SPHERE

First published in Great Britain in 1961 by Hutchinson
First paperback edition published in 1969 by Arrow
This reissue published in 2014 by Sphere

Copyright © John Harris 1961

Foreword © Louis de Bernières 2014
Historical Note with kind permission of Andrew Jackson

The moral right of the author has been asserted.

A CIP catalogue record for this book
is available from the British Library.

ISBN 978-0-7515-5712-1

Typeset in Sabon LT Std by Palimpsest Book Production Limited,
Falkirk, Stirlingshire

Printed and bound in Great Britain by
CPI Group (UK) Ltd, Croydon, CR0 4YY

Papers used by Sphere are from well-managed forests and other
responsible sources.

MIX
Paper from
responsible sources
FSC
www.fsc.org   FSC® C104740

Sphere
An imprint of
Little, Brown Book Group
100 Victoria Embankment
London EC4Y 0DY

An Hachette UK Company
www.hachette.co.uk
www.littlebrown.co.uk

An Introduction
by Louis de Bernieres

John Harris was an author who was quite extraordinarily prolific. He wrote a book almost every year from 1951 onwards, and in many years published more. He wrote under three names: Mark Hebden, Max Hennessey and his real one. In addition, he was a cartoonist. My reaction to seeing the list of his publications was one of sheer astonishment. According to his son, Max, he treated writing as a proper job and started work at nine on weekdays, ready to 'burst out of his office' at five. Even so, his fecundity is worthy of a tropical jungle.

The foundation of his success was *The Sea Shall Not Have Them* which was published in 1953, and subsequently filmed, which enabled him to become a full-time writer. Thereafter, unlike most authors who have a big success, he never took his eye off the ball. My father knew him in West Wittering and remembers that he was 'very sedentary', which would certainly suit a fabulously productive writer, but this was right at the end of his life. Harris's children remember him as walking so fast that they could not keep up with him. He earned a pilot's licence in his fifties, and somehow even got caught up in a riot in Paris.

Covenant with Death appeared in 1961 and is a classic. It

has the hallmarks of many of the war books published in the 1950s, which I devoured in the 1960s when I was in my teens. That is, it is intelligent without being pretentious and is both readable and compelling. It is great literature without ever being 'literary'. The style is close to what Roland Barthes called 'Writing Degree Zero', a style so plain and clear that it is the style of having no style. Harris is sparing with adjectives and adverbs, except when there is action to be vividly described. You will not often even find the word 'very'. A great deal of his writing consists of dialogue, which gives much of the book a casual and jaunty air. The only infelicity I have found – the pleonasm 'incredulous disbelief' – should have been picked up by whoever was the editor or proofreader.

The story follows the trajectory of characters who are completely believable, and about whom we care, none of whom is particularly out of the ordinary. All of these war books are in fact about love – the kind of deep, intimate, asexual love almost unknown to most of us, which we call 'comradeship' without understanding how profound that is. The Australian concept of 'mateship' comes close. No one can understand how war is tolerable to those caught up in it, unless they understand that one's primary motive is to not let down one's comrades, and that a bond develops even between those widely separated by rank, which has no equivalent in civilian life. These are the friends you would die for if you could save them, who you will value all your life, and for whom you will grieve all your life if they are killed.

This is the literature of the ordinary person made extraordinary by war. It compares with Nicholas Monsarrat's *The Cruel Sea*, a classic ten years older, about civilians who became sailors on the Atlantic Convoys. It is a book that teaches the serious writer how to write about violence, because the only way to do that is to state it plainly, otherwise the moral force is lost. Another obvious comparison is with Erich Maria Remarque's *All Quiet on the Western Front*.

The difference is that Remarque served in the trenches and Monsarrat served on the Atlantic convoys – they were writing about what they intimately knew and vividly remembered. Whereas Harris, although not a stranger to personal heroism (he once saved the life of a drowning boy in Switzerland), was born in the year in which the story of his novel culminates and served in the RAF in the Second World War.

Covenant with Death is a miracle of authenticity. Harris was no doubt familiar with the stories of the various 'Pals' regiments; for example, the Sandringham detachment from the Royal estate in Norfolk, which appeared to vanish into thin air at Gallipoli. The Turks maintained that a mist came down on them as they advanced, and when it lifted the Sandringham detachment had disappeared. However, the fact is that Harris grew up hearing the stories of the Somme. His father took part, as did his father-in-law, brother-in-law and four uncles. His brother-in-law and one uncle were gassed, two uncles lost their legs and another was killed. When Harris was a newspaper man on the *Sheffield Telegraph* he worked amongst the very people who had volunteered for the Sheffield City Battalion – the heroes of this book. *Covenant with Death* is very evidently full of genuine history and biography; it would have been impossible that a novel as realistic and detailed as this could have been purely invented.

I do not want to repeat clichés about 'the futility of war'. The fact is that the Battle of the Somme was meticulously planned in the face of very real difficulties. For example, having to work alongside the French army which, because of the fear of mutiny, was committed only to defence; also, the need to send troops to Italy when the Italian front collapsed. It is, I think, unfair to talk of lions led by donkeys. Furthermore, great victories nearly always depend upon surprise, and this was the first war in history where complete surprise was always impossible. The aircraft up above at all times meant that one always knew what the other side was up to. This is why the Germans did not reach Paris at the outset of the war, and in my judgement it is the reason why the Western Front became bogged down. Under these conditions it was, as Von Moltke once said, inevitable that 'one's battle plan survives up to exactly that moment when one encounters the enemy'.

I also think that we have paid too much attention to the war poets, eloquent though they are. Most people did feel that the war was worth it. My grandfather was maimed in that war, and ultimately committed suicide, but he did not doubt that the war had been just, and was proud to have fought in it. His generation understood it as 'The War for Civilisation'; I think of it as a war for democracy. Germany would never have gone to war if it had been a democracy, and would not have done so again if it had remained one. Harris seems to leave the judgement about 'futility' open, as a good novelist probably should.

The whole point of the novel lies in the thirty pages of the last two chapters: a genuine, shocking climax that I do not think has been equalled elsewhere. The penultimate chapter is a passage of relentlessly sustained, virtuosic writing, describing in detail, without repetition and with mounting crescendo, the first hours of the Battle of the Somme. It is difficult to read it without an awful feeling of dismay, horror and darkness invading the room where one sits. One can feel one's own bones shadowed darkly through the flesh.

The last chapter is a meditation upon what it all meant. Its last paragraph consists of a long list of reasons for fighting, is followed by two terse, verbless sentences, and a final one of only four words. They are like muffled blows on a kettle drum at the end of a symphonic tempest. This writing is masterly and the emotional effect devastating.

Louis de Bernières
June 2014

Author's Note

This book is based most clearly on facts, and to obtain them I have read almost everything possible on the subject by the men who were there, to whom I owe a great deal for their acute observation and their deep feeling for the period.

However, while the unit with which it is chiefly concerned is solidly founded on an actual one, it is still a work of fiction and the characters in it are fictitious; though some of those men, now growing old, from the city where I lived, who told me of their experiences with such amazing modesty, will inevitably recognise many of the incidents in the story. To those men also I am very much in debt.

Part One

We have made a covenant with death and with hell are we at agreement.

ISAIAH xxviii. 15

1

I shall remember that morning till the day I die. Not just the courage and the horror and the incredible strange beauty. Everything. The faith we had in our leaders and the pride we had in ourselves.

Even now, after all these years, I remember the feeling that was in us that we should succeed where others had failed, the naïve certainty that we were greater than our predecessors; that upon us rested the future of the world and because of this it was well worth all that we were facing; that we, because we'd been chosen for the task, walked among higher spheres than our fellow-men.

We were joined in spirit. We were each of us, that morning, only too well aware of the others around us; only too well aware of *their* faith, and *their* courage, and *their* certainty, too; and of the completeness of the company we were in, of its absolute welded oneness. That was what sustained us. It wasn't just me, Mark Fenner, I remember. It was *all of us*.

And to understand that you have to go back to the beginning, to the very first day we all came together, nearly two years before.

*

I was awake at six o'clock that first day.

Not that I'd slept much. I'd hardly closed my eyes. I put it down to excitement, in an effort to convince myself I wasn't too full of emotion or disturbed by what lay ahead of me.

I was a reporter on the *Post* at the time, and when the war came in August 1914 – this war we'd all been half-expecting for years – the only immediate difference I noticed was the sign outside Stahlers' teashop, behind the office, which used to supply the reporters and sub-editors with sardines on toast and pots of tea on battered tin trays. They were German-Swiss, the Stahlers, and the day after the war broke out there was a single card tied on the brass door handle just under the scratched advertisement for Oxo. *Under New Management*, it said firmly. In bold letters scrawled in blue crayon on the back of a Woodbine box – bold letters that let you know that there'd been no nonsense about it. The Germans were out, and the Swiss were in. That was all.

In London it was different. There, pacifist speakers in Trafalgar Square were being mobbed, and the mounted police had been called out. When Sir Edward Grey, the Foreign Secretary, had rejected the German demands, a crowd had surged to Buckingham Palace demanding to see the King and shouting, 'We want war!'

German Jews were putting up their shutters, and the nabobs of the West End were taking down the pictures of their German ancestors. The Americans had left in their nickel-plated cars, and the stock markets were unsteady because the arithmetic kings and diplomats were hurrying back to their capitals from Bad Ischl and the German spas with their cures incomplete. There'd been a run on the banks and the air had become electric. The tension had been so great in London that only a declaration of war could relieve it.

But that was London. They're a harder-headed people in the north and not so easily roused. Apart from Stahlers' sign, the crowds outside the food shops and the small groups of men in boaters and caps who ranged about the High Street for a day or two, apparently with nothing better to do than break into the '*Marseillaise*' and 'Rule, Britannia' from time to time, there didn't seem to be much difference from peace time. Occasionally you saw a woman with a taut face and a sniffling child – but not often – and now and then a Territorial in ill-fitting khaki going off to join his unit, probably a little drunk, with all his friends round him urging to give the Germans hell, or keep his head well down, or both.

The first squad of soldiers that appeared on the streets was cheered to the echo as they marched to the station, laden down with their equipment and their stiff new kit bags, their straps wrenching their khaki uniforms askew, their peaked bus conductors' caps clumsy and awkward on their heads. But there wasn't much else – just a heart-cry from the city industrialists that trade with France would never be the same again and that commerce with Germany would stop altogether. Up there in Yorkshire, steel and wool still seemed to be far more important than that Belgian and German and French boys were lying in crowded ditches along the flat Flanders fields, startled to find that the war they'd rushed to so eagerly, their cannon decorated lovingly with flowers by the girls, wasn't quite what they'd expected, and that they were dying and that the blood on their dusty hands was their own.

I was on holiday at Scarborough when my turn came. The resorts had been saying *Everything as usual* for days, in an effort to squeeze the last joyous ounce out of the summer trade before it finished for good, and they were still doing a booming business; and none of us thought that the rash of red, white and blue posters – *YOUR KING AND COUNTRY NEED YOU, your country calls on all unmarried men to enlist at once in the ranks of the Army* – referred to us. We hadn't private incomes, so we weren't commissionable types, we'd decided in the Reporters' Room of the *Post*, right from the beginning, and we knew we weren't the class they normally recruited the rank and file from in those days, so there seemed nothing to do but carry on as usual. It wasn't a desire to shirk. It was modesty or, perhaps more properly, lack of thought.

We hadn't got used to the idea of war in England, you see. The mobilisation notices hadn't dropped through the letterboxes in every street in the kingdom as they had in France. They hadn't taken away whole staffs and closed shops, and there'd been no groups of hairdressers and chefs marching down the Mall singing, no massed phalanxes of conscripts and Reservists tramping off to the stations under home-made banners to report to their regiments, as there had in Paris. Even the warships at Portsmouth didn't look very different from normal, because there were *always* warships at Portsmouth. All they'd done was take the covers off their guns, post submarine lookouts and keep their lights doused at night. We'd never experienced the day when millions of men had kissed their wives goodbye with dry lips and burned their letters as they had across the Channel. All *we'd* done was put a bobby on the German Embassy, while the *hoipolloi*, in a fit of entente-cordiale-ism and a revulsion of feeling against all things Prussian, had taken to drinking Vichy with their whisky instead of Apollinaris which came from Germany. Even the skirmishings in Belgium hadn't meant very much to us. We often wondered where Kitchener was going to get all the recruits he was said to be after. We never dreamt he meant *us*.

Mons changed all that. The news that British troops had at last come into action against the Germans had been cheered from one end of Scarborough promenade to the other. The result seemed a foregone conclusion. Wasn't one Englishman equal to two Germans, three Frenchmen and any amount of niggers?

But then there came this startling and unexpected news of disaster from some obscure little town in Belgium, and suddenly it was Englishmen who were fighting and dying in ditches along the Belgian roads; and the boys who were sitting staring at their own blood, their backs still marked by their unaccustomed packs, their behinds still galled by the rub-rub of the unfamiliar entrenching tools, probably came from our own northern city, maybe even from the same street.

Defeated British soldiers were struggling across France. Beaten units that were the remnants of famous regiments were straggling among the vast flood of retreating refugees whose household goods were packed into decrepit landaus and victorias and farmcarts and perambulators. Heat-exhausted men were stumbling behind army waggons pulled by worn horses that were still restless in their brand-new harness, limping into little towns in Belgium to tell their harrowing stories to scared correspondents. The churches were full of wounded, and the sons of noble families were sprawled dead in the dusty fields. Odd groups of men were trying to hold up whole squadrons of Uhlans; and footsore sleepless soldiers were going for days with nothing to eat. The Guards – even the Guards! – were being cut to pieces, dying to a man as they strove in the sunshine and the heat to stem the advance.

From the moment I read about Mons I had the sensation of being engaged in the war.

Disturbed and restless, I went to a cinema to stop myself thinking and found myself stumbling over Reservists in uniform who'd been pushed in there because there was no other accommodation, and were endeavouring to sleep in the aisles through the chatter of the audience. All down the alleys at the side they lay in dun-coloured heaps, huddling restlessly among their stacked equipment.

Outside, all along the front, brass bands were still blaring away in the parks and the crowds were out in their hundreds, listening to the whelk-stall owners shouting their wares over the screech of tram-wheels and the clatter of hooves. We were all mopping our faces, fanning ourselves with newspapers and wondering about Mons as we stared limply at the coloured-slide advertisements for little liver pills and drapery and motorcars. Then the lights went off and 'Let's All Go Down the Strand' faded out on a discord, and, instead of the film we'd expected, a girl appeared on the stage, unannounced, looking a bit like Vesta Tilley in a blue jacket and the baggy red trousers of a Zouave.

The orchestra gave a few preliminary chords and she set off with a rush into a patriotic song about the French marching off to war. It had a French chorus that she kept shouting in a brassy voice till it brought the house down.

> 'Allons, partons, belles,
> Partons, pour la guerre . . .'

She was accompanied by four more girls in red jackets who showed their teeth and chorused the song with her, and the crowd howled for more, and the men in the aisles, curled up under their greatcoats, sat up and started to whistle and applaud.

'Never mind the French!' they yelled. ''Ow about *us*?'

'You come down here, lady! We'll find room for you and your pals in *our* mob! You can kip alongside me, in fact!'

Someone started 'The Boys of the Bulldog Breed', and one of the soldiers called for a cheer for the King. Then we had three cheers for the French and three for the Russians and three for the Belgians, and three for all the others we thought were on our side but weren't so sure about, then three for the Army and three for the Navy and three for the flying men. Then the girl on the stage capped the lot by calling for three for Kitchener's volunteers, and the Reservists laughed and jeered and catcalled again.

Finally, spontaneously, without any chord from the orchestra, we started to sing the National Anthem and we all stood to attention as we'd none of us stood for years probably, while the little men in the pit below the stage sawed on their fiddles and tried to catch us up. My back seemed straighter than I ever remembered it. I felt six inches taller.

8

Carried away by the emotion in that electrically charged hall, the emotion of a great many young men all patriotically and suddenly determined to do their damnedest – die, if necessary – I pushed my way through the yelling audience and went straight out to buy a ticket back to where I'd come from.

I arrived home to find that someone had been up to the War Office with the idea of raising a battalion of selected volunteers from the city – so that the men who pushed you around as civilians could continue to push you around as soldiers, Locky Haddo said. Earl FitzJames, from Brentwood, who'd served in the South African War, had offered to take command until they could find somebody younger, and the following morning – this morning – there were to be fifteen hundred forms of declaration of willingness to serve waiting in the Town Hall Reception Rooms for signatures. I fully intended that mine was going to be among them.

I'd decided that there couldn't be anyone more fitted than I for soldiering. I was unmarried. I had no parents to consider. If anything happened to me there'd be no one to grieve. It all seemed so straightforward to me, as I worked it out quite coolly and remarkably cold-bloodedly. Of all the people I knew, I seemed to be the one with the most right to become a soldier.

I'd spent most of the night thinking about what I was in for. I kept seeing myself advancing with a line of other men across bullet-swept fields, pressing ahead with the battle flags while others crashed to the ground all around me. I saw my friends fall and I was there kneeling at their sides when they died. It never occurred to me that *I* might fall and they might be kneeling at *my* side.

Then, after a while, I started wondering what it must be like to be killed. Could I stand the pain? What would it be like to lose a limb or be mutilated or disfigured? There'd been an old boy who'd lived near my home when I was a child who'd been hit in the face at Spion Kop. He'd lost his nose and one eye and I'd had nightmares about him many a time. Now I began to see him again and wondered what it must be like to have to live with some dreadful disfigurement like that. Or what it must be like to be dead. Try as I might, I could only imagine darkness and cold and vast singing space, and the suggestion of an immense glowing glory.

I wasn't sorry when the alarm clock went off, though I'd wakened half a dozen times to look at it. When it finally did go, the harsh ringing made me jump a foot in the air.

For a long time I lay in bed staring at the wallpaper. A bright orange it was, I remember, with pagodas on it, and over the end of the bed there was the inevitable picture of *Love Locked Out* that always seemed to find its way into the spare bedroom. I felt warm and secure in the moment of indecision before electing to dress, and I found myself wondering what it must be like to be on campaign, sleeping on the ground with a single blanket over me and only the stars for a roof.

In the end I crept out of bed unwillingly and washed and shaved. I put on a clean collar and fastened it with my best gold pin that my mother had given me. Then, as I was searching for a fresh handkerchief, something made me look inside the family Bible they'd handed to me when my father died. It had a marker in it and it fell open at Isaiah, and I realised for the first time, as I saw the words my father had been reading right there in front of my eyes, that he must have known he was going to die.

We have made a covenant with death, it said sombrely, *and with hell are we at agreement.*

There was something forbidding about the words that I didn't care to ponder on and I slammed it to at once. The pages fell together with a soft plop, and I went downstairs feeling I'd seen the light or something.

Mrs Julius, my landlady, wasn't up and I prepared my own breakfast, sneaking into the larder and cooking myself a vast

10

meal of bacon and eggs. Since I was about to set off at any moment to march to Berlin, I felt that for once the tight-fisted old faggot could give me a decent feed.

By the time I'd finished, I'd forgotten all about the foreboding of Isaiah and was just a normal healthy young man full of food and energy and optimism. I studied myself in the mirror and came to the conclusion that I looked fit and sturdy, but not very handsome or martial, with black eyebrows as forbidding as Isaiah and a chin that seemed to resist every effort I ever made to scrape it clean. In the end, I decided that the Army probably wasn't very choosy, anyway, and I picked up my hat and left the house.

As I walked towards the tram stop on the corner of Morrelly Street, it came to me again, with a sudden strange force, that this wasn't a normal day. It wasn't eight-thirty and I wasn't going to the office. It was six-forty-five and, God being willing, I was going to sign my name on a paper that would give the King and all his generals the right to stand me up for someone else to shoot at and probably to kill.

Once again the strange dedicated feeling came over me. I seemed to be obsessed with death that morning, but curiously enough it hadn't a depressing effect on me. I felt vaguely elated, in fact.

At the tram stop I was surprised to meet Henny Cuthbert from next door.

He was a thin young man with a long sad horse-face who managed one of the small silversmith firms in the narrow streets behind the Town Hall. We didn't have much in common with each other, because he worked during the day and mostly I worked in the afternoon and evening, but we knew each other well and had been known to chase the same girl at church dances. He'd got his best suit on and a furry Homburg and he carried a gold-topped walking stick, but he didn't look as though he was going to work or round to the Methodist Church where he normally wore this get-up.

'You're early this morning,' I said, trying to keep the suspicion out of my voice.

Henny looked back at me aggressively. 'So are you, come to that,' he retorted.

'Am I?' I said. I was a little ashamed of the emotions that had stirred me to want to enlist and didn't want Henny to know of them. 'Oh, well,' I said. 'It's just one of those days. Things to do, you know.'

He looked anxious suddenly. 'What about this battalion they're talking of raising?' he said.

'What about it?'

'Thinking of joining?'

'I might.'

We were silent for a moment, looking at each other sheepishly, each suddenly mistrustful of the other, then Henny smiled shyly.

'I'm going down to the Town Hall,' he said. 'I'm going to sign on. I thought I'd better get there early. Where are *you* going?'

'Same place.'

'Oh!' Henny seemed worried, and we stood there, eyeing each other sideways and blinking in the sun, both of us wishing the tram would hurry up and put in its appearance.

I'd expected, setting off at that time, that I'd be way ahead of all others, and that there wouldn't be any chance of being left out. But, now that I'd seen Henny, I began to have my doubts. If Henny, whom I'd always considered over-cautious at the best of times, had considered it too, so, surely would hundreds of others. Immediately I began to be scared I'd be too late and that every one of the fifteen hundred forms would have been filled in before I arrived. Just then, it seemed too dreadful to consider being the fifteen-hundred-and-first. Henny seemed to be thinking the same way.

'Think we'll be on time?' he asked.

'Bound to,' I said, but I sounded more hopeful than I felt.

12

'Surely there won't be fifteen hundred of 'em as daft as we are to get up as early as this.'

'Think not?'

'Bet you a level Bradbury.'

When the tram came, one of the old ones with an open top, a rattletrap affair that sounded like an ironmonger's van and felt as though it had square wheels, we were borne into the city, both of us smoking furiously, silent because the clatter made conversation impossible, both fidgeting restlessly, while the wooden seat kept bashing us in the small of the back every time we crossed a set of points.

There were one or two other young men on board – all of them about our age, I noticed – and it dawned on me then that they, too, had conceived the same stratagem as I had, and I began to get more fidgety than ever. Dropping off on the Common, Henny and I began to walk towards the Town Hall, hurrying to get in front of the others who, I noticed, were all ominously heading in the same direction. By the time we arrived we were almost running.

At the top of Suffolk Street we stopped dead. The pavement outside the Town Hall – a stretch of pavement that had been specially laid down for Queen Victoria's visit in 1899 and was reputed to be the widest north of London – seemed already full to overflowing with young men. Men in best blue suits or blazers and flannels; men in dark clothing who'd obviously come down early like we had on their way to offices; men who'd clearly just come off shift-work; a few young miners in their best clothes, the blue scars of their trade clear on their pale faces; and smart youngsters in black-braided morning coats, tall collars, striped pants and chamois gloves who might have been shop assistants or barristers or politicians. All standing in groups, looking once too often at their watches, eyeing the Town Hall anxiously, restless, worried, all talking noisily to anyone who'd listen, and swopping cigarettes and hopes and fears in a sudden sweeping wave of nervous friendliness.

Hurriedly trying to assess the number, Henny and I took up a position as near to the door as we could get, so we'd be at the front if a rush developed. It was an idea that had obviously occurred to a lot of others, too, and the crowd was a bit thick just there.

A beggar with a hurdy-gurdy pushed his way morosely along the gutter, hopefully waiting for a copper or two, then a newsboy in ragged breeches came along with the early papers, shouting the latest headlines – BATTLE OF LE CATEAU: GEN. SMITH-DORRIEN'S DECISION – and there was a nervous rush to buy copies and get back into position before someone pinched your place.

'If they can just hold on till we get there,' Henny said uneasily, 'it'll be all right.'

Just then, a scuffle broke out further up the queue and a big youngster in foreign-looking clothes was ejected, sheepish and smiling, from in front of us like a pip from an orange.

'He tried to push in,' someone said – bitterly, as though it were a criminal offence to push in.

The young man grinned. 'Well, wouldn't you?' he demanded cheerfully. 'I've come all the way from Canada. I'm not going to miss it now, brother.'

Someone gave him a half-hearted cheer, and Henny made room for him.

'Come in here,' he said. 'We'll get in all right. Come and stand with us.'

The Canadian grinned and joined us. 'Thanks, bud,' he said. 'The name's MacKinley. My old man came from this city, so blood's going to run in the gutters if I don't get in this mob. I paid my own fare all the way from Toronto.'

By this time, I'd noticed what appeared to be half the *Post* editorial staff standing in a group by the door – Hardacre, Sainsbury, George Dicehart from the Sports Department and Arnold Holroyd; even Jack Barraclough, one of the foremen

14

machine hands, his yellow hair greased for the occasion and sticking up in spikes, his colourless eyelashes blinking nervously as they always did when he was excited. They greeted me like a long-lost brother when they saw me – enthusiastically, but with a hint of uncertainty, as though, like me, in this strange new state of affairs, they sought safety in numbers and the reassurance of familiar faces.

'Frank Mason's around somewhere too,' they said. '*And* a gang from the Advert. Department.'

'What's happened to the paper?' I asked. 'Who's looking after it? Ashton?'

'Oh Lord, no,' Hardacre said. 'Ashton went off three days ago while you were on holiday. Locky Haddo's acting Chief Reporter now.'

He seemed faintly indignant, as though he thought Ashton ought to have waited for the rest of us. Hardacre took life seriously. He was a choirmaster and an ardent member of the Choral Society and would sing 'Drake Goes West' or 'Come Into the Garden, Maud' at the drop of a hat every time we got together for a hotpot supper.

'He pulled a few strings,' Hardacre said. 'He got a commission in the West Yorkshires. Magnus went too, and one of the photographers' apprentices, and two of the juniors.'

'What did the Editor say?'

'He promised to make up their pay. That's all.'

There were several motor cars parked along the kerb, one of them Earl FitzJames' black-and-yellow Rolls, with the family crest on the rear door, high and square and twice as aristocratic as all the others put together; and one or two horse-drawn carriages, full of women and girls, all of them a little tense and white and obsessed. I recognised a few faces – young Welch, whose father owned the largest drapery business in the city, talking to a woman in a big Daimler who was obviously his mother; Percy Sheridan, who was on the Stock Exchange; and Walter Bickerstaff, who was a nephew of the

Editor and had just passed his finals and set himself up in the High Street as an architect. There were one or two lecturers from the University and a couple of masters from the Victoria Grammar School. As a reporter I knew by sight most of the people in the city who were important, and most of the younger end seemed to be there that morning – business men I'd interviewed more than once, stockbrokers, engineers, chemists, metallurgical experts, medical students. I saw Henry Oakley, who bowled leg-breaks as an amateur for the county, and a couple of golf professionals and a whole bevy of medical students.

There were a few obvious steelworkers too – but not many – strapping young men in mufflers and caps, and a few clerks.

'And see who's there,' Henny Cuthbert whispered. 'Ephsibiah Lott.'

It was Eph all right, in a fancy yellow waistcoat, curly-brimmed Homburg and spats, and a collar that carved into his fat red neck as though it were about to remove his ears at any minute.

Eph was one of the Dooley Gang, who'd been terrifying the city pubs on and off for years. The police had been trying to put a curb on such people as Eph for ages, but they'd never quite managed it. I was surprised to see him there, surrounded by a few of the sharp-witted, tough-looking customers who helped him run pitch-and-toss schools and collect protection money from the small shopkeepers in the dark streets behind Cotterside Common.

'It'll be fine if they let *that* lot in,' Henny said resentfully, his long face mournful. 'I thought this was supposed to be a select mob.'

I didn't listen to him very carefully because I'd just seen Frank Mason and was busy pushing people out of the way to make room for him.

I liked Mason. He was a handsome man, six foot odd in his socks, with crisp black hair and a strong face and mouth. In the pepper-and-salt suit he'd bought at Aby Moss's on the Common the year before, he was enough to fetch the ducks off the water, and I noticed more than one of the girls in the cars with their eyes on him.

Before joining the *Post* on the same day that I had, he'd moved about the country for Liddell, Moore and Hart's, selling machine tools, and was the only man I ever knew who managed to have a girl in every county in the kingdom. To me, who'd lived in digs ever since I was sixteen, Mason was the absolute limit in human splendour.

He'd obviously dressed for the occasion and was wearing a bowler hat, cloth-topped boots and a stiff collar tall enough to cut his head off. Frank considered himself a bit of a lady-killer and liked to dress the part. He went dancing a lot and was always practising things like the Bunny-Hug and the Turkey-Trot and the Something-or-other Glide round the office, and when there was nothing to do you could always find him in the photo library downstairs with Molly Miles, who worked there, showing her how to do the Tango or something, or doing a bit of quiet mashing with one of the other girls in a corner behind the files.

'Hello, Fen, old fruit,' he said. 'Only people with real eyes and no more than ten toes are wanted this morning. I decided to offer my services. Obviously, it's going to hold up the war if I don't. They tell me Asquith's already telegraphed the Commander-in-Chief: "Mason's on his way."'

'The war's as good as won,' I said.

He grinned. 'Strong, clean and cheerful,' he went on. 'A fine figure of a man. Put me down for a general and I'll not complain. Butter up the sergeant and tell him that Mason's to be well looked after.'

'Hardacre's here,' I pointed out, and Mason grinned.

'We shall have music wherever we go,' he said gaily.

It was already very warm, in spite of the early hour, and several of the men around me had their jackets over their arms.

Then I saw one or two of them had dusty clothes and looked as though they hadn't shaved.

One of them, a square-built man with a back like the Rock of Gibraltar and a pale scarred miner's face, grinned at me in a sudden onrush of friendliness that lit up his sombre features as though the sun had come out behind his eyes.

'Been making a night of it?' I asked, and he nodded.

'We've been 'ere since yest'y, if that's what you mean,' he said, with a curious dignity that went oddly with his cheap blue suit and cap. 'Slept on t'pavement. T'police let us.' I was impressed by a patriotism that was greater than mine.

'We come over from 'Amley,' he went on. '"Tom Creak," I said, "you'll need to be early. If you don't stay overnight, all them forms'll be snatched up before t'first bus gets in." So we slept 'ere. There was about twenty of us. Tom Creak saw to it. I'm Tom Creak. I'm a deputy at t'pit.'

The first of the traffic was beginning to appear now, buses drumming past on their solid rubber tyres, blue and white and with the city coat of arms; drays drawn by great clattering Clydesdales, piled high with barrels of the strong north-country beer the city was famous for; carts of straw and hay and coal and great white rolls of paper for the printing presses; drays of steel bars, blue-grey from the rolling-mills, and bales of freshly cooled wire – the iron rims of their wheels polished bright on the stone setts; horse-drawn cabs; a few motor cars; and the first of the office workers – pausing at the end of Suffolk Street to stare at the growing crowd outside the Town Hall.

Several of the men around me were skylarking about on the pavement and dancing to the hurdy-gurdy, and two or three had begun to climb on each other's shoulders to look into the windows of the Town Hall.

'There's an old josser in there,' one of them said eagerly, his nose against the glass. 'I think he might even be alive. He's breathing. Hi, you in there!' he bawled. 'Come and open these damn' doors!'

A policeman appeared and told them to get down, and they promptly joined hands and began to dance round him. The policeman grinned.

'Now look 'ere, you young fellers,' he said, 'nobody minds you acting the old goat, but don't stop t'traffic, that's all. Keep on t'pavement and make way when folk want to pass.'

He was saluted and cheered on his way, and Frank Mason and several others started pretending to form fours for him. The crowd at the end of Suffolk Street began to laugh. Then in the distance I heard the faint wheezy sound of a brass band and saw that the crowds were turning away and staring down the High Street. The policeman took a hasty look and began to push the pedestrians back on to the pavement, then, standing in the middle of the road, he held up his hand to stop the traffic.

Round the corner swept the brass band in blue-and-lavender uniforms, thumping and wheezing away at 'The British Grenadiers'. There must have been a dozen of them, ranging from the oldest who was a man easily seventy with a white beard, sawing away at a trombone, to the youngest, a thin-faced boy with pimples, whose blue bus-conductor's hat wobbled over his nose as he marched to the music.

Behind them, swinging round the corner, came a banner, held on two poles and supported by four crimson cords. *National Union of Mineworkers*, it said, *Caldby and Hannerside Lodge*, and behind the banner, trying to march in step, were another two or three dozen young men, all of them, like Tom Creak the deputy, with the pale faces and blue-scarred noses of underground workers.

'We're 'ere boys,' one of them yelled excitedly. 'They can start t'war now.'

A cheer went up from the crowd outside the Town Hall as the band turned into Suffolk Street and came to a shuffling halt. There was another cheer from the passers-by, which was returned by the men behind the banner. Then it dawned on me that these two or three dozen miners had probably been marching behind their brass band ever since daylight, all the way from Caldby, a matter of fifteen miles, simply for the privilege of enlisting.

'Has it started yet?' one of them shouted.

'It's been going on since August, old sport!'

'Not t'war, fat'ead! T'recruiting.'

'There's ten minutes to go,' someone announced. 'They daren't open t'doors in case they're killed in t'rush.'

By midday there were three bands and three banners outside the Town Hall. They'd arrived in a blast of noisy patriotism that had died as quickly as it had risen when they realised others had arrived before them. Most of the bandsmen didn't bother to go home but stayed to sign on themselves, taking their places at the end of the queue, which stretched away into the evening and eventually into the next day, so that they had to be found beds in city hostels and Y.M.C.A. rooms.

I was one of the first in.

Earl FitzJames, who'd offered to act as commanding officer, was sitting beside the clerk who was filling in the forms, his top hat on the table in front of him, so that I could see the red silk lining and the name of the makers. He owned collieries all over South Yorkshire and had raised and commanded his own battery in the South African War.

He stared at me silently for a moment, stroking his gravy-dipper moustache, his watery old eyes looking me up and down. His frock coat hung loosely on his shrunken frame and his long bowed cavalryman's legs stretched out in front of him.

'Strong young feller, by the look of you,' he observed. 'Play any games?'

I told him I did, and he nodded approvingly.

'That's the stuff,' he said. 'Sporting spirit. Don't hit a man when he's down. Yer in for the greatest game of yer life, young feller.'

He fished out his cigarette case and offered me a smoke from the rolled gold with the FitzJimmy crest on it, and I sat there like a lord myself as they took down my particulars.

'Name?'

'Fenner.'

'Christian names?'

'Mark Martin.'

'Age?'

'Twenty-four.'

'Religion?'

'Church of England.'

'Trade or profession?'

'Journalist.'

I was out within half an hour, but there were others who stood in the broiling sun and the dust outside the Town Hall for most of the day, fidgeting restlessly, fearful they were going to be overlooked, telephoning friends who might pull enough strings to get them in by a short cut, and waylaying passing recruiting officers or plucking the sleeves of harassed sergeants to argue about their places in the queue. They were marshalled back into line by weary policemen, and old FitzJimmy sent for meat pies, cheese sandwiches and beer from the nearest pub to keep them going.

We were attested and sent in cheering, police-escorted groups to the Corn Exchange, where a group of civilian doctors in sacking-covered booths slapped our chests, examined our private parts, our height and weight, our feet, our teeth, our hearts, our eyes, our hearing, our lungs, and, as far as they could, our internal workings.

'Touch your toes,' I was told by an old man with a red face and mutton-chop whiskers, who wore knickerbockers and looked and smelled like a vet.

I tried.

21

'*Without* bending your knees,' he pointed out grimly.

I hadn't done it for years and it was harder than I thought, and I decided that if I got through this lot I'd cut out drinking and smoking and concentrate on keeping fit. Something in my spine gave an ugly creak, but with a bit of an effort I managed it in the end.

'Quite a job,' the doctor said dryly. 'Still, that's quite a breadbasket you've got on you, isn't it? Sure you're not in pup?'

I tucked in my stomach as fast as I could, blushing furiously. We'd all thought the medical would be easy. We'd been saying all morning that if they looked in one ear and didn't see daylight from the other, you were in.

Most of the time we waited in nearby rooms, half-clothed and in acute embarrassment, obeying orders to walk up and down, open our mouths, read from cards and fill small test-tubes, dreading constantly that the next step might be the last.

'Why'd *you* join, old boy?' the man next to me was saying.

'We-ell' – his neighbour scratched his head – 'I don't know, really. Because everybody else seemed to be joining, I suppose. It seemed the thing to do. Besides, you can't let the old Hun get away with it, can you?'

'He said my teeth were bad,' Henny Cuthbert complained, his voice like the mournful neigh of a horse. 'Anybody'd think I wanted to *eat* Germans, not shoot 'em. They say they're going to interview every one of us individually to make sure they get the right type. Every one of us. It's worse than applying for a new job.'

He edged uneasily away from Eph Lott, who was sitting next to him. Eph's body was white up to the point where his collar fitted. There it became bright purple in a sharp-etched line, almost as though his head belonged to someone else and had got itself attached to Eph by mistake. As Henny moved away, Eph seemed to think he was making room for more customers and he hitched himself up too, so that Henny had to move again.

'Bloke in there told me I was too fat,' he said bitterly. 'Me!

Too fat! Anybody'd think they didn't want me. They've only to say, and I'll do a bunk quick as poss. They don't realise what I'm giving up, to go and fight their bloody 'Uns for 'em.' He turned to me. 'How *you* doin', mate?'

'All right,' I said.

'Don't stand no nonsense. They *want* you, y'know.'

'Yes,' I said. 'I know.'

By this time, in fact, I'd reached the stage when I'd have considered it a shameful humiliation to have been rejected, and I suffered agonies as the doctor examining my feet and legs seemed to hesitate.

'Varicose veins?' he asked.

'No, never,' I said.

'Feet give you any trouble?'

'No.' I was beginning to wonder if he'd spotted something dreadful I wasn't aware of.

'You sure?'

'Certain.'

'What about that one?' He pointed at my right big toe which I'd once broken playing football.

'It's all right.'

'Funny shape, that's all. Don't like the look of it.'

He stared down at my foot, bending over to peer closer, and my eyes followed his anxiously.

'I've never had any trouble, Doctor,' I pointed out quickly. 'And I do a lot of walking.'

He looked up at me and smiled. 'Do a lot of walking, do you?' he said. 'Well, you're going to do a lot more walking before you're much older, young man. Very well, go through there.'

'Am I all right?'

'I wish I'd got a heart like yours.'

In a small room off the main hall, someone had chalked on a blackboard *To Berlin Via the Corn Exchange* and we thought it rather good. As we appeared, still a little sheepish and uncertain, a sergeant, with a ferocious moustache and South African ribbons on his chest, lined us up, shoving at us with gnarled hands. I noticed he looked rather elderly and not very bright, and that his nose had a deeper hue than perhaps it ought to have had. He looked like a Reservist who'd been called back to the Colours and just then, to me, he seemed the very symbol of authority and military skill.

'All right,' he said harshly. 'Stop all this spitting and committing a nuisance. This here's government property for the moment. Less 'issing, whistling and false laughter, and take them grins off yer faces.'

It was an old joke he'd probably trotted out dozens of times before, but we managed to laugh. He handed me a Bible and told me to hold it up so that two or three other men could put their hands on it at the same time. Eph Lott was with me, and Henny Cuthbert and Jack Barraclough.

'We're going to swear you lot in,' the sergeant said. There was no emotion on his face, none of the deference we half expected as the saviours of mankind. To him we were just bodies about to be absorbed into the vast impersonal machine of the Army – and pretty uninteresting bodies at that. 'Nothing to it,' he went on, 'jest keep yer 'ands on them there Bibles. Back in a tick.'

He opened a door, while we were left standing with our arms high in the air, all feeling a little foolish and over-dramatic.

'Just think,' Henny Cuthbert said, his long face alight. 'In half an hour we'll be in.'

But after what seemed ages the sergeant was still speaking to someone in the office beyond. They seemed to be discussing the weather.

'They've forgot us,' Eph Lott complained. 'What's that old fart up to? Leaving us standing 'ere like wet weekends? They want to remember we're busy men.'

Eventually an officer appeared. Like the sergeant, he too was elderly and seemed bored by the whole business. He wore an old-fashioned uniform with a stand-up collar and a starched stock.

'Take the Book in your right hands,' he said. 'Oh, you have done! Well done, Sergeant. That's the stuff. Right, now say after me: I swear——'

'I swear——'

'—to serve His Majesty the King——'

'—to serve His Majesty the King——'

'—his heirs and successors . . . and the generals and officers set over me by His Majesty the King, his heirs and successors, so help me God!'

'—So help me God!'

'Now kiss the Book.'

We did as we were told and the officer disappeared without another word, and the sergeant collected the Bibles unemotionally and gave us each a bright new shilling and a strip of paper with a set of figures on it.

'That's your number,' he said. 'Don't lose it and don't bleedin' well forget it.'

'Are we in?' Barraclough asked.

The sergeant nodded. 'Yes,' he said. 'You can go now.'

'Go?' Henny's face fell. 'Where to?'

The sergeant shrugged. ''Ome,' he said. ''Alifax. 'Ell. I'm not fussy.'

'Don't they want us?'

The sergeant pulled a face. 'Not now they don't,' he said. 'But they _will_, don't fret. Now they've got you, they won't let you go in a hurry. They'll be in touch with you.'

It must have been late afternoon by the time I got back to the office. Sergeant Corker, the commissionaire, had gone, I noticed, from his little cubicle at the bottom of the stairs in the Editorial entrance, and I wondered suddenly if, complete with shiny red nose, large moustache and South African War ribbons, he too

25

was engaged at that moment in swearing in groups of other eager young men elsewhere in the country.

In the Reporters' Room, Frank Mason greeted me with a gleeful thumbs-up sign to indicate that he was through, but Hardacre, who was sitting at his desk, puffing furiously at a cigarette, merely gave me a heavy reproachful look.

'Get through, Hardy?' I asked him gaily, secure in the knowledge that I *had* got through.

For a while he said nothing and I could hear the machines' monotonous scratchy ticking from below, and a telephone bell in one of the offices along the corridor, ringing with a harsh jangling sound as though it were shrill and angry at the lack of attention. Then Hardacre looked up and shook his head and I saw there were tears of disappointment in his eyes.

'Some trouble with my feet,' he said.

I suppose until a week before Hardacre had never dreamed of becoming a soldier. He was a humourless man whose spindly legs led us to call him 'Four o'clock Feet'. He was married, with three children, and every year he sang like a lark in Handel's *Messiah* at the City Hall, then pounded back to the office to write a criticism of himself. He'd got a chest like a barrel and walked miles in spite of his legs, to improve his lungs. He'd never struck me as a possible soldier, but in the prevailing excitement, here he was on the point of tears because he wasn't one.

'I'd worked it all out carefully,' he said, with an air of bewilderment, as though he'd discovered someone cheating against him somewhere. 'My nipper's growing fast. He's fourteen now and well able to do things about the house that I do. He could look after his mother. There was no excuse for me not joining up. And now they don't damn' well want me!'

'Cheer up, Hardy,' I said, trying to calm him down. 'You'll be here pushing a pen when the rest of us are pushing up the daisies.'

He turned away, avoiding me. 'They didn't want me,' he said.

'They said my feet weren't quite up to scratch. Dicehart was the same.'

He turned back to the desk and started poking with a fretful indifference at the newspapers around him, pushing them away in little jerky frustrated movements until he'd cleared a space on the untidy desk in front of him. He made no effort to work, though, and sat staring at the cleared patch of desk with a haggard expression as though he'd lost all interest in life.

Lockwood Haddo was sitting at the Chief Reporter's desk in Ashton's place, and I saw him watching Hardacre with interest. Although he was only a bit older than I was, Locky was a dedicated journalist who'd worked in London for several years and come back north to be Ashton's deputy. I loved Locky. He'd taught me all I knew and made me feel like an awkward colt most of the time with his air of knowledge, good sense and imperturbability. For ages on and off I'd been in love with his sister Helen.

Now he sat watching Hardacre with a wry sympathetic smile on his mouth, his lean, sensitive face half-turned towards the telephone receiver he held in his right hand.

'Cheer up, Hardy,' he said. 'There'll be plenty of others. We don't *all* suffer from the same epic masculinity as this lot, thank God.'

'I'm glad *I'm* in, anyway,' Mason said loudly, and Locky glanced at him with a hint of reproach in his eyes that he could be so gleeful in front of the suffering Hardacre.

'In your Homeric craving for martial glory,' he pointed out, 'has it ever occurred to you that soldiers in wartime are sometimes rather summarily done to death?'

It made me feel schoolboyish and naïve, and his air of tranquillity of spirit made me wonder if I'd been a little hysterical.

Frank was unperturbed, however, and Hardacre was beyond consolation. He slung the evening paper across to me, and jabbed a long flat finger at a paragraph on the main news page under a thirty-point head.

'They've estimated they'll be under strength,' he said, bitterly. 'They're reckoning on thirty per cent of those who signed not being completely A.1. That's me. Not completely A.1. My God!'

I picked up the paper. There was an interview by old FitzJimmy there, jammed into the left-hand column.

We consider, he'd said, *that, with the men we have to choose from, it is pointless selecting any but the very best – and I mean the very best in intelligence, physique and bearing. Doubtless there'll be a chance for those whom we have rejected to serve in other capacities and other battalions, but this battalion is to represent this city and it must have only the very best material in every possible way.*

I felt flattered that I'd been included, but I knew what it meant to Hardacre. He had to face the fact for the rest of his life that he was only second-best and perhaps not even that.

It was while I was putting the paper down, still wondering what to say to him that might make it a little easier to bear, that the door slammed open, swinging back with a crash against the desk, and young Murray burst in.

He was only seventeen, the youngest in the office and the one who got all the dirty uninteresting jobs to do, all the waiting in the rain, and all the church and chapel paragraphs. I'd last seen him arguing the toss on the Town Hall steps with an adamant police sergeant who was trying to send him home, almost weeping as he insisted to his disbelieving audience that he was old enough to join, his smooth rosy face indignant; his eyes alight with a sort of wild despair.

He snatched his hat from its peg and swung round to face us.

'They've got room for a few more,' he shouted gaily. 'They've slung out a few old duffers with knock-knees and squint-eyes and they'll be under strength. I'll manage it after all. That bloody policeman's gone off duty now. We're in, Meredith, we're in!'

He crammed his hat on his head and disappeared in the

direction of the stairs, whooping wildly, and as the door slammed after him Locky looked up at Hardacre again.

'Old duffer,' Hardacre mourned. 'Knock-knees! My God!'

His voice was thin and his long face was sharp with bitterness in the sunshine that was streaming through the high glass windows that ran down one side of the Editorial Room.

'There'll be plenty of time, Hardy,' I said. 'There'll be other battalions.'

'Other battalions aren't *this* one. This one was special.'

Locky put down the telephone and reached for a sheet of paper.

'It'll be weeks before the office recovers from this damned war,' he sighed. 'Only God and Sir Edward Grey realise the damage the Germans have done.'

2

It had been an extraordinary summer, that summer of 1914, a summer I remembered with an unbearable nostalgia for years. There was no real rain from March onwards and the scorching sun brought on the plums, and the plums brought out the wasps, so that they found their way even into the office windows in the city centre, buzzing maddeningly against the glass in places where you didn't ever expect to find wasps. I remember it as if it were yesterday, morning after morning after morning of it, when even the drab *Post* rooms were full of dusty gold and the summer hum of insects.

For weeks before the war started I'd been subbing half-baked scare stories from the agencies of German bands concealing weapons in their instruments, and German waiters spying on gunsites and army installations around London in readiness for the invasion of England they'd been talking of for years.

There were a lot of Germans in the country in those days, working in the hotels and pork shops, singing Schubert on the music-hall stages and sweating in their little round hats in the parks and through the dusty streets with their brass bands. Many of them had even married English girls and settled down, and their relatives were always over to visit them. We had quite a few of them in the city. Some of them had been in England for generations.

Schemingers, for instance, the chemists in the High Street; Singer and Greene, who'd been Sänger and Gruhn only a few years before; Stahler, the German-Swiss who kept the *Post* office supplied with trays of tea. Nobody had noticed them until a few weeks before, then as the events on the Continent had blown up into a crisis old Singer had suddenly found it advisable to retire to Bournemouth and leave the business to Greene, who at least spoke King's English, and hadn't a houseful of blond bullet-headed children; and John Schafer, the owner of the big food store in the High Street, a man who'd lived all his life in England and couldn't speak any other language, a man who'd given a fortune to the city in the form of art galleries and parks and property of various sorts, was booed in the street. It seems like prehistory now, as far away as the ancient Greeks, but it was all very real and exciting then.

I hadn't taken much notice when Franz Ferdinand and his wife were murdered in Sarajevo. No hint of the desperateness of the crisis seemed to leak into the papers. Ireland was much nearer and far more turbulent, and assassination was an occupational hazard for middle-European monarchies. Besides, what's a Crown Prince or two to a young man sighing like a furnace over a girl, or absorbed with sport? You know how it is.

Yorkshire's position in the county-cricket table was a matter of great moment that summer, and I'd been occupied with Locky Haddo's sister, Helen, for some time. We'd all met her first at an office party and she'd bowled me – *and* Frank Mason – clean over for a week or two. Since then, when Frank wasn't claiming her, I'd seen her on and off, playing tennis, going to the cinema, walking on the moors, but never getting very far with her. She was young, too lively and forthright to be dazzled, and not given to the kind of talk most girls favoured. But whenever I felt I was making headway with her, she'd turn to

31

Frank, and the next trips we made together always seemed to end in arguments, with Helen laughing at me and me hating her like hell – till next time. She was small, fair, pretty enough to take your breath away, alert minded like Locky and with the same sharp sense of humour.

For the most part Locky ignored us, or behaved like a cynical elder brother, never referring to Helen when I saw him at the office. His father was a doctor with a surgery on the Common and they never seemed to be short of money, which didn't make it any easier for me, because my parents were dead and I was in digs and never had any money in my pocket. Things were cheap of course. Good cigarettes were ten for threepence and a suit cost you thirty bob. But I always felt a bit like a poor relation, for, if prices were low, wages weren't so high either, and Frank Mason lived at home and had far more to spend than I had.

The night the war started we were all there in the office, and I remember hearing the tick-tick-tick of the machines up the air shaft next door, and the shouts for messengers or for tea from the sub-editors.

Ashton, the Chief Reporter, was at the telephone, sitting at the end of the room at a desk with a frosted-glass screen round the front to give him privacy – a pink, round-faced man with pince-nez glasses who looked like Mr Pickwick on his trip to Ipswich. He was a man of precise and exacting demands, inclined to get harassed under pressure. He hated ticking anyone off, and, instead, he just used to look at you when he was angry, his face wearing a hurt empty look that had the effect of making you feel as if you'd struck him. He leaned heavily on Locky Haddo, who at that moment was sitting opposite him, busy with the engagements diary, his lean face absorbed as he wrote.

Frank Mason was reading the paper, his hat on the back of his head; Hardacre, his face long and cadaverous, was gloomily

32

shoving with one hand at a plate of sardines on toast, on a tray that had been brought in for him from Stahlers', while he wrote some copy with the other; Sainsbury, George Dicehart, from the Sports Department, and Arnold Holroyd were arguing about cricket with Barraclough, in from the Machine Room with a query. Only young Murray was missing, out somewhere in the loveliness of the evening, on the sort of unimportant query they always reserved for beginners like him.

The city wasn't as big then as it is now, but it was expanding rapidly and even if *we* didn't think much of the possibility of war, the authorities at the Admiralty had had it well in mind for years and there was a great demand for guns for Jackie Fisher's new Navy. The steelworks along Cotterside Common were working overtime, and had been for years, lighting the sky with their devilish colours all the way along the valley from the Dower Arches to Eccleston. They'd run trams out to Greenedge that spring and had just started a bus service to Ambleside, and the little streets of flat-fronted houses that were spoiling Cotterside were filling every scrap of open land round the chimneys and furnaces with their narrow-gutted ugliness, and every breath of fresh air that was left when the steelworks had finished with it with their streams of smoke.

There was never much to recommend the city from the point of view of classic beauty. Smoke has a habit of clouding the vision as well as darkening the stone and sooting up the windows. It was just a place where guns were made and vast quantities of armour plate were churned out, where steel ingots, bars and strips were despatched through the sooty streets to other brighter cities that turned them into machinery.

We had the finest smoke and grime in the north, the longest straightest narrowest streets of small houses in Yorkshire. They stood in acres, growing more crowded every day, surrounding the vast high-sided works where row on row of huge chimneys belched out multi-coloured smoke. Every road had its quota of pubs where steelworkers – scorched-cheeked, white-mufflered, blue-spectacled – went in all their off-shift hours to replace in beer the sweat they lost before the furnaces. Ours was a city of dark caverns lit with hellish lights, a city where the fresh green grass was always smutted by the smoke two weeks after spring came. It was a city of noise, of great steam-hammers and dark rolling-mills and clanking trainloads of rattling steel bars; of sturdy, stout-hearted people with worn faces lined with years of trying to keep their homes and their children clean in surroundings which made it much easier to be dirty.

Nothing on God's earth could ever make the place beautiful. Like its people, it was as forbidding as its numberless Methodist churches and Baptist chapels. Square, sombre, touched with grime, and depressing, but still oddly enduring.

There wasn't much to do that night, I remember. Most of what was going into the paper was coming in from *Exchange Telegraph* and the other agencies, and only the subs seemed to be busy. I remember the Deputy Chief Sub, who was in charge, had taken his collar off because of the heat and it lay on the desk beside him, still with his tie in it, stiff and shining and cold-looking, a bit like a disapproving snake. The rest of us were only pretending to work, smoking and waiting for things to happen, our minds too busy with national events to be concerned with local ones.

I was reading the *Evening Clarion*. Officially, I was looking for district carry-over stories for the morning paper, but I was chiefly engaged in reading the war news. It had grown worse since Bank Holiday. Germany had stopped her noisy demand for a free passage for her armies through Belgium and had plunged ahead and invaded. Her columns were already on the borders of France. The headlines hit you in the eye like the announcement of a Second Coming:

CONTINENT PLUNGED INTO WAR. GERMANS INVADE. BRITISH CABINET DECIDES TO SUPPORT FRANCE.

In the next column, however, there was something that made you breathe easier. There, the world crisis had been reduced to local proportions. BLOW TO CITY, the headlines said. CONTINENTAL TRADE PARALYSED. BLACK OUTLOOK. In spite of the crowds round the food shops, it made you feel it wasn't going to be any worse than a strike or a slump. And in between the announcements that the British Army was being mobilised, and the information from Sir Edward Grey that 'we could not stand aside', was Jack Hobbs' 226 for Surrey at the Oval and the cheering news that at Old Trafford the traditional enemy, Lancashire, had collapsed and Yorkshire were heading for their ninth successive victory.

I'd often wondered what I'd do if it came to a showdown, but I'd never thought seriously about it because I'd never really felt it would ever come to a war. Even now, what fear I felt was overlaid by an immense strange excitement. It was a new feeling, this imminence of war. We'd none of us in the office ever known it before. Most of us could only just remember the Boer War. We'd seen troops leave the city for South Africa, but not many; because the Boer War, by comparison with what was hovering over us at that moment, was a colonial skirmish or a Saturday-afternoon sporting event. But now, here we were, with something bigger and closer to home looming out of the shadows and likely to affect us all, something that reached out and personally touched London and Berlin and Paris and Brussels and St Petersburg in Russia, and had already snatched away with a startling immediacy what few troops were garrisoned in the city.

The Territorial camps had been cancelled to keep the men on hand and youngsters were slipping away from their families to get their names down before they were discovered. Men were being moved urgently about the country in vast numbers, sailors to Scapa Flow, soldiers to the cross-Channel ports, recruits to the camps round Salisbury and Aldershot, and the railways were jammed with unexpected traffic.

On the Continent travellers were rushing home, and in Berlin, where they were still cheering the regiments off to the front, old soldiers shouting 'Nach Paris' and 'Nach Petersburg' were toasting 'Der Tag' and singing 'The Watch on the Rhine' and 'Deutschland über Alles', and 'Was Bläsen der Trompeten?'. The Unter Den Linden was full of barked orders and stiff phalanxes of spiked-helmeted men, in field grey now instead of the parade-ground Prussian blue, all kicking their feet up in a goosestep that seemed foreign and difficult and faintly ridiculous to British eyes.

All day people had been out of their offices and shops, talking and staring blank-eyed at newspapers. The Government had long since sent an ultimatum to Berlin requesting that the German Army should evacuate Belgium by midnight, but, according to the *Clarion*, the Germans were ignoring it and continuing to pour forward. It was no wonder nobody could settle down to work.

For a long time nobody spoke, then Mason shut his paper with a clash of stiff new sheets and we all looked up.

'Sir Edward Grey,' he said, and he sounded faintly aggrieved, 'should have made our position clear, then the Germans wouldn't have dared to move. They don't want to fight us any more than we want to fight them. That's obvious, so it's all a bit barmy when you think about it.'

Nobody said anything, chiefly because we agreed with him. Hardacre went on picking drably at his sardines, and Arnold Holroyd and Dicehart and Sainsbury had stopped the argument on cricket they'd been having. Ashton was holding the telephone receiver to his ear, not speaking, his attention on Mason. The sound of the machines below came up, noisily insistent, jarring against the brain, a thin scratchy clicking that seemed to go with Hardacre's wilting sardines and the smell of dust that always pervaded the old building.

'I think it's nothing but a swizz.' Mason folded up the paper with a methodical slowness, as though he were busy thinking of other things and the paper was only something to keep his hands occupied. 'It's a put-up job. The big steel combines started it to get everyone to spend money on arms. It's the giddy limit. That's what it is. Nobody wants it.'

'The French do,' Dicehart commented. 'They're itching to get back at the Prussians for 1870.'

Hardacre looked up and gestured with one of Stahlers' knives. 'They say that when the banks reopen they're not going to issue any more sovereigns,' he said slowly. 'They're going to issue notes. One pound and ten bob.'

'What's that got to do with it, old fruit?' Mason asked, annoyed at having his diatribe interrupted.

Hardacre shrugged. 'Well, it's all part of the scene,' he said lamely. 'It just shows they're scared, that's all.'

'How?'

'Well, they're hanging on to all the gold reserves, aren't they?'

'They're not going to fight with coinage.' Mason was a complete extrovert and never thought much beyond the next girl and the next new tie. '"Dear Frau Hoffenstinkel,"' he went on with galling sarcasm, '"I regret to inform you that your son, Hans, has died gloriously in battle. He fell at the head of his troops today, with a half-sovereign smack between the eyes."'

Dicehart laughed and Hardacre began to lose his temper. He was busy with a bath bun which had come with the pot of tea and the sardines from Stahlers', and you could see the perspiration along his upper lip as he cut at it in a furious sawing movement. 'It's nothing to do with that,' he snapped. 'It just shows it's going to be an economic war. That's all.'

Locky slowly raised his head from the diary. 'Anybody'd think you lot were eager for a war,' he commented in that grave mocking manner of his.

'Can't say I'd mind.' Arnold Holroyd spoke cheerfully over his shoulder, his pink face round and cheerful. 'Somebody's got to teach the swine a lesson, haven't they?'

'You'd soon change your tune if they called *you* up.'

Mason grinned. 'I don't know,' he said. 'It'd make a change from reporting.'

Locky stared at him. He was just working up to one of those scathing retorts he was so good at when the Editor appeared. The door slammed back, and he walked straight through to Ashton without looking round. The Chief Sub was with him, dressed in evening clothes as though he'd been called away from a dinner party, and his face was pale and taut and there was a nerve twitching under his eye. Ashton rose at once and stood waiting for them, one hand on his blotter.

'We're only a few hours from war,' I heard the Editor say. He seemed to draw in a deep breath, then he faced Ashton, his fingers fidgeting nervously with the edge of the desk. 'The ultimatum's due to expire at midnight. There isn't a ghost of a chance now that it won't be allowed to.'

The office seemed to petrify. Ashton stared at the Editor without speaking. Hardacre, leaning forward across the desk, pretended to be absorbed with his bath bun. Mason was staring at the folded newspaper in front of him, his face suddenly grim, his eyes flickering towards the group by the desk. Locky still had one hand reaching across the diary for a slip of paper. Sainsbury, Dicehart and Arnold Holroyd were in a huddle, pretending to be discussing something again, but their ears were flapping like signal flags.

Then Mason smiled slowly and gave me a thumbs-up sign across the desk, and I saw that all the faces around me had relaxed and were suddenly free from strain. After all the days of doubt and fading hope, the certainty of war had brought a kind of peace. Our problem was gone. It was no longer a question of 'Will we?' or 'Won't we?' Now it was only: 'Well, it's here. Let's get on with it.'

The Editor turned and faced us, as though about to make a proclamation, and we all lifted our heads and stared at him with dutiful expectancy.

'It's war,' he announced dramatically.

'Thank God,' Mason said at once. 'This ought to teach the Kaiser to mind his own damned biz, if nothing else. If he wants a scrap, maybe a few belts of the best from us'll make him change his mind.'

Someone chuckled and before we knew where we were, we were all laughing and cheering Mason's defiance, and even the Editor started to smile. The subs stopped work and joined in, and a few of the people from the offices along the corridor crowded through the door. They grouped themselves among the desks and started talking noisily, all excited and keen and uncertain about what would happen next.

We were all like that, all bristling with eagerness and the sensation of being on the brink of glory, when young Murray burst in. He was in a tearing hurry as he always was, faintly indignant as usual, falling over his own feet and making as much din as ever, and his first words stopped the laughter and brought home abruptly to us that war wasn't all flags and banners and cheering, but something else that included hatred and ugliness and fear.

'The crowd's throwing bricks through Schafers' window,' he shouted.

And that's how it started for us all. A few taut words from the Editor, a few cheers and a lot of laughter, and bricks through Schafers' window. And now, here we all were, in the Army, a little startled and scared by our own boldness and wondering what the hell was in store for us.

We'd signed on for three years or the duration of the war, and we weren't Militia or Territorials, but Regular soldiers – in a brand-new unit, the 12th (University and City) Special Service Battalion of the two-counties regiment that had been garrisoned in the city since the Crimea.

They'd given us our shilling and sworn us in and now here we were, all sitting around on our behinds waiting for a summons to report for duty that didn't seem to come, all trying to behave normally and trying not to think of the future – because none of us could see any future beyond the Army.

It wasn't easy waiting, because everybody else seemed to be busy. Stories filtered north of heavy gunfire being heard off Southend and of a naval action off Kent; but while British ships were being sunk, and the Army began to fight back in France, my sole contribution to the war effort was a hashed-up story of the Angel of Mons.

The city went on much as before. Although people were still hiding everything German they possessed, and disowning indignant German relatives as hard as they could go, the *Messiah*, which should have been put on at the City Hall when war broke out and had been cancelled because someone had suggested Handel was a Hun like Mendelssöhn and Wagner and the rest, was reannounced with the reassuring news that Handel was a jolly good type after all, because he'd given up his German friends and preferred to live in England.

The management of Ross and McCall's Empire billed a patriotic concert, and newsagents were offering on the streets *The End of the Kaiser, Predicted in Brother Johannes' 300-year-old prophecy of the war, price one penny*. Every church and chapel from Cotterside to Greenedge began to announce sermons on thundering Old Testament texts, *Whoso Diggeth a Pit Shall Fall Therein* and *Whoso Sheddeth a Man's Blood, by Man shall His Blood be Shed*. There were plenty for them to go at, once they started looking.

Advertisements for foot-plasters for soldiers, and blast-proof earplugs for civilians in danger of bombardment, began to dot the papers, and notices appeared on the main news pages of the *Post* suggesting that anyone who might wish to enlist in the Yorkshire Dragoons or the Royal Engineers would be made very welcome if he cared to call at the Drill Hall. The *Weekly News*, the Sunday paper attached to the *Post* and the *Clarion*, announced a new serial, *The English Girl*, which was a hurried re-write of one which had appeared during the Boer War, only now the enemy were Uhlans instead of Boer vedettes, and to accompany it the Artists' Department had turned out a very smart picture of a girl in a summer frock and picture hat, her arms held rigidly behind her by two German soldiers so that her bust stuck out. Her frock was torn discreetly at the shoulder, which was about as far as you could go in those days towards being suggestive.

Photographs of people who'd joined the Army appeared on the picture pages, and Mason and I and Sainsbury and Arnold Holroyd were snapped on the front steps of the office and emerged among the main news as '*Post*' *Men in the City Battalion.* I have it yet, yellow and dog eared, four self conscious young men in a theatrical pose which is heightened by the fact that the cameraman was on the bottom step and we were on the top, four young men in narrow trousers and light-coloured boots and tall stiff collars, me in a felt hat with a broad silk band, Holroyd in a natty sporting cap that almost drowned him, Mason in a furry Homburg that drew sardonic comments from everybody in the office.

All the same, we were pleased with the picture for there were plenty of witless idiots about with white feathers and insinuations of cowardice, and it let people know we'd taken the plunge.

The girls round the office suddenly took a new interest in us, and Frank Mason vanished more often to the dark corners behind the files in the photo library. Suddenly we'd become privileged persons, and people found they wanted to stop and congratulate us and buy us drinks.

Somehow, the simple act of enlisting had become a crusade. The new battalion had become a squadron of young Galahads in shining armour, itching to get at the Hun. The words they used to describe us! *Steel-true! Blade-straight! True-blue!* We weren't very far from the turn of the century and the Victorians were still in full cry.

We were all rather naïve in those days and thought that the

British Empire was God's gift to the world. We'd convinced ourselves that the whole structure of civilisation would fall to pieces if someone destroyed the Empire, and we felt the Germans were attempting to do just that.

'After all,' Frank Mason said, 'nobody believes all that cock about atrocities they're trying to give us. But the Huns are such a bloody dull lot with their Kaiser Bill and their "*hochs*" and their Nibelungs and Siegfrieds and so on. I once heard Wagner at the City Hall. It made me feel ill. Anybody can see they need a bit of sorting out.'

So there we were, about to take up arms against Prussianism and militarism. Our King and Our Country needed us; and the '*brav' Belges*' and all those men of the Contemptible Little Army who were slowly sinking into the ground in Belgium were crying out to us to hurry. Jingoism and Kipling had suddenly become very popular again.

But if the emotion increased, there was little sign of any anxiety on the part of the authorities to let us get on with the job.

The *Post* was full of belated stories of fire and sword in Belgium, of the great German advance and the giant 42-centimetre Austrian siege guns that had smashed Belgian forts to bricks and rubble. Art treasures had been systematically destroyed, the agencies said, and the Germans were cutting off the ears and hands of children for sport and shooting old men and women out of hand. German officers were said to have raped women held down by helpful private soldiers on the cobblestones of the public squares in towns on the Meuse, and their troops, stupefied with brandy to enable them to face the crackling fire of the French 75s, were being slaughtered in thousands as they advanced – arm-in-arm to hold themselves upright. Their officers, in jack-boots and spiked helmets, were well to the rear, of course, driving their men before them, not leading them from in front as they did in the French and British armies.

History was being made while we went on waiting.

Much to our bitter annoyance, those men who'd got into the

Army before us were already in camp and some of them were even in uniform. The Territorials, who'd been regarded with a certain amount of ribald merriment as Saturday-afternoon soldiers who could form fours, turn left and right and stand to attention and not much else, had overnight become the Thin Red Line, Up Guards and At 'Em and Gentlemen Rankers Out on the Spree.

Then young Magnus, the copytaker, appeared in the office, cocky in all ill-fitting new uniform with a high collar that looked as though it was throttling him, and Murray and Sainsbury almost died of envy.

'My God,' Sainsbury said. 'If they keep us hanging about any longer the blasted war'll be over. The Russians are on their way to France already.'

'Who says?' Locky asked, imperturbable as ever and quite unmoved by the hysteria.

'They've been seen on the stations,' Sainsbury said.

'I don't believe it.'

'Well, that's the story. They've even seen the snow on their boots.'

'In this weather?'

'Well' – Sainsbury began to hedge a little – 'whether they have or not, it's time somebody got a move on. I thought they wanted us to set about the Germans. They made enough fuss about it. "Your King and Country Need You". "Kitchener expects this day that every man will do his blasted duty". That nonsense. Well, I'm waiting to be needed. I'm anxious to do my duty. And what happens? They tell me to sit back as meek as Moses and hang on till someone in Whitehall finishes his holiday or something. Well, blow 'em. I'm not going to.'

And he went off and joined another unit that was willing to take him at once, and he vanished overnight without calling in to say goodbye. We never saw him again.

'I wish I'd joined the Navy,' young Murray said, staring glumly at a sheet of paper and pencil, no more capable of doing any intelligent work than flying to the moon.

At the barracks, queues of men were still shuffling forward, and self-conscious little parties were marching away daily en route for some regimental depot, cheered by the kids all the way to the station. Smart young officers appeared in the pubs, a little excited and flushed, and horse-drawn service waggons took their place among the cabs and drays and tramcars and buses in the streets.

There were always two or three sheepish Territorials nowadays to give weight to the recruiting sergeant's words and sash and King's Shilling, and a flood of martial music to ruffle the hair, stir the blood and disturb the conscience.

Patriotic summonses came from the Town Hall steps and the plinths of the sooty statues in the parks. Even the women were at it, all those women who'd been concerned only with suffrage and the equality of the sexes up to a week or two before. And all the old thunderers from the City Council, reaching out gleefully for all the new and ringing phrases that had appeared in the papers.

Words like *Entente Cordiale, Our Noble Allies*, and *Prussian Militarists* came to their lips as though they'd spent all their lives thinking about the situation, instead of having had it sprung on them overnight like the rest of us. *Entente Cordiale*? 'Our lot' to everybody else. *Noble Allies*? 'Froggies' was good enough for most of us. *Prussian Militarists*? 'Kaiser Bill' to the troops. What they didn't realise, all those pretentious old windbags with their mutton-chop whiskers and frock coats and scarlet-lined top hats, what none of us realised, was that it was a young man's world all of a sudden. The old world that they were used to, all the pompous Victoriana that never split an infinitive or ended with a preposition, was over and done with for ever.

When the summons arrived at last, it was just a formal typewritten cyclostyled request to appear at the Edward Road Drill Hall at 8 a.m. the following morning. Nothing more. No instructions about what clothes to take. No words redolent of glory or ringing with martial ardour. Just a simple blunt little sentence that had the effect of leaving you filled with disappointment.

Murray almost fell into the office that morning. 'Thank God we can go now and wipe the swine off the face of Europe,' he said sternly, every inch the ardent warrior.

'Have you told your mother yet?' I asked, and his face fell at once. Murray's mother was a fussy little woman with pince-nez spectacles and a shrill voice who had a habit of registering complaints to the Editor whenever she thought her son was being overworked. Murray was a little sensitive about her.

'Not likely,' he said. 'She'd have me out like a shot.'

'When are you going to?'

His face grew longer. 'I don't know,' he said gloomily. 'I'm not quite sure how to set about it. She'll kick up such a fuss.'

I said goodbye to Mrs Julius the next morning – not because I was fond of her, but simply because I didn't expect to be back – and she surprised me with the emotional scene she worked up. She called in the neighbours and announced that 'her second son' was now going after 'her first son'. Willie Julius had been a compositor on the *Post* until he'd got a job on a London daily and he was in one of the Territorial regiments down there. He was a corporal now and a devil for drill, though he'd once told me he only joined for the money and because the uniform fetched the girls in hordes. He was camped out on some race-course in the south and was apparently thoroughly enjoying himself.

Saying goodbye to Mrs Julius took the best part of half an hour. For once, she'd got up ahead of me, and she'd cooked me a breakfast big enough for a navvy, clearly convinced that from that moment on I was unlikely to get a square meal until the Army discharged me at the end of the war.

I'd packed a small case with my shaving things, debating for some time whether to include pyjamas. I wasn't at all sure that soldiers wore pyjamas and the letter hadn't been very helpful.

Somehow, I felt that soldiers slept in their shirts and I had no desire to appear different, and in the end I came to an arrangement whereby I would write to Mrs Julius and she would send them along to me if it didn't seem wrong to wear them.

By the time I'd finished the meal she'd worked herself up to a frenzy of excitement, and was rushing round the house collecting everything she thought I might need – sandwiches, books to read, a piece of home-made fruit cake – and was occupied in wrapping and re-wrapping them for me to carry in my pocket. It was like going for a new job or on holiday.

I finally got away ten minutes later than I expected and missed the tram, and found myself standing on the corner of Morrelly Street, thankful at last to be out of sight of the waving, weeping Mrs Julius, doubtful as to my future, and clutching a case and an enormous parcel of food. For a long time I tried to stuff the parcel into the pocket of my jacket, then into the case, and finally, in despair, I threw it over the wall into Henny Cuthbert's front garden.

The Drill Hall was already full when I arrived, and the first person I saw was Mason, smart in a Homburg and spats and surrounded by half a dozen other members of the *Post* staff.

He grinned when he saw me. 'We thought we might as well hang together, old fruit,' he said. 'They'll probably put us all in the same company then. Ashton's here, by the way. He wangled a transfer. Apparently he thought this mob would be more élite than the West Yorks.'

I glanced among the crowd of young men standing in embarrassed-looking groups, eyeing each other furtively, and caught sight of a familiar figure waiting quietly in the background as though he were trying to hide.

'Locky,' I said. 'Fancy seeing you!'

He came towards me, smiling and looking more like Helen than ever. He was in his ordinary office suit, unlike the rest of us who seemed mostly to have plumped for comfort and come in flannels or knickerbockers and tweed jackets. He looked as though he'd been in to the office, in fact, to get the day's work in order before leaving.

'What are *you* doing here?' I asked.

'Same as you,' he said.

'Have *you* joined as well?'

He gave me a sidelong grin that was faintly embarrassed. 'It's remarkable the sort of people who've come to the conclusion they were cut out for a military career,' he said.

'You never said anything.'

Locky shrugged, that self-deprecatory shrug of his, and I guessed he'd worked it all out alone, asking no one's advice and no one's permission. The thought made me feel naïve and enthusiastically schoolboyish but I was glad to see him. Somehow his presence there seemed to set the seal on what I'd done.

'Nobody's business but mine,' he went on. 'I thought about it a lot before I decided. Not much point in staying behind and doing all the work myself. That's all. I wasn't keen at first, but when you lot went off like a gang of swashbuckling privateers the Trojan Horse was already within the citadel, and I thought I might swash a buckle or two myself!'

While we were talking, someone blew a whistle. The blast shrilled among the iron girders that held up the roof, and a tremendous voice echoed round the hall.

'Get yerselves in line,' it bawled. 'Come on, you're soldiers now! Let's see a bit of life.'

'My God,' Mason said. 'It's Commissionaire Corker!'

Complete with flat boozy face, stringy waxed moustache and bulbous nose, and dressed in a threadbare tweed suit that looked a little too tight across the stomach, the old man moved about the hall with a couple of elderly corporals in faded uniforms, pushing at groups of young men who clung awkwardly and persistently to their friends as though they felt they'd drown if they drifted apart. King's and Queen's South African campaign ribbons shone on his waistcoat and his eyes looked as bright

47

as boot buttons under the peak of the enormous flat cap he wore.

'Morning, Corker,' Mason said as he stopped in front of us. 'How's it going.'

Corker stared straight through him, almost as though he didn't recognise him.

'*Sergeant Corker* to you, Mr Mason,' he snapped. 'Yer in the Army now. And don't you forget it.'

Then he winked and passed on, still pushing men into line.

'All right, 'old your noise,' he was bawling. 'Stop shuffling yer feet. The CO wants to talk to you. Get yer 'eads up and stand still. Get yer feet apart and yer 'ands behind yer backs. That's better. Now you look a bit like the soldiers you ain't.'

On the balcony that ran round the hall, Old FitzJimmy had appeared. He looked tired but curiously bright-eyed and excited. You could have heard a pin drop as he took off his silk hat and moved to the edge of the balcony to stare down at us.

'Well,' he said, 'I might as well tell you all about yourselves. It's something you've got to know, because at the moment we've got nothing else to offer you. We've got nothing in the way of equipment for you and we're not likely to get any for a damn' long time.'

There was a sigh, almost a sob of disappointment, from the crowd of men, and FitzJimmy held up his hand.

'That's the way it is,' he said apologetically. 'Lord Kitchener doesn't know where the equipment's coming from, and I'm damned if I do. But that was one of the stipulations he made when he gave his consent to the raising of this battalion. Make no mistake, though. He wants you. All of you. And probably a lot more. But there's nothing to spare in the way of equipment for you yet.'

'We'll fight as we are,' came a shout from the back that sounded like young Murray, and I heard old Corker come down on him like a ton of bricks.

FitzJimmy grinned. 'We've been told we're responsible for

48

your organisation, training and administration,' he said. 'Until the War Office can manage to take you over. But that won't be yet. They've got plenty on their slates bringing the Regular battalions up to strength. So there you are. There'll not be much to spare, but we'll get it somehow, even if we have to pay for it out of the rates. I, for one, will offer here and now a set of drums and fifes. Dammit, you'll want a band to march to, won't you?'

He paused and looked at us again, the whole fifteen hundred of us all bursting with patriotism and idealism and trying hard to look like soldiers.

'I haven't much more to say,' he went on. 'You're a fine-looking crowd – the finest crowd of recruits I've ever seen, most of you officer-material, in fact – but you're still only a *crowd*, and it's our job to make you into a fighting battalion. Give us the chance, though, and we'll do it.'

The adjutant appeared then, a thin-faced solicitor who'd been one of the stalwarts of the Territorial organisation for years.

He read out a list of officers who'd already been gazetted and the names of men who'd been given rank as NCOs. We had to know their names because most of them had no uniforms or badges of rank to identify them.

When he'd finished, we stood about in groups again, waiting for something to happen, still a little scared by our own boldness and eager for someone to tell us what to do.

But everyone was too busy making lists – lists of companies, lists of platoons and sections, list of stores, lists of equipment, lists of questions about other lists. There seemed to be no order and not much sense in what was going on. You could sense in the chaos a hint of disenchantment.

Finally, when we were all beginning to feel the pangs of hunger and the need for a meal, someone announced they were ready to form the companies, and the interminable lists started again.

I found myself in A Company with Henry Oakley, the crick-eter, and a lot of miners. All the others, Locky, Mason, Murray and the rest of them were in D Company, but Mason came across to me, leading by the arm a grinning man with blue scars on his face.

'It's all right, Fen,' he said. 'I've arranged a swop. He wants to be in A with his pals and we want you in D. Come on over and see Ashton. He's with *us*.'

Ashton looked bigger somehow, I noticed, healthier and quite different from the harassed-looking Chief who was always being pestered by telephones and awkward enquiries, and I found myself remembering his wife, a thin-nosed little woman who was reputed to nag him, and wondered how much she'd had to do with his sudden decision to enlist. I recognised young Welch standing just behind him, very much the schoolboy he'd been a few months before, and Walter Bickerstaff and Percy Sheridan, the stockbroker; there was Howard Milton, the son of the Rector of Endwood, and a metallurgical expert from the east end of the city whose name I've forgotten, and one or two more, all eager to be friendly, but all trying to look like officers at the same time.

Corker was there too, and I saw with a shock that Eph Lott and his corner boys were in with us. There was Tim Williams, who'd played rugby for Wales and was lecturer in Modern History at the University and often drank with us in the Blueberry Tavern, which had been the Press pub from time immemorial, lean and dark and Celtic against Jack Barraclough's broad Saxon blondness; MacKinley, the Canadian; Bob Catchpole, who was the son of the Vicar of Cotterside; Arnold Holroyd; Spring, who'd been an actor; and Tom Creak, the miner who'd spoken to me outside the Town Hall, when I'd first arrived, not at all ill at ease among all the younger men about him, all of them better dressed, better paid and better educated.

'Wouldn't you rather be with A Company?' I asked him.

'Tom Creak's all right 'ere,' he said firmly with that curious dignity of his. 'You get sick of miners, man. All they talk about is mining.'

Two men who were with him, stunted men with fair hair and Irish accents, whose name appeared to be Manderson, nodded and grinned agreement.

'Billy Mandy,' Tom Creak said, introducing them. 'Tommy Mandy. Manderson's too long where we come from.'

Ashton finished the list he was making and turned to us. Corker, standing behind him, was very respectful, very much the soldier all of a sudden.

'For the time being,' Ashton said, 'you'll have to go on living at home. We've got no quarters yet. Those of you who don't live in the city will be found billets. You might even be able to find them yourselves with people you know. See what you can do. It'd be better that way.'

He paused, giving us the long-suffering-father look he'd always worn when he'd given us a particularly dirty news job to do. 'Just remember, though,' he said, 'this is rather a special battalion. I doubt if there's *ever* been a battalion with the quality this one's got. We've got no tradition. We've got to make it ourselves. So start by behaving yourselves. We haven't got many NCOs yet, but there'll always be room for intelligent men who show signs of ability. For the time being we expect someone with a gift for leadership to take charge, and the rest of you – because you're young men of honour and intelligence and courage and responsibility – to help by doing what you're asked.'

He nodded to dismiss us and a few loose arms flew up because we had an idea that, since he was an officer, we ought to salute him, then he turned away, faintly self-conscious and certain that the Army had a more spectacular method of leave-taking than this sheepish shuffle we put on for the right turn Corker had told us we used to withdraw.

As we began to disperse, Locky touched my arm. 'The old man's car's outside,' he said. 'Helen'll be there, I think.'

It was the first hint he'd ever given that he'd noticed my

interest in her. He waited for me, smiling gravely, and led the way. Helen was sitting in the back of the big grey Lanchester his father used for his rounds, with its brass bonnet and the square upright windscreen and folded hood. She looked bored, but she cheered up as soon as she saw us.

As Locky turned away to adjust the throttle and crank the engine, she reached out for me as though I were something familiar in a rapidly changing scene.

'It's amazing how quickly you pick it up,' she said at once, with a wide smile, staring at me with head on one side. 'You look like a recruiting sergeant already.'

'I don't feel like one,' I said.

She laughed. 'Never mind,' she said. 'Any day now you'll be swanking, bold as brass, along the Common, with a clay pipe in your mouth and winking at the girls. I expect you're so pleased with yourself it'll cost tuppence to talk to you.'

Not to her it wouldn't, I said.

'Did you *want* to join up?' she demanded in her forthright, frightening manner. 'Or did someone push you into it? Were you dared or did you get carried along by the mob? Or did you do it of your own free will and accord?'

'Own free will and accord!' I said.

She pulled a face. 'You ought to have known better,' she pointed out.

I leaned on the door of the car, trying to get a little closer to her. I was certain Frank Mason would come barging along at any moment – he always seemed to pop up just when I'd got her on my own – and I tried hard to take up a position that would exclude him from the conversation as much as possible if he did.

'Well,' I said, 'I wouldn't say I'm exactly cut out for a soldier. But someone's got to do it.'

'Personally,' she retorted. 'I think you're all barmy, rushing off like this. There'll be thousands who won't.'

I was faintly disappointed. I'd hoped she'd set the seal finally on what I'd done by giving her unqualified approval. But she didn't seem to appreciate that at great trouble and expense I was about to defend my country and a lot of principles and people, among them Helen Haddo herself. Her refusal to get dewy-eyed about my patriotism was a bit of a damper.

'At least,' I said flatly, 'we'll all be in it.'

She sighed. 'Yes,' she said. 'And then some fool of a general will push you into the front line and, before we know where we are, everybody who's worth anything in this stupid silly city will be killed and only the dreary odds and ends will be left.'

She looked surprisingly near to tears and more vulnerable than I ever remembered her.

I put one hand over hers where it rested on the car door.

'Oh, well,' I said. 'A short life and a merry one. It won't be all that bad. There'll be leave before then.'

Her head came up and the helplessness vanished in a flash, and she was at once the old Helen again, self-assured, confident and capable, and ready for a joust.

'And I expect we'll all be expected to drop everything at once and come running with true feminine humility just because you're all soldiers and arrogant with martial ardour?'

She was a firm believer in the suffragettes and women's franchise and that sort of thing, and always liked to get her little dig in about the equality of the sexes, but I sidestepped and tried to get her smiling again.

'Not me,' I said hurriedly. 'I'm not arrogant. I'm much shyer than I look and I haven't a single opinion on anything at all.'

She laughed, and her manner immediately became more gentle again. She knew she could twist me round her little finger and she enjoyed it because she was young.

'If they let us off the chain,' I said, 'can I call round and see you?'

She laughed. 'I don't suppose so,' she said.

'Oh!' I felt my face fall. 'Why not? Frank Mason?'

'No such luck. He's chasing Molly Miles at the office. It's

just that I shan't be here. That's all. I'm going to be a little busy myself.'

'What doing?'

'I'm going to find a job.'

'You?'

'Why not? There's a war on. There'll be an unholy row at home when Father gets to know about it, but I expect I'll get away with it in the end.'

The engine fired as Locky swung the crank handle and she started to jiggle faintly in her seat with the vibration. She put up her hand to hold on her hat, a wide affair of straw and ribbon.

'Damn this potty headgear,' she said. 'I think I'll go into the works as a labourer and wear a flat cap. This is a time of emancipation, and flat caps are a symbol of it. Perhaps I can learn shorthand or typing. There'll be plenty of jobs flying about. I think I'll go and make screws or battleships or something.'

Her manner was vigorous, but she suddenly melted again and became mischievous and tormenting. 'Just think,' she said, her eyes alight with laughter. 'How wonderful it'll be! When you're earning a bob a day, and I'm driving a bus, I'll be able to ask if I can take *you* out. If anything leads to equality, that ought.'

She stared at me, smiling all over her face, then suddenly her smile died again and she became more serious. She studied me with her head on one side, her eyes thoughtful. 'You know, Fen, dear,' she said. 'I think you'll make a jolly good soldier.'

I could see my reflection in the polished brass of the head-lamps. Compared with Locky's or Frank Mason's, mine seemed an unprepossessing face, with ordinary-looking hair.

My clothes, too, had the sort of ordinariness that went with me – an ordinary grey suit and an ordinary stiff collar that seemed stodgy and unimaginative by comparison with Mason's soft shirt and spats. He had the air of a brisk young business man on holiday. I always managed to look exactly what I was – a reporter on a provincial daily.

'Not me,' I said. 'Frank's more the type.'

She shook her head. 'Don't you believe it, Fen,' she said. 'It isn't the Frank Masons of this world who'll save civilisation. The Masons lead charges of Light Brigades. But Light Brigades don't win wars. It's hanging on that wins wars and I know no one more fitted out by nature for hanging on than Mark Martin Fenner.' She leaned out of the car and her face seemed kinder than I ever remembered it. 'Nobody'll budge *you*, if you don't want them to,' she said. 'I know they won't. I've tried myself.'

I felt light-headed and a hell of a fellow for a moment, then she gave me a little push that quite destroyed the moment. 'Now go and play at being soldiers,' she said curtly. 'Looking round at you all, I think I'll marry a stockbroker.'

I felt a bit of a fool when I arrived home that afternoon. I'd thought I was already a warrior when I'd said goodbye to Mrs Julius and marched off in the morning, but now here I was back again, wondering how to face her.

I remembered that I'd thrown away the food she'd given me, and was just debating what to tell her if she asked about it when I saw her sitting in the hall, one elbow on the bamboo stand, her hair among the leaves of the aspidistra she polished so lovingly every morning and put out on the pavement every time it rained. I hadn't much affection for her. I'd always felt she overcharged and underfed me. But she'd been crying, poking her handkerchief up under her spectacles to wipe her eyes, and her old embittered face was crumpled and miserable.

'Willie's gone to France,' she announced as I appeared in the doorway.

'To France? Already?' They didn't seem to be wasting much time, I thought.

She waved a letter at me. 'It just come,' she said. 'He posted it before they left. He'll be there now. What'll happen to him?'

I tried to reassure her, but I wasn't very successful.

'Nothing, Mrs Julius,' I said. 'He'll be alright. He's trained. He knows how to march and drill, and I suppose he knows how to shoot. Anyway, it'll all be over by Christmas. Everybody says so. He'll never even get to the front.'

She didn't seem to hear me. 'He says he *wanted* to go,' she said. Her face was a picture of moist bewilderment. 'He *wanted* to go!'

'He's not the only one,' I said.

'But he's only twenty-three.'

'Best age,' I said stoutly. 'Look at me. I've signed on.'

'You're only a boy yourself.'

'I'm twenty-four.'

She didn't seem to hear me and went on dabbing at her nose and eyes, poking her handkerchief up under her glasses and shoving them one-sided, her elbow on the bamboo table, her hair disarrayed by contact with the stiff aspidistra leaves.

'It only seems like yesterday that I bought him his first sailor suit,' she mourned.

She sniffed and suddenly looked at me with suspicion, as though she'd only just noticed I'd come back.

'Don't they want you?' she demanded sharply.

'Yes,' I said startled by the change in her. 'They just haven't got organised yet. That's all. We've got to report tomorrow.'

'I thought you went to report *today*.'

'Well' – when you considered it, it *did* seem a bit silly – 'that's what they told us. They just got us there today to sort us out a bit.'

'Just like the Army,' she snorted. 'Where's your uniform?'

'I haven't got one.'

'Why not?'

'Nobody's got one. We don't possess any. Not yet.'

'Soldiers can't fight without uniforms.'

'We're not going to fight yet,' I said, beginning to lose my temper. 'They've got to train us first. Everybody has to get trained.'

'I suppose you've come back for something to eat,' she went on tartly. 'We'd better give you a decent Yorkshire tea before we send you back.'

'I'm not going back,' I pointed out. 'Well, not tonight, anyway. They've got nowhere for us to sleep yet, either. We've got to live at home for the time being.'

'Live at home?' She looked a little embarrassed.

'That's right.'

'You can't,' she said.

'Why not?'

'I've let your room. A young man from the works came.'

I wondered if he'd have jumped into my grave as quickly, and said so, and she flared up as she always did when I complained about anything.

'A woman can't just wait,' she snapped. 'I'm a widow, and my boy's in France. I didn't know you'd be coming back.'

'Oh, well, it doesn't matter,' I said, feeling a little deflated and anxious to avoid bad feeling when I expected to be leaving soon. 'I'll find somewhere else.'

'You can have the attic,' she pointed out grudgingly. 'I'll clean it out for you.'

I didn't fancy the attic very much, but it crossed my mind I'd probably be sleeping in stranger places than attics before I was much older, so I said it would be fine. Besides, I thought, it wouldn't be for long. They'd be moving us into camp before many days were out.

All the same, as I pushed my belongings up under the eaves that night, I felt I'd been a bit hard done by. I thought I'd joined the Army to save people like Mrs Julius.

3

Troops had been garrisoned in the city for years, but they'd been pretty inconspicuous and no one – least of all me – had ever noticed them before. They only appeared for occasional parades out at the barracks and on the days when they provided a band for the park during the summer holidays, or on the one night of the year when the regimental ball was held at the Corn Exchange and officers came from all over the country in their braided red jackets and tight trousers, pushing with their womenfolk through the crowds who waited to see them arrive. But, even then, it was the women with their low-cut evening gowns and jewels and piled hair who caught the eye, not the soldiers.

Nobody had ever heard of '*Yorkshire Johnny*', the regimental march, still less troubled to sing it, but for weeks after the battalion was formed it found a new popularity and even became a feature at Ross and McCall's Empire, vigorously sung by the Choral Society choir, noticeably now without Hardacre in the front row.

We soon discovered you could get a seat in the pit stalls for nothing if you were a member of the battalion and, what's more, would very likely be called on to the stage to let the audience have a look at you. And that was always a fitting and riotous end to a night out because the chorus took your arms and sang 'Yorkshire Johnny' or 'We Don't Want to Lose You, But We Think You Ought to Go', while you stared sheepishly, blinking and blinded by the footlights, and tried to see your pals or your girlfriend down at the back of the auditorium.

You could always reckon on getting a free drink in a pub or even a free meal; and people liked to stop you in the street and shake your hand, and old ladies got into the habit of thanking you touchingly for offering your life to protect theirs. Proud wives and mothers of men who'd enlisted were embroidering fire-screens, and cushions for the horsehair sofa in the front room, with the white rose that was the regimental badge as a centrepiece and the flags of all the Allied Nations as a surrounding frieze, while the City Guild of Mothers' Unions was busy stitching a silk battle standard which was to be draped in the cathedral with all the other torn and dusty banners that hung there.

The flags were everywhere now, of course. Hanging from houses and in all the shop windows, with pictures of the King and Queen, and the Commander-in-Chief, Sir John French, and Albert of the Belgians. Union Jacks, white ensigns, all the Dominion standards. The French and Belgian tricolours. The Russian Imperial emblem. The Rising Sun of Japan. We didn't run to the flags of Serbia and Luxembourg and Montenegro, because most people round where I lived had never heard of Serbia and Luxembourg and Montenegro until a few weeks before.

As the summer drew to a close, playgrounds and open spaces all over the city began to fill up rapidly with men as the Army reached out for every available training ground. Every rifle range in the district had been commandeered and new ranges were springing into existence all the time. They even had one in the crypt of the Cathedral. Volunteers who'd been turned down for the City Battalion found their way into other units, and businesses were being denuded of managers, clerks and other employees. Hardacre, who'd appeared among us once or twice at the Drill Hall, outcast and gloomy in his humbler capacity as a newspaperman looking for a story, suddenly vanished and we heard that he and Dicehart had finally persuaded some less pernickety unit to accept them as soldiers and they'd gone gaily off to war, satisfied at last to be doing their bit.

Schafers' shop window was broken again, and when they boarded it up someone wrote *Huns! Remember Mons* across it. With the pictures of the dead and wounded beginning to appear in the *Post*, it didn't pay to have a name like Schafer just then, and anybody who disagreed was a traitor and a 'Little Englander' and was soon told so.

Kitchener's face was everywhere by this time, a little younger than was true, perhaps, painted in flat washes that showed him as he'd been at the time of the South African War, with that great handlebar moustache of his and pointing finger, and those glowing magnetic eyes that seemed to follow you everywhere you went. There were never any rude words written by the kids on that one, I noticed. There wasn't even any point in drawing whiskers on it because it already had a far better set than anybody could have added with pencil.

He was still at the War Office, laying the law down about what a rotten little army we had, issuing his commands and concocting his appeals: *An addition of a further 100,000 men to His Majesty's Regular Army is immediately necessary in the present grave national crisis . . .* or: *Lord Kitchener appeals to ex-non-commissioned officers of any branch of H.M. Forces to assist him now by re-enlisting for the duration of the war . . .*

There was a neat placard on every public vehicle to supplement the official posters covering the windows of post offices and council buildings and occupying large spaces in the columns of the *Post* and the *Clarion*. It appeared on the windscreens of motor cars and was plastered on the sides of buses and trams.

It was flashed on cinema screens and exhibited outside theatres. It was on tram tickets, in the windows of private houses, in the pulpit and on the stage; in neat little letters on leaflets and in great big letters on gigantic posters: YOUR KING AND COUNTRY NEED YOU.

There was something about it that made it personal enough for a man to look over his shoulder. YOUR KING AND COUNTRY NEED YOU, it seemed to say, not HIM. Nor *him*. Not the clerk on his way home, arguing about the price of plums over the barrow by the arches. Not the miner in the flat cap round the corner with his face in a pint pot. YOU. And you felt a little prouder for having answered.

It didn't take me long to realise that my chief concern was not so much the battalion as the company I was in. Even in those early days I rarely passed beyond its boundaries, and I lost touch with friends who'd found their way into other companies. With our officers we'd been lucky. Although they knew no more about soldiering than we did, at least they seemed willing enough to learn, and for sergeants we had two crafty Reservists, Bernard and Twining, and Corker, who'd been a lance-sergeant in the Buffs twelve years before.

Corker had gone off to war cheerfully, looking for a cushy billet where he could run the same sort of rackets he'd worked from his box at the door of the *Post* Editorial entrance, where he'd been in the habit of putting money on horses for anyone who wanted a flutter, and buying cigarettes for the subs on night duty and selling them at a copper or two over the odds. His attitude to the war was easy-going and cheerful, and, while he made an honest effort to turn us into soldiers, it was half-hearted because he wasn't an educated man and he had no one above him with the experience to direct his labour into the proper channels. Then one morning a strange new voice appeared, high and shrill, and rasping like a file through the iron girders of the Drill Hall roof.

'Ex-Guards,' Murray informed me with a touch of awe in his voice. 'He was doing some job in one of the works along Cotterside. He's come to be company sergeant-major.

To Murray, honour and tradition were right and proper things to have about us. Most of us had been only brushed by the feel of glory: Murray was daubed all over with it. Even to the more martial among us, this period while we were living at home was a reprieve that meant a few more days with wives or girlfriends, but to Murray it was a restless time of waiting, when he occupied himself with preparing himself for service, training his body with long walks and his mind with proper study for the stern duty ahead.

He'd spent all his spare hours in the public library with the regimental history and was proud to discover that our parent unit had been among the last out of the battle at Minden and had held a position on the right of the line at Waterloo. He was a little disappointed that we didn't possess the prefix '*Royal*', but was satisfied to learn that, after having had it refused them when they'd claimed it following some bloody skirmish in the Peninsular War, the regiment had thereafter elected to remain steadfastly republican. He was itching to go and stand in a square or relieve Lucknow or charge the Russian guns with the Light Brigade or something, and add another scroll to the sacred flag nobody had ever seen but which bore the names of twenty-odd towns and villages in various parts of the world where the regiment had earned fame on the battlefield.

'Ex-Guards,' he said again in an awed whisper. '*He* ought to get things moving.'

'Perhaps too fast for some of us,' I said. 'Does your mother know yet that you've joined up?'

He looked a little uncertain of himself, as though he weren't sure whether he were a man itching to get his hand on something lethal and do damage with it, or still just a boy, scared stiff his mother would find out he'd done what she'd forbidden. 'Not yet,' he said. 'She thinks I go to the office every day.'

'Are you *going* to tell her?' I asked.

He grinned sheepishly. 'Thought I'd wait,' he said. 'I'll be eighteen soon and then she can't stop me.'

Murray had all my sympathy. I'd long since ceased to enjoy living at Mrs Julius' and reporting each morning by bus to the Drill Hall. It was a bit like being at the office, and I'd discovered that damned attic at Morrelly Street was a dark and cheerless hole to spend an evening in when I hadn't any money in my pocket. Mrs Julius had long since decided that the fitful allowance they gave us for rations wasn't half enough, and her patriotic affection had diminished rapidly, and the meals she served up had taken a decided turn for the worse.

'All right! All right! *All right!*' The sharp Guards voice stopped all the chattering as though it had been cut off with a knife, and we all swung round, standing in groups in the grey interior of the Drill Hall, nervous of this intruder into what in such a few short days had already become a normal part of life. We were still new enough to be scared of fierce-looking strangers and edged closer together, anxious not to do the wrong thing; and the new company sergeant-major marched between us, the only one of us in uniform, not asking us to get out of the way as we'd been used to from Corker and the others, but using his bony shoulders against anyone who wasn't quick enough, his hands clasped firmly behind his back on a cane; a tall sullen sliver of a man, thin as a lath, with a narrow pale face and a ginger moustache.

'All right,' the high hectoring voice went on. 'Let's 'ave you. Let's 'ave you in your sections. Y'oughta be there by now, didn't you? You shouldn't need tellin', and I shan't tell you again. My name's Bold. Patrick Bold. Son of Mrs Bold, of Streatham. Bold by name and Bold by nature. So you'd better watch out. Let's 'ave you outside – AND SHARP, TOO!'

There was something in that stentorian voice and ramrod figure that made you leap to attention – authority and three hundred years of pride and skill; and we literally charged through the door to reach our appropriate places.

'Come on, come on, jump about a bit!' Bold's voice was like a terrier snapping at our heels, chivvying us, worrying us, nagging at us, so that we instinctively shied away from it whenever it came too close.

Between them, Bold and Corker got us sorted out in the roadway in sections, and the crowd of small boys which had taken to hanging round the Drill Hall doors was joined by a dozen or more housewives and a few men from the pub and from the brassworks belching smoke at the end of the road. By the time they'd got the usual stragglers in their proper places, the street was crowded with interested spectators, and people were hanging out of the upper windows shouting encouragement.

'Give it 'em, boys! Down with the Kaiser!'

'You're in the wrong mob, Eph,' someone called. 'Dooley's Gang hangs out on the Common!'

Eph Lott grinned and waved, a smart figure in a fancy waist-coat, yellow-and-black boots, celluloid collar and a furry Homburg. He never seemed to do much except stand in his place, surrounded by scowling minions who fetched him cigar-ettes and pushed to the front in the pubs to buy him his sand-wiches when they dismissed us at midday.

'Don't you worry,' he shouted back. 'I didn't make no mistake.'

'Shut your row,' Bold told him immediately. 'And face front! Yes, *you* I mean,' he roared as Eph looked round, startled, for the criminal. 'YOU! FATTY! You with the fancy boots and red face. Git yourself moving and take that grin orf your dial, do! This is the Army, not the Vaults Bar of the Pig and Whistle.'

It was surprising how fast Eph could move when he had to.

Bold glared after him and began to walk slowly down the line, his hands behind his back, eyeing us one after the other as though he detested the sight of us. His face was hard, as though there was no flesh under the skin, only iron-like bone and muscle; but there was humour about his mouth and, in spite of its tightness, it was curiously not mean. In front of Tom Creak he stopped dead, with a shocked look on his face, as though he'd found someone without his trousers.

'You ain't shaved,' he breathed, horrified.

Tom smiled. 'Every other day,' he pointed out, ''cept on Sundays when I go to chapel.'

'In the Army,' Bold told him, his jaw thrust out, his voice low and vicious, 'you shave *every* day. Every day, see? – and *twice* on Sundays.'

'Oh! All right!' Tom gave Bold a beaming smile that showed his willingness under the circumstances to change the habit of a lifetime, and Bold's face went red, the colour flooding up from his collar and over his prominent cheekbones.

'All right?' he said. '*All right?* What kind of answer's that? What's your name?'

'Tom Creak.'

'Tom Creak, eh? Not Kaiser Bill or Wee Willie Winkie? Just Tom Creak. Mrs Creak's little lad. Well, Tom Creak, just remember that these 'ere stripes and this 'ere crown on this 'ere arm ain't there just because I scored three goals and a foul for the Rovers. I slaughtered the enemy in thousands in South Africa. I earned 'em in the field, and I'm entitled to the respect what goes with 'em. I'm *Sergeant-Major* Bold to you lot, see? SERGEANT-MAJOR!'

He turned on his heel and faced us, and we instinctively stood up straighter and stuck our chests out farther.

'Right,' he snarled. 'You're now going over to the Rovers' ground at Hendrick Lane where you 'ave in the past been in the 'abit of disporting yourselves among the cup-tie crowds. This time, though, it'll be different. At great trouble and expense the colonel's 'ired the ground so you can start your first day's squad drill. And, for a change, you ain't goin' to ride there on trams or in motorcars. You're goin' to march there, see? So do me a favour, will you? See if you can all manage to arrive at the same time.'

It was more like a ramble than a march. We set off enthusiastically enough, every one of us feeling himself a hell of a fellow, but there were more than a few who seemed to have trouble in getting their feet to the ground at the same time as everyone else. Before we'd turned the first corner the whole column was changing step – one file after the other – so that ripples seemed to be running up and down the column like waves on a beach, and we were all complaining, apologising and treading on each other's heels.

Corker marched at our side, shouting the step in his raucous boozy voice in an effort to make a presentable job of it, and at first we tried to keep our eyes firmly fixed ahead in the approved style. But there were too many children running alongside and getting in the way, too many jibes from the carters sitting on their vehicles that had to be answered. Miniature Union Jacks were waved in our faces and an old man with an accordion trotted alongside us trying unsuccessfully to play 'The British Grenadiers'. Then, as we passed a couple of halted trams, the drivers started to stamp rhythmically on their bells and the motorists who'd been drawn up by a policeman to let us pass began to pump the bulbs of their horns, and a frightened horse started to kick its shafts to pieces.

Someone began to cheer and the noise brought more people running to the doors of the little houses in Hendrick Lane. A girl in an apron and mop-cap came out of a passage to watch, still holding in her hands a fruit tart she'd been on the point of putting on the table, and in a flood of emotion she handed it at once to someone a few files ahead of me. There were cheers and calls for more and a man standing in front of a pub with a pint in his hand offered it to Tom Creak, who drank it as he marched and solemnly handed the pot back to someone else farther along. A fat woman tried to kiss Sergeant-Major Bold, but she picked the wrong man and he brushed her aside without even faltering in his step.

'Ep! Ri! Ep! Ri! Keep up, there! Git back in the ranks, that man!'

The gates of the Rovers' ground were already open and we swung inside and across the green turf, watched by curious groundsmen, and came to an untidy stop that made Sergeant-Major Bold wince.

As we shuffled into a ballooning line, heads craning to see what was happening and where the marker was, he stalked towards us, his face fierce, the bony whiteness of his chin gleaming in the sunshine.

'That was a bloody fine exhibition,' he snarled. 'I don't think. Pies! Beer! Shaving every other day!' the words exploded like grenades. 'What a rotten sloppy lot you are. I don't know whether you 'ope to frighten the Germans but, by God, you certainly frighten me. You've been too long in offices. That's what you've been. You've been too long on your mums' knees and in your nurses' arms. From this minute – this very minute – you'll realise you're in the Army. Got that? What you did before don't matter. What you do when we let you go don't matter. It's *now* that matters. Now that I've arrived – me, Patrick Bold, late of the Grenadiers – you don't eat tripe-and-onions and pea-and-pie suppers on the march. See? You're in the Army. And to prove same, you will now learn such intricate movements as right wheel, about turn and form fours. Very difficult for tiny minds like yourn, what's only been used to grappling with how to sell a yard of ribbon or 'ow many beans make five in a ledger.'

He paused and walked along the front rank, his eyes darting from face to face, cold, sneering and full of contempt. 'You will nevertheless learn to perform these movements proper,' he went on. 'Because they are the sacred war dance of the soldier. Mysterious, complicated and unamusing to all but the trained man, who looks on the correct performance of 'em as the right and proper reward of 'is labour on the parade ground. If you learn to do 'em proper, it might save a battle. It might save

England. It might even save your useless little lives. So take them coats off. I'm going to make you sweat. Get 'em off. Quick! *No!*' he roared as there was a concerted rush for the fence. 'Stay where you are! I didn't tell you to break ranks, did I? Drop 'em at your feet. I'll git you clear of 'em without you gitting 'em all round your silly little ankles.'

As I dropped my coat in the dust, Kaiser Bill had already been replaced in my mind as Public Enemy Number One by Sergeant-Major Bold. His high snarling voice was like a knife twisting in a wound and there wasn't one of us who didn't nervously try to make his eyes click in their sockets when Bold called 'Eyes front'.

The squad drill wasn't hard at first, and curiously enough, in spite of Bold, for the first hour or two it seemed fun. Even with Corker barking at our heels and Bold watching with lordly disdain from the touchline. But after a while, after lunch – when they dismissed us and told us to find something to eat in the little pie-and-brawn shops and pubs round Hendrick Lane, where those with money paid for those without and Eph Lott's ill-gotten gains supplied beer and pies for Tom Creak and the Mandys and a few more from out of town – by the end of the afternoon, when we were growing hot and tired, it became boring and wearisome from sheer repetition.

'There's a 'ell of a lot of you blokes' – Bold came up from where he'd been supervising another squad and eyed us disgustedly – 'what 'ave never noticed your right side's different from your left.'

He walked up and down in front of us, sneering and icy, his expression jarring like a blistered heel against our weariness. We stared sullenly back at him, seething with anger. It had been galling to discover that people like Corker and Bold, Regular soldiers who we'd been in the habit hitherto of looking down on as men who couldn't hang on to a job in Civvy Street, could perform with ease the evolutions that were now causing us so much heartache. It was humiliating to discover that our better education didn't help us at all, and the humiliation made us mutinous. I hadn't joined the Army to be pushed around by ill-natured boors like Bold, I was thinking savagely. I'd joined up to go and fight the Germans, and Bold's snarling sarcasm had no place in that plan.

'Your right side,' he went on, rubbing salt in the wound 'in case your tiny little minds ain't yet grasped the fact, is the one you shake 'ands with.'

'I never shake hands,' Spring said in a low vicious voice, his sweating face furious under the boater he still wore. 'I always say "What ho, old boy!"'

Spring was on my right and I saw Bold's bony face draw nearer, unmoved by the hatred in the faces of at least a hundred and fifty of the two hundred-odd men in front of him.

'Ho, you do, do you?' he said. 'Well, you don't say "What ho, old boy!" round here. I'll tell you that for nothing. You stand to attention, see? And if it's an officer, you salute. Any of you lot know *when* to salute?'

'When I see the whites of their eyes,' I muttered, sarcastically. I was as hot and tired and bored as Spring and already full of ideas of waylaying Bold one dark night somewhere in the back streets round the Drill Hall and getting my own back.

There was an appreciative snigger from several other sufferers that made me feel better, but Bold heard, too, and came closer, quite unperturbed by the show of dislike around him.

'Aha,' he said, staring at me with a disconcerting peer. 'Another little man with wit and 'umour who thinks he knows more about soldierin' than Sergeant-Major Bold! Another little man who thinks that, because Sergeant-Major Bold was only a Regular soldier while he was earning big money in an office, he knows how to fight a war. Mentioning no names, of course, but following the direction of my eyes.'

He paused and surveyed us all cheerfully. 'You all hate my guts, don't you?' he went on. 'Good! Well, I'll tell you something now, free, gratis and for nothing. There's too many of you blokes who think you're the lords of creation, just because you've generously offered your services at a time of crisis. Well, you ain't, see? You shoulda stayed civilians if you want to go your own sweet way. But you didn't and you ain't managers and under-managers and chief dustbin-emptiers no more. You're in the Army now and you've got a job to do, and the sooner you learn it the more use you'll be to your King and Country and the more I'll like you.

'For the moment, you're the lowest form of animal life ever thought of – untrained soldiers. You speak only when you're spoke to. You don't answer sergeant-majors back. And you salute an officer whenever you see one, and sometimes when you don't. You salute him riding a bicycle or astride an elephant, standing still or flying through the air. See? And when you salute, you salute like a soldier, not like a drunken ostler touching 'is 'at to the gentry. Before I've finished with you, I'll 'ave you saluting postmen, station-masters and commission-aires. I'll make you realise the Regular Army wasn't just full of loafers and bloody 'alf-wits, and that there 'ave been from time immemorial men who enjoyed soldiering – curious as it seems – and who took a pride in serving their country. Men like me, for instance. Men like them in France, what have been 'olding the Empire together while you rotten lot skulked in Civvy Street, and will go on holding it together till you lot are ready. See?'

He gave us one more glare and stalked away.

'Right,' Corker shouted as he vanished, his voice faintly apologetic, as though he considered Bold's energy was going to play havoc with what he'd hoped would be a cushy billet among friends. 'Let's 'ave yer! Body erect, 'ead up, feet at an angle of forty-five degrees, chests out, shoulders back, arms 'angin' loosely by the sides. *Chests*, I said, not the bit Napoleon said you marched on! Squa-a-ad – right – turn!'

'I've managed for years,' Locky panted, secure in the knowledge that Bold was now beyond hearing, 'to turn to

70

right or left quite easily, regardless of any scientific rules on the subject.'

'Silence, that man, or I'll crime yer,' Corker bawled. 'Let's 'ave it again. Both knees straight. Body erect. Swing on the right heel and left toe. And *stamp* yer feet! For Gawd's sake, *stamp yer feet*!'

'It still seems simpler the way I did it before.'

Corker glared, infuriated. 'Stop that talking, Mr 'Addo,' he shouted. 'Please! You ain't so bleeden 'ot at it you can afford to waste your breath gassin'. Let's 'ave another go. Heads up. Chests out – not *that*, Murray! It looks indecent. Your *chest*.'

While Antwerp was captured, and with it the naval brigades who'd gone into battle without water-bottles or bandoliers and had carried their ammunition in their pockets and their bayonets in their gaiters; while the French, still in the red trousers and long blue capotes of the Second Empire, were led to the Marne by officers in epaulettes and white gloves; while the Russians were smashed at Tannenberg, and the remains of the British Army squared up to meet the Germans and their own final destruction at First Ypres – we wore the grass completely off the turf at Hendrick Lane. By the time the summer broke, and the evenings began to grow misty with autumn, the field had turned into a quagmire and the directors were looking anxiously into the possibility of governmental recompense.

So we moved back to Edward Road and the police closed the street outside the Drill Hall with barriers, and we performed ignominiously in front of a perpetual crowd, floundering in the roadway while the buffer girls from the works around came to shout catcalls in their dinner hour; falling off the parallel bars to the great delight of the kids on their way to school; lying in the dust of the gutter and performing Swedish drill until we were exhausted with exercise and fresh air. The battalion horses and waggons which had arrived at last – a gift from the Corporation – were parked around us, and great piles of fodder had appeared in the street, much to the joy of the householders who kept chickens and pigs in the allotments on the railwayside behind their houses.

We'd got all our officers now. FitzJimmy had thankfully retired and we'd got a new colonel. The second-in-command was a dug-out who'd been retired to Gloucestershire for ten years and who, if he'd stayed long enough with us, which fortunately he didn't, would have discouraged the easily discouraged by sheer negation. Ashton was already a captain and in command of D Company, but the junior officers, in spite of their keenness, had no more idea of soldiering than we had and had to be led by the hand almost by people like Bold and Corker.

Most of the faded NCOs who'd appeared on the first day, with their dyed hair and the hidden medals which gave away their age, had vanished into the stores or to other cushy jobs, and newcomers had taken their places. Mason had been one of the first to be picked out for a stripe and we'd all cheered him and told him to 'treat the men kindly' and 'not to forget he'd been in the ranks himself', and had pretended for days to snap to attention whenever he approached.

'How many pints did you have to buy?' Locky had asked him. 'I'm told Quartermaster-Sergeant Twining sells stripes at a fiver a time.'

They'd vaccinated us and inoculated us, and Bold had at last begun to make us realise that, in spite of the civilian clothes we still wore, we could no longer regard ourselves as fit to hire or fire others and that we no longer had the backing of trades unions or friendly societies. In spite of our knickerbockers, and the clean white collars we put on dutifully each morning out of sheer habit, we were expected to stand stiffly to attention in front of the humblest NCO and salute people like Ashton who not long before had been in the habit of drinking with us. We were not Territorials but Regulars, and Bold never let us forget it.

'My God,' Mason said bitterly, after a particularly trying morning, 'if that's what the Regular Army's made up of, no wonder they retreated from Mons. That man would worry rats.'

Locky grinned. 'God made him,' he said, untouched by the general surliness. 'In his own image, too.'

'It must have been one of his off days, then,' Mason growled. 'He's the sort of bloody man who'd stand to attention to speak to the CO on the telephone. It'd be kinder to have him quietly put away. We could have him shot,' he suggested cheerfully. 'He'd like that. He could arrange the ceremony himself.'

'Ten rounds rapid and one up the tarara for anyone who misses,' Murray chirruped.

'And bury him at the crossroads with a stake through his heart so he can't come up again.'

When it rained, they taught us musketry without muskets and bayonet-fighting without bayonets. They showed us pictures of the Lee-Enfield rifle and the Vickers machine gun and we had to make do with those until we could get the real thing. Once – a great day – they produced a genuine rifle and placed it on a tripod in front of us, an object of veneration and interest we weren't allowed to touch.

'That's a rifle,' Bold said. 'What's it for, Fenner?'

'To protect my life, Sergeant-Major,' I said.

Bold sneered. 'Your life?' His eyebrows shot up. 'Who's worried about *your* potty little life, you silly little man? The rifle's given to you for the destruction of the King's enemies and nothing else, see?'

Often, I'm sure, he ran out of ideas of what to do with us. When he'd exhausted us with drilling, he gave us lectures on regimental history, Boer War battles and tactics, on military

73

law and organisation, and every bugle call he could think of. He taught us rank badges, for none of us had yet seen enough to be familiar with them, and most of us couldn't tell a colonel from a company sergeant-major.

'This 'ere star means a second lieutenant,' he told us with the aid of a blackboard. 'That means 'e knows nothin', so don't take no notice of 'im. A dog's leg or skater means a lance-jack and three stripes and a crown's a company sergeant-major. 'E's the man to watch. I'm a company sergeant-major.'

I acquired a thousand and one unimportant items of military information – why, for instance, soldiers always break step when crossing a bridge and why you never put your hands over the muzzle of your rifle – when you *had* a rifle.

'You get perspiration into the muzzle, see?' Bold said. 'And if you do you'll have the armourer-sergeant after you.'

We were told never – even in fun – to point rifles at each other and why it was a court-martial offence to whistle the *Dead March* in barracks.

We learned it was improper to address a Guardsman as 'Private' – according to Bold it would be sheer brazen impudence for us to address a Guardsman at all, but if there were no alternative it had to be with 'Guardsman'. Cavalrymen were 'troopers'; engineers 'sappers'; signallers 'signalmen'; men from the rifle regiments, 'riflemen'; and artillerymen, 'gunners'. I learned that all fusilier regiments had a bomb in their badges and all light-infantry regiments a bugle, and all units raised in India before the mutiny a tiger.

From time to time they sat us down in rows on the floor of the Edward Road Drill Hall and brought some elderly politician along to tell us stories of German atrocities, probably in the pious hope of producing blood-lust in us. Nobody believed them, of course.

There were lectures on discipline, with examples from Waterloo, Omdurman and the Crimea to fortify the claims for its necessity. They even brought in the Church to give us lectures on how to behave ourselves, but somehow most of these became invocations to fight like devils 'for God and the Mother Country'.

No one ever alluded to the fact that we might at some point in our career be killed.

When the city Council had assembled enough tools for us to make it worthwhile, we were marched to Suffolk Park to learn how to dig trenches. To the surprise of everyone in France, particularly the generals, the war had settled down to a curious sort of stalemate which failed to include all the expected cavalry charges and infantry actions – just a queer mole-like combat where soldiers sat in holes in the ground and waited for the enemy to stick his head up so they could blow it off – and digging trenches had suddenly become an important part of recruit training.

With all the drilling and lectures we'd endured, a day out in Suffolk Park looked like making a pleasant change. Most of us had memories of picnics there, or visits with girls, and we set off joyously, in spite of the damp, behind Sergeant Corker, followed as usual by waving flags and crowds as the city turned out to see us go.

We had a band by this time – most of the instruments still privately owned – but Corker was late starting and we lost touch with the music before we'd reached the first corner. It didn't worry us much, though, and we bowled along making enough racket with our silly little songs to wake the dead.

Murray was inclined to favour 'Boys of the Bulldog Breed' and choruses full of patriotism and dedication, but most of us were content to settle for 'Ilkla Moor Baht 'At' or 'Tipperary' or ridiculous little ditties that enabled us to give a sheepish guffaw at ourselves. The things they *never* appealed to were honour and glory. We could leave that sort of nonsense to the

French, we thought. Our songs were irreverent, banal and occasionally obscene, but never passionate or patriotic. Mostly they were merely music hall ditties you could march to and had nothing at all to do with the war.

'Send for the Boys of the Girls' Brigade,'

we sang

'To set old England free.
Send for my mother, send for my sister,
But, for God's sake, don't send for me.'

By the time we crossed Greville Road we'd got a whole host of enthusiastic dogs barking round us, and in St George Street the vicar decanted the kids from the Church School on to the wet pavement to cheer us on, and they all stood there in an untidy mob by the door, in long black stockings and sailor suits with *HMS Tiger* on the pocket, in jerseys and knitted ties, and pinafores and hair-ribbons, waving grubby handkerchiefs and uttering little treble cries.

On Sidepool Hill, Corker fell us out on a patch of waste ground alongside a pub and told us we'd got ten minutes to rest before we finished the journey. It was cold and inclined to drizzle and in our innocence we waited uncomplainingly, huddled against the damp wall while the leaves drifted down all round us; then Eph Lott went round to the back door to see if he could get a whisky to warm him up, and came back bog-eyed with the news that the pub was kept by Corker's sister and Corker was inside by the fire drinking hot rum-and-lemon.

'We didn't join up for this,' young Murray shouted indignantly. 'We joined up to fight the Boche, not to provide Corker with a free bloody rum!'

'They can't get away with it,' Mason said indignantly, his

new stripe burning a hole in his arm. 'They can't do this to *us*.'

It was hard for us to understand soldiers like Corker. Though he'd probably have flogged for booze, if he'd had a chance, every scrap of equipment we possessed – and it wasn't much at that time, God knows! – his rotten, loyal old heart was solidly in the Army and he had no favourites.

There were others who gave nothing as a collateral for the lessons in drill they offered to ambitious privates, with false promises of stripes at the end of the course; or for the illegal subscriptions they got out of us for parting gifts when Fitz-Jimmy and the adjutant left us, and which never saw the light of day. These men we could appreciate, but the company could never have existed without Bold and Corker – for all the harsh nagging of one and the boozy face and the professed desire for a cushy billet of the other. Between them they coached Ashton in court-martial procedure, the subalterns in drill, the chaplain in church-parade order, the MO on how to conduct sick parades, and the NCOs in hygiene and discipline.

Bold we understood. He was a machine. He was a dedicated Regular with no warmth or feeling in him anywhere for us. But that Corker, with his sly humour and friendliness and merry boot-button eyes, could take advantage of our lack of knowledge was beyond us. Perhaps it was all part of an unconscious desire on the part of the once-despised Regulars to make us realise we were now no better than they were and that they, with their sure knowledge of what they could get away with and what they couldn't get away with, had the advantage of us, despite our superior education.

Only Locky didn't raise his voice in protest and I suspect that of us all he was probably the only one who understood.

'Never fear,' he said gravely. 'Doubtless we shall win the war in spite of – or perhaps because of – the Regular Army.'

There was a hurried indignant debate about what we should

do, because none of us had the sense or the courage to go and call Corker's bluff by joining him at the bar, then MacKinley, because he was a Canadian and, as such, got away with things on the ground that he didn't understand our way of life, agreed to go in and complain. Corker was no Bold. Corker was one of us, like most of the officers, and we had no awe of him.

He came out behind MacKinley, fastening his waistcoat and adjusting his checked cap, and stood staring at us as we formed up again, all of us glowering and anxious to be off.

'I've never seen nothing like you lot ever before,' he said, in bewilderment, his flat red face baffled. 'Never in all me puff. I never thought I'd see the day when soldiers'd be keen to get to work. Right honest, I didn't.'

He marched to the head of the column, shaking his head. It was beyond his experience that men could *demand* to be worked, could even practise arms drill with broomsticks in their spare time, as we did, so they'd be able to mount guard when they had rifles and something to guard.

The other companies were already hard at it when we arrived at Suffolk Park and had already started to carve up the turf with trenches, watched by a morose head park keeper.

The officers were fidgeting impatiently as we swung into line in front of them, Ashton with a hurt disembowelled look on his face as though he'd been wondering where the hell we'd got to. They were in a group, surrounding the new colonel in his old-fashioned overcoat with its fur collar and the yellow piping on the shoulder straps. His tunic was as out-of-date as his overcoat, with a choker collar and starched stock, and he stood there under the dripping trees, his long nose red with the nip in the air and his head well down on his shoulders. He'd joined us from the Indian Army, together with a new adjutant, Lieutenant Pine, and, with the permanent dew-drop on the end of his nose, seemed to be perpetually thinking of a warmer climate and the less boisterous, dark little men he used to command in some Gurkha regiment.

As we came to a stop, he moved restlessly among the group of officers, sharp against the mistiness of the background, where the distant trees were mere shadows in the drizzly rain.

'Your company's late, Mr Ashton,' he snapped fretfully, slapping at his boots with his cane. 'We're wasting time! Get them busy, please.'

There were no traverses in the trenches we dug, of course, because we still had no knowledge of the blast effects of high-explosive shells. We used picks and shovels – all of them with the City Councils's initials still burned into the handles – which made it a great deal easier than it would have been with entrenching tools; and as Tom Creak and the Mandy brothers and the other miners among us, spare and hard as the tools they'd used since boyhood, regarded the efforts of the rest of us with something not far from contempt, we were inclined to stand back and cheer them on while they did it for us.

When we'd finished and had stood back to admire our handiwork, hot and tired and with our suits covered with mud, an elderly brigadier with boiled blue eyes like marbles, whom we'd never seen before, came galloping across the turf. 'No, no, no,' he said irritably as he came to a stop. 'For God's sake, not like that!'

There was a hurried conference among the officers, then Corker came clambering along the heaps of soil towards us, slipping on the clayey slopes.

'Fill 'em in,' he said. He looked angry and fed up.

'Fill 'em in?' Eph Lott stared down at the scarred turf at his feet, 'I only just dug 'em,' he said indignantly.

'Well, fill 'em in again.'

'Just cos that old bastard with the red 'at-band and the 'orse says so? 'Oo's 'e think 'e is, anyway?'

'Fill 'em in.'

'There's a bleeden park keeper over there,' Eph said, pointing.

'Looking like a sick cat because we've mucked his bloody park up. He's going to go 'ome tonight and tell his old Dutch: "You know what them soldiers – Kitchener's mob – did today? They dug all my bleeden park up till it looked like an allotment. And what you think they did then? Some bloke with a red 'at-band and a face like a vegetable came along and told 'em, 'Fill 'em in.' And they did." Well, they *didn't*. I'm not going to fill 'em in,' he announced. 'Let 'im with the red 'at-band fill 'em in. If 'e wants payin' for the job, I don't mind slipping 'im 'alf a bar.'

Just then Bold strode across from where he'd been talking to Ashton. His stride was jerky and puppet-like and his bone-white face had two red spots on it, high on his cheekbones.

'Fill 'em in, lads,' he said, his voice more gentle than I'd ever heard it.

'What, now?' Eph said.

'Fill 'em in, I said.'

'Yes, Sergeant-Major.'

So we filled them in while the brigadier sat and waited on his horse and the colonel stood and slapped his boot morosely with his cane, and Sergeant-Major Bold glowered at them and fidgeted with his stick.

'My God,' Eph muttered. 'Ain't it enough to turn you pie-eyed?'

For a long time we worked in silence, the clay clinging to our shoes in great lumps, muttering to each other, and swearing softly, then I heard the colonel talking to the brigadier.

'What about barbed wire?' he asked. 'Shouldn't they learn something about that?'

The brigadier fiddled with his reins and the horse curvetted, kicking up clods of turf to the disgust of the head park keeper. The brigadier's red gorgets looked new and he'd probably just been promoted, and his manner was anxious and impatient, as though he weren't very certain himself what should be done.

'There isn't any wire,' he said. 'We haven't got any. In any case, you don't *need* wire, Colonel. If the Hun sees posts he'll think there's wire all right. It looks like wire from a distance. It always fooled the Boers.'

The colonel looked surprised and the brigadier gestured angrily with the crop he was carrying.

'Personally,' he said, 'I think all this damn' trench-digging's a lot of nonsense. Stops movement. Impedes the cavalry. Somebody's got the wind up in France. That's the trouble. You'd be better employed getting your men to learn to advance against shell-fire.'

So, to please the brigadier, we 'advanced against shell-fire' and charged up the slopes under the trees, tearing up the gravel surfaces of the paths and flinging ourselves down in the puddles that had collected.

'Here goes my last suit,' I said to Mason as we lay in the dirt, and got a swipe across the behind from Bold's cane for my trouble.

'Never mind about your suit,' he snapped. 'Just git your 'ead down. The other end'll look after itself. You won't worry about your best suit when the Hun starts shooting at you.'

'I hope when the Hun starts shooting at us,' I muttered, 'I shan't have my best suit on.'

Bold stared down at me. He looked as cold and disgusted as we were, and the bones of his jaw seemed to stick through the skin.

'You've got a damn' sight too much to say for yourself, altogether, Private Fenner,' he told me harshly. 'A lot too much. Maybe you'd like to come back tonight and do a little cleaning up around the Drill Hall, just so you'll learn in the Army it pays to 'old your tongue and not question orders. Take his name, Sergeant Corker.'

They kept us there till dusk, most of the time lying down on the wet earth, until Bold found young Murray fast asleep at the end of the line, wearied by all the digging and running in the open air.

''Aving a nice dream?' he demanded loudly, giving him a shove with his boot.

Murray looked up and blinked as he tried to make out where he was. Then his smooth young face broke into a wide unashamed grin.

'Not half, Sergeant-Major,' he said. 'I dreamt the war was over and I was chasing the girls down the Unter den Linden.'

'Oh, you did, did you?' Bold snapped. 'Well, just to show you it ain't, you can join Fenner here at the Drill Hall tonight. I expect we've got some nice fire buckets that need scraping and painting.'

He slapped his calf with his cane and stalked off with Corker. As he vanished, we could hear him muttering.

'Bloody old dugouts,' he was saying. 'These lads'll get their death of cold. That blasted brigadier wants his 'ead examining.'

Murray looked at me and we both stared after Bold, startled. The fact that he ever stopped to think about our health and welfare came as a surprise to both of us.

'He loves me,' Murray breathed in mock ecstasy. 'He loves me. He's actually noticed that I exist. Mother, I can now die happy.'

When orders to parade for uniforms appeared at last on the noticeboard at the Drill Hall, a howl of joy went up.

I'd ruined two suits and three pairs of shoes already and had had to buy myself a pair of officer's boots at the Public Benefit Shoe Company for thirty bob. Even some of the instructors still wore cloth caps and bowlers and there'd been no sign yet of the money we'd been promised for wear and tear. Even pay was still a bit irregular and it was fortunate that most of us could *afford* to be soldiers.

'Being a volunteer's becoming bloody expensive,' Frank Mason complained.

Shoes had started to fall to pieces as soon as the first blisters had begun to emerge, and our clothes were suffering badly from the strain. Once, when we'd marched through Nethersedge village, they'd thought we were Germans captured at Ypres and one old dear with a softer heart than the rest had offered an apple to Locky because she thought he looked as though he hadn't eaten for days.

Milton had bought more than one pair of boots for men who needed them and Eph Lott had seen to it that some of his market-stall friends had dug deep into their pockets to provide clothing.

'The bastards can afford it,' he'd said. 'With watches at five bob a time with 'alf the works missing, and two 'undred per cent profit on fruit? 'Course they can. I know. I was selling 'em both meself last month.'

Then young Welch had managed to get a few cheap suits and shirts sent down from his father's store, and the men whose breeches behinds were hanging out had been able to hold up their heads again.

Curiously enough, it never occurred to me – and I'm sure it didn't to anyone else – to feel particularly neglected. I just assumed naïvely that Kitchener was pretty busy in other directions and would get around to *us* when he'd got the time, and I was quite prepared to endure until he did. I'd been fortified all along, I think, by the knowledge that I'd got in on the fight before all the best places in the ring were taken and was quite prepared to supply myself with all that the Army couldn't manage. In fact, I'd been taken in by every profiteer on the market, buying more than my share of special non-wear socks and patent foot-salves. *When its feet give out, the Army gives in*, they told us and, like everyone else, I'd swallowed it whole and bought the damn' stuff in crate-loads.

But now, with uniforms, real uniforms, within our grasp, there wasn't one of us who wasn't prepared to forgive and forget the penny-catching efforts to get our pay off us. We were dazzled by the thought of parading down High Street with at least one girl on each arm.

The Drill Hall was jammed with excited men in a variety of frayed suits and battered hats and worn shoes long before Company Quartermaster-Sergeant Twining deigned to arrive from the digs he occupied on Cotterside Common.

It was raining a little outside and thin veils of autumn mist were drifting in through the door, making a wet smear on the floorboards near the entrance that shone in the grey light from outside. Ashton appeared, his coat sparkling with damp, his spectacles gleaming, then Milton and Welch, all hurrying through to company headquarters. There was a long-drawn-out sigh of thankfulness as we heard the bolts of the quartermaster's store being drawn.

'They're coming,' Murray said.

But it was Sergeant-Major Bold who stepped out, ramrod-straight, his moustache bristling, his eyes glinting under the peak of his cap.

''Ello,' he said cheerfully, feigning surprise. 'What's this? The lions at feeding time? A mob of bloody fuzzy-wuzzies starting a war dance?' He paused and stared, his eyebrows shooting up. 'Or can it be soldiers?' he asked. '*Real* soldiers, ready to do and die for King and Country?'

He glared at us and his milky tones suddenly changed. 'Get yourselves into line, you sloppy lot,' he stormed. 'Let's 'ave a bit o' discipline, do!'

'There's too much bloody discipline in the British Army,' Arnold Holroyd muttered as we shuffled into a queue. 'The war might be tolerable if it weren't for that.'

But we got into line. We not only wanted to behave like soldiers, we wanted to look like soldiers. There were plenty of people in high places ready to sneer at us, and we were anxious to show them they were wrong. We'd been called 'Kitchener's ridiculous regiments' and 'the laughing-stock of all the armies of Europe', and a uniform seemed to be one of the first requisites for a true martial bearing and the quickest route possible to a bit of respect.

But when Murray, who was inevitably the first into the store, re-emerged, he had a look of shocked misery on his face.

'Look,' he choked. 'Look what they're giving us!'

He held up for us all to see an outfit that was nothing more than a militarised blue-grey flannel suit, hurriedly adapted by a multiple tailor. They'd added another couple of buttons to the jacket and left the turn-ups off the trousers and there was a glengarry of the same material, with a red stripe, to go with them. There were no badges, no brass buttons, nothing that could conceivably catch a girl's eye – only an arm-band which stated what unit we belonged to. You could only call them uniforms because they happened to all be alike.

'My God!' Spring said. 'Here I've been complaining all this time that a boater's not quite the thing to wage war in, and now look what they've given me.' He turned over the glengarry in his hands disgustedly. 'It looks like a coffin for a cat,' he said bitterly.

Bold was grinning all over his hard handsome face, enjoying the rage around him. 'They wouldn't waste good uniforms on you lot,' he said. 'They're a cheap job just thrown together quick.'

'A cheap job!'

'Just thrown together!'

Bold chuckled. 'Well, ain't that what you lot are? – ain't that what the 'ole of Kitchener's Army is? – a cheap job, just thrown together till they can get something better. Give me time, though,' he promised earnestly, 'and I'll make you fit to wear His Majesty's uniform. I'll make 'em *anxious* to give you a decent uniform. Get 'em on, and let's see what you look like.'

We dressed and stood staring at each other, shamefaced and like a lot of convicts in the ill-fitting clothing.

'It's no different from me working suit,' Eph Lott complained. 'The one I wear with me red tie and me yellow boots. Only it don't fit so well. They gave me a better suit than this when they sent me down for assaulting the police.'

His fat red face was indignant, his flabby cheeks quivering with indignation. Eph wasn't a very big man and you could hardly see him for uniform. 'I didn't join to get shot up the backside in a bloody spud sack like this,' he mourned.

Locky was staring at his reflection in one of the windows, a look of wry humour on his face.

'It's impossible,' he said in a tone of awestruck wonder.

'What's impossible?' Bold demanded.

'No man can look like Ethelred the Unready and Abdul the Damned at one and the same time.'

Bold's bony face cracked as he gave a bark of laughter, then he stifled it hurriedly and began to shout at Twining. 'Come on, Quartermaster,' he snapped. 'We haven't all day! Give 'em their trousseaux and let's get on with it!'

One after the other, we had our arms filled with shirts, underwear and socks.

'These boots are too big,' young Murray complained.

'Git 'im a new pair,' Bold snapped.

'Sergeant-Major,' Tom Creak said. 'This 'at. It's too small.'

'Git yourself a new 'ead,' Bold said unfeelingly. 'What do you think this is? Savile Row? One of them fancy French mobs? This is the Army, man!'

'Now,' he roared when we were outside again, awkward in the new uniforms, the cardboard-stiff kitbags filled with civilian clothing. 'Git your stuff 'ome and let's 'ave you back 'ere tomorrer morning with your uniforms fitting. *Fitting!* 'Ear that? Git your mums on the job. Git your wives. Git your sisters. Git your girl friends.'

'Sergeant-Major,' someone piped up, 'I've got no girlfriend.'

'Well, git yourself one,' Bold told him, unmoved. 'You ain't no soldier if you ain't got a girl friend. You ain't got much time. Next week we're going to start soldiering proper. We're leaving here.'

'Leaving?' Even the ridiculous uniforms they'd given us were forgotten as this latest item of news sank in through the noise.

'Leaving?' Henny Cuthbert said. 'Where are we going, Sergeant-Major?'

'Where are we going?' Bold said. 'Blackpool front. Southend-on-Sea. We're going to Blackmires. That's where we're going.'

'Blackmires!'

There was a loud groan. Blackmires was a thousand feet up, just outside the city on the edge of the Pennines. It was the place where Colonel Cody had flown his string-and-canvas aeroplanes from several years before, and it was well known he chose it because there was nothing but open moors to get in his way for miles around, and the strongest wind in the country to help him off the ground.

'They've been building a camp there,' Bold informed us. 'Well, now it's finished and we're going to take it over.'

'Blackmires,' Murray moaned. '*With winter coming on.*'

Locky sighed. 'The first drop of red-hot iron has entered my soul,' he said.

4

Until we moved to Blackmires it had all been a bit of a picnic. We'd been reaping the glory of the men in France with a minimum of discomfort. We'd lived at home, admired and treated like fighting-cocks, regarded as heroes and Hotspurs and defenders of the faith, without lifting a finger to defend anything and with more girls and free drinks than a lot of us could easily manage.

At Blackmires, it was different immediately. There wasn't much glory in that bleak little plain, and, cut off from the city streets as we were by those few empty miles of rain-soaked moors, there was a great deal of discomfort. There was no one within reach to regard us as heroes, and only one pub, the Four Merry Lads, where the farm-worker customers couldn't afford to buy anything for anyone but themselves. It was a wild windswept area devoid of trees and bushes and already with a hint of snow in the wind.

'Is *this* it?' Henny Cuthbert gave a neigh of horror as he stared from the top of the last hill through the growing dusk at the bleak huddle of huts in the shallow distant valley; a mere grouping of corrugated-iron and asbestos-and-wood shacks like a lot of squat black beetles round an unpainted water tower on stilts, their roofs gleaming in the needling rain that beat into our raw faces and soaked us all to the skin. The few trees about us were stunted and leaning well to the east, and the moss-patched dry-stone walls glimmered and shone in the fitful light that came through the racing clouds.

'This is it,' I said. I was carrying Henny's kitbag in addition to my own belongings and the best part of a parcel that Murray had brought, which had burst open halfway up the hill as we marched so that he'd had to distribute its contents among his pockets and his friends.

The camp was nothing but a shambles. The fields were sodden and the roads were quagmires. Nothing was finished. Nothing was ready. I saw Sergeant-Major Bold, his uniform soaked, his white face furious, splashing through the puddles on the cinder path that led to headquarters, shoving between groups of limping, bewildered men and cursing under his breath the people who'd sent us there. Suddenly soldiering seemed to lose all its glamour, and in the plaintive wails around me I caught a hint of the thin sad scent of disillusionment.

Because they hadn't had a chance to practise it, the regimental cooks didn't know their job and our first army meal was a wretched affair of half-boiled mutton, hard potatoes and undrinkable tea.

No one had knives or forks because we hadn't needed them up to then, and we had to tear the meat apart with our fingers, all sitting on the floor because there were no tables, all surrounded by the little items of equipment we'd had to tie about us with a string because we had no slings and pouches, all smelling of wet wool and complaining of feet crippled by boots that hadn't been properly broken in.

The draughty, damp-smelling cookhouse, that echoed the complaints like a vault, seemed to be full of steam and the smells of cabbage and half-cooked meat.

As darkness came we tottered towards our huts, through

parked transport with the City Council's name on it in square white letters, through the piles of canvas bags and tent poles and floorboards that lay in the mud, through the rolls of rusting barbed wire that were to form a fence and the rows of untarred wooden buildings and the piles of unused planks and bricks. There was no electricity, no coal and no roofing felt on the huts, and rainwater dripped monotonously inside to form pools on the bare floorboards. Half the windows were missing, and here and there an ill-fitting door banged in the wind.

There didn't seem to be anything else to do so we decided to go to bed. There weren't enough palliasses, of course, so we put them together in twos, and sharing the blankets, which were nothing more than suit-lengths from city tailors cut to the right size, lay down across them in batches of five for warmth, like litters of piglets in front of a sow.

We undressed in silence, listening to the whine of the wind and the creak and groan of the hut-frames in the gale, too exhausted and dispirited to say anything. Inevitably, Locky was already asleep. He had the gift of adapting himself to whatever came along. He wasn't a good soldier in the way that Mason was a good soldier. He was clumsy on parade ground and indifferent to authority, but he had the gift of fitting in without complaint, always hard-working, always good-tempered, always unobtrusive.

Murray had stripped himself to the skin and put on his pyjamas and then adorned himself with an assortment of socks, pullovers, scarves and balaclavas to keep himself warm. He was sitting moodily now on the edge of his portion of palliasse, his round young face edged by the faint light from the two candles which were all the hut could boast.

'Wouldn't like to borrow a couple more pullovers, would you?' I asked sarcastically. 'I've got some in my bag, if you'd like 'em?'

Murray turned his head wearily. 'I'm all right,' he said despondently.

90

'You ought to be warm, anyway.'

'My mother said I always ought to make sure of that.'

Someone laughed and Murray turned. It was Henry Oakley. He had money and he'd always been popular with the crowds at Hendrick Lane as a cricketer, but on closer acquaintance he'd proven to be quick-tempered and hard to get on with. He'd originally been in A Company, but had eventually turned up in D, and Locky insisted that Bold, with one eye on the company's cricket team, had swopped him for a spare clerk and a hundred cigarettes, and the disgrace had soured his nature.

'You think it's funny or something?' Murray was demanding.

Oakley looked up. 'You're in the Army now, sonny,' he said. 'You've got to leave your mummy behind.'

'You leave my mother out of this.'

Murray's mother was a standing joke in the company. He'd managed for weeks to hide from her where he went every day, but he'd been seen at last by a neighbour, charging madly across Suffolk Park with a broomstick, in company with two or three hundred other madmen, and before we'd left the Drill Hall for Blackmires there'd been quite a scene when she'd insisted on getting the colonel's promise that he shouldn't go overseas till he was eighteen.

His face went pink now and his fists started to clench.

'You trying to pick a fight or something?' he demanded, and Oakley grinned confidently.

'You want to do something about it if I am?' he asked.

Murray sighed and got to his feet and we all turned round to watch the fun, none of us really interested, but all welcoming violence as a diversion from the draughts and too tired to try to stop it.

Only Catchpole took no notice. He was on his knees by the window and we all thought he was saying his prayers, though it wasn't much like him. Although he was the Vicar of Cotterside's son, he'd never showed much enthusiasm for the family business. He was a burly rakehell of a man who'd been to sea and spent some time gold-mining in South Africa before returning home just before the war. He was always borrowing money from Eph, and scrounging cigarettes, and claimed to have a wife in Cape Town his family knew nothing about.

He'd placed a lace handkerchief that had obviously belonged to one of his numerous girlfriends on top of a wooden box he'd pinched for use as a locker, and on the handkerchief he'd stood a brass ashtray he'd brought with him and a bottle containing one of the two candles we'd found. For a long time he'd been silent, then just as Murray lifted his fists and Oakley got slowly to his feet, Catchpole, in sepulchral oratorical tones he'd obviously learned from his father, started to deliver a catechism of his own.

'Dearly beloved brethren,' he said loudly, and Murray and Oakley stopped dead and turned towards him, 'we are gathered together here in the sight of God and in the face of this congregation to join together these two men in mortal combat.'

Murray stared, startled, and Oakley's scowl faded. Arnold Holroyd grinned and Eph Lott twisted round on his palliasse to see what it was all about.

Catchpole stood up. He was wearing his shirt outside his trousers and, in the half-light looked vaguely like a parson in his surplice. He lifted his hands and began to proclaim in sombre tones that made everyone turn their heads.

'The Army moveth us in sundry places,' he said hollowly. 'To acknowledge and confess our manifold sins and wickedness . . .'

Someone laughed, a short sharp bark, and Murray dropped his fists and began to smile. Catchpole gestured with his hands over the flickering candle.

'We should not dissemble, nor cloak our sins before the face of Almighty God, the colonel,' he went on and we all sat up and began to listen gleefully, feeling better at once, all eyes turned to the candle-lit figure by the end of the hut, his fair hair ruffled by the breeze that came in through the broken window.

'We should not dissemble them before the face of the adjutant, the officers, or Sergeant-Major Bold. Let us confess them with a humble, lowly penitent heart, to the end that by the infinite goodness and mercy of the War Office we might eventually be granted blankets, knives, forks, spoons, and perhaps even somewhere to lay our weary heads.'

'Amen,' Mason said solemnly.

Catchpole turned and held out his hands towards us in blessing, his face as straight and expressionless as a curate's.

'O Lord,' he said loudly, 'we have erred and strayed from Thy ways like lost sheep and in consequence have had idiots set in judgment upon us . . .'

'Amen!' The chorus was taken up by all of us this time, cheerfully and with great zest, and the fight was forgotten as Catchpole began to warm up.

'. . . They have not done those things which they ought to have done and very soon there will be no health left in us . . .'

'Amen! And amen again!'

'Grant, O Lord, that we may hereafter live a godly, righteous and sober life – paying particular attention to one Ephsibiah Lott, who has long been a straying lamb . . .'

Eph started to chuckle, then it dissolved into a breathless laugh that shook his fat little body, and in the end he rolled off the end of the palliasse and lay flat on his back on the floor.

'Straying lamb,' he wheezed. 'Me! My Gawd!'

'O Lord, open Thou our lips – O God, make speed to save us.'

'O Lord, make haste to help us.'

Catchpole made a few more passes over the candle and swung round again to us, the wind that howled through the broken window ruffling his shirt. 'Blessed are the fornicators,' he said, 'for they shall populate the earth. Blessed are the lowly and the poor in spirit, for they are all privates in Kitchener's Army.'

'Amen, mate,' Eph shouted enthusiastically, still on his back.

A ghost of a smile crossed Catchpole's face and he dropped on his knees before the candle, raising his hands to heaven.

'Now let us pray for all those set over us,' he said, his voice wavering up and down as though he were chanting a psalm. 'For Lord Kitchener, the War Office, King's Regulations, Army Council Instructions, Daily Routine Orders, the generals, the colonels, the majors, the captains, the lieutenants, the second lieutenants, the sergeant-majors, the sergeants, the corporals, the lance-corporals, the cooks, the military police, the orderly-room staff, the chief cook, the bottle-washers, the colonel's terrier, the major's cat and the man who fought the monkey in the dustbin.'

Catchpole's voice grew stronger and he seemed to gather us together in a sweeping gesture before him, his sepulchral voice coming through the noise of the wind and the mutter of a loose door and the low sniggers of laughter, as he leafed through a novel belonging to Murray as though he were looking for his place in a Book of Common Prayer.

'We will now conclude,' he said, 'by singing hymn four thousand six hundred and seventy-three: "O Lord, I have never wronged an onion, So why should it make me cry?"'

As he droned to a stop, there was a burst of noisy laughter that was followed at once by a shout from the bed nearest the door.

'Quiet! Bold!'

The candles went out immediately and there was a hurried scuffling for palliasses. The door shook under a heavy fist and Sergeant-Major Bold's voice broke through the rattling of the wind and the beat of the rain.

'What are you lot doin' in there?'

'Saying our prayers, Sergeant-Major,' Henny Cuthbert said meekly, in a high-pitched girlish voice.

There was a long silence from outside. Bold was clearly trying to make up his mind how much truth there might be in the statement. For all his vast experience, he'd never had recruits such as he'd got now, and he was never quite certain what to expect next. He was clearly coming to the reluctant conclusion that, in fact, we *might* be saying our prayers.

In the end we heard him splash away and settled back in peace.

Suddenly Blackmires didn't seem so bad after all.

From the first trembling notes of reveille next day, when we learned just how cold cold water could be in a howling gale, life suddenly became a round of fatigues which I hadn't known existed when I'd lived at Mrs Julius'. Suddenly there was a cookhouse to clean, potatoes to peel, latrines to clean, huts to scrub, and always – always – some part of the camp to erect.

'God strike me blind,' Eph Lott complained. 'There's even a list of bloody duties to be done before breakfast.'

We got up at six-thirty – six if you had any sense and wanted to avoid the shoving, jostling crowd of men round too-few washbasins, shaving out of a mug filled over someone else's shoulder, scraping at cold-toughened beards in the half-light. We formed up with a great clattering of hobnailed boots outside the hut to march to the steamy warmth of the cookhouse, the darkness noisy with the clash of mess tins and spoons, the cooks grey-faced and unshaven in soiled white aprons and reaching for a mug of stale tea whenever there was a spare moment between the dollops of burnt porridge.

A whole day of work followed, boring and repetitious because they still hadn't realised we had any intelligence and insisted on doing everything the simple way, but relieved by moments of sly joy when we took pleasure in deliberately marching where we shouldn't – across the CO's lawn, over the fence into the next field, through the cookhouse – when Corker's attention was attracted elsewhere and he forgot to give us right or left wheel. In the evening, if there wasn't an inspection the next morning with boned boots and scrubbed table-tops and white-washed stove surrounds, and rolled greatcoats and laid-out kits, we had a free hour or two to pick up the threads of civilian life with a daily paper or a pack of cards, or a trip to the Four

Merry Lads where it was always beer and choruses round a piano with the back taken off.

Inevitably Eph became our crown-and-anchor king, and whenever there was a moment to spare he was down on one of the palliasses with his little strip of canvas or his lotto board on a blanket. We never got the chance to sample much else but Eph's gambling. We weren't allowed to wander far, and for days all we did was eat whatever was given us like ravening wolves and fall asleep wherever we happened to be lying. The company became more than ever our boundary, and of the wider world beyond it we never learned a great deal. If the battalion was our world, the company was our city, and the platoon our particular street.

All the original crowd seemed to be still together. I've got them all to this day, set down for ever on one of those group photographs that men always fly to whenever they're thrown together in groups or communities, all our little platoon in a curiously mixed bag in one corner of the picture. Henny Cuthbert. Eph and his corner boys, curiously saintly in the blankness of their expressions. MacKinley. All the newspapermen. Henry Oakley, looking just as he always did in the columns of the *Post* when he'd sent the wickets tumbling at Hendrick Lane. Catchpole, big and blond and somehow evil-looking. Tim Williams, who, to Eph's amazement, wrote poetry in his spare time. Spring, who was a Devonshire man and had joined the battalion for no other reason than that he happened to be in the city with a group of barnstorming actors, and had marched off to war in a fury because someone had dropped a cigarette among his props and destroyed the lot so that, in the excitement after Mons, he'd seen the hidden hand of the Germans in it. All of them, stiff and uncomfortable in ill-fitting uniforms and glengarries, with Tom Creak and his little group of ex-miners to one side, stunted, hardbitten, dour men for the most part, with the grinning faces of the Mandys shining out from the middle of them like a couple of Irish moons; and

Tom, still a deputy to them in spite of his uniform, looking like an unofficial major-general with his stiff dignified face.

Tom and the Mandys were our most important men those days. We had to make our own roads and not many of us were used to the work. We quarried our own stones for the road surfaces and put down drainpipes, claying the joints up quite wrongly, so that we had to take them up again and send for Tom and the Mandys to show us how to do it properly. Suddenly life took on different values. The men who were heading for promotion at this point in our lives were the ones who knew how to build walls and lay drains.

The camp remained a vast expanse of mud where the wooden duckwalks disappeared from sight when it wasn't raining and floated on the surface of the puddles when it was. The parade ground was a mud-flat that never once changed its texture except when the damp browns of autumn faded into winter mists and the bitter black frosts came down on us, with stars of ice in the congealed footprints in the mud, and the grass looking white like a winter fur. Then the snow came to soften the harsh outlines of the camp and isolated us for days, so that we had to live off oranges, which were the only thing the cooks had plenty of just then. During that period we crouched miserably round the red-hot stoves of our huts and prayed for fine weather. A few cases were taken away with pneumonia but surprisingly not many.

I learned to live under the conditions that would have depressed a poacher's lurcher, but we'd joined of our own free will and accord so no one complained. Those of us who'd practised guard duty at Edward Road in preparation for the time when we should have something to guard, began to wonder – when we learned what it was like to stand on sentry duty throughout a bitter night, armed with staves instead of rifles – where we could have found such enthusiasm. When we were cold we stamped about the comfortless huts for warmth, our boots hollowly thumping the floorboards, and when we were bored – and we were often bored because for a long time we had no lights to read or write letters by – we managed to be sustained by the faith that our hardships were suffered in a good cause. We sang 'Tipperary' and 'Hello, Hello, Who's Your Lady Friend?', and 'Who Were You With Last Night?' to Tommy Mandy's mouth-organ, or listened to Catchpole or Spring who had the biggest fund of dirty ballads I'd ever heard.

We worked off our excess spirits by acting the fool and playing stupid jokes on each other. One night we shaved off the moustache of one of our elderly corporals when he was drunk on swiped rum, and another we nailed Sergeant Bernard's boots through the laceholes to the ceiling, and put fireworks among the coal by Corker's stove. But, with their stripes, they always had the whip hand and worked it out of us by giving us left and right wheel in extended order so that they had us running miles.

When they let us out of camp and the weather was reasonable we crammed the open-topped, hard-tyred buses, or borrowed bicycles or motorbikes or even runabouts from those who were lucky enough to possess them, and roared, shouting and singing, each of us as cocky as ten men because we were who we were, into the city or the Four Merry Lads, some of us still in incomplete uniforms.

Then, as the bitter weather ceased, the rats discovered the waste behind the cookhouse and came from all the farms around and bred in their thousands under the huts, and it became a matter of life and death to us that we should clear them out. One night when the colonel was in town, Tom Creak and the Mandys and I helped ourselves to a stray terrier which had attached itself to him and slept in his office. Unfortunately, the blasted dog got stuck and we had to go under the hut after it with shovels, crawling among the the rubbish and old food that had been thrown there out of the way, scratching around in the slime and barking our knees on bricks the workmen had left behind, accompanied by sarcastic shouts of encouragement from the rest of the hut crouching outside.

When we got it out we had to give it a bath in a washbasin and dry it in front of the stove, and finally toss up for who should sneak it back before the CO returned. Inevitably, I lost, and was caught by Bold as I crept back, keeping to the shadows away from the camp patrol.

He swooped on me like an avenging angel, as though it literally warmed his heart to find someone he could put on a charge. He had long since accepted the challenge thrown out by a couple of hundred high-spirited young men determined not to be downhearted under the conditions, and waged a perpetual breezy war with the lawbreakers.

'Whatcha doing out of your hut?' he demanded immediately.

'Going back, Sergeant-Major,' I said. I was wet and muddy and sick of the colonel's dog by this time.

Bold put his hands on his hips and thrust his bony face forward. 'What sort of answer's that?' he demanded.

'Well, you asked, Sergeant-Major.'

He flashed his torch over me, dazzling me, a disembodied voice behind a bright light.

'An' what's all that mud on your uniform?' he demanded. 'You been under the wire? You been out of camp?'

'No, I haven't, Sergeant-Major.'

'We'll soon see. You're in the mush, my lad. Better come along to the guardroom.'

For a while, as he turned away, I debated bolting for it, but I rejected the idea in the end, giving Bold credit for having too much cunning to let me get away with that.

As we walked between the darkened huts, he looked down at me.

'Quite the boy for fun, ain't you, Private Fenner?' he said.

'I get by, Sergeant-Major.'

'I've thought more than once I might make a soldier outta *you*, if nobody else. But you can't go chucking promotion at a bloke what's always in trouble. Now can you? 'Pon me word, you're enough to demoralise a whole army corps.'

'Sorry if I've disappointed, Sergeant-Major.'

'You got the ideas,' he went on in a low baffled voice. 'You got the strength. You got the right sort of nasty temper. You get rattled when dirty great NCOs like me come down on you. Just the type to wipe out a regiment of Prussian Guards single-handed because their artillery's knocked some dirt in his morning cup o' char. You don't half make life difficult for ambitious sergeant-majors.'

'I'm sorry about that, Sergeant-Major.'

'You want to git left behind, or something?'

'No, Sergeant-Major,' I said.

'Well, the way you're shaping, you will,' he said. 'In case you don't know it, we're over-strength and the colonel's determined to put on a good show when we get out there. They're going to weed out the shirkers and the troublemakers, so you'd better look out or you'll be one. I'll tell you that for nothing.'

Taking Bold's advice, I stopped dodging church parades and found to my surprise it was simpler than dodging the fatigues which were the only alternative. So I sang 'Fight the Good Fight' with gusto but more than a little sarcasm, considering the total absence on the camp of anything more lethal than a pick-handle, leaving the back row to Locky and Tim Williams and Eph Lott who always made for the dark corners; Locky and Tim because it was one of the few places where they could read in peace, and Eph because he ran a card school there, conducted in whispers among the guarded fag-ends.

'I'll go nap,' you could hear in a muttered undertone all the time through the padre's sermon. Or 'I shoulda led trumps' or 'Keep your bloody voice down or the old bastard'll hear you.'

Fortunately, the padres never did hear or, if they did, they pretended not to. Most of them were too engrossed in exhorting us to 'fight for right' and 'scrag the Hun', anyway.

By the spring we were soldiers with a sturdy independence, modelled neither on the Territorials nor the Regulars. Bold did his best to make us Regulars and discipline was as strict as any Guards regiment, but neither he nor anyone else ever quite overcame the fact that our officers had been our friends and that we'd cheered the same football teams and courted the same girls. Not all the edicts that were ever issued, not even the War Office, Lord Kitchener and all the Bolds in creation, could alter that.

Before the end of March another company was recruited to supply reinforcements and joined us at Blackmires, while the case-hardened original members of the battalion cheered them in with horrifying tales of the conditions.

To Corker's bewildered amazement there was a fanatical abstention from all the ordinary military crimes.

'Never in all me puff,' he said, ''ave I seen so many brutal and licentious soldiery who were so lacking in brutality and licentiousness. There's a perfectly good guardroom there waitin' for occupants and all goin' to waste. It's a bleeden shame. That's what it is.'

'We've always Fenner,' Bold liked to tell him with the heavy humour of the parade ground when he was feeling particularly cheerful. 'The Crippen of D Company. The Charlie Peace of the City Battalion. If you watch him carefully, you're bound to nick him one o' these days making off with the colonel's trousers.'

They loved to indulge in this sort of talk in front of us when we couldn't reply, but they knew as well as we did that the abstention from criminality sprang entirely from the very real dread we had of being left behind if the battalion were sent overseas. Once even, Eph Lott gave one of his boys the mother and father of all hidings for trying to steal from a comrade.

'This is *our* mob,' he said. 'Nick it from another mob if you like, but not from *this* one. We don't do that 'ere.'

'We'd learned as much in six months as the average soldier

learned in six years. Bold himself said so and that was praise indeed. We could endure hail, rain and snow; could march our twenty miles a day – fifty minutes on the trot and ten resting – and dig trenches with the best.

We were slowly being shaken into our appointed places. The authoritative were given rank. The clerks found their way – amid ironic cheers – among the signallers and telephonists, or to the blanket-covered tables and piles of pay books in the over-heated orderly room. The youngest with good lungs like Murray were employed as runners. Henry Oakley used his skill as a bowler to such an extent that he could drop a dummy bomb on any given spot within thirty-five yards of where he was standing and got himself a stripe for his trouble. The mechanically minded were absorbed into transport and swarmed in dozens over the solitary lorry we'd acquired. The tradesmen became cobblers, farriers, butchers, harness-men, bakers and cooks. A few of us – I was one – were given instruction on machine guns and squatted for hours behind wooden models complete with tripod stands and corrugated barrels, solemnly swinging rattles to simulate firing.

'The Maxim is practically a rifle with a automatic breech action,' we were informed by a lordly corporal instructor who spoke like an emasculated curate. 'To prevent it becoming over-'eated it is enclosed in a brass water-jacket and ammunition is fed to the breach by means of canvas belts carrying supplies of cartridges. It can jam. Learn what causes these 'ere jams, or you're a dead man and, what's *much* worse, the enemy might capture the gun.'

We got our khaki at last – a magnificent new suit, paid for by the City Council out of the rates – and, thankfully handing in the conspicuous blue for the unfortunates coming along behind, swarmed into Sidepool to have our photographs taken, singly and in groups to send home to families, wives and friends, all looking broken-necked in the stand-up collars buttoned to the throat and the bus conductors hats from which we pulled the wire when Bold wasn't around, to make them look older and battle-worn.

Dear Mum and all – the letters went out in dozens – *this is me and the boys.*

Life had become immensely simple. I no longer had to worry or think for other people, or even for myself. There was always Bold, hard-faced and unforgiving, but, I discovered, never foul-mouthed and always willing to help, to do it for me; and everything was fixed in advance, from the time I got up to the way I had to have my hair cut. It meant nothing to me that the elderly NCOs in the stores still fiddled the rations and flogged the blankets from time to time, and that if Sheridan, Ashton's second-in-command, had run his business in Hill Street as he sometimes tried to run the company, he'd have been ruined.

Then one day rifles appeared, the first real rifles we'd had, to take the place of the home-made wooden ones they'd issued us with for drill. There were only forty-odd of them and even those were on loan from the Vickers works in the city, but we paraded with them in small batches, complaining all the time about the way Bold's dull military mind kept us throwing them around when what we really wanted to do was shoot Germans with them.

We took our turn on the range which, of course, we'd had to build ourselves, firing five rounds apiece – *when we could get five rounds.* The rifles weren't much good as weapons, but we got so that the movements became instinctive and we automatically ceased to breathe when we took sight. We fired at bobbing jinnies, and were initiated into the mysteries of 'grouping'. We learned what a sector was and how to judge distances, and began to boast about our skill, which, God knows, was nothing to write home about.

'You start to see a man's eyes at a hundred yards,' Corker told us. 'You start to see his buttons at two hundred yards, 'is face at three hundred. When 'e's four hundred yards away you start to see the movements of his legs, and the colour of his uniform can be seen at five hundred. If you want to count men moving when they're so far away they're only a blur, remember that cavalry riding in twos pass a given point at sixty a minute. Guns and waggons pass five to the minute and infantry in fours at two hundred to the minute.'

'What happens if Cavalry attacks us?' Murray asked breathlessly, and Corker gave him a glance which was full of contempt.

'Don't worry about that,' he said. 'They won't. They know better. Cavalry only attack prepared infantry positions once in their sweet lives. They never come back for more.'

One of the most heart-lifting things that occurred was the arrival of the 10th Battalion. They were brigaded with us and brought to Blackmires, and when we found we could outmarch them by miles we suddenly began to take an inverted pride in the bleakness of the conditions we'd had to endure.

'You know,' I said as we watched their squads wheeling on the muddy parade ground, 'perhaps we're not so awful as we thought we were. I mean, that lot's a bit of a mob, isn't it? Look at their discipline. Just look at it!'

'Fen, my son,' Locky said placidly. 'It's remarkable the number of people round here who've suddenly started to discover the meaning of *esprit de corps*.'

Rumours flew about like pigeons in a high wind. Germany was finished, we heard, and we were only waiting for the spring to smash him, so if you wanted to see any fighting you had to move smartly, but if you could transfer to one of the Regular battalions your chances of getting to France were greater. However, the Big Push was due at any time and when it came we were *all* in it, Regulars, Territorials and Kitchener men, so perhaps it was pointless to worry. The war wasn't going to be over by Christmas, after all, it seemed – not even the second Christmas.

Gradually, and in penny numbers, we were equipped with water-bottles, haversacks, mess tins, waterproof sheets and then

– in the midst of tremendous excitement – the first real consign-ments of rifles arrived. They were long Lee-Metfords, weapons which were already obsolete and had been replaced months before in France. Two hundred of them appeared and were used for drilling. Then another two hundred and yet another two hundred, until everyone had a weapon. Many of them were in bad condition because they'd been picked up on the battle-fields of France, but they were just fit to fire and we stayed up till the small hours making them presentable for parade the next morning, scratching at the rust, and dabbing boot-polish on the butts to make them shine.

'The night has suddenly become hideous with the click of rifle-bolts,' Locky said dryly.

Only now were we satisfied. We were not only properly dressed but at long last we were armed. Nothing could stop us. If the enthusiasm had been strong before, it was red hot now. Nothing could mar our faith in being in at the final victory when it came. Nothing managed to dim the sight of distant glory, not even the cold or the discomfort. It even survived our first disturbing meeting with men from France.

In the spring the isolation hospital farther along the road, standing like a fortress on a small hill where the Blackmires winds could tear through its wards and blow away the germs, was emptied of fever cases and turned over to the military who promptly filled it with wounded from Ypres.

We heard they'd arrived but we rarely saw them, until one night we found that the little back room at the Four Merry Lads, which we had come to accept as our own private head-quarters, had been taken over by men in bright blue suits and red ties who were dodging the rules that insisted they were not to be served with intoxicating liquor.

We stopped dead in the doorway as we saw them. They held crutches against stiff legs or drank left-handed because they had no right hands, and the face of more than one of them was marked by livid new tissue where torn flesh was just beginning to heal. They were the first wounded we'd ever seen and we regarded them with awe and a certain amount of guilt.

'Where'd you get it?' we asked them, and for the price of a pint and the inevitable question, 'What's it like out there?' they proceeded to chill our blood.

There was silence as they finished, the silence of disbelief and shame. In our enthusiasm to get into the war this had never been quite how we'd imagined it would be, and it ran contrary to our expectations.

'Oh, well,' Murray announced, as casually as he could, trying hard to appear indifferent, 'it'll be *our* turn soon. We've just about finished our training.' He was eager to be accepted by those dour, hard-bitten men, anxious that no one should think he was dodging his share of the work, keen to let the rest of the Army know that they'd only to hang on until he could take over from their faltering hands and face the storm for them. 'Any day now,' he said. 'And we'll be there.'

They were unimpressed by his zeal.

'Don't be in too big a hurry, mate,' they told him flatly. 'You're a bloody sight better off here than hanging on the wire.'

'Hanging on the wire?' Murray's rosy face was bewildered.

'Dead, mate.' A big man with bristling black moustaches spoke up from the corner. He had a pair of crutches beside him and the good-conduct stripe of an old sweat on his arm. 'It's no place for a regimental soldier, out there, mate. You can reckon on living about three months, if yer lucky. Officers and NCOs two. If you want to go out there kid, you want to get your dad to pull a few strings for you and get 'em to make you a general first. They're the boys what enjoy the war. Twenty miles behind the lines in chatoos. Bloody great houses like Buckingham Palace set in their own parks. Dinner and wine at night. And girls in their beds as well, for all I know – so bloody beautiful they make you weep real tears just to look at 'em.'

Gradually, it all came out in tight, brusque sentences that

put a dread in your heart. They told us of their hatred for the Belgians, who profiteered from the troops trying to save them, and of the French jeers at half-trained Britishers; of confused orders that hung whole companies on uncut German wire like scarecrows, to rot in the sun and the rain; of men who did succeed through sheer courage and were left unsupported, to be shelled to perdition because their own artillery had nothing to fire in retaliation.

We didn't believe half of it and put it down to the usual old soldier's desire to impress.

'I think you're stretching it,' young Murray said at last, his round pink face shocked and horrified. He'd been listening with increasing anger, his face growing more and more suffused with indignation until he clearly couldn't contain himself any longer. 'That's what I think. I think you're bloody well drawing it out a bit.'

'Drawing it out or not,' the man with the moustaches said, 'I didn't get one in this here leg of mine because I didn't know *my* job. I been in the Army long enough to know what's what.' He held up his arm with the good-conduct stripe on it. 'I got a stripe to prove it. I got my packet because I got caught on the wire when they said there wasn't any and I couldn't get away. Every time I shifted I got caught on another bit and, in the end, there I was hanging half upside down with it twanging all round me like a banjo band and the bullets whistling in me ears like bees. I'd have been there yet if my pal hadn't come and got me off. *I left him there*. He stopped the one that didn't get me.'

There was silence again, then Murray stood up.

'I still think you're stretching it,' he said.

'You calling me a liar?' There was an ominous movement from the corner, and I bundled Murray outside before trouble could start and left Locky behind me to explain it all away.

'He's a bit mental,' I heard him saying gravely. 'They only let him in because his father's the Lord Mayor.'

We were all a little subdued as we went home that night. A little of the dread they felt had found its way into us. These men weren't bayonet and bombing instructors trying to put the face of war on us. They'd tried war and found it different from what they'd expected.

But we were too young to brood long and, as soon as spring made it possible, we were thrown into a training programme that seemed at first ridiculous and childish in the extreme.

Reveille was at dawn and we rolled out of bed, gummy-eyed with sleep, with Corker bawling at us from the door. 'Up you get! Turn out! Turn out!' A two-mile run in heady air that was sweet and strong in your lungs. 'Faster! Faster! What you think you're doing? Crawling?' Back, famished, for breakfast, and then a whole day of marching and digging and eating bully beef and bread from haversacks at the roadside among the first of the daisies, like a lot of roadmenders, and listening open-mouthed to instructors with their tall tales of derring-do.

'Let's see a bit more murder in them eyes,' the bayonet-fighting sergeant liked to say. 'A short jab to the froat and out again. Nobody needs more than six inches o' cold Sheffield to let the life out of him. I seen ten men killed in twenty seconds by a man what knew his job with the bay'nit.'

We had brigade and divisional manœuvres and, because some bright individual with red gorgets conceived the idea of raiding the camps of other battalions for practice, we spent half our nights sitting under bushes in the dark waiting for someone to stumble upon us.

'A fatuous form of play-acting,' Mason announced porten-tously as we crouched in the rain in a grass-fringed ditch on the edge of the moors, trying to behave like outposts.

We had rattles with us to represent machine guns and were waiting for a nervous patrol of the 10th to come our way so we could ambush them. We'd picked the spot carefully because we were anxious to do the job properly. We'd been taught that grass was camouflage and head cover came from behind and we'd argued for ten minutes on the subject before we finally sat down.

It was raining steadily and the wind moaned dismally through the chinks of the dry-stone wall behind us. We'd lain dutifully silent for a long time but in the end we'd all become stiff and numb with cold, and, disregarding the chances of being heard or seen, we'd stood up one after the other and stamped our feet and rubbed life back into our hands before finally settling into a state of numb indifference. Nobody had been near us for what seemed hours, and Mason was anxious to pull back into shelter.

'They've forgotten us,' he kept saying bitterly. 'They've forgotten we're here.'

'Ashton won't forget us,' I said. 'He never has done yet.'

'All right, then.' Mason started slapping his cold hands against his ribs and stamping. 'All right. They *haven't* forgotten us. But they've left us stuck out here where we'll be spotted sure as eggs are eggs. We'll spend the night in somebody else's guardroom.'

'At least it'll be warmer and drier than this,' Locky said.

'They'll not spot us,' I pointed out. 'They can only come on us from the west, and they'll have what light there is behind them. We've got this wall and the bushes behind us. They'll never see us before we see them.'

Mason stopped flapping and stared at the leaden horizon more cheerfully. 'I hadn't thought of that, old fruit,' he said enthusiastically. 'Yes, when I consider it, troops, perhaps I've chosen a good position after all.'

'Only *you* didn't choose it,' Murray said sourly. 'Fen did.'

The rain came down harder as it grew later, solidly, effortlessly, with no sign of stopping, and the water, running off the field behind us and down the bank where we were crouching, began to form in a little rivulet in the limp grass at the bottom of the ditch. Mason began to grow impatient again.

'For God's sake,' he said. 'What a perfectly blood-stained way of spending an evening. Anybody in favour of a retreat?'

'You're the corporal,' I said. '*You* decide.'

Murray interrupted irritably. 'How do you expect to learn anything,' he said in his eager exalted way, 'if you just pull back every time it rains? We'll have plenty of rain when we get out there.'

Mason was looking uncertainly about him, hating the weather but stirred by Murray's challenge.

'Well, Appleby said we should stay here,' he agreed.

Second Lieutenant Appleby was a tall young man with dark-ringed yellow eyes and a ginger toothbrush moustache who'd been attached to the company. He'd been a sergeant in the Gloucesters and he'd arrived with a group of quiet-mannered, tired-looking men from France to teach us that the real fighting was vastly different from the theoretical stuff we'd been learning.

'Bombs are important,' he'd told us. '*And* the pick and shovel.'

He'd proved to us it wasn't a good idea after all to dig trenches on the slope of a hill overlooking enemy positions, because there they'd be spotted at once and promptly blown out of existence by artillery fire. The place, it seemed, for constructing trenches was over the brow of the hill, or in hollows, and the method was to follow the line of the country so that aircraft couldn't spot them.

He'd pooh-poohed the theories on rifle-fire that we'd been taught and claimed it was more important to learn to shoot fast than to shoot accurately at great distance If we were rushed, it seemed, a field of fire of two hundred yards was sufficient to wipe an enemy off the face of the earth.

'At two hundred yards' range,' he'd said, 'rapid fire is the most dreadful medium of destruction yet devised in warfare. At Mons they thought we were armed with machine guns.'

It had all sounded like good sense, and as Appleby's nerves weren't all they might have been after Mons and Le Cateau, and he sometimes appeared on parade in the afternoons

110

glassy-eyed, bad-tempered and swaying, we'd got into the habit of taking no notice of him.

So we stayed where we were, with Mason fretting miserably, certain we'd been forgotten, and Eph Lott and MacKinley and a few more huddled under the wall trying to keep out of the rain.

There was a scrape of a match as someone lit a cigarette and a splash as a stone was knocked from the wall and fell into the rivulet of water by our feet. Then Eph shuffled restlessly.

'Let's find a barn,' he suggested. 'Make a fire. 'Ave some grub. I'm so hungry I could eat a mangy pup.'

Mason gave a harsh laugh. 'A fire?' he said. 'Up here at Blackmires? What'll we burn? Nothing grows up here but heather.'

'Well, we can try for nothing.'

'Appleby said to avoid barns,' Murray said, his voice rising.

All that we'd learned about taking cover in farm buildings or plantations or woods had also had to be rapidly unlearned on the arrival of Appleby. Much to my amazement, it seemed that the safest place in battle was a small hole in the middle of a large field that wasn't marked on a map, because there the enemy's range-takers would find it hard to gauge the exact distance.

We sat a little longer, huddled in sodden greatcoats, miserably contemplating the wet countryside and the fading light, then someone suggested a move again and the argument cracked to life once more.

'I say toss up for it,' Tom Creak said. "Eads we go. Tails we stay. Or draw lots.'

'Let's vote for it,' Spring offered.

Mason took off his cap and shook the water from it. His face was only a blur now in the increasing dusk. 'This isn't the Houses of bloody Parliament,' he said. 'This is the Army. We don't have debates and take votes.'

'Well, we ought to.'

'Up the Reds!' Henny Cuthbert said gloomily, his long face longer than ever.

We began to laugh and Mason started to get a little irritable. 'Well,' he said. 'You're all so blasted full of ideas, what do *you* suggest?'

'I suggest a game of 'alfpenny nap,' Eph grunted.

'Come on, Mason,' Spring encouraged. 'You're the man with all the power and authority. You're the lance-corporal. Let's hear those stentorian commands ring out. What are we to do?'

Mason shook his head uncertainly. He clearly wanted to go home as much as anyone else, but he was scared stiff of Appleby and the possibility of losing his stripe.

'I don't know,' he said. 'It's bloody wet, isn't it? What do you suggest, Fen?'

'Stay here,' I said.

'Why?'

Locky grinned. 'He's got the best spot. He's under a bush. That's why.'

Mason looked perplexed. 'You think we should?' he said.

'Yes,' Murray replied firmly, far less daunted by the weather than by what he considered a lamentable lack of martial ardour on Mason's part. 'Give 'em the old rapid fire. Remember what Appleby said: "The most dreadful medium of destruction yet devised in warfare."'

Locky raised his head. 'It struck me at the time,' he said thoughtfully, 'that if we can wipe them off the face of the earth as easily as all that, what's to stop 'em returning the compliment when we play away.'

'If you'd read your little history books as a boy,' Tim Williams, the history lecturer, commented, 'you'd have noticed that the power of the rifle in defence has been growing ever since the American Civil War.'

Murray fidgeted restlessly. This sort of talk always made him uneasy. He had absolute faith in his destiny as a saviour of

112

mankind, and in the skill of the people set above us. He liked life to be orderly and simple, and felt that everyone else should have the same faith that he did.

'They'll not stop us when we get out there,' he claimed stoutly.

Mason shivered and started to slap his arms against his sides again.

'It's just a game,' he snorted. 'Designed to find the officers something to write down in their little notebooks.'

'It's a curious fallacy among the young,' Locky commented gently, 'that it's possible to do any job without bothering first to learn it. You were always inclined to that view as a reporter, I seem to remember, Lance-Corporal Mason.'

He was speaking in his normal quiet voice, devoid of anger or irritability or weariness or even boredom. He sounded as though he were laughing, in fact, and Mason swung round on him angrily.

'I suppose *you're* enjoying all this Mr Bloody Deputy Chief Reporter Private Haddo,' he said sourly.

Locky chuckled. 'I fortify myself,' he said, 'with the thought that if I can do it properly it might help me to survive the war. Six months ago, I foolishly presented myself burning with patriotic fire at the Drill Hall and was promply bereft of my name and forced to answer three-score questions and ten about myself ranging from stupidity to sheer impertinence. I had my head viciously shorn of its hair by an uncontrolled farmer with sheep-clippers. I've sworn a great oath and had my number stamped indelibly all over my person. I've long since realised that I've made the greatest mistake of my life, but, loving my home and having a few quid in the bank and hoping one day to marry and raise more little Haddos like myself, I'm determined to emerge at the end of it alive enough to enjoy it all. I'm therefore learning to make use of cover and trying not very successfully to fire round it instead of over it – in the manner of Appleby and the good Bold. When

I finally get a rifle that shoots straight, I should be quite an expert.'

There seemed to be no answer.

In the end we stayed where we were and caught the patrol we were waiting for, and Mason got a pat on the back from Appleby for his determination.

5

By the time the Germans sank the *Lusitania* in May 1915 the war had begun to change.

Gas had been used against the Canadians at Ypres and was likely to be used again, and its appearance opened up a whole new series of horrors. Gallipoli had started in a welter of blood and failure, and the need for that Big Push for which they were supposed to be saving the Kitchener armies seemed to be growing daily more pressing. Things were going none too well out there and the casualties in France were mounting rapidly. In spite of the strangely static front, the papers were filled monotonously with lists of dead and wounded and the *Post*'s roll-of-honour column ran on to other pages now.

Men I'd known appeared briefly under the single heading FOR KING AND COUNTRY and then were forgotten for ever. Magnus who'd been one of the first to leave the newspaper with Ashton and Sainsbury and old Corker, was back in the city, minus an arm and looking ten years older, and suddenly, in spite of his youth, beyond our reach, strangely withdrawn and unanxious to meet us. He told us Sainsbury had died of fever on some Greek island no one had ever heard of on his way to the Dardanelles and before he'd even heard a shot fired in anger. The *Lusitania* was only one more stone that marked the passage of the war.

The night the news came through, Locky, Frank Mason and I had sneaked out of camp for the evening. Officially, we were supposed to be confined to company quarters, but the 10th Battalion was furnishing the guard that night and for the promise of a drink we found someone who agreed not to press too hard for our passes at the gate when we returned.

Locky set off on his own because he hadn't so far to go, and Mason and I got a lift into town from a second lieutenant in the 10th, who had a yellow bull-nosed Morris runabout. He crammed us into the dickey seat, both of us furtively eyeing the guardroom, and we roared and jiggled down the hill, through Parkland and Sidepool, our feet on the mudguards, holding on to our hats with one hand and to the car with the other. The second lieutenant hadn't had the car long and hadn't much idea how to drive. His contribution seemed to be to take the brake off and open the throttle as wide as he could. We weren't sorry when we arrived.

He dropped us at the bottom of Cotterside Common and we took a tram the rest of the way, and arrived in the High Street to find the air crackling with hatred for the Germans. We'd heard of the loss of the *Lusitania* in camp – it had arrived, I suppose, through the usual channels of the know-alls of the orderly room, and had spread from battalion headquarters down through company headquarters and on to us. But none of us had taken much notice of it, beyond a feeling of shock and awe.

We went for a meal at a soldiers' club and sneaked into a cinema, keeping a sharp lookout for military policemen, and when we came out there were crowds in the street. There was a man on the Town Hall steps waving a banner which proclaimed REPENT. THE DAY IS COME! and shouting burning Old Testament texts.

'I was a sinner,' he was saying. 'But I got washed in the blood of the Lamb.'

'You still look a bit bloomin' mucky,' someone shouted and there was a burst of laughter.

Farther along, near Schafer's shop, which had *Huns* chalked on the door again, another man was waving a copy of *John Bull* and preaching violence to a small crowd he'd collected around him.

'Let *them* suffer too,' he said. 'Let the pro-Hun baby-killers take a taste of their own medicine!'

We listened to him for a while, then Mason touched my arm and we moved away.

'Let's go and get a drink,' he said. 'Then we'll try and find some girls.'

He jerked at his jacket and ran his finger over the little moustache he'd started to grow.

'I feel I have the desirability of the lonely young soldier,' he said, 'that always arouses the maternal instinct in young girls. One drink, Private Fenner – no more – and then we'll look for company. Come on.'

In the Vaults Bar of the Blueberry Tavern next to the *Post* office, where we inevitably ended up – being Pressmen – the air was electric and already growing noisy. Everybody seemed to be talking about the sinking and a man by the bar was trying to claim he'd expected it all the time.

'What do you expect of a nation that'll try to poison a Christian enemy's food supplies?' he was saying loudly. He carried a silver-topped cane and wore a pair of dark pearl-button boots that didn't seem to go with his yellowing boater. He leaned on the counter, a little the worse for wear, his elbows in a pool of spilled beer, chivvying the landlord, jabbing with his finger to emphasize a point, his voice gimlet-sharp with insistence as he tried to drive his argument home. 'All these Germans who were in the country before the war,' he said. 'Where've they all gone? You can't kid me they've all gone back to Germany.'

''Course they haven't,' the landlord said. 'They're in internment camps where they can't do no harm.'

'That's what they say,' the man with the boater said. 'But that's all nonsense. *I* know where they are. Shall I tell you?'

'Go on. Where?'

'They're in cellars signalling to submarines with wireless sets.'

The landlord moved uneasily in his position by the beer engine. 'Wirelesses don't work in cellars,' he said uncertainly, as though he weren't sure of his facts, and the man in the boater slapped his hand to the counter emphatically.

'The sort they've got *now* do,' he insisted. 'They work anywhere. They're sitting there tapping away, telling the Hun where all our food supplies are, all our guns, and all our ships, and all our army.'

'What army?' the landlord said. 'Kitchener said we hadn't got one, and we've got a damn' sight less since Ypres.'

The man in the boater stared at the landlord patiently, as though he considered flippancy had no place in his conversation. He drew a deep breath and stared round the crowded shelves and at the gilt mirrors behind the bar, the gaudy mezzotints of Minoru winning the Derby and the Guards at Inkerman, and the adverts for Vichy water and whisky, as though he were making a great effort to contain his anger. Then he jabbed a quivering finger at the landlord and began to speak slowly.

'We'll have even less if things go on as they are doing,' he said. 'They're landing poison in Ireland and the Irish are getting it across here in suitcases with false bottoms. Before six months is up, there'll be thousands dying in the streets.'

'Can't see it meself.' The landlord was unmoved by the picture.

'I can,' the man with the boater said. 'I saw it all the time. Right from the word "go". And now this. 'Ow many on board?' He swung round, breaking off the argument he'd started, and poked his cane at Mason who was reading the *Lusitania* story in the evening paper. Mason looked up and the man in the boater nodded encouragingly.

'Go on,' he persisted with grisly interest. "Ow many on board?'

Mason shook out the paper and turned to the main news page. You could see the story plastered across three columns, pushing out of sight the indignation that was still being felt about the gas at Ypres and the nonsense they were talking to make Gallipoli sound like a resounding victory.

'Go on,' the man with the boater said again. He seemed to be getting a little impatient. 'Read it, man. I've not got my glasses. How many on board?'

'One thousand nine hundred and fifty-nine passengers and crew,' Mason said. 'Ninety of 'em kids. Thirty-nine infants in arms.'

'There you are.' The man with the boater swung round and jabbed his cane at the landlord. 'Just as I told you. Ninety of 'em kids! It's a bloody shame! It's just like the Hun. Where was it?'

'Just off the Old Head of Kinsale. A torpedo.'

'I thought so. They was lying in wait for her. Just like I said. Information supplied by wireless. Tic-tac, tic-tac. Fizz-fizz up a bit of wire. Tic-tac, tic-tac in Berlin. Anybody who'll use poison gas to fight a war doesn't deserve any mercy. In South Africa, whatever else you said of the Boers, they fought fairly.'

'Were you there?' I asked.

The man with the boater turned to me. 'No,' he said. 'I wasn't. I was making horseshoes for the cavalry though. I've got a forge near the station. I did my bit, I can tell you.'

'They ought to have given you a medal,' Mason said.

'I got an illuminated address from the chapel.' The man with the boater was oblivious to Mason's sarcasm. 'And I'm doing my bit again this war. I hate the Germans,' he said. 'They don't fight fair. There's still a damned sight too many of 'em about in this country. I reckon it's the German shopkeepers who put the prices up. It's nothing but an attempt by Schafer and that lot to undermine the country's economy.' He jabbed with his cane at Mason. 'Read some more,' he said. 'Out loud. So they can *all* hear it.'

Mason turned the page, skirted the sober little announcement that said how pleased the Editor of the *Post* would be to receive photographs from relatives of dead, wounded and missing soldiers for insertion – free of charge – in the *Roll of Honour* columns, and went on reading.

'Within sight of the shore,' he announced. 'Nearly fifteen hundred victims. They were given no warning. There were about a hundred Americans.'

'That'll fetch the Yanks into the war,' the man with the boater said.

'"It is considered to be a deliberate act of policy",' Mason read on, '"for which the German Government is directly responsible. It had disseminated warnings beforehand in the shipping offices of New York. It is considered to be an act of spectacular brutality which shocks the conscience of the world, and appeals more forcibly to American conscience than even the desolation of Belgium."'

The man with the boater slapped the counter with his cane.

'Now what do you say about the Germans?' he shouted at the landlord.

The landlord lost his temper and began to shout back.

'Fair play,' he roared. 'That's all I ask for.'

'Fair play! There's no such thing with the Hun! They don't want to intern 'em and shove 'em into camps! What good does that do? They want to cut off their 'ands and feet and leave 'em to die, like they left them people in the sea! Nearly two thousand of 'em, women and little kids! They ought to be all strung up from the gaslamps! Here, outside, in the street! This street! Every street! Anybody with a German name, anybody with German relations! Governesses! Pork butchers! The lot! It's terrible! Terrible!

All them children! We ought to go out and smash up the shops!'

Almost as though his words had been heard outside, the door was flung back against the wall as he finished and we all turned from the bar to stare at the man who was framed there against the growing darkness. His eyes were wide and excited and he was pointing back in the direction he'd come. Even before he spoke I guessed what he was going to say and I seemed to hold my breath in anticipation.

'They've just flung a brick through Schafers' window again,' he yelled.

We burst through the door, jamming it as we stuck there for a second, our bodies filling the opening, then we were tearing off down Blueberry Street, our boots clattering on the pavement.

Even before we got to the crossroads we could hear the noise of the crowd – it sounded like the ugly baying of a pack of hounds – and as we turned the corner we saw them filling the street in front of Schafers' shop.

It was a new place built just before the war, with smart grained woodwork and tiled shelves, and the window seemed to be full of tinned food. A lot of the crowd were drunk, men and women alike, shouting and shrieking as they swirled like a human tide in the roadway. One little man with a voluminous cap and an unshaven face, who clearly didn't belong in the district, had made a noose of a clothes-line and slung it over the crossbar of a gas lamp. It wasn't strong enough to hang a dog, let alone a human being, but he was making a great play with it.

'Shove 'em in 'ere,' he was shouting. 'Two at a time! And up they go! Like a monkey on a stick! One, two! Another little Hun gone!'

Some of the crowd were laughing but most of them, swarming across the tram-lines and holding up the late district trams, were shouting angrily.

'Child murderers!' they were yelling. 'Down with the Huns!'

Schafers' window, starred by a brick, shone gap-toothed and splintered in the glow from the blue-painted gas lamps, and the pavement was littered with fragments of glass that picked up the light in a thousand jagged flashes of yellow.

A policeman on the fringe of the crowd was blowing his whistle, and trying to hang on to two men at once, but he seemed to lose his balance and fell over, taking the two men with him.

There was a flat above the shop but it seemed to have been deserted by the manager who normally lived there and we could see people in the bedrooms filling their arms with clothes and bedding. One woman I saw was carrying a pair of leaping bronze horses which had obviously decorated a mantelpiece, two great metal pieces of violent action that seemed about to jump out of her arms. Downstairs most of the tinned and potted food seemed to have disappeared now, and I saw a man standing in the window passing out what was left of it to his friends. A couple of men were squabbling over a tin of ham, each of them hanging on to it with both hands and heaving it backwards and forwards as they argued at the tops of their voices.

The driver of a tram behind the crowd was stamping on the pedal of his bell so that the monotonous cracked *clang clang clang* added to the bedlam of noise. The passengers were crowded at the windows and hanging from the open platform with the driver, staring and shouting advice, and there was a woman with a child on the top deck, who was screaming for the police.

The crowd was surging about now round the scuffle in the roadway, and people were barged over and fell underfoot. I was separated from Mason, and fully occupied with keeping my balance as I was jammed up against a shop window which I thought was going to collapse at any moment and deposit me and the rest of the crowd round me into a display of elastic-sided boots. The temper of the people in the street was beginning to look uglier all the time and the laughter had stopped altogether now.

The policeman had got to his feet again and was appealing to the crowd to help him, but no one moved, and I got the impression that most of them were far more interested in the food in Schafers' window than in the nationality of its owners. Prices had recently gone up again and the *Lusitania* was just a good excuse to most of them. Nobody was smashing the window of Schemingers', the chemists, I noticed.

'Bloody German bastards,' a woman screamed as she appeared in the doorway of the shop with her arms full of clothes. 'Bloody Hun murderers!'

As I fought my way free, I saw John Schafer himself arrive. He'd obviously been called down by telephone and he came pushing through the crowd, a white-haired old man with a square-topped bowler.

'What the devil do you think you're doing with that?' he snapped at the men squabbling over the tin of ham.

'What the 'ell has it got to do with you?' he was asked.

'It happens to belong to me, that's all.'

The two men stopped arguing. 'Christ,' one of them said. 'It's the old 'Un bastard himself! 'Ere 'e is, boys!'

He gave old Schafer a violent shove that sent him into the crowd and in a second he was down on his knees. A girl with her hat on lopsidedly burst out of the milling people and went to his rescue. Someone pushed her away and I saw her go flying. As she recovered her balance, a woman grabbed at her collar, and her dress tore at the shoulder, and I managed at last to fight my way through to the front, elbowing and fisting and kicking.

The girl was brandishing an umbrella now, magnificently undeterred, and I saw her set about the crowd round old Schafer who was now crouching on his knees as they kicked and pummelled him with sticks.

As I broke free, a man got hold of the girl, but I swung him round and knocked him flat on his back. Someone jumped on me from behind but I tucked my head between my knees and he went clean over my shoulders on top of the first man.

My cap rolled away with him and I lost it, then suddenly there seemed to be policemen everywhere and the looters were dropping their prizes and running. The woman with the clothes was arguing violently with a sergeant and the woman from upstairs with the bronze horses was being bundled towards a waiting van. I pulled another shouting man away from the girl by old Schafer, then someone grabbed her round the waist and seemed to be trying to pick her up. As I tried to stop him, he swung his arm back and his elbow caught me in the mouth, and I tasted blood and lost my temper. I hit him on top of the head with my fist, and as he turned, I punched him as hard as I could in the nose and he reeled away, his hands to his face howling blue murder.

Then suddenly the street cleared and there were only the crowd on the pavement and the policemen bundling their captives into a van, complete with their loot. The people in the shop doors were jeering at them and shouting.

'Bloody Germans,' they were yelling. 'Leave 'em alone! It serves 'em right!'

I saw a police inspector in a round pillbox hat grab at the coat of a man who was running away with a tin of biscuits under his arm and pull him up short. The man lost his balance and the tin of biscuits went flying, skating across the pavement, sweeping the splinters of glass before it in a shower. Then, as he swung round and landed on his back, his feet in the air, a thin whippet-like dog came out of the crowd from nowhere, and grabbed hold of the inspector's trouser leg.

The inspector shook his foot in an irritable way, jerking it quickly backwards and forwards, so that the dog was whipped round and round, still growling.

'For God's sake,' I heard him say with an irritated desperation.

'It's got German sympathies,' someone yelled. '*Sprechen sie Deutsch*, Inspector! *Hoch der* bloody *Kaiser!*'

The man in the inspector's grip struggled to get up, but the policeman held him down, still kicking violently with his foot to shake off the dog hanging on to his trouser leg. Then the inspector's hat fell off and went rolling among the glass splinters in a curving run, and someone trod on it. Finally, another policeman took a swinging kick at the dog, which went off into the crowd yelping like a house on fire, and the inspector straightened up and handed his catch to a sergeant. He was marched away through the crowd, who had turned their hatred of the Germans on to old Schafer as a policeman helped him to his feet.

'Baby-killers,' they were shouting. 'Rapists!'

The man who'd been shouting over the bar in the Blueberry was waving his cane. 'Huns! Boches!' he was roaring. 'Child-murderers! Who left the kids from the *Lusitania* to drown?'

I turned to the girl and, taking my jacket off, dropped it over her shoulders where her dress had been torn.

'Better put this on,' I said.

'Thanks,' she said. She brandished her bent umbrella and laughed. 'Well, I helped a bit,' she said.

Then she pushed the hair from her face and I saw it was Helen Haddo.

'Helen!' I said.

She gave me a quick hug that was excited more than anything else, and held me like that for a second. Her eyes were bright and her face flushed, and she looked as though she'd been thoroughly enjoying herself.

'What the hell were you up to?' I asked angrily. 'Joining in that lot?'

Her smile died and her eyes flashed. 'You surely didn't expect me to stand back and see them beat the life out of an old man, did you?' she retorted.

'Don't be silly,' I said. 'Of course not. All the same, you ought to leave that sort of thing to me. It's not your cup of tea.'

She opened her mouth to start disputing it with me, and I decided to get her away to where I could speak to her in peace. If she was in an argumentative mood, I'd found, I always needed a little calm to talk her round.

'Let's push off,' I said. 'They're in an ugly mood still.'

'I don't care!'

'Well, I do. I'm supposed to be fighting Germans, not this lot.'

The road was a shambles of broken glass and scattered paper. I saw two or three odd shoes and a bashed-in bowler, and a broken umbrella, then a string of sausages someone had snatched and dropped, looking ridiculous as sausages always do, like something out of a clown's equipment at a circus. Even as I watched, a dog slunk up to them, belly-down to the pavement, grabbed them in its jaws, and darted off with them flying behind it, like a picture out of a comic paper.

'What the devil were you doing in town at this time of night, anyway?' I demanded, as I took Helen's arm and began to pull her away.

She shook me off but she was smiling again now. 'I've been working,' she said. 'That's what I've been doing. Didn't Locky tell you? I'm a shorthand typist now.'

'Well, you ought to have more sense than hang about here when there's trouble brewing, like this.'

'Yes, Mark.'

She suddenly seemed meek and pliant, and let me lead her away. I tried to steer her into a shop doorway, away from the crowd who were still booing the police and arguing among themselves, but she seemed loath to turn her back on the uproar.

'You might have been killed,' I pointed out.

She looked at me defiantly. 'I might,' she said. 'But I wasn't.'

I was helping her to put my jacket on properly when the inspector arrived. The top of his cap was stove in, I noticed.

He fished out a little notebook and pencil and stopped in front of us.

'Thanks, son,' he said. 'It got a bit out of hand for a time there. It's been happening all over the city. We just haven't had enough men to handle it and the specials always dodge anything rough like this. It's worse in the East End. You were pretty prompt. It might have been nasty.'

'That's all right,' I said, wishing he'd go away. There always seemed to be someone in the way whenever I tried to get Helen on her own. It had always been Mason before. Now it was the inspector.

'You a City Battalion chap?'

'That's right.'

'Better give me your name. I'd like to mention it to your CO.'

'Oh, forget it,' I said. 'It was nothing.'

'I'll mention it to him by letter,' the inspector pointed out. 'It'll go in your personal file. It'll help.'

'It doesn't matter,' I said. 'I didn't join up for this. Forget it.'

'Well, it's your affair.' He looked a bit offended, as though he'd been trying to do me a favour, and he tucked his notebook away and turned on his heel to where his men were dispersing the crowd.

'Come on! Come on! Let's have you! Move on there! Nothing here for you!'

'Bloody Boche!' the man with the boater was shouting still. 'I hate the Boches!'

'If you don't shut your rattle,' the inspector told him severely, 'I'll charge you with using violent language to an officer of the law.'

'Bloody Boches!' the man with the boater shouted again, and I saw a sergeant grab him by the arm and swing him round. His face fell and the cane he was brandishing dropped to his side, and I wondered if his hatred of the Germans was sufficient to withstand the blandishments of the police. Apparently it wasn't and I saw him move off hurriedly.

'Why didn't you give the inspector your name?' Helen asked, eyeing me curiously. 'They might have made you a sergeant or something.'

'Not me,' I said. 'They know me too well. Besides, I'm out of camp without a pass. If Bold finds out he'll be on to me like a ton of bricks.'

The traffic was moving now and a tram rumbled slowly past, its passengers all eyes and hanging out of the windows, then the cabs and the carts and the motor cars. One of the motorists stopped in front of us and stuck his head out from under the canvas hood.

'I saw what happened, son,' he said to me. 'Jolly good effort, I thought. Fair play, I always say. Even with the Boche. If the young lady wants taking home, I'll give you a lift.'

Just then, I saw a figure in khaki appear alongside me, holding my cap. It was Frank Mason, and the cap looked as though a cart had been driven over it. My heart sank as I thought what Bold would have to say when he saw it.

'Here's your cap, Fen,' Mason said. 'It's a bit of a mess, old fruit. It's been trodden on, or run over, or something. You'll very likely be charged with malicious damage to government property and have to pay for the one you've spoiled and the one they'll give you to replace it.'

'Oh, well,' I said. 'It's only one more thing for Bold to gloat about.'

Mason was staring past me now. He'd recognised Helen and was grinning all over his face. 'Why, Helen!' he said. 'What are *you* doing here?'

His hand went up to the dinky little officer's moustache and he'd got his Bunny-Hug and Turkey-Trot and Waltz-round-the-back-of-the-files-with-me look on his face. I'd seen it often before round the office whenever a girl came into the room.

'I'm seeing Helen home,' I said quickly. I wasn't going to let him muscle in – not now. I pushed Helen in front of me towards the car, but Mason got in the way and I found myself treading on his heels.

'Sorry I couldn't get to help you,' he said smoothly to Helen, beaming all over his face. 'Only I got shoved against the wall by the crowd and couldn't get out. They looked nasty and I decided it was wiser to hold my tongue. Let me open the door for you.'

He pushed Helen inside the car, then turned to me.

'That's all right, Fenner,' he said, smiling. 'Two's company. Three's none. I'll look after her.'

'You damn' well won't,' I said, losing my temper. I gave him a sharp shove in the chest and climbed into the car. I'd got the door firmly shut behind me before he recovered his balance.

'You'll be late back to camp,' I grinned. 'Better hop it. No sense in two of us being put on the hooks.'

As we moved off, I saw a look of blank astonishment on his face, and Helen glanced at me obliquely.

'That was neat,' she said admiringly. 'I think you're learning a lot in the Army, Fen dear.'

There was no one in when we got to the Haddo house and Helen held open the door for me. 'Father's out,' she said. 'Better come in and spruce up. You've got blood on you.'

She lit the gas-mantles and deposited me in the kitchen to wash while she went upstairs.

'I'll keep this,' she said, holding up the bent umbrella. 'It'll do as a souvenir.'

When she returned she'd changed into a green skirt and a plain shirt blouse and done her hair. She had a bruise on her cheek but otherwise she seemed all right, and I got my first real look at her. She appeared to have grown up a little in the six months I'd been in the Army. Her face looked narrower but it still had the same fierce humorous strength and honesty in it.

'Let's wash that cut on your mouth,' she said. 'Or you'll be in trouble for fighting.'

'I'll be in trouble anyway,' I said. 'I ought to have been back in camp by this time.'

'Ought you to go?' She looked up quickly, her eyes wide and concerned.

'Might as well be hanged for a sheep as a lamb,' I said.

She pushed me into a creaking wicker chair and fetched a bowl of warm water and sponged the blood from my mouth and my cut knuckles. Her face seemed gentle just then, with none of its normal cheerful pugnacity. For a moment she was silent, her eyes on mine as she dabbed at the cut. Then she smiled.

'Thanks, Fen dear,' she said quietly. 'Thanks for coming to my rescue.'

'That's all right,' I said. 'Any time you feel like it. Just fetch Fenner.'

She laughed, sitting back, holding the bowl and the piece of damp flannel, and I loved her then, for her beauty, her honesty, her wry humour and her kindness.

She'd often teased me and jeered at me, and argued with me, but I'd still always felt I'd rather be with her for an hour and have her disagreeing with me, even quarrelling with me, than any other girl for a year. For the simple reason that she was like Locky, uncomplicated and straightforward, and easy to understand.

'Good old Fen,' she said. 'Always the same old Fen. Let me get you a drink.'

She put away the bowl and the flannel and found a bottle of her father's beer, and two glasses, and we sat at the kitchen table, our elbows on the red plush cloth, drinking it and eating some bread and cheese she found.

'I haven't seen you for ages,' she said.

I gave her a guilty sidelong look. I knew I'd been neglecting her. Dazzled by the adulation the Army had brought on us, we'd all been a little guilty of neglecting old girlfriends for new ones. Since she'd spent most of her time before the war playing

Frank Mason against me, however, I'd felt a certain amount of justification in the thought that she wouldn't be lonely; but now, looking at her, and caught up again by all the old worship of her, I began to realise I'd been a bit of a fool and tried hard to put it right.

'I've been busy,' I explained. 'We get involved in things a bit.'

'Locky has nights off. Don't you?'

'When I'm not on defaulters.'

'You're not on defaulters always.'

'I seem to get caught for it more than most people.'

'Why?'

'Because I can't keep my mouth shut.'

'You never could.' She looked sideways at me. 'Suppose some time when you could manage *not* to be on defaulters you come and see a girl.'

I grinned. 'It's not a bad idea,' I said.

She toyed with the glass in her hand, moving it slowly and thoughtfully in little circles on the red plush cloth, then she looked up at me under her eyebrows in the same quizzical way that Locky had, so that I wasn't sure whether she was laughing at me or not.

'Or have you got a girl already somewhere?' she asked.

'You know I haven't.'

'Well, it's time you had.'

I was just going to tell her that that was something which could well depend on her, when she went on, 'What's it like at Blackmires, Fen?'

'It's not so bad.'

'Locky says it's awful.'

I was surprised. He'd never shown any sign of disliking it. He'd seemed to take it all in his stride, neither approving nor disapproving.

'It's no worse than digs,' I said. 'Especially now that the winter's over.'

'How long do you expect it'll be before you're sent abroad?'

131

'It shouldn't be long.'

'Will it be France?'

'I expect so. Another few months and then we're for the chopper.'

She sat up abruptly, and put the glass down on the table with a thump. 'Don't say that,' she said quickly.

'Don't say what?'

'What you said just then. It makes it sound as though you're dead already.'

I shrugged. We'd all said things like that to each other on many occasions. We were all a little more fatalistic than normal because of the sure knowledge that some of us might not be alive in a year's time. But we'd none of us brooded much over it. We were normal healthy young men and far more concerned with enjoying the present than thinking about the future.

'Well, we might be,' I said. 'If you think about it.'

The warmth seemed to go out of her at once and her head came up.

'This world's barmy,' she said sharply. 'I think sometimes you men enjoy war, the way you dwell on your rosy dreams of glory, all well fortified with patriotism and honour and aggressiveness.'

She swung round and turned her back on me and started to stare at the fire, and for a long time we sat like that, in the glow of the green-shaded light over the kitchen table, listening to the big clock ticking on the wall. I waited for her to face me again but she made no effort to do so.

'What's the matter, Helen?' I asked gently.

'Nothing,' she snapped.

'I can't say this is the best view of you.'

'Well, you'll have to lump it.'

I began to get angry. 'For heaven's sake, Helen,' I said. 'I brought you home——'

'Jolly nice of you.'

'Yes, it was, considering that when I get back they'll probably charge me with being out without a pass. With my record they'll probably hang, draw and quarter me.'

She turned round slowly at last, her face anxious and pale.

I grinned. 'Bold would love to see me in the guardroom,' I said. 'It would make his day.'

She smiled faintly, but without much mirth, and I could see her eyes were moist and troubled. 'Why do we always get so cross with each other, Fen?' she asked.

'I don't know,' I said.

'It isn't always *my* fault, is it?'

'No. It's mine as often as not.'

'Do you fight with Locky like this?'

'No. Locky and I seem to live at peace with each other.'

'It *must* be *my* fault then,' she said. 'But, looking at you, all of you pretending to be soldiers when you're not, all of you busting to go out and die, makes me want to cry all the time. That's all. There are so many of you and you know so little about it. I get so angry and so afraid.'

She got up and put the gramophone on, almost as though she weren't thinking, and it started to play some ragtime piece; and we were still sitting there, not really listening to it, not speaking, perplexed by something we couldn't understand, when the door opened and Locky appeared. He was smiling and looked as though he might have drunk too much. But his speech wasn't slurred and he seemed to be in control of himself and extraordinarily happy.

'Caught you!' he said.

Helen looked up, then she swung round on her chair and put her back to him.

He leaned on the door and stared at us gravely. 'I've been drinking,' he said. 'One of Father's friends who insisted on wining and dining one of the saviours of the Christian world. Molly Miles' father, just for the record. Remember her, Mark? In the photo library at the office.'

'I remember her,' I said. 'Mason always seemed to be dancing the Bunny-Hug or something with her round the files.'

Locky nodded slowly. 'Er – yes,' he said thoughtfully. 'That's the one.'

He nodded to the gramophone which had finished its record and was grinding away, click-click-click, in the groove at the end.

'Finished with that, by any chance?' he asked.

Neither of us spoke and he crossed the room and switched it off. 'It occurred to me I was late,' he said, 'and I came home to borrow the car to get back to camp. As it so happens, Private Fenner, I can probably give you a lift now. I didn't know you two had been seeing each other. What have you been up to?'

Helen stood up and turned quickly away. 'Shut up, Locky,' she said.

Locky looked at her, then at me. 'Mark Martin Fenner,' he said. 'What have you been doing with my sister?'

Helen swung round quickly before he could probe any further.

'There was a riot outside Schafers',' she said. 'He rescued a damsel in distress.'

'Did he, by God? Was she beautiful?'

'No.'

'Yes, she was,' I said.

Locky grinned. 'There appears to be some doubt on the subject,' he commented. 'Who was it? Anyone I know?'

'Me,' Helen said.

'Oh!' Locky raised his eyebrows. 'Anybody get hurt?'

'Only the man who tried to get hold of me. He went off complaining his nose was broken. Mark hit him.'

Locky grinned. 'I'll see you're recommended for a putty medal, Private Fenner,' he said. 'For the moment, however, it occurs to me we ought to be getting back. Seen the time?'

'Yes.' I nodded. 'It makes me feel quite ill.'

'We'll borrow the car.'

'You won't,' Helen pointed out. 'Father's got it.'

'Oh, my God,' Locky said. 'I thought he'd be safely home and in bed. It looks as though we'll have to walk then.'

In the end we managed to hire a car that Locky's father used occasionally for his rounds, and it arrived shortly afterwards, an open tourer with flickering yellow lights and a driver in a leather coat with his cap on back-to-front. Helen watched us leave without a word of goodbye.

Locky sat back and said nothing, but halfway up the hill, with the engine roaring fit to explode, and a hot burnt-oil smell coming back to us from under the bonnet, without a word of warning he turned to me and spoke cheerfully.

'Why don't you get married, Mark?' he said.

He was still in his mellow mood. Something had happened to him that had pleased him, and he seemed unable to stop smiling, but I didn't feel much like laughter myself just then.

'Go on,' he said. 'Why don't you?'

'Never thought of it,' I said.

'Time you did then. You're quite a big boy now.'

'So are you. You're older than I am. Why don't *you*?'

His smile grew broader. 'Curiously enough,' he said, 'I've considered it. I find the idea appeals to me.'

'I wouldn't have thought wartime was the best time to get involved,' I said. 'It's only extra responsibility and I can't see much point in leaving some girl in the lurch, probably with children.'

Locky shrugged. 'It doesn't seem to have occurred to your somewhat atrophied intellect, Private Fenner, that this is the most opportune time of all for marriage. With men dying, and the world emptying rather more swiftly than normal, it seems to me perambulators and crèches ought to be kept busier than ever.'

I didn't say anything. I was still preoccupied with thoughts of Helen and I stared round the windscreen at the stunted trees and the dry-stone walls and the blank moors beyond, holding my battered cap on in the freezing wind that blew into the rear seat round the edge of the glass.

I knew Locky was staring at me, but I didn't turn round, and in the end he gave a short laugh.

'You're a stand-offish old buster at times, Fenner,' he said at last.

'Yes, I know.'

'All this bothering about possible death is morbid, selfish and unnecessary. It's not like you.'

'Stupefaction's setting in,' I said. 'That's the trouble.'

'You ought to be ashamed of yourself.'

'Same to you, with knobs on.'

We got the driver to stop before we reached the camp and we walked the rest of the way in silence. As we reached the wire fence, we paused, wondering how to get in without being caught.

People who got themselves put on charges weren't very popular. Murray, for one, thought it was letting the side down. And there was always the knowledge that anyone who was a troublemaker could be booted out of the battalion with very little difficulty at all.

'What do we do now?' Locky said as we stood staring over the darkened huts, and the tall square shape of the water tower against the the sky. 'What's next?'

'Let's get through the wire,' I suggested.

'Suppose they catch us?'

'They won't. The grass is long. We can almost reach the hut from this corner without standing up.'

'How do you know?'

'I've tried it before. Let's have a go.'

We wriggled on our stomachs through the damp grass under the wire and headed at a crouch towards the dark block of shadows that was the huts. We had crossed half of the patch of grass when we saw something move in front of us, and we froze to the ground, panting.

''Alt! Who goes there?' The voice came sharply across the thin night air, and made us jump.

'Where is he?' Locky said.

'He's near the gate,' I said. 'We're all right. He's got the wind up, that's all.'

'Wind up or not, he's coming this way.'

''Alt or I fire!'

'What do we do now, for God's sake?' Locky was hugging the ground and his voice sounded muffled as though he were laughing.

'It's not so bloody funny,' I said.

'Isn't it?' he said. 'I thought it was. Come on, Fen, you're the man of action. What do we do?'

'Run like hell,' I said.

'Suppose he really does shoot?'

'Don't talk barmy,' I said. 'He's bluffing, there's nothing on this camp that's straight enough to hit us.'

Locky raised his head cautiously. 'I think it's Bold,' he said.

'Oh God! Now what?'

'Let's throw ourselves on his mercy.'

'He doesn't know the meaning of the word.'

'Let's stay where we are,' Locky suggested. 'He might never see us.'

'Not on your life,' I said. 'He's got eyes in his behind. You go that way. I'll go this. He can't catch us both and there's no point in both of us being on a charge. And if only one gets away, he doesn't give himself up. Agreed?'

'Fair enough. Ready?'

'Yes. Off you go.'

It was when Locky had gone that I realised *he* was heading for the shadows and I'd picked the wrong direction. I knew I was caught. Bold was too much of an old soldier to be baffled by two enemies at different points. He went for the one he could see and appeared smack in front of me. Thin as a lath and as high as a house he seemed, from where I was crouching in the grass. I was tempted to run for it, but there wasn't much point, so I stopped.

'Aha!' he said cheerfully. 'What the hell do you think you're up to there? Rabbitin'?'

I stood up and he shone his torch on me, blinding me.

I heard him drew his breath in quickly, then he gave a gusty sigh. 'Cor stone the bloody crows,' he said wearily. 'Not you again, Fenner?'

6

I was still finishing my period of detention when we were informed we were to move from Blackmires to Romstone on the East Coast.

Murray, as usual, was the Perseus who brought us the news. I never did find out how it was that Murray always got to know the news first, but he always did. It was almost as though he hung around outside the orderly room waiting for something to happen. He spent most of his days in a tizzy of excitement and fear and indignation, and inevitably he came up more than once with what was nothing more than a camp buzz. But this time he was right and he waltzed me round, full pack, rifle and all, as I returned from the guardroom.

'We're going,' he chirruped. 'We're going! One step nearer the war!'

'Can't say I'm sorry,' I said. 'It'll be a change to see the inside of a different guardroom.'

He began to help me off with my equipment, still hopping about and frantic with excitement.

'Just think,' he said. 'No digging. No building. No road-making.'

'And a fresh batch of girls!' Mason said.

Murray's mood changed abruptly, as though he regarded the comment as a flippancy not in keeping with the correct attitude for war.

'They say they don't like troops to grow attached to any one place,' he said sternly.

'*Who* says they don't?' Spring demanded.

'Well, they don't.'

'Well, go on, General, tell us why.'

Murray scowled. 'They just don't,' he said. 'They've moved the Manchester battalions long since. Now it's our turn. I expect the idea's that they think we should learn to do without wives and girlfriends. Sort of in preparation for the real separation when it comes.'

All Murray's thoughts and opinions were directed by his dedication to the battle he was going to fight before long. All harshness, all discipline, all disappointments were subordinated to and explained by this greater thing that hovered over us, this privilege we'd been fortunate enough to have bestowed on us.

We left Blackmires at six o'clock in the morning led by a Royal Engineers band playing the regimental march. On the city outskirts a colliery band in scarlet and gold was waiting for us, and tagged on behind. It was made up now, I noticed, largely of older men and younger boys, but they're great ones for brass bands in the north and the noise was still enough to wake the dead, and people appeared on the pavements in spite of the early hour. Flags hung from windows all along the route and banners with goodwill messages were strung across the streets. ON TO BERLIN they said, and UP, THE CITY BATTALION, and things like that.

Outside the Town Hall, we were formed up in a hollow square and addressed by the Lord Mayor.

'Never forget,' he said ponderously, 'that you're taking the

140

good name of this city with you. We shall await reports of your gallantry and heroism, in full certainty that when the war ends – perhaps next year – you will all have played your part.'

He seemed to go on half the morning, dwelling far longer, it seemed to me, on the city we came from than on us. Somewhere along the line he lost sight of the battalion and, as he developed his paean of praise for the Corporation transport system, I could see restless twitchings going on all around me.

It was warm and we were tired, because most of us had been on our feet since long before daylight, and our packs were heavy and dragging at our shoulders. I could see Bold in front of me, rigid as a ramrod, not a muscle moving, intense disgust expressed clearly even by the back of his neck, and Appleby, fidgeting a little restlessly, his expression wild.

Finally, long after I'd lost interest, someone called for three cheers for us, and they were given by the crowd that was filling the road behind us, holding up the trams and the traffic, the shrill cries of the women and the children coming through the deep-throated roar of the men. We returned the compliment enthusiastically, thankful the ordeal was ending, then we formed ranks once more and set off for the station, women and children in dozens alongside the marching column, arm-in-arm with husbands and brothers and sons. Every window seemed to have sprouted flags, Union Jacks, tricolours, pictures of the King and Queen and the Prince of Wales, and miscellaneous bunting.

The sun was just beginning to warm the drab little houses among the cutlery works, and the soot-rotten bricks glowed in its yellow light.

There was another crowd outside the station and as we approached hats, sticks and handkerchiefs started waving agitatedly, and a low self-conscious murmur began as they worked up to a cheer. We were marching at ease now, joking and shouting, women stumbling along beside us, getting in the way, some weeping, some laughing, all excited and a little hysterical.

141

As we reached the bottom of the hill, we were called to attention, and swung up the station approach in fine style, past horses and waggons and field kitchens and piles of kit which had been dumped in the roadway outside the goods entrance, all ready for loading. We marched through the sooty columns that were still plastered with *Skegness is so Bracing* and notices for cheap fares, led by our own band and accompanied by two others. The reserve company, which was staying behind, was drawn up alongside the booking office and saluted us with the colours that the Mothers' Unions had stitched for us as we stamped on to the platform, the shouted orders echoing in the sooty glass-and-iron dome of the station.

We piled arms on the platform and were allowed to fall out to say goodbye to friends, while they loaded up the last of the equipment in the goods yard. Molly Miles from the *Post* picture library was there and seemed to be seeing Locky off; and Arnold Holroyd's wife, Ethel; and Murray's mother. I thought and hoped Helen would have come to see Locky off too, but there was only his father.

'She's coming later,' Mason announced confidently.

'How do you know?' I demanded.

He grinned. 'Saw her last night, old fruit,' he said.

I stared. I'd been trying to telephone her from the orderly room half the evening. I'd bribed one of the clerks because I wasn't allowed to leave camp, but the maid had answered and said she was out. Now I knew where.

'No wonder I couldn't get in touch with her,' I said bitterly.

Mason grinned again. 'The skivvy said someone had been telephoning while we were out,' he said. 'Was it you?'

'Yes.'

'Well, well.' He chuckled. 'The things you do get up to, to be sure. Of course, if you *will* go and get yourself in Bold's bad books. It was hard luck, that, at a time like this.'

I pushed through the crowds, cursing Bold and dogging Mason's footsteps, determined that he shouldn't catch Helen on her own without me having a chance to speak to her too. But she hadn't come by the time the train arrived and we were both beginning to lose our tempers with each other.

'My God,' Mason said bitterly. 'Can't a chap look for a girl without other people hanging around all the time?'

'No,' I said. 'Not if the chap's you, and the girl's Helen, and the other people's me.'

Eventually the order to entrain was given and they shoved us in, eight to a compartment, and in a few moments the platform was empty and the windows of every carriage were full of laughing faces. Pine, the adjutant, who was staying behind to clear things up, went along shaking hands, and we reached out to grab his fist.

'So long, sir,' Murray shouted. 'See you later.'

'Mind you don't miss your putty medal!'

'We'll keep a few Fritzes back for you if you're delayed.'

Then the Lord Mayor and the Lady Mayoress came along, and old FitzJimmy, waving and shouting, and, I thought, a little too full of whisky, considering the early hour.

He shook every hand he could reach and Eph sat back, awed, staring at the palm of his hand and his thick red fingers.

'Gawd,' he said. 'If that don't take the bloody biscuit! Me, Eph Lott, shaking 'ands with a ruddy earl! It's amazing what a war does for a chap.'

Mason and I were still fighting each other for a place in the window, staring down the platform for Helen and pumping Locky with questions.

'She's late,' I pointed out.

'She promised,' Mason said agitatedly. 'Last night.'

A whistle blew and Mason groaned as the crowd began their final yell, their final waving of arms, handkerchiefs and Union Jacks. We all waved back like mad, cheering and shouting, and the train jerked.

'She's there!' Mason shouted, heaving violently in the window so that I banged my chin on the glass, and I saw Helen appear on the platform just behind Molly Miles and Locky's father. She ran forward, looking a little lost, then stopped, her hand to her mouth, then she started to wave frantically.

'My God,' I said. 'What bloody awful luck!' I gave Mason a shove and got an arm out. 'For God's sake, get over, man!'

Mason pushed me back. 'Helen,' he bawled. 'Helen!'

His big body was filling the window and I couldn't get my head out and I had to edge one shoulder below him and try to wave like that.

I caught a brief glimpse of her, a slender figure in blue, then we were passing the sooty windows of the workshops along the Queen's Road embankment, which were full of cheering men and girls and agitated flags. The furnace-workers outside Liddell, Moore and Hart's were waving their caps among the purple-grey bars of cooling iron and the smoking new bogey wheels stacked in the yard, and all the way along the Enfield Road the crowds were standing, with the kids they'd turned out of the schools and lined up to cheer us as we went by.

Mason sat down in the seat next to the window, among the piled equipment that we'd dumped hurriedly in an effort to get nearest to the platform.

'That's that,' he said flatly. 'What a damned shame! Didn't give a chap chance to say goodbye.'

Romstone was a dreary little place where we dug trenches all over the sand dunes, then waited for the sea to fill them in again so we could dig some more the following day, while all the time along the beach the tireless batteries of horse artillery wheeled in and out of white posts set in the ground, limbers bumping and swaying and instructors bawling their contempt from the sidelines.

'You blokes want bicycle 'andles,' they shouted. 'We'll never train you lot till someone invents a horse you can ride inside, like a bus.'

We were now part of the new 4th Army and were brigaded

with another Yorkshire battalion and two battalions from Lancashire. The whole area echoed to the tramp of men in khaki, and tents and huts were springing up outside every town and village. Work was being carried out in theatres, cinemas and halls wherever there was room. There were men in companies and squads, occupied in battalion and brigade and division drill; men of the machine gun section, engineers constructing bridges over every spare stream and pond and canal they could find; cavalrymen, motorcycle and bicycle corps, scouts, signallers; men at bayonet practice, men at musketry training, men learning transport; whole divisions marching or at manœuvres, skirmishing, charging up steep slopes and across the dunes, erecting barbed-wire defences, or just lying on the ground recovering.

Here we learned to work with artillery and aircraft, little string-and-wire affairs that circled over us as we moved about, the sun shining on the varnished surfaces of their wings as they banked and caught the sun, with just the grinning face of the pilot, swathed in leather, leaning over the edge of the cockpit and an arm waving down to us.

We were billeted in the basement rooms of Victorian boarding houses along the front, all of them darkened every night in case of Zeppelins or the hit-and-run raiders who'd shelled Whitby, Scarborough and Lowestoft from the sea. The esplanade and the beach where the kids had built their sandcastles not so long before were deserted most of the time, and the shelters were dilapidated, most of the glass smashed. The gaslamps were blue-painted and there was barbed wire everywhere in great looping black tangles, as sorrowful as the cries of the seabirds that spotted the promenade with white.

'It looks like the last place God made,' Locky commented, staring over the top of the railinged steps that led to our gas-lit basement quarters.

'Perhaps it is,' I said.

We did our drilling on the front and our trench-assaulting

among the dunes. After a while the silver ornaments began to reappear in our billets, and eventually we were surreptitiously moved into bedrooms which had been standing empty since all summer visitors had stopped. Brass bedsteads were given a rub up for us and the picture of '*Hope*' was polished and the patchwork quilts were hung out of the windows to air in the sunshine.

'We had to be careful,' they told us shamefacedly. 'They're not all gentlemen like you lot.'

We became part of the family, and, to save work, eventually moved in with them and helped with the chores, taking the place of sons who'd disappeared into other regiments and were probably now stationed in the place we'd just left. We sneaked out at night in their civilian clothes and sneaked in again when no one was looking. Love affairs developed inevitably. Barraclough was taken tea in bed every morning; and Murray found himself with a motherly old dear who so took to his rosy cheeks she provided transport in the form of a dog-cart from his billet to the little seafront school which had became company headquarters.

We lived with them, ate with them, and in one or two notable cases like Eph Lott and Spring, the great lover, slept with them. Two men got married, rather abruptly.

'It's the sea air,' Locky said.

At Romstone we were taken over at last by the War Office, at one of those fantastic parades the Army loved so dearly, with the whole division standing for hours in a drizzling rain, while we were inspected by some elderly general who arrived late and, because of the weather, hurried through the affair and departed for the officers'-mess fire as fast as he could. Afterwards, they formed us up outside our huts, and the colonel came along and announced unexpectedly that, because the battalion was so much over strength, anyone who wanted his discharge could have it at once. All we had to do to get our freedom was inform the orderly room.

The suggestion was received with the stunned silence of indignation. Even after a training that consisted in no small measure of building huts and making roads and rifle ranges, no one wanted to go home. That unreasonable optimistic faith that had brought us in wouldn't let us back out now.

As a result, the following week, the whole battalion was medically examined to pick out the best, and we queued up outside the little school that was sick quarters for hours to know our fate, trying not to smoke and to learn by heart the letters on the eye-chart in case of some dreadful mistake.

'They can't throw me out,' Murray said loudly. 'Not now. Not after all this time.'

Locky looked up from where he was reading a book, sitting on the pavement, his feet in the gutter, absorbed, indifferent to the discomfort, the boredom and the uproar as he always was. 'If I were you,' he said dryly, 'I'd be inclined to lay low and say nothing. You know what happens to little boys who tell lies about their age.'

Murray grinned. 'Yes,' he said. 'They end up as soldiers in France.'

We all pretended it was only because we'd gone so far that it would be a waste not to go the rest of the way. But the truth was that there was a tremendous pride in the battalion which had never been put into us by the artificial means of propaganda. We knew we were the pick of our northern city and we'd acquired a reputation for outmarching and outshooting everybody else.

But it wasn't just prowess that made us what we were, not just comradeship. It was something more, an awareness, perhaps, that we all came from the same place and that any letting down of the side would be heard of at once at home. Our friends knew each other, some of us were related even – there were several sets of brothers like the Mandys – we'd gone to the same schools, attended the same churches, followed the same football teams and chased the same girls. And we had an immense confidence in ourselves and nothing in the world could induce us to feel we weren't needed – every single one of us.

We felt we were soldiers now. Only ordeal by battle could tell us how good we were, but there was a feeling which ran through the whole battalion like a bright thread of courage, that we shouldn't at this stage be cheated of the chance to prove ourselves.

In my despairing moments, when things didn't seem to be going right, I sometimes wondered how we'd behave if we were ever faced with some situation that hadn't occurred to our instructors, some desperate chance that might arise when we'd been separated from the directions of the staff. What we'd learned was mostly theoretical and only the colonel and Appleby and Bold and Corker and one or two others could say with any certainty how they'd react to danger.

If the colonel were to fall, I thought, was Ashton capable of taking his place? If Ashton fell, could young Welch step into his shoes? If Welch died, could some sergeant take command? And if our sergeants were hit, could we? I often doubted it.

But when those thoughts frightened me, I pushed them away hurriedly; and pride, both in myself and in the battalion, didn't let them come often. Surely, I reassured myself, that native intelligence that had enabled so many of us to do well in our civilian jobs would help us on any battlefield.

In the end, only about fifteen were sent home, and they were mostly the troublemakers and the shirkers, who the colonel was glad to be rid of and who on the whole were glad to be rid of us. Since they'd picked us so carefully in the first days of the battalion's existence, and told us more than once that our physique equalled that of the Guards, they couldn't honestly throw out anyone on medical grounds.

But we were still greatly over strength, and someone had the much brighter idea of sending for the Ministry of Munitions people, who descended on us unexpectedly and began at once to weed out the tradesmen, the turners, the fitters and the machinists. There'd been a tremendous outcry about the shortage of ammunition after Loos, and Sir John French was in danger of being superseded as Commander-in-Chief and Lloyd George had taken over the Ministry of Munitions. Even Kitchener was being edged out of office for the faults that had become obvious in the system.

There were three of the investigators, conscientious little men with glasses and well-pressed suits, sitting at a table on which they'd spread a blanket and a Union Jack. They had all our files there and looked very important. They were the sort of men who always find themselves on tribunals and city councils or in Parliament; the sort of men who spend a lifetime doing public work, poking their noses into everyone else's affairs, dressing up their remarks in high-flown parliamentary language, all very important and efficient and unimaginative, reducing patriotism to the loveless proportions of a disputed footpath.

They tried hard to pin down Barraclough, who'd been a foreman mechanic at the *Post*, but he hedged cautiously, blinking his pale eyelashes indignantly. 'My job was to see that the paper didn't tear and the printing inkwells were full,' was all that he'd admit to. 'That's all.'

'That's not what it says here,' they pointed out, and they put him aside with fifty-odd other men. But, when they weren't looking, he sneaked away to see Ashton, his pale hair spiky with rage, and Ashton, wearing his hurt-father look, was unable to say 'no' to him and demanded that he be allowed to remain, on the grounds that he was essential to battalion transport – at that time one lorry and a lot of horse-drawn carts.

It was about this time that we lost the colonel, who was sent to command an Indian battalion in the Middle East and departed thankfully for the warmer climate. In his place, the adjutant, arranged that his brother, a little terrier of a man with service in the Durhams, should take over. The new colonel was a city man like the rest of us, but he'd been in France and, after being blown up, had lost an eye and acquired a stammer which in no way, however, detracted from his efficiency, and he was given a spontaneous cheer when he first appeared on parade.

'He's got the Military Cross,' Murray whispered. 'I can see the ribbon. That's a leg up for us, if you like.'

In spite of his wounds, Pine was a hard-boiled soldier, and he told us firmly what he expected of us. He stood with his feet apart, his hands behind his back, the black patch over his sightless eye sinister against his pale face, his small frame tensed and eager, holding our attention as he talked. At his feet sat the little white terrier he'd inherited with the battalion and which had finally become part of the official presence of the commanding officer.

'You ch-chaps – have done damn' well,' he said, his jaw working as he struggled to get the words out. 'It's taken you only a year to reach a – state that a new regiment in p-p-peacetime would have taken three years to reach. So we're – not going to let you go stale by overdoing it.'

There were cheers from the rear which were immediately squashed by Corker.

'Because of this,' Pine went on, 'I've come to the b-battalion with something that ought to make me very dear to your hearts. I've b-brought something you haven't had before – leave.'

The burst of cheering that followed the announcement drowned all the protests from the sergeants, and Pine stood in front of us with a broad grin on his face, fingering one of the buttons of his jacket.

'Thought y-you'd appreciate that,' he said.

We played cards most of the way home, crammed into a special train with all our kit, very conscious of ourselves with our best khaki and the hard-bitten look we all thought we wore by now. In the next compartment, in a fug of cigarette smoke, they were singing one of Spring's ribald songs and outside in the corridor the Mandy brothers were arguing about some girl they'd picked up at Romstone.

'She will,' Billy Mandy said.

'She won't,' Tommy Mandy said.

'She will, you know.'

'She bloody won't, you know.'

Young Murray had climbed on to the luggage-rack for comfort, his face a little lost and homesick. He'd shown no interest in anything but the business of becoming a soldier from the day he'd joined up, but now you could see the desire to get home burning out of his face.

Locky sat silently in a corner, reading a book, curiously untouched by all the excitement, though I'd thought that going home would be the one thing that might have roused him from the curiously detached state he always managed to preserve.

'Suppose we go and get killed,' Murray said suddenly out of the blue, the words coming unexpectedly through the excited conversation round the card game.

'Well, suppose we do?' Mason said. 'What's bothering your baby mind, son?'

He didn't look up and didn't show much interest. We never thought much of death, obsessed as we were with life and winning the war.

'It's just a thought, that's all,' Murray said. 'What happens if we do get killed? Will it make any difference? I mean, what'll they think of us? I suppose somebody'd write and tell my mother, wouldn't they?'

Mason laughed, but Murray was not to be put off.

'It's not a joke,' he said thoughtfully. 'It's a big problem.'

Locky looked up. 'I think it is, Murray,' he said. 'People do occasionally get done to death in wartime.'

'There were a lot killed at Ypres,' Murray said thoughtfully. 'Something went wrong, by the look of things.'

'Are you afraid, Murray?' Locky said gently.

Murray looked down at him from his perch, his eyes wide. 'Me?' he said, surprised. 'No, 'course not! Only, well, just suppose I got a bullet in the heart . . .'

151

All Murray's conceptions of death seemed to be neat clean ones, and usually included a bullet in the heart. It often seemed to me that death in battle could easily be a much more untidy affair than that.

'Suppose I got a bullet in the heart,' he said. 'Suppose I just fell and nobody noticed. Who'd be aware that I'd tried to do my duty?'

'I think it'd leak out somehow,' Locky said gently.

'How?'

'Well, we've had to listen to you – often when we didn't want to – for the best part of a year now. In fact, many a time, when training was slow suicide, the flat and toneless day became sheer music for me as I heard you giving tongue to your own particular brand of patriotism.'

'You're sneering at me.'

Locky looked up. 'I promise you I'm not,' he said seriously. 'I solemnly swear by God's holy trousers that I meant every word I said. If it weren't for people like you, who see this affair in Europe as something rather above the murk of a dirty political squabble, there wouldn't be much point in fighting at all, would there?'

Murray stared down at him, like most of us, always uncertain whether to take him seriously or not, then he shrugged.

'I don't want anybody to tell me I'm being noble or heroic, like they do,' he said earnestly. 'That's all eyewash. But if anything *should* happen, I'd just like it to be known that I'd pulled my weight. That's all.'

Our arrivals and departures always seemed to be the excuse for an official occasion, and when the train pulled in the Mayor was there waiting, with the city councillors and the station-master and a couple of bands. The platform was jammed with relatives and friends but they all had to wait until some long-winded old donkey had made a speech. Then, as they let us off the train, everything became pandemonium, with kids

152

shrieking, dogs barking and people shouting and laughing and crying all at the same time.

I saw Colonel Pine kissing a pretty girl and Ashton arm-in-arm with his wife. Young Murray, his brow still troubled, was being swept away by a whole crowd of noisy relatives. Appleby disappeared with a woman who looked like a barmaid, and Welch's family were there en masse, with two enormous cars, to meet him. To my surprise I saw Molly Miles go quietly up to Locky and put her arm through his, and they left together.

'Now, that's a new one on me,' Mason said thoughtfully, staring after them. 'I used to think she was *my* girl.'

'It doesn't look as though she is now,' I said, enjoying the look on his face. 'God, how many girls do you want at a time?'

'Master Henry Lockwood Haddo's a bloody dark horse,' Mason said, a faint trace of indignation in his voice. 'I always did say so – with that quiet smile of his and that way he has of hiding behind his own face Ah, well, I'm going for a beer. Going to drown my sorrows in drink. Coming?'

As we set off for the exit, I saw Earl FitzJimmy, who was said to have lost two of his sons in France with the Guards and a third in the Dardanelles. There was no one now to carry on the title, and he seemed to be taking it hard and looked tired and ill. But he waved to anyone he recognised and wished us luck.

Locky's father was at the station entrance, waiting in the big grey Lanchester, and I watched anxiously lest Helen should appear. But there was no sign of her and, after skirmishing round each other for a while in case she turned up, Mason and I went off to have a drink.

'Here's to women,' Mason said, hoisting his glass. 'Bless 'em all – particularly one of 'em.'

'Which one?' I asked.

Mason grinned. 'Helen,' he said. 'Who do you think?'

He slapped me on the back. 'God, what a face,' he said. He paused, then put his arm round my shoulders. 'Hard luck, Fen,' he said sympathetically. 'But we're free, white and twenty-one and all's fair in love and war. No ill feeling, I hope, old sport.'

There was quite a lot of ill feeling on my part but I could hardly say so.

'Have you been seeing a lot of Helen?' I asked, trying not to appear concerned.

'Of course,' he said. 'She's been writing to me.'

'She didn't write to me.'

'Obviously you haven't got what it takes.'

'You've got more than your share.'

'Well, that's the way it is.'

He was staring down at me, handsome, confident, certain of himself. He'd spent hours doing things with his cap which gave it a rakish devil-may-care look that I could never get into mine. I always felt I looked like a bus conductor in mine, and even when I took the wire out it merely seemed to deflate and die, with none of the devilish lines Frank's always managed to have. He never seemed to have difficulty charming the girls around him, and to me finding it hard to charm even one, he seemed to have more than his fair share of the world's good things.

'You're not kidding me, Frank, are you?' I said. 'You really have been writing to Helen?'

He became serious at once. In spite of my attempts to appear indifferent, I expect it showed all over my face.

'I'm not kidding,' he said. 'Want me to show you the letters?'

'No.' I shook my head. 'No. I don't want to see the letters. I only wanted to know. Just for certain.'

He put his hand on my shoulder. 'I'm sorry, Fen,' he said gently. 'It's just the way things have worked out. Was it important?'

'Lord, no,' I said, the words like ashes in my mouth. 'There are other fish in the sea.'

'Good, then. No hard feelings?'

'None at all.'

'You going to bow yourself off the stage now?'

'Not much point in hanging around, is there?'

He grinned and slapped me on the back. 'Let's have a drink, Fen,' he suggested, 'We ought to shake hands, you and I. It's been a good clean fight, old fruit.'

We got Spring and MacKinley to join us, and eventually several of the other men who had to wait for buses to outlying villages. Finally, when Mason had gone, I teamed up with Spring, who like me had no settled home.

'What are you going to do with your leave, Fen?' he asked.

I shook my head. I'd been busily making plans all the way home but Mason seemed to have put an end to all those. He and I had been chasing round each other to get at Helen for so long, I'd merely accepted it without thinking. Somehow, I suppose, I'd imagined Mason would *always* be there in the background. Now, though, it seemed I was in the background, and there didn't seem to be much point in trying any more. I'd better put it away from me, I thought. No sense in brooding over things.

It crossed my mind that I might go to London, which was supposed to be a wonderful place for leave, but it seemed to be an effort just then to find another train and I couldn't be bothered. I was beset with the wavering uncertainty of a young man whose plans had collapsed about his ears. 'God knows what I'll do with it,' I said. 'What about you? What'll you do?'

Spring grinned. 'Sleep,' he said luxuriously. 'Eat. Drink. Go out with girls. Let's start by drinking some beer.'

But our night out together didn't quite come off. The city had changed in a subtle way. Like Romstone it had grown shabbier as people economised and builders' yards closed down for lack of manpower. The drab houses round the station were a shade drabber than they'd been before, and there seemed to be a complete absence of bright colour in a dark landscape that was made even more monotonous by the number of uniforms about. There were a lot more soldiers about than there had been, and a few officers who looked obvious frauds, temporary gentlemen of the worst type, who were clearly intending to sit out the war in the greatest possible comfort. They belonged to the navvies' battalions or curious new units which had sprung up in the vast dumps around the city.

The papers were still full of casualties and I was startled to see Willie Julius' face staring out at me from the *For King and Countrys* column.

'I knew him,' I pointed out.

'Poor bastard,' Spring said.

The place was still cheerful, but there was an undertone now of suspicion, as though people were beginning to suspect the war wasn't going to be the picnic they'd expected it to be. The enthusiastic blood-and-thunder stuff of August 1914 had given place after Loos to something a shade grimmer. It wasn't the Absent Minded Beggar and Soldiers Three who were being extolled now, so much as the craftier Old Bill of Bairnsfather's cartoons. People had begun to realise the war was no longer a matter of cheering and charging, but a case of setting your teeth and hanging on.

Prices were rising rapidly and food was growing more difficult to obtain. The parks had all been torn up for training grounds and every scrap of open space seemed to have horsed transport parked on it, with pamphlets on the gates from the Dumb Friends' League appealing to the men inside to treat their animals as chums. Everyone seemed a little more noisy than normal, particularly the tough, tired-looking men in goat-skin jackets from France, who expected to be pushing up the daisies before long and naturally went for the beer and the girls.

The churches were still going at it hammer and tongs from the pulpit and in the columns of the *Post*, appealing to us to 'fight the good fight' and 'never to sheathe the sword until we had conquered the anti-Christ', and various other exhortations that seemed to us not only naïve but downright stupid.

'Pity they can't come with us when we go,' Spring commented. 'Then they could have a shot at it first-hand.'

We got rather drunk in the Blueberry. The rumour had got around that we were shortly to go overseas – I suspect Spring himself started it because he was always short of money – and people rallied round, only too anxious to drown us with drink.

During the course of the evening we picked up a blonde woman from somewhere. She was a little tight and put her arms round my shoulders and tried to make me drink gin from her glass. She had a look on her face that I was too old not to understand.

There was a piano in a corner of the room and a man in his shirt-sleeves was hammering out ragtime. The woman leaned on me and told me some rigmarole about her husband being an officer in France and that she'd taken a job to keep her spirits up. I didn't believe her. She looked to me like a plain, ordinary, common-or-garden tart, but the story about the officer-husband gave a hint of gentility and loneliness that she probably thought was rather fetching.

'People would have frowned at me for being in here once,' she said. 'But times are different now. Everybody's broader-minded.' Was I broad-minded, she asked. I said I was.

'You look as though you would be,' she said. 'Some people sneer at me for coming in here. I don't belong here, you know. I'm not the type who normally goes in pubs. But a woman gets lonely. Do you get lonely?'

'Not particularly,' I said, 'Only in crowded bars.'

She laughed. 'That's clever. You look as though you're clever. You've got the look of a man with a brain.'

She stood back and stared at me. Spring joined her and they examined me from top to bottom. They both seemed barmy.

'It's those eyes,' she said.

'I don't know,' Spring pointed out. 'Have you seen his *feet*? Especially in ammunition boots.'

She pushed him away irritably and came closer. 'Yes,' she said. 'It's those eyes. That's what gets me about you. And those black eyebrows. You look like a soldier who *fights*. You look like a soldier who suffers. You have the look tonight of a hero, a lover.'

'Not really,' I said, wishing she'd go away. 'It's just my normal look.'

'I'd like to know you better. What's your name?'

'Charlie Chaplin.'

'Please,' she said earnestly, 'no kidding. This is serious. Your real name?'

'Oh, all right,' I said. 'Henry Wadsworth Longfellow.'

'That's better. I like Henry. Do they call you Henry or Wadsworth?'

'Wadsworth.'

'The French always use the second name. I prefer Henry. Harry Longfellow. I like that. Was your mother French, by any chance? You have a French look about you.'

'No,' I said. 'She was an Eskimo.'

She looked startled and Spring joined in. 'She came over for Queen Victoria's Jubilee,' he said, 'and never went back.'

'Well!' The blonde woman eyed me appreciatively. 'I bet you could make a woman well content.'

'Have a drink,' I said, to change the subject.

'Thanks, I will. As a matter of fact, I was looking for someone to see me home. Those two sergeants over there are trying to pick me up.'

She indicated a couple of elderly three-stripers whose only interest in life seemed to be in sinking as much beer as they could manage. The table was already full of empty glasses.

'What, those two?' I said.

'Those are the ones.'

'Well,' I said. 'Let's go over and fight them. Let's have it out with them here and now.'

'No, no, no,' She put her hand on my arm quickly and held me back. 'I don't want trouble.' She tried to kiss me and I could smell the gin on her breath, then the landlord leaned over the counter and said: 'Hey, Daisy. Less of that.'

'He's a Frenchman,' she said.

'You've got it wrong,' Spring said, grinning all over his face.

'Don't you kid yourself.' The landlord laughed. 'He's a Tyke like me and you and everybody else in here. He used to work on the *Post*.'

She turned to me, her eyes flashing angrily. 'Do you mean you're not French?' she accused.

'*I* never said I was French. *You* said that!'

'And your name. It's not Longfellow?'

'Well, no.'

'You've a nerve, sonny. What is it then?'

'Frank Mason,' I said.

'I don't like that name,' she decided, beginning to lose interest herself now.

'I don't like it very much myself,' I said.

We hadn't been long rid of her when Spring tried to pick a fight with a Grenadier, then, when I stopped him, one with me. By the time the pubs closed he was in a gloomy mood. The city seemed morose and dreary too, now, though there were still a lot of people in the darkened streets, mostly soldiers trying hard to be gay and noisy with nothing to be gay and noisy about.

'You want London for fun,' Spring said heavily. 'Always somewhere to go and plenty of girls. Booze any old time, if you know what's what, and always a show somewhere. Even the public lavatories are locked at eleven o'clock round here.'

In disgust we found a Y.M.C.A. hostel and hired beds for the night, narrow cots in a lysol-smelling room where there were half a dozen other soldiers sleeping off their liquor. The next morning Spring rose with a headache, and announced that he thought he'd go and look up a girlfriend of his who was appearing in a show at Birmingham.

'She's not much,' he said. 'But she'll do. Pity she's a bit on the thin side. Bit like a bagpipe. Flat at the top and sharp at the bottom. But beggars can't be choosers.'

159

I saw him off at the station.

'Sure you won't come?' he asked. 'My friend's got a friend who's a chummy little piece. I can vouch for that.'

'How chummy?'

He grinned. 'Well, I've shared the same digs with her and I know what goes on after the witching hour chimes.'

'Thanks all the same.'

I walked back into the city, very conscious that a fair proportion of my five days' leave had already gone and I hadn't much to show for it but boredom. Everyone I'd known seemed to have disappeared into the forces and the pubs seemed full of strange faces.

I called on Mrs Julius the following day to say I was sorry about Willie but I found the place locked up. From next door, I was told that she was on munitions work and was thinking of marrying again.

'A blacksmith,' I was told. 'Not likely to get into the Army. That's why she picked him, between you and me.'

I said I thought it was a very good idea and, taking my leave, got on a bus to Blackmires, which had to pass through Parkland where the Haddos lived. It was an old hankering to be around familiar places that I'd enjoyed, I knew – to see Helen perhaps, if only from a distance – though I kept telling myself all the time it was just because I wanted to have a look at the moors again and visit the Four Merry Lads.

But Blackmires was full of surly strangers from Northumberland, who'd just joined up and were already regretting it, and the Four Merry Lads was full of people who looked like war-workers out for a day trip.

'You on leave again?' the landlord said.

By the next day I was desperate. I'd looked forward so much to leave, but the bottom seemed to have fallen out of it on the station within a few minutes of arriving. It had seemed like treachery then. I'd thought that night after the *Lusitania* riot that Helen and I had drawn closer together, but it hadn't stopped her writing to Frank. Then I realised she'd probably written because he'd happened to be last on the scene, when I was languishing in detention. It was just one of those things. It had always seemed to be a toss-up between us, and it had just happened that Frank was there when I wasn't, and that must have been what had finally tipped the scales. Battles were being won and lost all over Europe simply because someone happened to be there and someone else happened not to be. Who was I to complain?

I was in pretty low spirits when I went back to the YMCA at tea-time for a wash, but my heart leapt at once when they told me there was a letter for me. I had no one in the world who was likely to write letters to me, and I immediately thought of Helen and all sorts of optimistic thoughts about her crossed my mind.

But the letter was from Locky. It was short, sharp and surprising. It was written in the journalistic hand we always employed in the office, all the words strung together and made briefer by the occasional strokes of shorthand that everyone recognised.

Where've you been, you damned fool? it said. *Come and see us. Party tonight. It's Helen's birthday, and I've got myself married. Molly Miles from the photographic library. Remember her?*

I found myself beaming at the thought of Locky married. To me, Locky was a bit like the dream friend lonely people invent for themselves. He was casual, kind and accomplished. He never made demands on me and to a certain extent had widened my knowledge. He had dry sardonic ideas about things and was a dedicated journalist who'd probably taught me my job. He seemed indifferent to other people's opinions and wandered through life with a slightly bored good-humoured manner, with his wry crooked smile and withdrawn look. He disliked the Army, I knew, but he'd accepted it as his duty, and he probably grumbled far less than some of the people who'd taken to the

161

life like ducks to water. He was that rare product, the completely unruffled, completely adaptable, completely untouchable man.

I tried to remember all I knew about Molly Miles, but all I could recall was seeing her dance the Bunny-Hug with Mason in the photographic libary, though I imagined there must be more to her than I'd ever noticed for Locky to love her.

Then I read the letter again and, thinking of Helen, began to wish they hadn't asked me – not just now – and in the same breath to wonder what I could buy her for a birthday present. As the shops were shut, there wasn't much choice and in the end I bought a tin of toffees. Then I went round to Henny Cuthbert's and he managed to get hold of a silver toast rack for Locky from a man he knew in the trade.

I tried to spruce up a bit, but only managed to feel clumsy in those damn' great ammunition boots I was wearing. For a long time I stood by the bus stop, then when the bus arrived to take me to Parkland I decided to catch the next, thinking I'd be too early. I called at the office to kill time but there was a frightening array of new faces. There was nothing left of me there now, no sign that I'd ever spent the greater part of my days there. It was as though I'd climbed out of it and it had healed over the hole I'd made. I stayed long enough to say 'hello' to the few I knew, then I fled at full speed back to the bus stop just in time to see the bus disappear.

I waited half an hour in a fret of anxiety but when the bus came, and I climbed aboard, it seemed to wait an unconscionable time before it finally left five minutes late. It seemed to crawl up the hill, pausing far too long at each stop, while I gnawed at my nails and fidgeted with impatience.

'You in a hurry?' the conductress asked curiously from her platform at the back.

'A bit,' I said.

'Well, if you can hang on a bit longer, we'll try and get you there. If you don't stop going at those fingers of yours, you'll be up to your elbows before you notice.'

The bus seemed to be full of old ladies who couldn't move very fast and who had large parcels or a lot of children to delay it at every stop. When it finally reached Parkland, I almost ran towards the Haddos'. Outside the house there was a big Morris with a brass bonnet that I recognised as Frank Mason's father's, and it had an ominous look about it to me.

As I reached the door, I heard Mason laughing and Helen's voice saying between her laughter: 'Stop it, Frank. Don't be an idiot.'

Then the door opened and Locky appeared with a glass in his hand, and pulled me inside.

'Where've you been?' he demanded.

'Nowhere,' I said. 'Just hanging around, that's all.'

'Why didn't you come and see us? Have you been at those awful digs of yours?'

'No.'

'Where've you been then?'

'I stayed at a hostel.'

'More fool you. You could have stayed here if I'd thought. It never crossed my mind. I expect you've had an awful leave, haven't you?'

'No, I haven't. I've had a good time.'

'I don't believe you. You've got a face like an early Christian martyr. Have you really had a good time?'

'Not really,' I said.

Locky grinned. 'I went in the Blueberry,' he said. 'They told me where you were. I've been looking all over the place for you. Come in and meet my wife.'

As I hung up my cap and belt, Molly Miles appeared in the hall with a tray of sandwiches and drinks, and Locky put his arm round her and pulled her forward.

'Hello, Fen,' she said shyly, and somehow she looked quite different from the girl I'd remembered dodging Mason round the files.

I thrust the toast rack at her. 'Hello, Molly,' I said. 'Congratulations.'

She seemed to have grown up suddenly and I sensed it was being married to Locky that had done the trick.

'Did it two days ago,' Locky said. 'Special licence. "Exigencies of the service."'

Then Helen appeared in the doorway. Her eyes were bright and her smile was wide.

'Fen!' she said. 'Where've you been?'

She was dressed in a simple green dress and there was a strand of hair falling over her nose that she kept blowing away. Seeing her eyes and that small sharp face again made me start kicking myself for a fool and wondering why on earth I hadn't just ignored Frank and taken a chance. But as she pecked my cheek I was aware of a subtle difference in her. She seemed to have grown up since I'd last seen her and I had a curious feeling of being an intruder as though, if I'd met her on her own, I'd have had to get to know her all over again. She was a stranger suddenly whose poise was a little disconcerting, and I decided after all that Frank could not have been lying. Somehow, she seemed to go with Frank.

'Thought I'd come to say goodbye,' I said awkwardly. I pushed the toffees into her hand. 'Happy birthday, Helen.'

Mason appeared behind her and put his hands on her waist, confidently. He looked big and handsome and sure of her. He'd got civilian shoes on, I noticed, and they had the effect of making my boots seem a yard long and a foot wide. He grinned immediately at me.

'Fancy seeing *you* here,' he said, as though the house were his and not Helen's. 'Come on in.'

The place was full of young people, some of them officers whom Locky's family knew, and there was one young man sitting in a green leather armchair whom I loathed even more than Mason for his noisy attention to Helen.

He played the fool a lot and kept putting on an act that made everyone laugh and, because I was congenitally incapable of playing the fool in front of strangers, I disliked him all the more. Scarlet, sweating and stonily shy, I talked to a few of the girls, who didn't seem to have much to say, and we toasted the bride; then all the girls and the few civilians toasted those of us who were soldiers. Finally, when the party began to break up and people seemed to be going, Helen found her way to my side.

'I'm glad you came, Fen,' she said gravely. 'I'd have hated it if you hadn't.' And my evening was made.

'I'm sorry I've been so busy,' she went on. 'But we just had to celebrate Locky's wedding. It was a little unexpected.'

'I didn't even know he'd ever noticed Molly,' I said. '*I* never saw him with her.'

'Locky's a dark horse.'

'That's what Frank says.'

She paused. 'Frank's been round here a lot this week, Fen,' she said quietly.

This is it, I thought. She's trying to break it gently. I felt feverish and absurd in those vast boots I wore that made me look like a labourer. 'Oh?' I said.

'He told me a lot about you.'

Treachery, I thought. Treachery! Just like Frank. Going behind my back.

'Frank seems to think a lot about you, Fen.'

That's it, I thought bitterly. Frank all over. Butter me up while he runs me down. It was an old dodge. 'He's a fine chap *but. . .*' Someone started the gramophone and swung the horn round and it started blasting in my ear, scratchy and crackling, '*If you were the only girl in the world . . .*'

I began to feel resentful, and envious of all the others, whose parents were still alive and who'd been brought up in the middle of a family, admired, respected and taking their due measure of affection. Their lives had been simpler and, not being engrossed in keeping their heads above water, they'd had the time to learn how to be gracious and charming and at ease.

Helen was staring curiously at me and I felt clumsy again,

still loving her but unaware of any means that was now left open to me to tell her so.

'He said the sergeant-major had a high opinion of you, too,' she pointed out.

'It's news to me,' I said.

I looked at her small pointed face and unreasonably began to hate Frank. When I'd arrived I'd been happy – nervous perhaps, because living in digs all my life I'd not been in the habit of attending parties – but content at the thought that the Haddos, people I loved very much, should think of asking me. Two hours later, after seeing Frank hanging round Helen all evening, I'd become a fugitive, wishing I could get away and leave them to it.

I'd better put her out of my life, I thought wildly. Forget her, and get back to the war. Get back to Bold with his snarling sarcasm. That was something I could understand. That was something within my reach. Women I'd never understand, I felt. Army life was simple and uncomplicated, a never-ending feud between Bold and myself. Civilian life with people like Helen around was difficult, sad and worrying.

'Locky says you're due for overseas,' she went on, and her voice seemed to drown the gramophone blaring in my ear.

'Yes,' I said. 'Any day now, I suppose.'

'Poor Locky,' she said softly. 'Poor Molly!' She sighed and toyed with the glass between her fingers.

'Will it be France, Fen, do you think?' she asked.

'What did Frank say?'

'He said it would.'

'Then I suppose it will. Frank gets to know more than me.'

She laughed. 'I don't suppose he does, if the truth's known.' She looked serious for a second then raised her eyes to mine. 'Look after Locky, Fen. He means rather a lot to us here. And we can trust you.'

I was wondering if it was part of the arrangement for Locky to look after me, when she spoke again, simply, but in a way that knocked all the stuffiness out of me.

166

'I'll pray for you,' she said simply.

Before I could think of anything to say in reply, someone shouted her name and she left my side, and the next time I saw her she was laughing with Frank.

When I got up to go, though, she was there to see me to the door. Mason had gone to start up the Morris to give me a lift into town.

'Aren't you going to kiss me goodbye?' she said quietly. 'Frank did.'

'He would,' I said.

I put my hands on her waist and touched her lips with mine, but she put her arms round me and held me close. With Frank's words at the station still roaring in my ears, I wondered wildly what was behind it, then I heard the horn of the Morris and the slam of a door, and saw Frank tramping up the drive, and before I could ask her he'd taken her hand and pulled her gently away.

'Come on, you two,' he said. 'Cheese it, troops! Hands off my girl!'

On the train going back, I felt I wanted to be alone and pretended to go to sleep, listening all the time to what the others had done with their leave. Under the threat of going overseas, several of them had got married, and even young Murray had fallen heavily for the girl next door.

Locky sat reading silently, as he always did, withdrawn yet always part of us, while Mason tried hard to make conversation with him, the sort of conversation that seemed to concern Helen or Locky's new wife, the sort of conversation that to me seemed ominously to suggest they were related already. Locky's replies were largely nods, and he didn't seem disposed to talk, and in the end Mason sighed and started teasing young Murray and pretending to give him fatherly advice on how to go about wooing the girl next door.

At Romstone, they formed us up outside the station and

marched us to headquarters on the seafront. We were surprised to see Ashton standing at the door with a list in his hand and the schoolyard full of packing-cases and stores and all the orderly-room clerks looking hot and busy for a change.

'What's up?' Mason hissed anxiously. 'What's going on?'

It didn't take us long to find out. Orders for overseas had come through, and as we split up and went to our billets everybody was shouting questions.

'When do we leave?'

'Where's it to be?'

Tom Creak announced he'd got something urgent to do, and we discovered he'd got a girl at the other end of the town, and he and the Mandys got their heads together and in the end we started a diversion to enable him to dodge the pickets the provost marshal had posted to see that we remained in our billets.

An hour later Murray arrived in our room, bursting with excitement as usual. He'd arrived by the back way, climbing over a couple of walls to dodge the military police.

'I heard the colonel talking to Ashton,' he said eagerly. 'It sounded like Souippes or Souisse or something. I couldn't quite make it out. But we've looked it up. Tim William's got an atlas. There's a place called Suippes near Rheims. It's just behind Verdun. That must be the place.'

'Looks as though we're being thrown in to support the French there,' Mason said knowledgeably. 'There's been talk of a big German attack coming off round that area in the spring. I expect they're using us to stiffen the Frogs. They've been pretty severely mauled.'

'I've got a cousin,' Spring announced, 'who's a liaison officer with the French on that front. I saw him on leave. He says they're badly in need of new blood.'

'Perhaps they're going to try to get in our attack first,' Arnold Holroyd said. 'Perhaps they're going to try and knock the old Boche off-balance before he can get started.'

Murray clapped his hands together and did a little excited jig, hardly able to contain himself.

'This is something like,' he laughed excitedly. 'We're in it at last. Suippes, here we come!'

Locky, who'd been leaning on the door of the room listening to the chatter, suddenly laughed, and we all turned round to him. He'd got that superior, knowledgeable look on his face that always quietened us down.

'What's the joke?' Murray demanded.

'You are.'

'All right,' Mason snorted angrily. 'Let's have it! What's the Great-I-Am got that we haven't got? You've got something. It's written all over your face.'

Locky grinned.

'Peace, children,' he said. 'You can stop your worrying. I know exactly what's going to happen. Instead of chasing the breezes round the town, I made a point of getting permission from the military police to see Ashton about a marriage allowance, and while I was there I asked my old friend and colleague just where we *are* going. It's not Souippes or Souisse or even Soups. It's Suez.'

7

It was Suez all right. Two days later we paraded in our little streets and schoolyards in full marching order at five o'clock in the morning and stood waiting. Farewells had been said and weeping girls left behind. All around us in the little houses people were sleeping. We'd been forbidden to leave billets the day before, but most of those with girls had managed it long enough to say goodbye.

A stiff coldish wind was blowing ragged shreds of cloud across the house-tops and gusts of chilly rain kept whipping into our faces. There was a lot of fidgeting as we bent forward to ease the weight of straps or jiggled packs higher up our shoulders with a jerk of the spine.

The previous day we'd spent parading, first at one little hall or warehouse and then at another, to draw completely new kits, waiting hours in the drizzle for the tropical uniforms which made us all look like strangers when we tried them on. Then there'd been endless kit inspections and more visits to the Quartermaster's stores. We'd been issued with field dressings and iodine for the first time and been lectured by half a dozen different individuals on the importance of secrecy and the necessity to keep away from foreign women. Sergeant-Major Bold gave us another little talk while we waited, but we were all getting rather irritated and impatient by this time, and wishing he'd shut up so we could get on with it.

None of us was particularly looking forward to Suez, but we'd reached the stage now when all we wanted to do was get moving. The indignation that they weren't sending us to France where it was becoming increasingly clear the decisive battles would be fought was slowly dying now, but Murray had it firmly as a fact that we were going on to the Dardanelles to pull a wasting campaign out of the doldrums and we consoled ourselves with that. Life seemed to be as perilously short at Gallipoli as in France, and we felt there was no dishonour attached to our destination.

'Wish we could get moving,' MacKinley said.

'I wish a lot of things,' Mason said. 'That this bloody drizzle wouldn't beat into my face for one, and that my pack wasn't so blasted heavy for another.'

For a long time we whispered together, growing more and more weary with the weight on our backs.

'Let's get a move on, for God's sake,' Henry Oakley muttered. 'Let's get there and get it over with.'

'Wish it were France,' Murray said dreamily.

Eph Lott grunted and hitched at the straps of his pack. 'Somebody's stuck the colonel's horse in this bloody thing, I think,' he murmured.

We were beginning to groan with boredom and frustration when we saw the doors open in the little schoolhouse which was our headquarters, and a beam of yellow light streamed across the dark yard.

'Company . . .' Bold's voice brought heads up. 'Company . . . a – tten – shun!'

Four hundred-odd heels slapped together. Catchpole looked out of the corner of his eye, and spoke without moving his lips.

'Appleby's blotto,' he said.

'Silence, that man,' Corker roared from behind. 'Look to your front.'

We were inspected by Ashton, with Sheridan and Welch and Bickerstaff and Milton and all the others trailing along behind him. Appleby was indeed blotto and slightly wild-eyed.

His pince-nez shining in the faint light from the open door of the schoolroom, Ashton made a speech which was again on the need for secrecy, but no one could hear properly because of the wind, and when they marched us off to the station all secrecy went immediately by the board, because the colonel had cheerfully decided that if we were going, we were bloody well going to let people know it. The band was waiting for us on the front and took its position at the head of the column, blowing and wheezing and thumping for all it was worth, and as we set off towards the town windows slapped up all along the route, as though they'd known all the time and were waiting for us, and the cheering and flag-wagging started all over again. A few girls hurriedly dressed themselves and began to run alongside. March discipline relaxed and half the town seemed to appear at their doors and windows as the brassy music rebounded from the house-fronts.

'So long, Eph! So long, Henny! Give 'em one for me!'

Several girls had broken into the ranks and were marching with us, weeping or swinging their arms to the music. It was the same as when we'd first left home, the same noise, the same cheering, the same riotous station platform, the same crowd alongside the railings, the same waving arms, the same tearful singing of 'Auld Lang Syne' and 'Goodbyeee, Don't Cryeee'.

Oakley chalked *On to Berlin* on the side of the carriage and an officious station foreman came up and demanded that he wipe it off.

'This here's government property,' he said.

'So are we,' Murray shouted delightedly. 'And so are you. We're *all* government property!'

The foreman became difficult and the complaint became a shouting match, then, as the train jerked, MacKinley jumped out and grabbed the foreman round the waist and pushed him head-first through the door.

'Let's take the goddarned bloke with us,' he shouted. 'Then he can register his complaint to Kaiser Bill himself.'

The foreman began to shriek about his wife and family as the train jerked again, and in the end we pushed him out and he fled to the opposite end of the platform. As the train slowly moved away, we all collapsed on the seats, weak with merriment.

We spent the greater part of the day in sidings watching other trains pass by, and arrived at Southampton in the evening, the train edging slowly past the backs of shabby houses where sooty chickens pecked at soil among the dying summer flowers round the entrances to their coops.

We tumbled out of carriages that had been over-heated by too many occupants, and stood in little bunches on the platform, yawning and cold, in the light of blue-painted gaslamps that came on in groups as the daylight died. Behind us the compartments were a litter of cigarette-ends and paper and bits of crust.

'Gallipoli, here we come,' Murray said gaily, his spirits undiminished.

'Who says we're going to Gallipoli?' Tom Creak asked.

'Well,' Murray said, 'where else can we go? They wouldn't waste troops like us on garrison duties in Egypt.'

'Why not?'

'What, after all our experience?'

'I always thought we were frighteningly *in*experienced,' Locky said thoughtfully.

There was a great deal of hither and thither among the officers and the military police on the platform, then the colonel went into a long angry conference with the Railway Transport Officer and they moved away, waving arms and sheaves of paper at each other.

In the end, we discovered someone had sent us a day too soon, and we were marched to another schoolroom exactly like the one we'd just left and told to bed down there on the bare floor for the night.

'Any moment now,' Locky said slowly, 'I shall give vent to a pageant of age-old martial vituperation.'

The following afternoon they marched us through the cheering crowds who lined the streets, all hope of secrecy vanishing for good as we clumped towards the docks with our solar topees strapped to our packs and singing fit to raise the roof:

'The bells of hell go tingalingaling
For you and not for me,
I hear the angels singalingaling,
With them we soon shall be.
Oh, death, where is thy stingalingaling,
Oh, grave, thy victoree? . . .'

In the docks we filed aboard the troopship *Ordenia*, which had ferried troops to the Boer War fifteen years before and had actually carried old Corker to Cape Town. She was old then and by 1915 was almost falling apart at the seams. D Company was on the lowest deck of all, well below the waterline, in a stuffy hold smelling of rotting potatoes and crammed with kit and humanity.

As the ship moved out of the harbour, we lined the decks, shivering in the raw autumn wind that blew from across the Continent, watching the spill of the searchlights on the water, and red and green lamps that seemed to be everywhere in the darkness. All the way down Southampton Water to Spithead, ships' sirens blared at us, long blasts on steam whistles and little whooping sounds from destroyers, and shrill little toots from torpedo boats.

The rumours started again at once. A ship had been sunk

that morning and the submarines were waiting just outside the boom for us. Once we heard a thumping bang against the ships side that seemed to echo through the whole structure of the vessel and Murray told us it was a depth-charge going off somewhere.

'They've got the U-boat,' he announced cheerfully.

We went down the Channel escorted by four plunging little black torpedo boats which didn't look big enough to face the waves that were rolling up past the Isle of Wight, and from the signal station above Portsmouth a light began to flicker at us, and the battalion signallers read out the message.

Good luck, it said. *Bon voyage*.

We stood at the rails and sent cheer after cheer into the night. When it was all over I remained on deck, staring back at the land, long after everyone else had gone to the canteen at the stern for a beer or cocoa. After a while Locky joined me.

'How do you feel, Mark?' he asked.

'Homesick,' I said. 'Which is funny, considering I haven't got a home.'

'Same here.' Locky hitched up his collar and stared back at the land with me. 'I suppose it's just the knowledge that we've put England behind us now. Wonder if we'll ever see it again?'

'Why shouldn't we?' I asked.

'I don't know. It's just that the partition's so final. It makes you feel there's no return.'

'We'll be back all right.'

'I hope so. But it has the effect of making you feel suddenly lonely, doesn't it?'

'A bit,' I said. 'How did Molly take it?'

'She expected it,' he said, his voice flat and unemotional. 'It's a funny thing about women. They seem to take these things far better than anybody ever expects them to or gives them credit for. She tried hard to be very matter-of-fact about it. I think her only regret was that we hadn't got a family.'

He paused, staring into the darkness. 'It's a flattering feeling,' he said, 'when you realise that, in spite of a very doubtful future, a woman wants something like that, something she can hold on to, I suppose – a sort of insurance in case anything happens to you.'

'Nothing'll happen to you, Locky,' I said.

Locky grinned 'I've never had quite the same innocent faith that Murray has,' he said. 'And martial glory never appealed to me much. I joined up because I felt it was my duty to join up, but I can't say I'm looking forward to a hero's death in battle as a prize for my patriotism. Especially now. There seems too much to live for.'

He was quiet for a long time, then he stirred.

'Ever thought you'd like to marry Helen?' he asked suddenly.

I tried to think that one out. I'd often thought I'd like to marry Helen. She had a lot to offer. More than most girls. Laughter and happiness, and something that was always exciting. It had often been a temptation to pop the question. But I never had done.

I think as much as anything else it was the awareness of the war and the possibility of the sudden death that was looking over my shoulder which had held me back. Perhaps I wasn't even ready for marriage or the time didn't seem opportune. Perhaps I felt I already had enough responsibilities and that Helen was too young to be saddled with sorrow. Whatever it was, I'd never got around to it, and now it was too late. Mason hadn't had the same caution and, being older and more mature – or more devil-may-care, call it what you will – he'd taken the plunge and I was out.

'We always seemed to start fighting,' I said lamely.

Locky laughed. 'That's nothing to worry about,' he said. 'Not at this stage.' He became serious again. 'Still, it's not my affair,' he said. 'I'm not matchmaking. Only curious. Did she ever say anything to you?'

'No.'

176

'Did you ever say anything to her?'

'No.'

He nodded and was silent for a while. 'It's a funny thing,' he said in the end. 'Intelligent people always seem to have about as much intuition as a boiled egg. She sent her love,' he concluded.

'Thanks. I expect she sent it to Frank too.'

He turned, a shadow in the darkness, as he began to move away.

'Curiously enough,' he said, 'she never even mentioned Frank.'

It was almost impossible to sleep on the *Ordenia* and virtually impossible to eat. Housey-housey was interminable, with Eph Lott and his pals raking in the money from the youngsters like Murray who firmly expected to make a fortune and never did.

Whenever we passed another ship there were vain shouts of 'What mob are you?' and efforts by the battalion signallers to read the messages which were flashed back and forth, followed by more efforts by amateur strategists to translate them into hard news. Spring got up a concert party but, as the only place they could find room to perform was in the officers' lounge, the only people to get any benefit from it were the officers and Spring and his men, who returned below with wild tales of unbridled luxury and mouth-watering accounts of what they'd drunk and eaten.

We arrived in Egypt towards the end of the year, white and ugly and uncertain of ourselves in our unaccustomed drill shorts and the bucket-like monstrosities they gave us to protect our heads from the sun. We were crammed into trains and shunted through a hot gritty wind towards Ismailia where we detrained, hot and sweaty and dirty, and already suffering from prickly heat, to suffer our final disillusionment. We'd not come to Egypt to take part in any campaign. We were there simply and solely for garrison duties on the canal.

There's little to remember of it now, beyond the flies and the bad food and the dust-storms that blew up, and once an Italian girl in a bar singing 'Ilkla Moor' to us in an accent that was enough to make them spit blood all the way from Middlesbrough to Sheffield. The authorities had clearly not lost sight of us, for we constantly trained for battles which now seemed farther away than ever. We went on forming fours, sloping arms, turning left and right, standing to attention, grounding arms, porting arms for inspection and fixing and unfixing bayonets. We dug trenches and went through the same old rigmarole about parapets and paradoses and how to advance across the desert under imaginary shell- or machine-gun-fire. We carried out exercises with non-existent field telephones and rode camels and bought carpets, and explored the bazaars in Port Said and acquired dozens of curios which, as it happened, never got sent home. We celebrated Christmas on duty with a ration of one bottle of beer apiece, one toffee and a couple of nuts, together with the usual Christmas egg for breakfast and a Christmas pudding made by the battalion cooks, chiefly out of dough and currants.

We were buoyed up in our boredom by the thought that someone might learn who we were and finally throw us into the Dardanelles, but in the early New Year of 1916 the campaign there was abandoned and all the veterans of the peninsula began to arrive in the camps around us. They were mostly tall Australians and New Zealanders with a tremendous reputation as fighting men, sun-bronzed soldiers from a dead campaign, who looked on us as amateurs, and pretty poor amateurs at that, and enjoyed chilling our blood with tales of the Turk.

'They came over in their thousands,' they said. 'Yelling like banshees, and we brought 'em down in rows, till they were in heaps three feet high and crying for mercy.'

The British troops from the peninsula were almost all Kitchener men like ourselves, but they had a weariness about them that didn't come entirely from fatigue. They'd seen their friends die around them and, no matter how hard we tried, we couldn't comprehend what *that* meant.

178

The guards continued and we marched up and down the side of that damned canal, wishing someone would steal it or, at least, that the Turks would produce some initiative and put on a show of capturing it so that we could feel our time there was worthwhile. The thing that bore down on us most was the degrading thought that we'd been relegated – even if only temporarily – to the duties of second-line troops.

'As far as I'm concerned,' Murray said bitterly, 'they can have the bloody canal and good riddance to it. I don't suppose we'd miss it, anyway.'

As we patrolled through the mud they dredged from the canal during the day, our clothes grew filthy from the dust that blew up from the noisome drying heaps, then as night fell, and the dew came down, they became coated with mud as the dust in the creases was touched by the moisture and congealed.

The Australians jeered that they'd been pulled out to win the war for us in France, and not even the greater freedom that came with being abroad took the ashes from our mouths, and we all started looking round for avenues of escape. De Burgh from A Company volunteered for the Royal Flying Corps, which was just beginning to expand and was calling for pilots and observers, and Arnold Holroyd, who had long since applied for a commission, found to his surprise that it had come through, and he disappeared to Cairo to get his uniform before leaving for a battalion stationed at Gibraltar. Several other men – Mason, Catchpole and Spring among them – promptly put in for commissions for themselves, but were told privately by Ashton that there wasn't much chance of getting them while we were in the Canal Zone where things had a habit of getting lost.

Mason was a little defensive about his application. He and Holroyd were the only ones from the group who'd been on the *Post* who'd tried, and Mason had made his application quietly, without suggesting it to anyone else, after he'd heard where Holroyd had gone. It was almost as though he were faintly ashamed of trying to leave us and he was a little noisy in his self-defence.

'Dear old lad,' Locky soothed him. 'No one here minds *who* has a go for a commission. So long as you promise not to bother us too much if you get it.'

Mason grinned, considerably relieved, and the nervous boisterousness went out of him as he realised no one disapproved. 'I don't know why you lot don't have a go,' he said. 'They told us when we joined that we were *all* potential officer material.'

Locky was thoughtful as he watched Mason clowning with Murray and Tom Creak, pretending to salute them both and force them to stand to attention before him.

'Why don't *you* put in for a commission, Fen?' he asked me.

'Bold would kick me from here to Cairo,' I said. 'He's told me more than once that with my record he couldn't even recommend me for a stripe.'

'He might change his mind.'

'If it comes to that,' I said, 'why don't you?'

'It's crossed my mind,' he said. 'It might make the journey a bit easier. I've debated which would be more use to Molly – a bigger wage or my useless life – and I came to the conclusion that she'd prefer my life. A subaltern's career seems to be short and sweet these days. And, curiously enough, I like the ranks. I like a man on either side of me. I suppose,' he concluded, and I felt curiously closer to him than at any other time, 'that, like you, I'm not the type.'

Egypt grew more boring and the flies more troublesome. Parades devised to kill time seemed incessant, and inspections followed closely one on another. As the first city battalion they'd had in the command, all the bigwigs came out to stare at us – the Governor-General, the High Commissioner for Australia, the Commander-in-Chief Middle East, the Divisional General and half a dozen others – and morale took a plunge into the abyss.

'If only there were something *happening*,' Murray wailed. 'If only there were even something to do.'

'Washing and shaving's a legitimate recreation,' Locky said. 'And you can always take off your boots. Why not go mad and get yourself tattooed?'

The Australians and New Zealanders had left for France by this time. They'd marched past the camp cheering and jeering at us through the wire.

'Look after the canal, you jokers,' they'd shouted. 'And lay off the sheilas. We've got a job to do in France, then we'll come back and finish the Turk off for you.'

Then the South Africans arrived, en route for England, big bronzed men who spoke occasionally in a strange language that only Catchpole and Corker and Bold could understand. After them came clouds of Indians, bearded men in blue turbans, and the first of the Chinese labourers who were going to France to make up working battalions. The whole of the British Empire seemed to be heading past us for the big battles which rumour told us were to take place that spring, all moving west while we remained anchored to that damned canal.

A youngster in C Company died of appendicitis in hospital at Ismailia and enjoyed the doubtful honour of being our first casualty, and a man in B got himself involved with an Egyptian girl and got her boyfriend's knife in the kidneys for his trouble.

We fretted and fumed more with every regiment and unit that disappeared. The papers were full of a tremendous battle which had started at Verdun where the French were being thrust farther and farther back. If the fortress fell, it was expected that the Germans would sweep onwards towards Paris and the war would end. It was vital that Verdun should be relieved, and latrine rumour had it that a new battle farther north was being planned by the British, to draw away the German reserves and relieve the pressure.

France had suddenly woken up again after six months of quietude. The Germans had superiority in the air, and Little

Willie, the German Crown Prince, had fourteen hundred guns almost wheel to wheel at Verdun. But the French were resisting and the battle was turning into a mincing machine which neither side seemed able to break off. Thousands of men were being poured in and the French Army was in danger of extinction.

'They've got to do something to stop it,' Murray said anxiously, staring at a newspaper outside the tent. 'They can't just go on letting it go on like this.'

With the mercurial temperament of youth, he was unable to view the possibility of defeat without panic.

'Ashton told me,' Mason said, 'that a new battle's going to be fought entirely by the British and by the New Army. Duggie Haig's in charge now and they say he's just the chap for it.'

'In South Africa they didn't think he was much cop,' Catchpole said.

'Ah, well,' Mason said knowledgeably, 'he's been C.-in-C., India, since then, and in command at Aldershot. He had charge of the fighting at Loos.'

'And a bloody fine mess that was,' Eph Lott said, unimpressed.

'Well, that wasn't *Haig's* fault,' Mason said angrily. 'It was French's. Why else was he pushed out and Haig put in his place?'

'I dunno,' Eph said. 'Why?'

'Because of that, of course.'

'Oh! Did Haig tell you that?'

Mason looked disgustedly at Eph. 'I've got ears, haven't I? I keep 'em open. I hear things.'

'Latrine rumours mostly.'

'It isn't rumour about this new battle. It's not going to be fought by the old lot who copped it at Loos. It's going to be fought by the 4th Army, because it hasn't been affected by casualties.'

'We used to belong to the 4th Army,' Murray said disconsolately, his eyes dreamy. 'When we were at Romstone.'

'Speaking personally,' Locky said, curiously quiet, 'I've had time since I came here to discover that I'd be quite happy to see the war out on the canal. Malaria and dysentery are the most dangerous things I have to contend with here, and I find them infinitely preferable to bullets.'

Murray turned on him indignantly. 'We didn't join up for that,' he said.

'No,' Locky agreed. 'We didn't. But since then I've acquired a wife, and I gather from my last letter there's a youngster on the way. It makes a difference.'

'You could always back out,' Murray said bitterly.

Locky smiled. 'It might be worth thinking about,' he said. 'Surely these damn' people in Cairo could use a good clerk or a censorship corporal with a sound knowledge of news.'

'You'd never do it.' Murray was aghast at Locky's treachery. It wasn't the thought of Locky rejecting the chance of glory that troubled him. It was fear that the comradeship that had sustained him through all the past months might be breaking up at last. Arnold Holroyd had gone already, and Mason and Spring and Catchpole had applied for commissions and would inevitably go in the end. One of the transport corporals had joined some comic outfit belonging to an archaeologist called Lawrence, who was fighting the Turks in the desert with camels and armoured cars, and Murray seemed to sense that the reassurance he drew from the sight of familiar faces about him was in danger of disintegrating.

'You'd never do it,' he repeated, almost pleadingly.

'I'm not so sure,' Locky said thoughtfully. 'Suddenly I find the overriding instinct in my make-up is the instinct to survive. I think I'll look into it before it's too late.'

But Locky was already too late.

We sent Murray up to the orderly room that tea-time to collect the mail. We knew a convoy had arrived in Port Said that morning and inevitably there'd be letters. He went off grumbling, because being the youngest he was always treated as a messenger boy by everyone else and, in spite of his complaints, he usually accepted it for the same reason. But within ten minutes he was on his way back again and we could hear him coming a hundred yards away.

He was running as fast as he could, raising the dust as he turned the corner into D Company's lines. His face was red and sweating and his eyes were bulging with excitement.

'Now what?' Locky said, watching him draw closer.

'Leave's cancelled,' Murray was yelling, and heads began to appear through tent doors and under flaps to see what was wrong. 'Nobody's allowed out of camp.'

'Well, Christ, what is there to get excited about in that?' Eph asked disgustedly, and as Murray turned to fling the answer at him he caught his foot in a guy-rope and went down, flat on his face, scattering the letters in his hand like a shower of confetti.

He was up at once, bounding to his feet as though he were on a spring.

'They've come,' he shouted. 'They've come! Orders to move! We're leaving! We've got to indent for everything we need! The orderly room's gone batchy!'

Eph threw the boot he'd been cleaning into the air. It described a neat arc and landed on the next tent. Several men started a jig, swinging round each other in a heavy-footed dance.

'Where to? Where to? Out with it, man!'

Murray seemed about to burst. 'It's France!' he screamed. 'It's France! We're in the Big Push, after all!'

Everybody began to cheer and slap each other on the back. Eph started to throw tropical equipment at Henny Cuthbert.

'Let's go and flog this lot,' he shouted. 'We shan't need it now and we can use the money to have a beano.'

Locky's face was sombre as he stood watching Murray cavorting with Catchpole and the Mandy brothers.

'Well,' he said soberly. 'It looks as though I shan't get my

184

job as lickspittle to the mighty in Cairo after all. I'd thought I might find myself a cushy billet for the rest of the war, but now it seems I shan't.'

'Sorry, Locky?' I asked.

He turned to me and grinned. 'No,' he said. 'Curiously enough, I'm not.'

Part Two

Yea, how they set themselves in battle array
I shall remember to my dying day.

BUNYAN

1

The first sight of France had a sobering effect on us all and the excitement seemed to die out of us suddenly.

This was what we'd joined up for, this was why we'd trained through eighteen or more solid months. This was why we'd learned to march and shoot and discipline ourselves. France! In spite of the Dardanelles and the sideshows in Mesopotamia and Salonika, this, we all knew – because we'd been often told so by the newspapers – this was where the war would be fought and won.

'Well, there it is, Murray,' I said, staring at the flat-fronted pink-and-blue houses of Marseilles through a thin driving rain that had flecks of snow in it. 'That's it.'

'That's what we came for.' Murray seemed to be sniffing the air like an eager terrier, his eyes bright, his fingers gripping the ship's rail in an intensity of emotion that made his knuckles white.

Mason was on the other side, staring at the shore, his eyes sombre, and his voice sounded strangely flat, as though he were trying to control emotions that were in danger of making it uneven. 'Well,' he said, 'for better or worse, like marriage, you've got it now. And, like marriage, before you're much older, my lad, you'll probably wish you'd never seen it.'

Murray was gazing at the square shuttered houses of the distant port, glimmering faintly in the rain through the sails and masts and smokestacks of all kinds of shipping – from transatlantic liners and sleek destroyers to barges and gaily painted Mediterranean fishing craft. Even he seemed to be suddenly impressed by the immensity of what he was facing.

Here was death. I could almost see the thoughts passing in procession through his mind; here, possibly, were wounds, and maiming. But here was the enemy. Here was glory.

My own thoughts were a confused mixture of excitement and dread. Here, I thought, was the unknown, and with the realisation came a mild depression that reached all the way back to childhood bogeys and dim backstreets and darkness.

With the destroyers flirting playfully around us, we were edged into the harbour and butted by tugs alongside a fungoid-spotted green wall. We tramped down the wooden gangplank with the band standing on the wet porter-coloured cobbles playing the 'Marseillaise' as we formed up into companies and set off through the town in a thin sleety snow. The place had turned out to greet us, wrapped in coats and mufflers and shawls, they cheered us wildly and called out the name of the battalion in a foreign accent that made it sound like an act from a circus.

We halted in the first square we came to, while Colonel Pine consulted his maps and got his bearings. The little white terrier which had attached itself to him when he'd first taken command of the battalion at Romstone seven months before was still with him. It had been smuggled on to the troopship and taken to Egypt, and had survived the heat and the dust and the attentions of all the pariah dogs that had haunted the camp, and had finally found its way to France with us. It was almost a mascot now. When we were on the march it rode in one of the waggons, or sat on the colonel's saddle between his knees.

As we waited, we were accosted by a horde of grubby little boys offering bottles of wine for sale, and long French loaves. They ran in and out of the ranks as we hitched up packs and adjusted straps, yelling and shrieking at the tops of their voices. Several of them were touting for their sisters, bright-eyed urchins who looked too young to know what they were offering.

'She very nice,' one of them said to me. 'Not much money.'

Some of the older women, like crows with their thin pinched faces and black dresses, were crying, the tears running unashamedly down their faces with the raindrops, and one of them touched Murray's cheek with a gentle motherly gesture and called him a *'pauvre p'tit'*.

He blushed and seemed flattered. 'What's she want?' he demanded.

'Nothing,' Locky said. 'She just says you're a nice little boy.'

Several men were writing letters as we waited and, in halting French and with a vast amount of gesturing, were asking the women to post them, giving them cigarettes in place of stamps.

'No censor 'ere,' Eph observed brightly. 'Might as well get our last bit of love and kisses in without everybody reading all about it. No flowers by request. On with the bloody motley.'

Frank Mason was busy with a dark-eyed girl who sidled up to him and was whispering urgently to him and smiling.

'I don't know what she wants,' he said, 'but here goes! Steady, the Buffs!'

And he swept her into his arms and planted a smacking kiss full on her mouth. She shrieked and struggled for a moment, then she responded willingly, and a cheer went up.

'Remember Kitchener's message to the soldier going on active service,' someone warned. '"While treating all women with perfect courtesy, you should avoid any intimacy."'

'Kitchener's a bachelor and doesn't know what he's talking about,' Spring said.

When the colonel had received his directions from an RTO sergeant with two wound stripes and a livid scar on his cheek, who appeared with a sheaf of cyclostyled instructions from an office just off the square, we set off again through the narrow streets to the squeal of fifes and the shrill cheers of the crowds, boots clattering on the cobbles and the lines of the steam-trams that ran from the port. There were lengthy halts as we were held up by traffic – motor vans with strange French names, high-wheeled heavy carts with squeaking wheels pulled by enormous horses, box-bodied cars, British army GS waggons with canvas hoods, and lorries with rectangular brass bonnets and square wooden mudguards. In spite of the icy rain, the streets still managed to have a strong summer smell of drains, and occasionally you could hear an accordion whining as someone tried to play 'Tipperary', and made it sound somehow like something saucy from a French revue.

'*Bravo, mon vieux!*' A grizzled-looking French cavalryman in a blue-grey uniform with a sabre and a long beard shook Billy Mandy's hand as he passed, clinging to his fist and walking alongside him, his face a picture of welcome. '*A Berlin! A bas les Boches!*'

'Same to you, mate,' Billy grinned. 'Nice to know Father Christmas is on our side.'

A blowzy woman in black clothes and sabots and with breath smelling strongly of liquorice and garlic ran out and planted a kiss on my face and a child offered me a bunch of primroses. Only the old men in smocks and mufflers stared unemotionally at us we passed. You could see their thoughts on their faces, and their memories of Sedan and Metz and humiliation. They'd had their turn, they seemed to say. It was ours now. A few of them spat and drew their fingers across their throats and shouted '*Allemands*' and '*Verdun*', and as we reached the station one of them who seemed to be drunk and merrier than the rest came up alongside me and marched arm-in-arm for a while.

There were no young men about anywhere and it came home

forcefully to me just how many Frenchmen there must be in the firing line. There were only these grey-beards and soldiers left it seemed – the men of 1870 and the men of 1914.

The old man at my side pointed at himself and jabbered at me in quick French I didn't understand.

'*Soixante-dix*,' he said. '*Moi. Soldat. Soixante-dix*,' and in the end I gathered he'd fought against the Germans in 1870.

'That's the stuff, Dad,' Eph Lott grinned. ''Ere we are. They can git on with the war now.'

The troop train seemed to be miles long and appeared to consist almost entirely of straw-filled grey-painted cattle trucks, stamped with the initials PLM and stencilled in white paint with *40 hommes, 8 chevaux.*

'Every mod con,' Eph grinned. 'Good beds. Five minutes from sea.'

The confusion at the sidings, even to us – and by this time we were well used to the confusion of a battalion on the move – seemed worse than ever. Elderly smocked porters seemed to be everywhere, all shouting gibberish at us, and we'd still got our escort of small boys and dogs. There were a few German prisoners standing about in the station yard, handling equipment, pale silent men in grey-green uniforms who wore red-banded pork-pie caps. On their clothes were great patches of red and black and blue. They eyed us without hostility and even managed to smile and wave.

'Germans,' Murray breathed.

'Don't get too excited,' Mason said. 'They look as meek as Moses to me.'

'Wouldn't you be?' Spring said. 'If *I'd* been taken prisoner and found myself in a cushy billet in the South of France, you wouldn't get *me* trying to escape.'

Locky, who could read French, managed to beg a newspaper from one of the porters and began to read it aloud to us. They were still holding on at Verdun, it seemed, but there was a great need, the leaders said quite plainly, for a relieving battle

193

to be fought farther north, and it was high time their British allies made a move.

'The sands are running out,' Locky grinned. 'They're beginning to consider we should stop talking and get on with the washing.'

'Well, you can tell Sir Douglas Haig he can go right ahead now,' Mason announced. 'Murray's arrived!'

It took most of the day to load the equipment, the horses and the field kitchens, the limbers and the waggons, then they marched us over from where we'd waited, smoking, bored, impatient and leg-weary, and crammed us into the trucks, drawing us up in companies and telling us off in fours, jamming us in until it seemed impossible we'd ever be able to sit down, turn round or even move.

'It's crowded in here,' Henny Cuthbert wailed.

'Pass along the car, please,' Eph Lott shouted. 'Standing room only. Have the correct fares ready!'

We sat in the open doorways on the straw, shouting catcalls, while the officers walked past us with sheaves of papers, nervous and uncertain, and Bold and the sergeants tramped up and down to check any high-spirited attempt to jump out again. When a British Press photographer in army uniform came along to take our pictures, we stuck our shaven heads out in tiers and plagued him with idiotic instructions.

'Me left's me best profile,' Eph shouted.

'Hang on a minute till I part my hair,' Catchpole grinned, running a hand over his cropped head.

Finally, in a bloody smear of sunset, when they were just beginning to switch on the arc lights around the station, a whistle blew.

'Half-time,' someone shouted immediately, and Bold came along slamming the doors. The engine gave a tremendous sneeze of smuts and sparks, and you could hear the wheels spinning on the metals, then there was a violent jolt that threw us to the floor, and we started to move.

'We're off,' Murray screamed excitedly. 'Let's give 'em a cheer, lads.'

We were all growing a little bored and cold and hungry by this time, and because it seemed to warm us up we sat in our packed truck and cheered. The yell was taken up by the next truck and the next until it passed through the whole forty-seven that made up the train, and cheering we bumped and rattled over the points and out of Marseilles.

We were four days in that damned train.

The floors of the trucks, under the straw, consisted of planks set an inch or so apart, presumably for washing out after cattle, and we had to lay our groundsheets on the floor to keep the draughts out. We could none of us lie down properly, so we sat up all that first night, through the mists of cold that put a frosty rime on the outside of the truck as the blood-red sunset turned to the blue-green glow of clear wintry darkness.

Our breath formed little clouds of vapour, and mufflers and collars became damp with condensation as we played cards with freezing fingers by candlelight and sang all the old songs all over again – 'Tipperary', 'Long, Long Trail', 'Keep the Home Fires Burning', 'If You Were the Only Girl in the World'. They were foolish and sentimental and not very clever but there was something nostalgic about them that was warming, and that was what we needed.

We crouched over the cards until the candle burned out, then we sang again because it was too cold to sleep. Finally, with flurries of snow coming in through the ventilation slats above our heads, we dropped off into an uneasy, uncomfortable doze to the rattle-clack of the wheels over the rails, heads lolling against each other, feet entangled with equipment; overcoats and boots undone, heads on knees or across the next man's thighs.

It was surely the slowest train in the world. We reached Lyons the next morning and, as the train came to a halt, someone came along the platform shouting that tea was being served. We all poured out on to the snow-sprinkled platform, rubbing our prickling eyes and stretching limbs to get the life back into them. There was ice on the puddles and the wind that blew along the line had fangs and claws in it. If there *was* tea, it was forty-seven trucks away from us and none of D Company got any.

There was a French Red Cross train opposite us and we all stood alongside, curious, sympathetic, a little awed, trying to talk to the pale-faced men inside through the windows.

'Where'd you get it, Johnny?' Spring shouted up. 'Verdun?'

'*Oui! Verdun!*' There were nods and gestures. '*Terrible, Tommee! Terrible!*'

They were unloading the wounded into horse ambulances and the Frenchmen were groaning as they were lifted out.

There seemed to be only two doctors in charge, together with a couple of dressers and a few women from the town. A gaunt-faced nurse was going round giving the injured men hot soup as they lay on the ground. Many of their wounds were rotten and covered with pus, and one or two who were ominously still were laid quietly to one side, covered with stiffened bloody blankets. In the distance a priest and a sergeant walked behind a coffin covered with a threadbare black cloth edged with white, which was carried by four soldiers.

Over the whole train hung a sickening stench of dirt and decay. The soldiers were dishevelled, bearded, long-haired and wild-eyed, and a few of them cried out as they were jolted on their stretchers into the ambulances.

Murray visibly blenched. 'Did you see that?' he asked, jerking his head away, his eyes sickened. 'Maggots in his wounds.'

One of the stretchers was dropped by accident and the man on it screamed, a shuddering scream of pain that stopped us dead in our tracks. We'd never heard a man scream in that hideous rasping agony before, and in our misery and embarrassment we didn't know where to look.

I saw Bold farther along the train jerk his head round at the sound and stare at us. Then he pointed hurriedly, and old Corker came along, his flat boozy face grim, the spiked ends of his moustaches sticking out angrily.

'Come on,' he said, pushing us back into the trucks. 'Don'tcha know it's rude to stare. Git moving. You make the place look slovenly.'

We'd none of us had the tea we'd been promised, but we weren't sorry to get away from that trainload of misery and pain.

Mason was thoughtfully scratching the inside of his thighs by the truck. 'I've picked something up,' he said slowly. 'Some bloody skin disease or something.'

Corker snorted. 'Skin disease, my Aunt Fanny,' he said. 'You're lousy!'

Mason stared. 'Lousy?' he said. 'Me?'

'Lice, me lad,' Corker said, suddenly more cheerful, as though here was something we could all understand, something earthy and far removed from pain. 'Off the straw in the truck. I've got 'em too. So has everybody else. You want to go 'unting 'em before they start breeding. Catch 'em while they're young. Before they become grannies and grandpas.'

Mason gaped for a moment, then he scrambled back inside the truck and took down his trousers.

'By God,' he said. 'He's right! It is! It's lice!'

They scooped us all back into the train and we began to jolt onwards again. North of Lyons we pulled into a wayside station surrounded by skeletal trees and caught our first sight of British Red Cross nurses. They were serving tea with rum in it, and we queued up half an hour for that tea, stamping our feet and blowing on our hands and shivering in the wind. But it was worth it, not only for the warmth it provided, but for the sight of those young, clean, feminine faces. By this time we were all unshaven and dirty and uncomfortable with scratching. One or two men lined up to shave with icy water from a single dripping tap, but for those of us at the end of the queue it didn't seem worthwhile.

We still saw no male labour below the age of sixty, and the country women here were fat and ugly, old dames dressed in white bonnets, or young women as sturdy as the oxen they drove, carrying yoked buckets of milk on their broad shoulders.

It began to grow still colder as we got farther north and that night it was again hard to sleep for the draughts that forced their way up through the floor of the truck. Every time we were at last on the point of dropping off into an uneasy doze, we seemed to stop in some ugly siding lit by spluttering arc lamps, and we all promptly sat up to see if we'd arrived at our destination. We were shunted backwards and forwards, waiting interminably at times in grassy areas where the rails had gone to rust and the bare branches of the trees brushed the sides of the trucks, while other trains sped derisively by in both directions.

'They've forgotten us,' Murray mourned. 'They've just left us here to starve.'

He sat disconsolately in a corner of the waggon, his eyes against a crack in the boards, an expression of utter misery and frustration on his face.

'*Oh, why did I join the Army, boys?*' Eph sang in his rasping bar-room voice. He was crouching in the straw, his eyes blank and bored, dealing cards with an instinctive flick of the hand.

> 'Oh, why did I join the Army, boys?
> Why did I join the Army?
> Why did I come to France to fight?
> Because I was bloody well barmy!'

Catchpole, his face half-hidden in a muffler, began to conduct an imaginary choir.

'Now, girls,' he said. 'Let's take the treble first. The alto to come in when they've finished their knitting. Loosen your stays, sisters, and let it rip. *Count your blessings, count them one by one; count your blessings, see what the Lord has done.'*

Always there seemed to be the stamp of horses outside and the flash of lights through the ventilators and the quick jabber of argument in French and English moving along the train in the dark. Inside the trucks, we crouched in rows, our eyes glued to the cracks in the woodwork. The door was sometimes opened and shut again, sometimes not, then there'd be the toot of the guard's horn and away we'd go again, with ringing clouts on the buffers that rattled the head on your shoulders and were enough to wake the dead – bonk-bonk-bonk-bonk – all the way along the train, the coupling chains clanking and the wheels rattling over the points beneath us.

We spent the night sitting half-frozen with bent backs again, lolling over each other's arms, and thighs and boots. The following morning, when they let us out to stretch our legs at a small halt in the Midi, I went wandering off round the outbuildings and found two or three blackened fire buckets which the track workers obviously used, standing upside down on a stack of coal.

I took a quick look round and picked one up. Everybody seemed to be queueing up for bully-beef and biscuits and I marched back to the truck with it as bold as brass, deciding that was the way to look the least conspicuous.

As I came from behind the building, though, Bold appeared in front of me, as tall as a house, his feet apart, his hands on his hips, his bone-hard face thrust down at me.

'Where are you going with that?' he demanded.

There wasn't much point in trying to lie to Bold. He could pick out a liar as though he'd got an alarm bell on him.

'I'm taking it back to the truck, Sergeant-Major,' I said. 'To keep us warm.'

His eyes glittered and his teeth were bared in a grimace of a smile. Even his little gingery moustache seemed hostile.

'You pinched it?' he demanded.

'Yes, Sar'-Major.'

His face softened, and there was a sly sideways look in his eyes.

'Stoves, coal, troops for the use of,' he said softly. 'You're a bloody miracle, Fenner! Are there any more?'

My breath came out in a rush of relief. 'Yes, Sergeant-Major,' I said. 'At least two. *And* some coal. But you'll have to look slippy.'

Bold's hard white face cracked into a wide grin. 'I always did say I'd make a soldier outta you, Fenner,' he said. 'Right,' he snapped. 'Git going. I ain't seen yer. I'll now go and arrange to acquire one for meself.'

We got the stove going and rattled along merrily with the half-open door providing enough draught to keep the coals hot. During the night, though, I woke abruptly, feeling as if I were choking, to find that Henny Cuthbert who was sleeping nearest the door had shut it to keep out the draught, so that we were all slowly suffocating in the smoky fumes of carbon monoxide. We were already as black as nigger minstrels with the smuts, and I shoved the door open and went round the pile of lolling figures, waking them all up to make sure they were alive.

We passed through Paris in darkness and halted just outside the city to the north, listening to the whistle of engines and the clatter of trams on a road nearby. But we were forbidden to leave the truck, except for half a dozen men who were sent to the head of the train where we could see the glimmer of flames. The cooks had got a fire going against a wall, and they returned carrying black dixies of tea and a greasy-looking swill of bully-beef which restored life a little.

Then we went on again, jerking and jolting in a grey morning light past linked pools of water flung like a broken string of beads along low-lying rivers and criss-crossed dykes that were full of reeds and willows and pollards.

'Looks like the Somme,' Locky said, his head out of the door. 'I spent a walking holiday here once.'

We halted alongside a low field curving round the shoulder of a hill where an old woman was working. She wore a black skirt, and a red petticoat kilted up to her knees. Her skinny legs were covered in thick grey stockings that ended in clumsy ploughman's boots.

'Look,' Mason shouted. 'Girls!'

There was an immediate rush for the door and a disappointed howl, and laughter.

We shouted. '*Vive la France!*' and the old woman looked round, her nut-brown wrinkled face startled. She stared for a moment, unmoving, then sank down on her knees and began to pray. The simplicity of the action stopped the shouting and we became silent again until the train moved on.

Eventually, we passed row on row of poplars and a wild-looking grass-covered canal bank.

'This is Somme country, sure enough,' Locky said.

As it happened it was only a lower tributary and we didn't stop there. We rattled on again, passing a trainload of Welshmen drawn up in a grassy siding, who were singing hymns in perfect time and tune, their high strong voices echoing out of their trucks as though they were chanting Handel's *Messiah* back in their chapels at Cardiff or Pontypridd. They didn't return our cheers but continued, absorbed, rapt in their harmonies.

'Them bastards sound a lot 'appier than I feel,' Eph said. 'I'm proper fed up, and far from 'ome.'

The cards had disappeared. We were all sick of cards by this time and merely lolled against each other, bored, weary, dirty, wanting only to be able to see farther than the four walls of that damned truck.

'Locky,' Eph said thoughtfully, 'do you think they're ever going to let us out of 'ere, or do you think they're just going to go on 'auling us up and down France till we die of old age?'

He raised himself on one elbow from where he was lying.

He'd managed, being Eph, to stretch himself full-length, pushing Henny Cuthbert and young Murray out of his way, and his fat little body looked a lot more comfortable than most of us.

Locky looked up. Inevitably he was reading, his book held sideways to a crack in the planks that formed the side of the truck, trying to get a little light on the pages.

'Have no fear, Eph,' he said with a grin. 'Now they've got you here they won't let you go again in a hurry. You made a mistake, old boy. "Much wiser is he who, rather than go to war, stays at home, caressing the breast of his mistress."'

''Oo said that?' Eph asked, impressed by Locky's knowledge as he always was.

'Horace,' Locky told him.

''Orace 'oo?'

Locky grinned and turned back to his book and Eph scratched his head. 'I don't know 'ow you do it,' he commented. 'Straight I don't. I've played cards till I've wore me fingers down to the knuckle-joints. I've played crown and anchor, and pitch and toss, and sung songs till I'm pie-eyed. And all you've done is read that bloody book. Don't you ever git mad?'

Locky chuckled. 'I have no evil feelings on earth,' he said. 'Except about army biscuits.'

'You're lucky, that's all I can say. We've sat in 'ere three days now – or is it four? – soppy as a lot of prozzies at a christening. The niff alone's enough to put half-inch hairs on you. Every time we stop they shove us back in afore we get properly out, and a little bloke with a 'unting 'orn goes tearing round like a load of mad dogs. I feel like ten men – nine dead and one dying. Gawd stiffen the bloody rooks, it's enough to send a bloke off his onion.'

Locky moved and the watery sunlight that streamed through the ventilator slats of the truck striped him with pale gold. 'Eph,' he said. 'For a man whose oratory is normally restricted to words of one syllable, you express your disgust at the war in general, and the French railways in particular, with a considerable amount of verve.'

Eph settled back with a sigh, shuffling his plump body about until Henny had backed away a little farther and Murray was jammed hard up against Mason.

'Tell my valet to run me bath,' he said. 'I'm sick of this "bring your own grub and fleas" atmosphere. Tell him to lay on the champagne, and invite the colonel. He must be getting bored with them uncomfortable first class carriages.'

We passed through deep cuttings and at last began to see farmhouses and cottages with smashed windows or collapsed roofs, and once a broken bridge. Trees seemed to have been cut down everywhere.

'Gentlemen,' Catchpole announced, his eye to the ventilator slats, 'I suspect we are at last approaching the war.'

The lice we'd picked up seemed to have bred a thousandfold already, and we were weary with crouching on the floor of the truck. Then we began to notice the countryside was filling with horses and waggons, and men in khaki and the grey-blue of the French.

Finally, we reached an old unbattered city where the tall spire of a cathedral rose high over uneven roofs into a clear sunny sky and the train clanked to a stop with an escape of steam like a tired thankful sigh.

'Amiens,' Locky announced. 'That's the cathedral. Murray, your cup of happiness should be full to overflowing. You're safely in the Big Push.'

'Three cheers for that,' Murray said fervently. 'Perhaps we can get out of the damn' truck now.'

But orders came that we'd to sleep the night in the train because there was nowhere else for us to go.

''Aven't they even got an old cemetery or a muck-'eap they don't want,' Eph wailed. 'I'm getting proper vexed in 'ere.'

Inevitably, they woke us before dawn, just as we'd finally

203

dropped off, and turned us out, stiff with cold, and swearing and grumbling about the authorities, hitching at packs and rifles and buttoning up coats.

There was a feeling of urgency about Amiens, though, that soon brought us to life. Wrinkled Picardy farmers and well-fed businessmen mixed across the crowded pavements with trim-legged girls and buxom country women with baskets. Here and there you could see the red, white and black crest of Picardy or a speck of horizon-blue or the scarlet-and-gold kepi of a French general. There appeared to be hundreds of staff officers about, with their red hat-bands and collar gorgets, old ones, young ones, all well-fed, all of them immaculate, and most of them on well-groomed sleek horses and accompanied by smart-looking cavalrymen with polished bandoliers and buttons, or sitting back in brown, high-built, spoke-wheeled staff cars.

As they produced breakfast for us from cookers parked under the shadow of the cathedral, and we tried to wash and shave at a communal pump, we began to absorb some of the atmosphere of the growing offensive that reached out to us from the sandbagged buildings and the men sleeping in hundreds along the streets under the trees, from the horses and lorries and waggons and guns, in quantities we'd never seen before. This was the beginning of the war for us. You could smell it in the air, see it in the teeming movement in the streets, hear it in the hubbub of hooves and feet and rolling wheels over the pavé. It was all around us, stretching out to sweep us away, swamping the normality of the city's life, quickening the senses, heightening the atmosphere of urgency and haste.

Many of the soldiers moving about the streets seemed most unwarlike, however, and I saw looks of surprise about me as half a dozen shifty-eyed men, who had a little of the look of Eph Lott about them, sidled among us offering German helmets for sale, black metal spiked affairs with gilded eagles on the front.

'Only ten bob, matey,' they announced. 'They're eleven and six in Albert.'

'Are they real?' Murray's eyes almost popped out of his head.

'Real? 'Course they're real. Captured 'em meself up near the Ancre. You can see the German words inside 'em if you look.'

As they drifted past us, one of the cooks wiped his hands on his trousers and shook his head.

'Watch out for that lot,' he advised.

It seemed there was a medical board in the city, housed somewhere behind the cathedral, that attracted all the malingerers and cast-offs who'd been called up on reserve and were too old to fight and too young to discharge.

The cook clearly had no love for any of them and he slammed his pans about as though he could measure his disgust only in the amount of noise he could make.

'Them bastards spoil it for the genuine articles,' he said, letting his cigarette ash fall into the stew he was preparing. 'There are plenty of blokes round 'ere who've been smuggled back out of the line because they'd do a bunk if they 'ad to go in again. Out since 1914, some of 'em. They've 'ad more than they can take. Don't worry, there's plenty of good blokes fretting to get back to their pals, and clerks working twenty hours a day who ain't letting the side down, but that bloody lot gets us all a bad name with the staff.'

It came as a bit of a shock to realise just how much wreckage war left in its wake, not merely smashed guns and torn ground, but broken men, and dodgers on the lookout for a quick penny, enjoying their triumph over a medical board and determined, since they couldn't get a discharge, to make as much as they could while the going was good. We'd met them at home, but out here I'd expected it to be different. They seemed to reduce the war to a sordid little scuffle round a market place, and, more than ever, I felt we were amateurs at the game in this atmosphere of sharp practice and experience.

Still stiff with travelling, we fell in in companies outside the station, among the waggons that seemed to line the vast square, and, as we waited, a tremendous cavalcade of cavalry went past, magnificent phalanxes of men, flat-capped British with sabres and carbines and black-bearded blue-turbaned Indians with fluttering lance-pennants, jostling each other on well-fed, well-groomed mounts whose steel-shod hooves struck sparks from the cobbles.

'Well, we ain't much money but we do see life, don't we?' Eph said, caught up by the sense of power behind those clattering squadrons. 'I could make a fortune with a few of them nags at Derby 'orse fair.'

'Let's give 'em a cheer,' Murray suggested, and old Corker turned on him at once, his flat boozy face contemptuous, his yellow eyes cold.

'Don't you ever git sick of cheering people?' he demanded. 'It's a wonder you don't get 'oarse, the way you go on. Besides,' he snorted as he moved along the lines, shoving men into place, 'yer cheering the wrong lot, lad. Cavalry never did do much but clutter the roads up and pull down all the telephone wires so the infantry 'ad to shove 'em up again. All they do is cover retreating infantry on horseback and hunt foxes and 'ares and shoot pigeons.'

He turned and stared after the last files of the cavalry, and his brows came down.

'They'll let you down when the time comes, you see,' he growled. 'Their 'osses'll not be groomed or fed, or they won't 'ave sharpened their swords or summat. When the fighting starts, it'll be the old mud-crusher on his two flat feet that'll finish it. You see.'

Murray became indignant and disbelieving at once. He seemed to spend half his life being indignant and disbelieving.

'If they're so damned useless,' he demanded, 'why do we have to have so many of 'em,'

'Because French's a cavalryman,' Corker said. 'And so is Haig and Gough and Allenby and all the others at the top. We won the war in South Africa with mounted troops. Right, we'll win the war in France with mounted troops. Now shut up and git in line.'

We set off north to the tap of drums and the high shriek of fifes and the oompah-oompah of 'Yorkshire Johnny' from the band in front. Within an hour, on the long road that led to Albert and Bapaume, the sun had vanished. It clouded over rapidly and the rain that started pecking at the puddles changed to sleet and snow, and we discovered that our boots, burned dry by the Egyptian sands, were completely useless. They'd lost their elasticity and leaked badly at the seams.

We stopped for a meal of uncooked bully-beef and biscuits in a village several miles outside Amiens, sitting on the pavement with our backs to the one-storey, red-brick houses that lined the only street.

'Nice place for a holiday,' Spring said flatly, staring round him at the shabby, tasteless buildings and the blank-faced women and children who stood in the doorways staring at us.

'A proper whirl of gaiety 'ere at night, I bet!' Eph said. ''Urry up, boys, they've lit the lights at the butchers'.'

An old man came along offering us pamphlets. He looked about sixty but he told us he was ninety.

'I bet he doesn't live on bully-beef,' Henry Oakley commented.

'*Comment vivre cent ans,*' the old man kept saying, shaking the pamphlets in our faces. '*Comment vivre cent ans.* How to live to be a hundred.'

'In view of the coming joust with the Germans,' Locky said dryly, 'I think his estimate's a little generous.'

All that day we marched, halting from time to time to let convoys of guns and horses pass us, standing stiff-kneed by the side of the road as they jingled past.

There seemed to be every kind and size of man – men from Bermuda, Newfoundland, New Zealand, Australia, South Africa, Canada, I saw – some of them mere boys, some of them proudly displaying the medal ribbons of long-dead campaigns.

There were miners from Wales and the Midlands, factory hands from the industrial centres, clerks and shop boys, ploughmen and shepherds, blond Saxons from the old south-east and swarthy Celts from the west and the north, college graduates and dock labourers, men who'd come from the distant places of the earth where death was a normal event, and men like me whose chief adventure in life had been a Sunday-afternoon bicycle ride. I saw men who ought to have been digging their allotments, their eyes alight with eagerness, and one I spoke to was a man of sixty who'd come all the way from South America and knocked twenty years off his age because his only son had been killed at Mons, and he was determined to avenge him.

Everywhere you looked the earth was brown with humanity. Every field seemed to be full of men and horses, and the arrow-straight road was jammed with waggons and guns and vehicles. Convoy after convoy came past, rumbling carts with whining axles and square-nosed, brass-bonneted Crossley ASC lorries, nose-to-tail, men nodding at the wheels as they drove. Thousands of pack mules with tossing heads and wild eyes, trudging southwards and westwards from the front, their legs and bellies caked with the chalky mud of the trenches, and remounts moving up in twos, tramped the brick-and-rubble-filled shell-holes flat; and near every village and farm you could see carpenters at work, both civilian and military, smocked and uniformed alongside each other, hammering two- and three-tiered bunks together outside barns and sheds.

'There'll be no mistake this time,' Murray said, his eyes alight with enthusiasm. 'It'll be a walkover. It's a dead cert.'

He was staring round him at the batteries upon batteries of guns, light and heavy, that were ranked ready in the fields, with thousands of men behind them stacking great piles of shining shells into dumps. Beyond them, the hills rose green and brown and studded with little clumps of woodland. After the dusty dryness of Egypt it was good to see the rich earth and the first spring foliage. The houses had not been touched by the war, and they looked prosperous and peaceful and full of hope.

'You know,' Locky said thoughtfully, 'thinking about it, seeing it, feeling it, scenting it, knowing what's going on, I don't think I'd have missed this for all the tea in China. I'm enjoying the swank of it.'

I nodded, caught by the same emotions. This time, I was telling myself, this time we were going to smash through Kaiser Bill's fortifications and bring the war to an end for good and all. There were enough of us – that was obvious – and we were clearly backed up by enough guns and shells and reserves for it not to go wrong again. This time it was going to be different.

For nearly two years now, the Allies had faced the Germans across a soggy strip of No Man's Land that ran all the way down from the North Sea to the Vosges, a narrow ribbon of stale, stagnant, churned-up land criss-crossed by rusty barbed wire and littered with all the ugly rubbish of war. For nearly two years they'd fought across that narrow stretch of blood-stained ground and, with the exception of the biting off of a salient or the thrusting out of other salients, the line hadn't changed much since October 1914.

Now, though, here on the Somme, there was a new spirit abroad. You could sense it in the air. You could see it in all these eager faces. Kitchener's new armies were arriving in their tens of thousands, untouched by the cynicism of the older soldiers. The munitions shortage had been overcome by Lloyd George, the little Welshman from Criccieth who'd turned the Government upside down after Loos and damn' near toppled Kitchener from his pedestal at the War Office. This was untainted country, hardly fought over before, dry, well-drained land unlike the soggy ditch-lined fields of Flanders to the north, land where cavalry could move, good open country perfectly fitted for the break through that would take us to Berlin.

This time, that sausage machine of the old soldiers, fed with men and churning out corpses, was not to remain screwed in place. *We* were going to shift it.

I don't think there was a man among us who wasn't convinced of that. There'd be casualties, we knew, but inevitably it would be the other chap, the man in front of you, or the man behind you, the man waving a brown arm at a blank-faced woman working with a long hoe in the fields, who regarded him with the same hatred she would have regarded the Germans. It might be your friend, your enemy, your sergeant, your officer, but never you yourself.

This time we couldn't fail. We daren't fail. If we did, it would take years of work to retrieve the failure. This was to be the first shaft of sunlight after two years of darkness, the end of the sorrow, the boredom, the pain and the frustration that had been endured so long, and I felt a surge of fierce joy in the fact that they'd entrusted the task to *us*. Here was history, I knew, and I felt privileged to be taking part in it.

We reached Albert in the afternoon, tramping under the tunnel of the railway arch that led into the town. We were marching in silence now, the band saving their breath for walking, the fifes and drums packed away in the waggons.

At Albert we saw the first sign of the desolation of war and felt the chill of hollow echoing buildings with broken windows like empty eye-sockets and smashed doorways like wailing mouths. It was a deserted, shattered, red-brick town where broken chimney stacks reached for the sky alongside the ruined tower of the Basilica. Here and there a gaunt half-savage cat living among the ruins fled across our path, disappearing into the broken shells and cascaded rubble that had once been shops, their signs *Au bon marché* and *Cuirs et clogs* and *Déboutant de Boissons* lopsided over the empty doors.

'Jules Verne used to live here,' Tim Williams told us.

'Why?' The word came back in a chorus of disgust.

A hundred feet above our heads, on top of the Basilica, the Madonna held out her Babe over the triangular square, almost as though she were going to toss Him among us. The tower had been hit by a shell in the early days of the war and the statue seemed to be perpetually on the point of falling. When it did, they told us, the war would end.

"Ow about scrimming up there and giving 'er a shove?' Eph suggested.

You could see heavy batteries hidden among the trees and behind the ruined houses. In one street there was an empty factory, mere brickwork tumbled about twisted girders of rusty iron, with broken sewing machines lying in the rubble and on the pavement, and in another a large barrack-like building that seemed to have been a girls' school, as empty and deserted as the rest of the town. We followed a street that curved in a gentle arc to where houses were levelled to the ground in pathetic heaps of brick and splintered wood, straggling weeds growing over the debris, so that all the time the mass of the Basilica with its peeling patches of gilt seemed to be there on our left, its pretentious modernity lost in the dignity of its ruins. Under the dramatic silhouette of that leaning statue, we marched out of the town in silence.

We took the northern road that led into the Rue de Bapaume. Just north of the square it was joined by another road that came up from the south, and we had to halt to let another battalion pass.

Mouth organs were whining and they were singing the maudlin songs that had already carried the Army round France for two years. You could see them grinning as they passed, old faces, young faces, all the same, all brown and healthy, all excited at the prospect of ending the war here on the Somme.

Four after four they came, the shuffle and crunch of their boots muffled by their strong rough voices, every one of them, rich and poor, stupid and intelligent, all reduced to the common level of khaki, all carrying their rifles in exactly the same manner, all bowed and sweating under the weight of their equipment; their khaki stained where the straps rubbed and the entrenching tools chafed, but all singing, all cheerful, in spite of their loads and the crowded roads.

They were chivvied along by worried civilian officers on horses or boyish-looking subalterns who didn't seem to know what was happening as they tramped along in their new water-proof trench coats, all of them bursting into cheers whenever they had the breath. It was like looking into a mirror and seeing a reflection of ourselves.

When the last man had gone on ahead of us, we set off again, crunching between lines of squalid ruins, left-handed over a railway and away from the town, past a battery which had halted on the road there and was just getting under way again, grunting and groaning with that peculiar sound of guns on the move.

We swung downhill through Querrieu, a small place by a river, which was full of cars and horses and military police and despatch riders, and cavalrymen in smart brushed uniforms and polished bandoliers. It was here, we gathered, that General Rawlinson, who had come out to take command of this vast new 4th Army, had set up his headquarters. Leaving Querrieu behind us, we turned right-handed, then left-handed, up the hill and past the dark mass of Aveluy Woods.

The moon appeared briefly, red and horned and chilly, and still we marched, tramping over the muddy surface of a road that was well padded with manure from thousands of mules and cavalry chargers and transport animals. I was tired now, and hungry, and beginning to realise that wet and chill and damp could be wearying too.

Villages slid behind us, nothing more than blank walls with chinks of light, seemingly indifferent in their emptiness to our weariness. Occasionally, when an officer or a military policeman swung a torch, or we passed a hurricane lantern hanging from a parked limber, you could see your own hunchbacked lurching shadow with other hunchbacked lurching shadows against the walls, gross enlarged stumbling shapes of men with slung rifles, and the flickering lines of moving legs.

It was impossible to see anything now, though it was quite obvious we weren't alone. There were small shaded lights everywhere and occasionally I caught a glimpse of guns or horses or waggons, and once or twice I heard the grind of lorries in the distance.

Occasionally, behind us and on our left, I saw a faint flickering of light in the sky, and in the rare moments of silence when we halted I could hear a dim thudding rumbling, a new vibration to the ears, a sound of infinite subtlety and yet of immense suggestion, almost like wheels passing over a distant board bridge. I saw heads go up as it travelled down the column like a sentence of death, and a thousand men seemed to sniff the air. It was still far away, but irresistibly there – the war.

'The guns,' Murray whispered.

'Murray, old fruit,' Mason observed wearily, 'you've got a gift for stating the obvious.'

'Cut it out there, you lot,' Corker snapped. 'You bloody newspapermen talk more than all the rest of the battalion put together. Now shut up and save your breath.'

We halted briefly on a long straight road through a double row of poplars, and here and there I could just glimpse broken walls and the glint of watery craters.

'Shell-holes,' Murray pointed out breathlessly.

'Oh, Christ,' Mason said.

I knew that there were many men around me. I could hear the poppling clatter of motorcycle engines and the rumble of wheels, and the jingle of bits as horses tossed their heads. On my right there was an aid post, and in the light from the doorway I saw a couple of stretcher-bearers pushing a wheeled stretcher. In the distance, thrown into silhouette by the flickering lights to the north, there was the skeleton roof of a farm against the sky. The whole area seemed to be one vast mass of confused activity. Then a whistle shrilled and there was a chorus of half-heard orders and the column concertinaed into uncertain movement, men shuffling against each other in the dark

'Come on, keep going,' Corker's voice kept nagging. 'This mob don't straggle. It's only a nice easy trip – especially for a staff wallah in a car.'

We marched on interminably. It was maddening, that marching through the darkness hour after hour with nothing to see but the black shape of the man in front, jerking up and down; sloshing through puddles you couldn't see; stumbling under the drag of packs and weapons; ticking off the miles. I shifted my rifle from side to side, carrying it slung or sloped, then slung again, using my hands to ease the shoulder straps of my equipment and take the ache from my collar-bones. I was staggering with weariness and hunger by this time, and movement became mechanical as I walked.

'They say you mustn't – take your boots off – after a march,' Murray panted. 'Or your socks. Not till you've – cooled down and the swelling's – gone from your legs. Bathing hot swollen feet – makes 'em tender.'

'For Christ's sake, shut up,' Mason snarled. 'It makes me feel poorly just to listen to you with your strings of good advice.'

It wasn't long before Murray became silent through sheer exhaustion and I took his rifle, and later Henny Cuthbert's too, while they plodded alongside me, arms swinging, mouths open, heads hanging. I remember seeing Bold by the light of a lamp that came from an open doorway, carrying a whole sheaf of rifles and pouring some of his own rum that he'd saved for just such an event into a man who'd staggered from the ranks and flopped exhausted by the roadside.

My feet were burning and, in spite of the spots of rain in the air, my body was running with sweat. We'd every one of us got a fifty-six-pound pack, ammunition, a water-bottle, a haversack, an entrenching tool, a rolled greatcoat and all the other things we had to carry.

The three rifles I was humping felt like a ton weight but I kept telling myself I couldn't pass them on to someone else. Hang on to them, I kept saying, every time I felt like throwing them away. Not far now. Surely not far now. The grit in my eye-corners was turning to mud with the sweat that stood out on my face. Only one thing to do, I thought. Clench your teeth and keep going. So I shut my jaw tightly and pretended there was nothing to worry about. Push aside the waves of pain that come up from your feet. Forget the ache in your shoulders. Hang on. Keep going.

God, I said, muttering aloud to myself as I put one foot down in front of the other with a numb feeling of automation, I thought we were *good* at marching.

While I was still occupied with the thought and the resentment it brought with it, Eph, who was in front of me, halted suddenly, and I crashed half-asleep into his back, cutting my lip on a buckle on his pack. Then I staggered forward again as Mason crashed into me from behind. As the whole column closed up like a broken bellows, dumb, panting, sweating, I saw a couple of lordly staff cars with Union Jacks on the bonnets go roaring past, officers dozing in the back.

Daylight was approaching. I was aware of halting in a lane. There was the ruined wall of a farmhouse and some battered-looking hedges. With the cessation of movement, Murray had simply sunk to the ground alongside me without a word.

Corker appeared, limping, his face drawn and grey with fatigue in the early light.

'Into the field there,' he said, pointing. 'We've arrived. You can git yer feet under the table now. Git moving. Sharp now.'

I stumbled through a broken gate. In front of me were rows of sagging brown tents and a broken barn. We shambled together again and stood once more in four untidy lines. Then

215

a whistle blew, and I saw the lines sliding sideways like a collapsing pack of cards.

I lay on my face. Locky, next to me, was on his back, and beyond him men were asleep just where they sprawled. Blissfully, I let myself float towards unconsciousness, then, suddenly, I remembered that young Murray was still outside in the lane. Oh, forget him, I told myself. He'll be all right. Then I thought he'd probably get run over by a lorry or a cart, and it nagged at me and wouldn't let me sleep.

In the end I forced myself to my feet and went back for him. It was almost more than I could manage because my knees had stiffened suddenly.

I staggered through the gate again, half-falling as my clumsy feet stumbled over the uneven ruts. I got Murray to his feet somehow but he slipped out of my arms as though he were dead and flopped to the ground again. I tried once more, falling over him, swearing at him all the time, cursing him with every foul word I could lay my tongue to, my hands as awkward as if they didn't belong to me, my eyes blurred, my body curiously unbalanced and difficult to manage. I got him over my shoulder at last and weaved, panting and blinded with sweat and still swearing in a low vicious mutter, back the way I'd come. I bumped into the gate which, curiously, didn't seem to be where I'd thought it was, and half-fell into the hedge, scratching my hands and face on the thorns before I recovered my balance.

I saw Locky lying flat out, with Barraclough and Henny Cuthbert and Spring and Mason, and stepped among them, trying to avoid falling over them. Then Bold appeared and saw me with Murray, who was snoring slightly now. He emerged through a blur and I tried to smile at him. But my face seemed stiff and wouldn't work properly.

He helped me lower Murray to the ground. 'If anybody's still on his feet,' he said grimly, 'you can bloody well bet it'll be Fenner.'

216

He gave me a push, and I staggered back, grabbing at the air for support, startled, trying to keep my balance, wondering what the hell he was up to.

'Here, steady on,' I said.

'Fall over, you stubborn bastard,' Bold said in a short vicious bark. 'Don't you know you're done?'

I gave him a weak grin and my knees seemed to buckle under me, and I sat down, still grinning foolishly, and fell over backwards, fast asleep.

2

The thin rain that woke me the following morning was carried on a light blustering wind that whipped the tree-tops and stirred the wheat on the shoulders of the hills.

I opened my eyes to find myself staring at a grey sky with hurrying clouds, and wondered where I was. As I sat up, I saw a sparse hedge and, just beyond, a barn with open doors, lofty as a church, its walls pierced with narrow slits for light and air, its beams and rafters unwrought. Then I heard the voice of Ashton and, twisting round, saw him standing by the gate with young Welch, comparing lists and maps, the light glinting on his spectacles.

The cooks had established some sort of cookhouse in a dip in a corner of the field, and the kitchens were already belching out smoke behind a sack-and-canvas lean-to. There was a smell of bacon in the air that wrinkled the nostrils and brought saliva to the mouth. Somewhere, almost beyond the reach of the eardrums, I could hear the faint thud of guns.

The sergeants were getting their own food from the cookers and I clambered stiffly to my feet and joined them. One by one, a few other men joined me – Henny Cuthbert, stumbling, and pale and drawn with exhaustion, and Catchpole and Spring and Locky and Henry Oakley, then young Murray, surprisingly bright and unwearied by the march – and they tagged on behind, hobbling up with their mess tins towards the queue that was already forming, licking their lips at the smell of food.

We ate like famished wolves under the thin shelter of the hedge, savouring the taste of the burnt bacon and the bread, and the hot sweet tea surfaced with globules of grease. As we mopped up the last smears of fat with bread, Corker and Bold came along, staring at us, chaffing us, on the lookout for the youngsters who hadn't the stamina of the older men. Bold seemed hard and taut and untouched but old Corker's moustache drooped a little. He was limping too, but his eyes were as bright and merry as usual.

'You all right, Cuthbert?' Bold demanded in his high voice, peering down at us, his eyes narrow and shrewd and concerned.

'Yes, Sar'-Major.' Henny put his mess tin down and started to get to his feet, his thin face gaunt with weariness.

'Stay where you are,' Bold snapped, putting a hand on his shoulder. 'Give yourself a chance, man, do. A soldier should always relax when he can, to make up for all the times when he can't. We ain't on parade 'ere.'

When we'd finished we cleaned our knives and forks on the grass and hoisted ourselves to our feet and rinsed out our divies. One or two men found buckets made of biscuit tins and scrounged hot water from the cooks. We started to shave and wash, sharing the water until it became grey and curdled, sluicing off all the dust and grime of a four-day journey. Someone managed to laugh and I heard a few catcalls. We were beginning to recover.

'There's women 'ere,' Eph announced unexpectedly, putting his head round the angle of the hedge where the platoon had established themselves, a sly salacious look on his face, his voice full of suggestion. 'Real mademoiselles with eyes and arms and legs and everything.'

He went into a wealth of obscene detail that set several men climbing to their feet, feigning indifference but with their eyes already alert and on the lookout, then sent them sagging back with his next words.

'All right, all right,' he grinned. 'You needn't rush. They're as big as the Rock of Ages and look twice as 'ard, and the officers'-mess servants are round there already, proper sprat-eyed, like moggies after a sparrow.'

Bold, who'd found himself an office consisting of a box under a broken haycart, appeared in front of us again. We were sprawling among the scattered equipment, the dumped mess tins and the stacked rifles, rubbing stiff knees and hunting lice, and I thought he'd come to get us on our feet to clear up.

'Cuthbert here?' he asked.

'Yes, Sergeant-Major.' Henny sat up, his face lengthening.

'Gas guard. Come on, let's have you.'

Henny's long face fell, but Bold jerked his thumb at an eighteen-pounder shell-case that he'd tied to a tree.

'Don't look so cheerful,' he said. 'It's a nice easy fatigue. Keep you out o' mischief in case anybody comes up asking for volunteers for 'umping kit.'

'I can hump kit, Sar'-Major,' Henny said earnestly, his thin body stooping with weariness. 'Honest I can.'

'That's what you think. I know better. That's why I'm a sergeant-major and you're not.'

We began to move about slowly, like drugged bees, limping still, cherishing our blisters and our chafed aching bodies. I found we'd arrived at a place called Colinqueau Farm on the edge of the village of Rippy, which was situated just north of Bertrancourt, which itself was north of Albert and well behind the line and facing a point somewhere between Gommecourt and Serre.

It was well-wooded country with sheltered fields full of long spring grass and thorn bushes, and hollows warm with the damp smell of earth. The village was a one-street place of crumbling single-storey buildings, with tumbledown barns housing ancient treadmill threshers, and farms which seemed to have been constructed chiefly in squares like keeps, the middens and the stables and the pigsties their most important points. Dry wiry grass and white flowers like daisies grew along the tops of old walls, some of them twelve or fifteen feet high, as though they'd been erected to keep out prying eyes.

The place had grown up haphazardly round a well, which stood by the village green, moss on its log-made hood, its base surrounded by puddles of curdled grey washing-water. With its ancient orchards, fringed with charlock, scabious and corn-flower shoots, its rusting iron crucifix, its one street and single-storeyed cottages, it looked poverty-stricken and cheerless under the wheeling pigeons and the cawing rooks that circled in the grey sky. The peasant buildings were built of warped beams and baked mud and laths, which were exposed here and there where a shell splinter had swiped away the surface, and all of them seemed to be falling into decay, except for the jerry-built red-brick Mairie with its gilded weathervane and the slate-roofed schoolhouse where brigade headquarters had been established. Every farm seemed to be jammed with men – in barns and huts and tents – and every field contained waggons and horses and guns.

There was a smell of burning vegetation in the air, and the newly turned fields nearby were rich and brown and red, here and there running into white where a vein of chalk came up near the surface. Down by the banks of the streams, in the misty basin of the valley, the air was noisy with the cries of waterfowl and other birds, and the hedges were full of early flowers, and long lush grass among the sycamores, pollards, planes and willows.

Higher up, where the Germans squatted, their four lines of defences built long since by Russian prisoners from the Eastern Front, there were no hedges and the land seemed to be reaching towards the sky. Here you could just see the beginning of the flattish acres of the uplands, with trees in round compact clumps beyond the withered wheat and corn and barley and beet which had been abandoned since 1914.

It was a rich sloping area of ridges and folds which had been fought over a hundred times by everyone who had ever made war in France. Colinqueau Farm itself had been occupied by Cossacks during Napoleon's retreat in 1814 and by Bavarians in 1870. Half a century later it had been occupied again and the farmer and his family had fled, and it had stood deserted for six months, its garden going to seed, its harvest rotting in the fields, until the Germans had fallen back again from the Marne and they'd returned to take possession once more.

Locky, who knew the district well, told us the Ancre had good trout in it when we felt like finding them, and Tom Creak and the Mandys, who almost every Saturday and Sunday of their summers before the war had gone off with their bait, their covered rods and their baskets in horse-drawn coaches hired by their miners' lodges, sat up at once, their eyes gleaming, on the lookout immediately for suitable poles on the willow trees.

Tim Williams, who'd lectured at the University on the subject, said the place was known in history as Santerre.

'*Sancta terra*,' he said. 'Sacred land. Peter the Hermit was a Picard, and a lot of Crusaders came from Amiens. Or perhaps it was *Sangua terra*. Bloody land. Take your pick. What's the difference? Charlemagne lived here in Picardy . . .'

'Who's Charlie Mann?' Eph asked.

'He was in your line of business,' Tim said. 'A long time ago.'

'What? Bettin'?'

'No, fathead, soldiering.'

'Who'd he fight? Germans?'

'For God's sake, Eph, dry up,' Murray said eagerly, and you could see he was excited by the knowledge that he was surrounded by history and on the point of making more. 'Go on, Tim. Tell us some more.'

'Well' – Williams smiled and gestured, looking more like a

lecturer than a soldier for a moment with his long hands and thinning hair – 'it's been ravaged round here by the Normans and the English . . .'

Catchpole looked up from the mug of cold water he was trying to shave from. 'Wouldn't mind doing a bit of ravaging myself,' he grinned. 'Or is it ravishing I'm thinking about? Anyway, whatever it is, away with protracted virginity! A soldier's life's too bloody pure these days. No loot. No women. I always thought they were the perquisites of the profession.'

Murray scowled, resenting the intrusion of flippancy. 'I wish you lot'd shut up,' he snapped. 'Go on, Tim. Who else fought here?'

'Louis XI and Charles the Bold . . .'

'Charles the what?' Eph looked round. 'Come again, mate!'

'Charles the Bold.'

'That's a name for a Sat'dy night, ain't it? Imagine me bein' announced to the colonel. Eph the Bold's 'ere, sir. Come to apply for leave. Go on, mate.'

'It suffered in the Hundred Years War . . .'

Eph's eyebrows popped up again. 'The 'Undred Years *what*?' he said.

'The Hundred Years War.'

'Was there a war that lasted a hundred years?'

'Yes.'

'What, with brass-'ats and kit-'umping, and wearing your boots down to the lace-'oles gitting from one place to the next?'

'I suppose so.'

'Cor!' Eph's eyebrows popped up again. 'Fancy filling sand-bags for a hundred years. I bet business went down the drain a bit. What they fight all that time for?'

'A small matter of property rights, I believe,' Locky grinned.

Tim nodded. 'They couldn't agree who was boss,' he said. 'This is Henry V's "tawny ground" . . .'

'I thought *that* was a port wine.'

Murray, who had been growing more and more impatient

during the interruptions, burst out now in an explosion of anger. 'For God's sake,' he shouted in disgust. 'Can't you shut up? I'm trying to listen to Tim, not *your* bloody silly comments!'

Eph turned to Catchpole, his small eyes wide in mock horror. 'Did you hear what he said to me, Vicar?' he demanded. 'I bet 'e never learned them words in Sunday School.'

'Take the child away at once,' Catchpole said. 'Wash his mouth out with lysol and saddle soap, and anoint him with chloride of lime.'

Murray quivered, trying hard to ignore the comments, his face red, disapproval shining even from the back of his neck.

'Why did they always fight here, Tim?' he asked deliberately, in a low, bitter voice, his words coming slowly with a precision that was designed to show dignity and composure under duress.

Tim was grinning all over his face and he found it hard to reply.

'Because it's perfect terrain for battle, I suppose,' he said. 'The last shot of Napoleon's 1814 campaign was fired from the walls of Peronne, which is just to the south of here . . .'

'Seems we're in good company,' Locky commented, and Murray raised his eyes in despair.

'Doesn't it just?' Eph stared at Tim admiringly, marvelling at his erudition. 'Ain't education wonderful?'

'It would be,' Murray burst out, 'if you silly bloody lot would let a man get the benefit of it!'

'Oh, my!' Eph shrieked in mock horror and put his fingers to his ears. ''E's at it again!'

Murray was still standing there, red-faced and furious, searching for an answer, the rest of us rolling on the ground laughing at him, when old Corker came up, shouting to us to fall in. Locky began to fasten his tunic, softly singing '*Let me like a soldier fall*', and Murray exploded again.

'It's all right for you lot,' he snorted as he reached for his cap. 'You've got no bloody feeling for history! We're in big things here. We ought to appreciate it.'

Locky laughed. 'Dear Murray,' he said. 'You and I never did see eye to eye on what constituted "big things". It's often occurred to me that the cleverest soldiers of all must be the ones who arrive not so early as to be involved in the bloodshed; and not so late as to miss the glory.'

Corker eyed him as he took his place in the ranks forming up in the lane, and cast a sly glance in the direction of the seething Murray.

'If you ain't careful, 'Addo,' he said, 'you'll 'ave this young feller busting 'isself with rage, and then where will we be when Sir Douglas 'Aig says "Let it rip, boys," and we ain't got Murray's soldierly spirit to fall back on?'

We'd thought that now we'd arrived at the war our fatigues might be finished, and they'd let us get on with the fighting, but they'd called us out to load equipment on lorries at the station, and, as we waited for the transport to arrive, they marched off C Company to search for wash tubs for baths, A Company to dig latrine and refuse pits, and B Company to spend the day unloading shells at a dump down the lane, a tremendous barbed-wire enclosure where huge piles of ammunition were covered with tarpaulin sheets.

D Company, enjoying the bliss of riding in lorries after the previous day's marching, and with that cool spring air about us after the heat and dust of Egypt and the appalling journey up from the south, made it a day out, enjoying the countryside, absorbed in everything – French cooking, French farming, French words even. Corker actually found us an estaminet with beer. By the time we got back, the camp seemed to be in some sort of order, with tents erected in rows and battalion headquarters firmly established in the ruined farmhouse with the farmer and Madame and her daughters, two sexless women around thirty. All our personal equipment had been cleared for us, and we flung ourselves down, prepared to stretch out and enjoy life, but Corker was after us again immediately.

'What, again?' Murray wailed.

'Yes, again. And why not? Ain't it the principle of the Army to keep men busy?'

'It's the principle of the Army,' Locky said, 'to find out what you can't do and then to proceed to make you do it. I was never built for labouring.'

Corker grinned. 'You 'orrible men, you,' he shouted gaily, as though the holiday spirit that lay behind the hopes of approaching victory had affected him too. 'We got work to do. We came 'ere to make war – and – war – we – 'ave – got – to – make. We will therefore,' he announced, 'march over to that there field next door and proceed to erect, lift, or otherwise put up, a few rows of tents.'

'Oh, well,' Murray said, his expression lifting. 'We might get some benefit from *that*.'

Corker grinned. ''Ave no fear,' he said. 'They ain't for us. 'Ave some sense, boy. That'd be too easy. These are for a new battalion just out from England, still wet behind the ears, who don't know how to go about it. We can't win the war on our own, can we? We've got to 'ave 'elp. We ain't all blood-crazy like you.'

We returned to Colinqueau Farm to find they'd jammed *us* into barns and outhouses. They'd been occupied many times before and the lice we'd picked up seemed to double their numbers within an hour, and we gave up trying to keep free of them.

'They're calling up their relations,' Catchpole shouted. 'Help!'

'I'm being eaten alive!' Mason was rolling on the floor, pretending to fight with millions of imaginary insects.

'I wouldn't mind 'em eating me flesh,' Eph mourned. 'But these spiteful bastards just take a bite and spit it out again.'

'Leave 'em alone,' Billy Mandy said. 'They've got to earn their living somehow.'

All the same, the barns and the deep, damp-smelling straw were signs that we were really soldiering at last. Tents suddenly seemed to hold a suggestion of amateurism, a hint of weekend camps, and we sprawled with unbuttoned jackets and loosened puttees, our equipment hanging on every kind of projection, the holes in the walls stuffed up with packs and greatcoats. Men hung over the edge of the lofts, joking by the light of candles with their friends on the ground floor, jeering at the lice and pretending to crow like roosters. This was real campaigning.

We had believed in our enthusiasm that, with the offensive hanging over us like a shadow, any battle training we might still have to endure would be a specialised form of instruction, with particular emphasis laid on what we were expected to do when they flung us at the German lines, but to our disgust it turned out to be the same weary routine all over again, day after day after day, everything we'd done at Blackmires and Romstone and in Egypt, advancing under imagined shell- or shrapnel- or machine-gun fire, digging trenches and building sandbag parapets. We fought the same old imaginary battles over the rolling ground between Albert and Amiens, in companies, battalions and brigades, and practised trench fighting in bombing squads of three men, the first man with a bayonet, the second with a 'potato masher', an Indian club studded with horseshoe nails or wrapped with barbed wire, the third with the Mills bombs, neat little fragmentation weapons which had at last taken the place of the home-made milk-tin grenades they'd used at Loos.

'Is this *all* we're going to do?' Murray asked plaintively. 'Just dash up and down again like we've always done?'

'War is made up of individual sorrows and personal miseries,' Locky said. 'My individual sorrow is training and my personal misery *more* training.'

'We can do the bloody job blindfold!'

'Well, now, in case of some extraordinary emergency that might arise, you've got to be able to do it backwards, upside-down and inside-out. Only then will the Army be satisfied.'

Locky beamed on young Murray and humped his equipment ready for the next spasm, his complaints good-humoured, his manner imperturbable, his spirit as untouched as ever.

We could always hear the sound of the artillery as we trained, and the tap of rifles and machine guns in front, especially in the early morning, when the firing swelled up into a tornado of sound. You could always distinguish the machine guns because they made a noise like the giant tearing of calico and it galled us to listen to lectures and practise movements by numbers, while away to the east and the north men were fighting the war we'd come to finish. We felt we'd been there long enough looking on.

Easter had come and gone, and with it the news in the *Daily Mails* they sent up to us of the German-inspired rebellion in Dublin, which had brought a howl from the leader-writers because it was considered to be in danger of drawing troops from the coming offensive in France. In spite of our first enthusiasm for barns, we'd soon had enough of sharing our lodgings with the pigs and the cockerels and the hens, and we were anxious to be on the march eastwards. We soon grew tired of promoting allied comradeship with the few French soldiers we saw, and bored with hunting eggs to put to our rashers of bacon. We'd learned all the tricks – how to ask always for Madame at the cottages, because the husbands and the sons were away and there was never anyone else *but* Madame and her daughters or sometimes some ancient grandfather or an imbecile or crippled son. The Picards were a taciturn lot, uncommunicative and fatalistic on the whole, to whom '*C'est la guerre*' was the answer to everything. They probably hated us as much as they hated the Germans, because we were trespassers on their land.

'When's our turn coming?' Murray begged again and again.

'It'll come in good time,' Corker reassured him. 'Just 'old your water, son.'

'But we're only learning stuff we've learned before. Half a dozen times.'

'All stands you in good stead.' Corker was unmoved by Murray's anguish. 'That's 'ow it should be.'

'That's no bloody answer,' Murray said disgustedly, flinging his cap to the ground as Corker disappeared.

His face was sullen as he marched backwards and forwards from the training areas, frustrated and sickened by repetition, convinced like the rest of us that the Army had got us there and didn't know what to do with us.

Even the instructors irritated us. The bayonet-fighting sergeants were even more bloodthirsty than the ones in England.

'You've got to get into a state of wild excitement,' they told us. 'Blood-madness, if you like. The bayonet is an offensive weapon and with it you go in to kill or be killed. You must all get the spirit of the bayonet. Put on a special face, instil fear into 'em, let 'em know they're for it. You're not dancing with a tart. Stick 'em in the eyes, in the throat, in the chest. Six inches are enough. If you shove it in a long way, you've only got to pull it out again, and somebody might get you while you're doing it. Even three inches'll do at a pinch. Don't lurch. Don't overbalance. Do it one-'anded, the other 'and outstretched to balance the body. Simply throw up the rifle with the 'and on the small of the butt. The weight of the rifle and the sharpness of the bayonet'll do the rest.'

We practised short points, long points, jabs and parries till our arms ached; then, as though it had been done deliberately to drive us to despair at the power the Army had over us, a new lieutenant was posted to the company from the armies of the north, and he told us sourly and without preamble that bayonet-fighting was a 'bloody waste of time and best left alone'.

In his constant search for efficiency, Ashton had drawn us up in a hollow square to hear the methods preached by this veteran of twenty-seven who'd been sent to add his experience to our theory, and I saw his eyebrows pop up at the sacrilege. All our training had been based on bayonet-fighting, and he glanced quickly at young Welch and Bickerstaff and the other officers alongside him, with that agonised crucified expression on his face, then he took off his spectacles and began to polish them vigorously, as though by doing so he'd avoided an unpleasant disagreement in public.

The newcomer was called Blackett and he was a former sergeant attached to the Egyptian Army who'd paid his own fare to England to enlist at the beginning of the war. He'd joined us from a battalion which had been decimated at Loos and, like Appleby, was inclined to be cynical. He was as ugly as sin, with narrow green eyes and a teak-hard face. He wore wide breeches of a livid salmon-pink colour and a peak cap with the crown crushed in, which, with his light trousers and shirt and tie and the hair-oil you could smell a mile away, made him seem a bit cheap and nasty. Nevertheless, he had a curious unboastful confidence in himself that came from experience.

'Never mind what they tell you,' he said. 'It won't be so bloody easy as all that on the day. You might as well face it. There'll certainly be somebody shooting at you, won't there? There'll be 'ell going off all round you, in fact, shells going up, and bullets whizzing about. And there'll be wire. Wire. Don't forget that. That there wire'll be the death of you if you get caught up in it. For God's sake, keep out of that wire, boys, because you'll be stuck there for 'em to pick off at their leisure if you don't. If the wire gets you, it's bon soir, toodle-oo, good-byee! I saw 'em hanging on it at Loos in their 'undreds, like a lot of old scarecrows.'

This was a picture we hadn't had presented to us by anyone with authority and it was a little unnerving.

Blackett paused and I saw young Welch lick his lips and look at Ashton. Then Blackett lit a cigarette and began to gesture with it. Smoking during training periods had always been forbidden by Ashton, who was a stickler for discipline, but his face stiffened stoically and he said nothing, as though he sensed that here in France things were different.

230

'I'm not trying to scare you,' Blackett said. His small green eyes flickered over the taut startled faces around him. 'But you don't really know much about it. You're still a bit wet, aren't you?'

There was an indignant murmur of dissent from the men around him and a hurt startled look from Ashton, but Blackett was undeterred.

'I'm only trying to show you what's in front of you,' he explained. 'That's all. It's better to go in knowing what to expect than like we did at Loos, thinking it's goin' to be easy. This time, of course, there'll be enough shells to blow their wire out of existence, so it should be a walkover. All you'll 'ave to do this time is stroll across and take over Jerry's *trenchées*. But there can always be accidents and you might as well be prepared for 'em.'

He paused and drew at his cigarette, sure of himself, undismayed in his stained and faded uniform in front of smarter men like Welch and Bickerstaff and Milton, who might boast greater wealth and education but had nothing to put against his knowledge and experience but theory and passages learned by heart from the *Infantry Training Manual*.

He glanced at Appleby and Bold and Corker, whom he seemed to accept and recognise as men of experience, and gestured with his cigarette. 'Don't believe all that eyewash they're telling you about bayonets,' he said. 'You'll never get near enough for that "up, one-two, point, one-two" nonsense. It isn't bayonets that'll win this battle. It'll be artillery. Sometimes I think there's too bloody much artillery in this war. All that about the bayonet-man going first – it's a lot of bloody nonsense. It isn't a waltz. "After you, Claude!" None of that stuff. It's the one what happens to be nearest. And coshes and bombs'll always do more damage than a bayonet. A man might recover from a bayonet in the guts but it takes a strong man to live through a bomb going up on his belt buckle.'

He paused to let this fact sink in, then he swung round,

staring at us with those bright ugly green eyes of his, faintly contemptuous, as though he didn't have much time for us, in spite of belonging to us, in spite of out vaunted training.

'Besides,' he concluded, 'you'll never get near enough to stick your bayonet in 'em. You wait and see. You'll see a few different-shaped 'ats over the next traverse and that'll be it. If you're quick with your bombs, you'll get 'em; if you're not, then they'll get you, and rotten 'ard luck too.'

We flung ourselves down exhausted. The woods around us grew silent with the approach of evening, and the larks stopped their singing and fell to earth among the tussocks of grass. You could hear the faint hum of an aeroplane somewhere and there were brown smudges in the air where the smoke of cooking fires rose up under the trees.

Just up the slope we could see the Colinqueau family moving about their evening chores, one unspeaking old man in sabots and corduroys, with hatred in his eyes and a frizz of beard round his chin, and a group of women in black – his wife, his mother and his daughters – all clinging to their battered farm-house with its blistered green shutters with the desperation of shipwrecked mariners clinging to a raft – as though they feared that if they lost their grip on it they'd drown.

They hung on with their few pigs and hens, a goat and the sole remaining, creaking, high-wheeled hooded cart that hadn't been requisitioned or destroyed. We all knew they called us '*Les autres Boches*' when they thought we weren't listening or couldn't understand. They were a silent lot, depending for their existence it seemed on the number of *œufs* they sold us. The grandmother, a lined and wrinkled ancient of eighty odd, was supposed to be the daughter of one of Napoleon's dragoons who'd fought at Waterloo, and she was reputed to have fought for her life and her honour when the Bavarians had walked through in 1870.

They were a shrewd hard-headed crowd, and it wasn't

232

difficult to guess they hid their wealth in stockings and put on an outward appearance of poverty for our benefit. For all the sabots and the tumbledown farmhouse and the ragged clothes worn by the nut-brown daughters who went with the water-carts to the pump – sturdy silent women with black hair, as solid as the ancient Percheron they led – they all seemed to enjoy their nip of calvados at night and didn't seem to go short of food, not even with the countryside teeming with half a million British soldiers all trying to buy against them.

Murray watched them for a while, lying flat on his back, his feet on a box.

'You know,' he said thoughtfully, his mind far away from the Colinqueaus, 'I think that new bloke's a bit of tray bon. The bayonet instructors would go absolutely fanti if they heard him, wouldn't they? He sounded as mad as a maggot.'

His language, we'd noticed, had suddenly become larded with the old soldiers' slang he'd picked up from the men we bumped into occasionally in the battered little townships behind the line – Colincamps, Hébuterne and Hamel – and he'd absorbed a lot of their mannerisms, their professional air of off-handedness, their casual attitude to the war, which never quite managed to mask the keenness he felt underneath.

'Yes,' he went on slowly. 'I honestly think he's got something. I really do.'

Locky grinned. 'I'm sure it's better,' he said, 'to throw a bomb than to go into a vulgar brawl with a bayonet. I never really did fancy that.'

'"Going up on his belt buckle,"' Murray chortled. 'That's a good one.'

'We should be so damn' good when we've finished this lot,' MacKinley said angrily in his nasal Canadian voice, 'we should walk through 'em.'

We were not only proud of our skill but, with the sureness of men who'd never been in battle, we were growing cocky

233

and impatient. We considered it was time somebody decided to let us have a go.

'There was a fight in the village today,' Catchpole said. He was sitting under the hedge, cleaning out his mess tin with a piece of bread, doing the job carefully, as though it were a matter of great moment that he should rid it of every last trace of grease.

'Who between?' Murray asked.

'New crowd,' Catchpole looked up again. 'Got mixed up with a bunch from the north in Belgium. They were in the estaminet and the new chaps didn't like 'em jeering.'

'Neither would I,' Murray said. 'What happened?'

'Oh, the usual. Fists and belts and boots started flying and one of the tables got smashed and they ended up by heaving bits of the marble top at each other. Then the redcaps came along and put the place out of bounds and marched off a few prisoners. Mostly the old sweats.'

Murray nodded sympathetically. 'They think they know everything,' he said.

We hadn't much time for the old soldiers' cynicism. They called the enemy 'Fritz' and never 'the Hun' as people did at home, and they seemed to hate the staff and the lines of communication troops more than they did the Germans.

The staff always tried to keep them well away from us – so that their cynicism wouldn't taint us, I suppose – but it wasn't easy, and we always resented their cockiness. After all, they weren't the only ones who'd been under fire. A few shrapnel shells had once burst with a series of loud elastic twangs in the field next to ours, and we'd all dived panic-stricken under the hedges for shelter, forgetting they'd be no more use against the singing bullets than paper. But afterwards, when we were on our feet again, watching the cotton wool smoke-puffs fading away almost reluctantly, and had got over the first fright, we'd decided being under fire wasn't too bad after all, and we'd felt big and bold and brave and noisy, and ready to resent any suggestion that we were untested by war.

The light faded further and the glimmer filtering through the trees from the cookhouse fires edged the crouching, sprawling men with red-gold light. Someone was singing quietly in the hollow behind the barn:

'Wash me in the water that you washed your dirty daughter,
And I shall be whiter than the whitewash on the wa-a-all.'

Somewhere behind the house the pigeons were croo-crooing and you could hear old Colinqueau pushing the pigs inside, and Eph Lott chirruping over his crown-and-anchor board. 'Come on, my lucky lads. All weighed, all paid? If you don't begin to speculate you can't afford to fornicate. 'Ow about one on the old mud-'ooke?'

A machine gun rattled somewhere in the distance and we all turned our heads to look. Then Murray sat back again and took his legs from the box.

'We'll go north after the breakthrough,' he said.

'Who says?' Catchpole demanded disconcertingly.

'Well, it's obvious.' Murray gestured. 'We'll go up round the back of the Germans and cut 'em off.'

'I suppose you had that straight from Sir Douglas Haig himself?'

'Don't be barmy, man,' Murray said, beginning to get angry. 'It's the only way. Outflank 'em. The number we capture simply depends on how fast we can move.'

Locky turned his head slowly. 'It occurs to me,' he said, 'that with the front stretching right from the North Sea to the Vosges, it's got to be quite a battle to outflank anyone.'

Murray gave him the pained tired look of a schoolteacher with a particularly stupid pupil. 'Well, it is *going* to be quite a battle, isn't it?' he said. 'You've only got to look around.'

'What would Napoleon have done under the same circumstances, Professor Williams?'

'Hand it over to the leader-writers. They always know what to do.'

'We'll be through 'em like a dose of salts,' Murray said. 'We've got the guns. We've got the men . . .'

'"We've got the money too,"' Locky quoted with a grin.

Henry Oakley sat up. 'Providence marches with the big battalions,' he said sharply.

'That was before the machine gun,' Mason joined in. 'The balance of power's shifted somewhat these days. Wars are different.'

'Why?' Locky said. 'Men seem to get killed just the same.'

'What's the odds, anyway?' Mason shrugged. 'We've got to have a go because of Verdun.'

'My God,' Catchpole said admiringly. 'You lot are wasted here. You could earn thousands working for the Win-the-War Department of the *Daily Mail*.'

As dusk came, the rumble of wheels started.

'They're at it again,' Locky said, lifting his head.

The wheels were both ours and the Germans'. Supplies of men and machines had begun to move up unseen in the darkness.

There was a sudden flurry of guns from somewhere in front of us that made us all sit up, and in the fading light you could see the flashes touching the underside of the clouds away to the north, where they were still battling it out in raids and scuffles along the Vimy Ridge.

Murray was staring towards the horizon, his eyes glittering and angry. He dragged at a handful of grass and tossed it savagely away from him.

'For God's sake,' he exploded. 'When are we going to have a go at the tronchay? We've been here days now. The bloody war'll be over before we get a chance, at this rate. We can't wait too long. We'll grow stale. I'm damned if *I* want over-trained. I came out here to fight the Germans, not imagi enemies in imaginary trenches behind imaginary barrages.'

Sergeant Corker had come up behind him in the dusk a stood with his hands on his hips, grinning. 'Did yer?' he sai loudly. 'Well, now's yer chance.'

Murray bounded to his feet in a single movement, as though someone had released a spring under him.

'Sarge,' he asked, 'have orders come through? Are we going up?'

Immediately, we were all round Corker, excited, eager, noisy with questions.

'Come on, Sarge,' Murray demanded plaintively. 'Let's have it. Have you heard something?'

Corker grinned. 'Yes, you 'orrible bloodthirsty little man, you. Tomorrow night we're sending ten officers and twenty-five NCOs into the line under Captain Ashton. The colonel's going up tonight and he'll be up there waiting to put out the red carpet.'

Mason began to chirrup with glee, and Murray scowled.

'Officers?' he said. 'NCOs? What's wrong with *us*? What's wrong with the men?'

Corker grinned again, his boozy face merry, tormenting him as he always did, enjoying his boyish eagerness.

'They will be accompanied,' he announced portentously, 'by a group of 'and-picked brutal and licentious soldiery. And I 'ope you're one of 'em, young Murray, you noisy talkative newspaper reporter, you, because if you are, you'll find yourself in the line alongside the Worcesters, getting to know what it's all about. And I hope you bloomin' well enjoy it.'

3

Four ancient, grey-painted London buses drew up in the lane behind Colinqueau Farm the next evening and, watched by those who weren't going into the line, those of us who were slowly began to climb aboard. A guide had come with the buses, a laconic second lieutenant with a Worcester badge and a muddy goatskin coat, who stood alongside Ashton and watched us file past with an expressionless face.

The evening was cold and there was rain in the air. It had been cheerless all day, and the breeze stirred the skirts of our coats and made us stamp our feet as we waited, leaning on our rifles and loaded down like pack mules. The officers fidgeted nervously with their holsters, but I noticed that Blackett had exchanged his revolver for a Lee Metford.

'Don't muck about with a revolver,' he was telling young Welch who, with his smooth schoolboy's face, looked like a child alongside him. 'It won't shoot straight and like as not you'll blow your own 'ead off.'

Someone had turned out the band for a lark, and they were playing 'Yorkshire Johnny' in their shirtsleeves as we climbed aboard. Curiously enough, there was none of the noisy chaffing that I'd expected, and no skylarking. Everyone seemed to be brooding a little and even the occasional catcall seemed a little unfunny and forced. I could see Locky looking thoughtful and Murray a little white and strained. Mason was unusually quiet and even Eph's cheerful ribaldry had an element of nervousness about it.

I wondered if they were suffering from the same sudden fears that had come upon me. We'd been itching to get at the Germans from the day we'd landed in France, sure of ourselves and our ability, but now, abruptly, faced with what we'd been praying for, everything seemed different. I suddenly began to wonder if we were as good as we thought we were. We'd got physique and intelligence, sure enough, and I thought we had our fair share of courage; but, looking back on it, our training still seemed a little threadbare in spite of the time we'd spent on it, and we hadn't the years of experience behind us that the Germans had, nor the instinct of generations of conscripts. Our morale was all right – it was probably the best part of us – but we'd been only playing at war up to now.

Most of the men about me seemed to be carrying far too much kit, I thought. I'd come to the conclusion long since that it was going to be a pretty sparse existence in the trenches and I'd stripped mine down to its essentials, even dumping my spare shirt and socks. Three stone was a lot to carry, I decided, but I'd had no home to get me used to all the little luxuries a man likes to cling to; I'd got years of living in digs behind me and I'd never gone in for extras.

The music the band was churning out grew sprightlier as we dumped our rifles and packs and tried to sit in comfort, strung about like Christmas trees. Then there was a cheer as the engines roared into life and we began to rock and sway down the lane towards the main road.

As we left Rippy behind us, we passed shell-smashed cottages where the roofs had fallen in and the wallpaper, saturated by the rain, had mouldered and was peeling from the walls. The floors were covered with broken bricks, tiles, smashed beams, laths and disintegrating plaster. Odd pieces of furniture remained, too damaged for soldiers to scrounge to grace their billets, twisted iron beds, and large rags which had once been clothes or sheets. Here and there were damp-stained photographs, scattered letters in faded ink fluttering in the corners, broken toys, bits of smashed vases, sometimes a dead cat or dog.

'Mice have been at that lot,' Eph said laconically.

I was anxious to acquit myself well, and I was curious, as I struggled with my feelings, to see whether I'd be afraid. I'd heard so much about shell-fire, I was wondering if I could stand up to it. Those few shells that had dropped in the next field had made us feel pretty tough and soldierly at the time, but now, thinking about it, I realised we'd all made more of them than they warranted.

From time to time the bus skidded on the pavé road. The cobbles were shining now in a light rain which had begun to fall, and once, on a corner, its stern slid sideways into a tree and the thump passed shuddering all the way through its structure to the passengers. The driver showed no sign of stopping and we all cheered with excitement and nervousness.

As we rolled eastwards, the dusk grew deeper and we could see the trees alongside the road lit from time to time as the glare of the flashes up ahead caught the rainwet boles. Several times we stopped for no apparent reason and we could hear the rumble of guns up ahead of us on the wind, and once, quite distinctly like rending cloth, the rattle of a machine gun.

'For God's sake, Murray,' Locky begged, 'don't tell us what it is.'

Murray turned a white, strained, eager face towards him but said nothing.

The guide was riding on the platform of our bus with Ashton and I heard him say 'Ours' laconically, without lifting his head. I envied him his confidence and experience.

After a while, our bus, which was leading, started to boil and, because we were holding up the traffic behind, they made the lot of us get out so they could drive off the road.

'You've only a few hundred yards to go anyway,' the driver said to the guide. He seemed more concerned with his vehicle than with his passengers and he only lifted his head from his engine with reluctance. 'You can take a short cut,' he said. 'Across that field and down the lane. It's signed.' He glanced at Ashton, seeming to sense his inexperience. 'You'll be all right,' he said reassuringly. 'It leads to Worcester Redoubt and that'll hold anything out.'

In the glow that caught the underside of the clouds and lit up the land, making the grey dusk of evening curiously bright, I was aware of vast movement about us as we scrambled across a ditch and began to form up in the field, while the guide went off to make sure of his directions.

The road was congested with waggons and lorries which were moving in both directions, trying to pass the buses. Then a covey of horse ambulances came past, heading back the way we'd come, each with a red cross on a white square painted on the canvas hood. The noise of gunfire from ahead had increased and it sounded like the rolling of a nearby storm, drowning the sound of hooves and the iron-rimmed wheels of the ambulances on the pavé, so that they seemed to be passing us in silence.

The bus driver glanced round and seemed to sniff the air. 'Dirty work at the crossroads tonight,' he said. 'Looks like the Leicesters are copping it.'

Under the darkening sky, as we formed up, I could see long-snouted guns painted in the drab browns and greens of camouflage, attended by the shadowy figures of men in their shirtsleeves. There were military police everywhere, trying to bring order to the congestion, revolvers in holsters, bright blancoed webbing distinct in the dusk. On our right, in a long sloping grass field that ran down to a crescent-shaped wood that lay like a black shadow in the valley, thousands of cavalry horses seemed to be picketed.

As we stood by the roadside, nervously trying not to do the wrong thing and trying to keep out of everyone's way, I heard a coarse buzzing sound that grew steadily louder and louder until it seemed to fill the air. We all began to look about us and instinctively cowered our heads and shoulders as the threat grew closer.

"'Old it!' Corker's rich fruity voice came over the noise, steady and reassuring. 'Remember 'oo you are and stop looking like a lot of nervous old women.'

I saw Locky trying to smile at me, a stiff wooden smile that didn't seem to belong to him, then there was an abrupt crash that lifted my feet from the ground and slammed them down again with a force that jarred my teeth. I saw a flash about two hundred yards away in the field we were about to cross, and an immense mushrooming cloud of grey-black smoke.

'No-ball,' Eph said with a nervous grin.

'Jack Johnson,' Blackett announced indifferently. 'All right, keep your 'eads up. It won't hurt you. Not now anyway.'

At the bang, the cavalry on our right had immediately started into action. Men had come running up the slope from the edge of the crescent-shaped wood and lances were snatched from where they were leaning in clusters, the bright blades catching the last of the daylight and reflecting it to the dusk-dulled pennants that fluttered just below. Horses were mounted and swung round into jostling untidy lines, curiously blurred and fuzzy in the poor light, and there was a sharp order. Watched by an officer, the cavalrymen began to file on to the road and canter off to the rear past the buses.

'Six to four the field,' Eph shouted. 'I'll give you evens on the little bloke with two pips in front.'

Corker was eyeing the horsemen disgustedly, his little currant-like eyes bright and angry, the points of his waxed moustache bristling. 'First bang and they're off,' he growled.

As we moved across the open field where the Jack Johnson had exploded, I felt as big as a house and as though every eye in the German line was on me. I was restless and impatient, not in a funk but certainly windy, afraid of a second Jack Johnson but probably more afraid still of letting the side down, anxious to put on a good show, nervously acquiescent and trying to look like an old soldier as they made us wait.

At the far end of the field, we passed a group of men apparently coming up out of the ground on the edge of a small wood. They were all wounded, with bloody crumpled uniforms and stained bandages, walking past us without any interest in anything but getting to where they were going. Dangling limp arms were coagulated with blood that dripped from their fingerends. Their faces were desperate and pasty in the dusk and the bloodstains looked black. They seemed to have lost all emotion and were only concerned with getting away. They pushed past us stolidly, moving like automata, their puttees loose round their ankles, their clothes torn or slit, some of them with rifles, some without, limping past like shadows, muttering to each other in undertones.

It seemed strange that they spoke the same language I did. Somehow, in that light, they seemed to belong to another race as they stumbled past, clutching their injuries. You could sense the feeling of apprehension that ran through the group waiting to go in, a sensation of being complete children in war.

We turned into a wide and muddy path cut into the clay that ran past a cluster of crosses on the edge of the wood. On one or two hung the mouldering caps of the dead, a few torn khaki ones, I noticed, one or two old-fashioned red French kepis torn by bullets and shrapnel, and an occasional German pork pie. At its edge, there was a sign pointing the way we were going. It was marked *The Shambles*.

243

'Nice name,' Oakley said. 'Nice and grisly.' And Corker turned on him angrily.

'Keep your mouth shut,' he said. 'And your ears open. It makes everybody's job easier.'

Here, on the fringe of the wilderness of war, it seemed one mustn't speak in normal tones – as though the numberless dead and the invisible underground armies and the desolation ahead of us called for whispers and nothing more.

The path ran downhill now, so that eventually we found ourselves stumbling along below ground level with a strong parapet of clay on either side of us. We began to toil through a trench that was just wide enough to pass along. From time to time I stumbled, sometimes knee-deep in glutinous mud, sometimes bent double where the trench was shallow and where there were ominous notices – *Look out, sniper*.

'Murray,' Mason's voice came through the shuffle of boots, 'you've arrived at the war.'

Overhead the clouds were clearing and the faint light that remained in the sky enabled us to find our way along the communication trench, following its winding course as it curled and twisted. Every hundred yards or so we passed under a plank bridge or round a great promontory of earth and timber which forced us to take four right-angled turns. The parapet was edged now with sandbags, laid header-stretcher three or four deep. Between them grass was sprouting and occasionally I saw the bloom of a poppy, black in the faint light. The trench looked cold and stark, like a scar cut in the bare flesh of the earth, and the faint luminous mist that hung about in the dips gave it an eerie unreality.

After a while we ran into a crowd of men standing in a shallow hollow of ground with crumbling earth walls that suggested it might once have been a mine-crater. From what I could see of them, they were dressed in mud-caked sheepskin jackets and looked a pretty tattered lot, with hacked-off overcoats and sloppy-looking unwired caps. They stood patiently, unspeaking, and with no sign of nervousness – all the indications of old soldiers.

'You this city-battalion crowd?' someone said just ahead.

'That's it.' I heard Ashton's voice.

'You're late.'

'Oh!'

There was a hint of rebuke in the stranger's voice and of grievous disappointment in Ashton's, that in our first attempt to move into the line we had not succeeded in pleasing.

'Get your men in with ours,' the cold voice said. 'Roughly platoon for platoon – if you can – and let's get going.'

There was a suggestion of contempt in those words, 'if you can', and for a while the mine-crater was confusion as Ashton and the other officers tried to sort us out in the darkness. The Worcesters cursed a little and jeered and were haughtily impatient with us.

'For Christ's sake' – the unseen officer's voice was nervous and irritable, as though he'd been on the edge of strain for too long – 'look slippy!'

Finally, we began to move off again. By this time there was a lot of sporadic rifle-fire from ahead which made me duck from time to time. The Worcesters ignored it all, I noticed, tramping along magnificently unconcerned.

We came to a crossroads in the trenches, with the signs *Princes Street* and *Sauchiehall Street*, and other such names that indicated the Jocks had been there before us. The trenches now were all narrow pathways six feet wide, sometimes less. I was beginning to be aware of the weight of my kit by this time, and was stumbling over the uneven duckboards that tipped up every time I trod on them and threw my foot into the sludgy bottom of the trench.

Conversation was limited, but I could hear Murray trying to ask questions of the man in front of him every time the shuffling came to a halt.

'What's it like in the front line?' I heard him say.

245

'Grub's none too good,' came the reply. 'Otherwise, pretty cushy.'

It wasn't till later when I'd heard it often that I realised the reply was always that it was cushy, no matter what sort of mayhem was going on around you.

Then, 'Stop that talking,' someone snapped, and Murray became silent. 'And don't make so much row all the time. Can't you stop your damned equipment clinking?'

The guide's directions came back in monotonous calls. 'Wire high here!' 'Look out, wire low.' 'Shallow here. Keep your heads down.'

Field-telephone wires were fastened along the trench wall with staples, and some of them had fallen out and allowed the wire to hang in loops that kept catching at equipment. In the dark I could see nothing, except for a faint gleam of light occasionally, which showed a puddle or the glow of water that was a shell-hole dug out to make a sump.

'Christ,' Oakley said in disgust. 'There's a foot of bloody water in this trench.'

'Nemmind,' Corker said with heavy sarcasm. 'Perhaps Fritz's got *two* feet in his.'

I began to notice now a peculiar, sour, penetrating smell, that seemed to be a compound of chloride of lime, sweat, manure and something else I couldn't define – something sickly sweet and cloying that seemed to get on to the tongue. Then I found myself in a trench that seemed deeper and better fortified than the rest – a wide place with heavily constructed parapets, fortified and riveted with props of timber and mats of woven willows and osiers that had clearly been cut along the banks of the Somme and the Ancre. Here and there, there were dark caves with curved corrugated-iron roofs, set into the side of the trench. It was a remarkably spacious place, with occasional signs of permanent residence in the form of little doors, sometimes real windows which had been salvaged from some wrecked cottage or other, even once or twice real curtains. On one of them was a carefully printed notice saying ORGANS, CIRCULARS, HAWKERS AND STREET-CRIERS PROHIBITED. On another was NO GERMAN BANDS.

'This is a fine old place to get a bullet through the heart,' Murray said.

'Ever thought you might be blown up instead?' Mason asked sourly. 'Or die of measles or something?'

Murray looked round. I could see his face, a pale, distraught shadow, in front of me. 'Well, I mean to say,' he said. 'If you fell dead here you'd be trampled into the mud before you could get a decent burial.'

'Might save us a lot of trouble,' Mason said grimly, and I saw Murray's eyes flicker in alarm.

It was raining more heavily now and this, together with the mud and the desolation, began to have a depressing effect on everybody. I could see faces growing longer, backs more stooped, expressions more resigned and fatalistic.

The silences as we waited grew longer. All the jokes had been used up and we fell back on sarcasm. Murray was trying to brush off the whitish mud that was daubing his uniform, pushing at it distastefully with his fingers as though it soiled his ideas of war and military glory.

'How much farther?' I asked the Worcester next to me.

'How much farther where?' he demanded.

'Forward.'

He grinned and I saw the flash of his teeth. 'If you go much farther you'll be 'avin supper with Fritz, mate,' he said. 'In front of 'ere it's No Man's Land.'

I stared round me. By the light of the flickering lights to the north, I could see a shabby unfinished wall of chalky mud held together with sagging sandbags. Above the parapet there were strands of rusty wire. There seemed to be nothing about me but bulging ramparts and stagnant pools of muddy water. Above me and behind was a splintered trunk of tree and by my side a tattered ground sheet, flapping wanly against a post. A candle and a brazier glimmered behind a nailed-up blanket and I could hear dim weary voices somewhere out of sight. The place had an air of great age and enduring perpetuity.

Somehow, I'd never pictured the front line like this. Nothing I'd ever read or seen had prepared me for this muddy atmosphere of boredom. The Germans seemed to be the last thing anyone was concerned with.

'Where are we then?' I asked.

'Front line. Worcester Redoubt.'

'What? This?'

'What more do you want?' The dimly seen soldier alongside me sounded indignant. He'd probably helped to build it and was proud of his handiwork.

'That'd keep anybody out,' he said, jerking a hand. 'It's well reinforced – with sandbags and stiffs mostly. You dig 'em out if you ain't careful. Frogs, from 1914.'

'When do we have a go at the Hun?' Murray asked.

'At the what?'

'The Hun.'

'We don't, mate. We sit 'ere quiet and Fritz sits there quiet and if we both be'ave ourselves, and some of them bum-boys on the staff don't start wanting to wage war, we might both have a quiet week.'

Eph was staring round him, his fat little body stooping under his equipment. 'It's a dark and stormy night,' he said, trying to force gaiety into his voice. 'Makes you think of 'ome, don't it? Makes you think of a nice warm fire and a bit of Mum's cooking.'

'You can forget your mum,' Corker said briskly. 'Nobody was ever any good who took his mum off to war with 'im.'

We stood around for what seemed ages, conscious of the chilly gusts of wind that came round the corner of the trench and whined drearily through the gaps in the sandbags. Jammed together, we tried hard to keep out of the way as relieved men stumbled past us, eager to be free of the trenches, complaining and swearing at the crowding. They seemed to sense it was all

248

new to us and took a particular pleasure in venting their weariness and spite on us. Once we heard a machine gun firing, and once the crack of a low bullet that struck the wire in front – '*ping!*' – and went over our heads towards the rear, spinning and misshapen, with a startlingly loud noise – '*clackety, clackety, clack*'. We all ducked except Corker, who laughed.

'Keep your 'air on,' he said. 'You've no need to duck. You don't 'ear the one that gits you.'

Hot sweet tea appeared, tasting of petrol and chloride of lime, and once there was a tremendous crash over on our left and we heard the cry of 'Stretcher-bearers' for the first time in our lives. A few minutes later a couple of swearing men, in the blanching flare of a rocket that rose solemnly and made us duck again, came stumbling along the trench carrying a bulging stretcher that dripped blood as it moved. On it there was a groaning man whose grimy hands clutched at its sides with a pain-filled desperation. Behind them came another stretcher, but the figure on that one was silent and its face was covered. Only a pair of ominously still boots stuck out.

I saw Murray peering nervously after them and Mason fiddling uneasily with the straps of his equipment. Then Corker pushed us back into line.

'All right, all right, all right,' he said, his harsh voice steady. 'You don't want to take too much notice of *that*. It happens all the time. There's a war on, ain't there? D'yer want to live for ever? Get into line and shut yer rattle. The captain wants a word with yer.'

Ashton appeared with Bold, and called out two names, and Bold pushed Eph Lott and Tom Creak into a firebay. Then more names were called out and half a dozen of us moved after Ashton down the trench, stumbling past a gang of men who were ferociously filling sandbags and slamming them into place on a portion of wrecked parapet that seemed to stink of explosives.

'What did that?' Murray asked.

'Rats, mate,' one of them snarled. 'Wotcha think?'

I was pushed with Locky into a big firing-bay with three other men – a sentry, a thick-set older man with a gravy-dipper moustache who was smoking a clay pipe, and a thin-faced lance-corporal who looked about seventeen.

'They'll tell you what to do,' Ashton said. 'Come on, the rest of you.'

As Ashton's voice died away, Locky and I sat down on the firestep, brushing at the mud on our clothes. None of the other three made any attempt to enlighten us about anything, and we waited dismally in the rain for something to happen, like two lost passengers on some windswept country station who'd missed the train.

Our eyes were growing accustomed to the dark now and we waited nervously, uncertain of ourselves. None of the three men in the firebay made the slightest move to greet us. The sentry remained with his head on the level of the sandbags and the other two went on dozing on the firestep. Apart from making room for us, neither of them showed any interest in us. This was as far from our conception of war as it was possible to get.

Never in all our wildest flights of imagination had we imagined that life would be reduced to sitting waiting in the rain in a squalid ditch lined with rusting elephant iron, and surrounded by blackened wire and rotting sandbags through which the grass grew, our chief concern trying to avoid getting our clothes covered with mud.

Then Eph Lott's face appeared round the corner from the next bay, a pale shadow in the semi-darkness but clearly doleful and unhappy. He looked at Locky as he always did when he was worried, seeking the comfort of his imperturbability as though he were something akin to an oracle.

'Stone me eyes right and fours about,' he said in a heavy whisper. 'We done it proper. We're in the dripping all right this time. There's a bloke in 'ere with a face like two of cheese and he ain't said a blind word yet. It's enough to make you feel like a bone what's got in the stew by mistake.'

Locky grinned. 'When you think of it, Private Lott,' he said. 'War *has* become a little vulgar these days, hasn't it.'

We spent the whole night in the firebay, listening to the occasional chatter of machine guns, which all seemed to be fired at random, and with no hope of hitting anyone, and to the sporadic crack of snipers' rifles, imagining every time we looked up and caught sight of one of the barbed wire posts above us that it was a man advancing on us with bayonet and bomb. Once there was a flurry of firing and the whole line was lit up with star-shells and rockets and Very flares.

'Raid,' the lance-corporal said laconically to the sentry without moving. 'It's the Warwicks on our left. After prisoners, I expect.'

With the approach of daylight the firing seemed to increase, and we heard again the cry for stretcher-bearers.

'A Company,' the sentry commented, glancing to his right. 'Mortar bombs, I think.'

Nobody answered. By this time I'd become so dulled by discomfort it meant nothing to me. The only thing that concerned me was that I was cold and wet and tired, and disappointed by our introduction to the war.

Just before dawn whistles blew and the lance-corporal's head lifted wearily.

'Stand-to,' he said, reaching for his rifle, and we all stood up and crouched on the firestep.

Colonel Pine came along in the first of the light and stopped to speak to us as he passed. The lance-corporal glanced at the eye-patch that suggested he was no civilian soldier like the rest of us, and, when he fished under his overcoat to find a cigarette to offer us, I saw the lance-corporal's eyes fall on the purple-and-white ribbon of the Military Cross on his tunic and his manner became doubly deferential at once.

251

The firing had grown fiercer now, though none of it seemed to be coming in our direction. The racket was tremendous, however, and I saw Locky's eyes blinking at every crash, as though the noise were more wearing than the danger. The other three simply huddled closer to the parapet, their faces expressionless and blank, their manner indifferent, as though they'd learned the art of waiting patiently for it to stop.

As the light increased, the firing died away again, and we began to be able to make out the details of our surroundings, the chalk-daubed sandbags and the grey, clayey bottom of the trench. Everything, the osier mats, the pieces of iron that strengthened the walls of the trench, the pit-props, the clothes of the men in the firebay with us, was smeared with clay. There was a piece of rusting iron plating held up in the side of the firebay by a couple of posts, and on it some bloodthirsty enthusiast – probably someone like Murray – from a battalion who'd previously occupied that strip of trench, had daubed *Hang the Kaiser* with a stick dipped in the grey-white mud. Some more realistic and disgusted soldier, crouching over his bully-beef and biscuits, had scratched beneath it, by the same means, the ill-spelt message *Hang the Comisariat*. Looking at the three men with us, with their blank, patient, undefeated faces, I could well imagine any of them being responsible.

After a while the whistles went again and the lance-corporal went down the trench. He returned with some tea in an old jam tin and offered it to us. For the first time, he seemed to have noticed us.

'Just out from England?' he asked.

'No,' I said quickly. 'We've been in the Middle East since last autumn.'

'Oh!' The boy nodded. 'Gallipoli,' he said, and I didn't enlighten him. 'Nasty business that,' he went on. 'Ought to ha' gone through with it. They'd have gone round by the back door then. Saved a lot of trouble.'

He was only twenty, it seemed, and had been out since 1914.

After a while he began to grow more expansive. Probably he saw how innocent we were, how bewildered by everything. Perhaps he guessed that, in spite of our spectacular claims, we'd not seen any fighting before, and he began to give us tips.

'Use an old sock over the bolt,' he said, as he saw Locky trying to poke the mud from his clogged rifle with a piece of stick plucked from the osier mat. 'Or a bit o' rag. Keeps the mud out. And you want to cut the skirts off yer coats. You don't pick up so much muck then. When it dries, it's a sod. Like boards, it is.'

A machine gun roared briefly in front of us and Locky looked up.

'Where are they?' he asked. 'The guns, I mean.'

The boy jerked his thumb. 'There's one over there somewhere,' he said. 'Jimmy Three, we call him. Always fires three bursts at a time. And one over 'ere. They don't like frontal firing. Makes 'em too easy to spot, and they can do more damage when they're enfilading.'

The firing seemed to increase and there were a couple of violent crashes on our left.

'Mortars,' the lance-corporal said. 'They've got a few home-made jobs round here. Full of ammonal. They put everything they can find into 'em. Even the contents of the latrines. A Company had a bloke killed the other day by a bit of old alarm-clock. They favour 'em in this sector because we've got a hillock in front that masks us a bit. Spoils it for the machine guns.'

He looked thoughtful for a while and very young with his pale hollow cheeks, sitting huddled over his dixie of tea as though he were warming his hands on it. His sleep-starved eyes were very distant and there was a puckered unhappy frown on his forehead.

'That's the only thing that puts me off going over the plonk again,' he said thoughtfully. 'The emma gees. I don't mind the rest. You puts your money down and takes your chance. But with machine guns you've got no chance at all.'

He paused, glancing at us. The other two watched him and said nothing, their eyes full of pity.

'I was at Loos,' the boy went on, 'and up at Ypres.' There was a real dread in his voice. 'That's the place. The Salient. Along the canal. They'd chopped the trees down into the water and you 'ad to climb over 'em all, every last one of 'em, every time you went up the line. This is home-from-home by comparison. Chlorine. Gas. Explosives. Stiffs all over the place. Our lot. Froggies. Saxons. Württembergers. Prussians. All in dark-green uniforms with leather equipment and hairy backpacks, all with spiked helmets. Big men they was, but they 'adn't a chance. They used to come over shoulder-to-shoulder. It was too easy. You couldn't miss. Trouble was, neither could they when we tried it. They cut us to pieces. I 'eard of one bloke who marched hisself out – the only one left of his platoon. He called the roll, right-wheeled and dismissed hisself, then he piled his arms and went and toasted hisself at the canteen.'

We listened to him silently, touched by his disillusionment but only half-believing.

'No use worrying anyway,' he said with a world of weariness in his voice. 'In two years' time the tronshay'll still be in the same place. You can't even run away from it, or some bastard at Headquarters who's never been up near the front line 'as you shot. They did a kid in our mob up at Loos. He was scared. He didn't like stick bombs and we'd only got jam tins filled with gun-cotton and bits of stone to throw back. He was only a nipper and he'd seen all his pals knocked off round him. They tied him up and put a sandbag over his 'ead and let him 'ave it. A week later the whole battalion 'opped it down the Menin Road, without packs or rifles, so it wouldn't have made much difference.'

He looked round him at the chalky walls of the trench, the sandbags laid tidily along its lip and the fringe of grass above, and suddenly he seemed to cheer up.

'Of course,' he said with a new enthusiasm, 'it's different

here. It ain't all swamp here, with everything going rotten and decaying. We've got a chance this time, and if the staff haven't made a balls-up of it again, we should manage to break out. With all them guns we've got, there won't be any machine guns left.'

He put his dixie down and stood up, stretching his legs. From the next bay I could hear Eph's voice, breezy and rasping, as though he'd recovered his spirits with daylight.

'Lovely little 'orse,' he was saying. 'I had 'er at fifteen to one, and she ran away from the rest of 'em like she'd got ten legs . . .'

The corporal seemed to listen to him for a moment, as though he took pleasure in the sound of an unfamiliar voice, then he put down his rifle.

'I'm for a bit of kip,' he said. 'They'll be along soon enough for fatigues.'

As he lifted his legs to the firestep, I heard a muffled pop from somewhere beyond the parapet, and he looked up with an unalarmed expression on his face.

'Minnie,' he said and, without waiting to warn us, he dived round the corner of the firebay, his friends after him. As I glanced round to see what was wrong, I saw what looked like a large black barrel with a fuse sticking out of it, swinging through the air in an erratic arc towards us, and I gave Locky a desperate shove round the other corner of the firebay.

The mortar exploded on the parapet behind me, and the blast roaring along the trench flung me the rest of the way round the corner. I caught a brief glimpse of Eph's face, round and boozy and startled, and Tom Creak's just beyond, then we landed on top of them, and we all went sprawling in the mud in a heap.

The crash seemed to tear the flesh from my bones and leave me skeletal, with all my nerves exposed and quivering. I was conscious of the first real fear I'd ever felt in my life, aghast at the incredulous appreciation that those noises I'd heard in the distance from time to time were now being directed at me, sending me grovelling and gasping and unashamedly terrified to the floor of the trench. This was like nothing I'd ever expected. Those few twanging shells I'd heard bursting at a distance had left me whole, but this, right on my doorstep, seemed to tear shreds off me and leave me incomplete, my body numb, my mind addled with echoing noise and fear.

For a moment or two the air seemed to be filled with flying pieces of wood and scraps of hot metal that plopped down into the earth round me as I clawed at the mud, panting with terror, then I became aware of someone screaming with the same shuddering tearing scream I'd heard outside the hospital train on the way north, in a way that seemed to rasp on the nerves and make you ashamed to be human. As I scrambled up to see who'd been hit, I was knocked flying again by a man who tumbled along the trench, bouncing blindly from side to side, groping absurdly with red fingers at the mess where his face had been, his voice bubbling and whimpering in his throat in little inarticulate inhuman cries.

I sat in the mud and stared after him until he disappeared round the next corner, then I realised with a shock that it was Henry Oakley, and it seemed a horrifying thing that this agonised creature who had stumbled past me, groping and twittering insanely in his throat, was a man I knew; a man who'd joined up on the same day as I had, a sane intelligent man of wealth and responsibility I'd seen playing cricket in immaculate white at Hendrick Lane as an amateur for the county. I caught Locky's eyes on me, and Eph's, and Tom Creak's, as scared, appalled and horrified as my own must have been, then I heard shouts for help from the damaged bay and scrambled to my feet.

Even to me, with no experience of death, it was clear as soon as I saw him that the sentry was already dead. The lance-corporal was half-buried under a collapsed parapet, which had been deposited in the trench with beams, osier mats, sandbags and everything else, in a hideous confusion of soil, smoking clods of earth, wood and iron.

I dived towards him, aware that other men were scrambling across the wreckage too, and began to tear at the earth with my fingers. I could see his boy's face pale against the grey soil, a smear of blood startlingly bright on his cheek, and, although I'd never seen a man die in front of my eyes before, I knew we were already too late. The flesh seemed to have fallen away from his face already. His teeth seemed to be protruding and the lines on his cheeks were growing darker.

I heard another explosion nearby and saw Locky duck; and another, then I saw Bold behind me, helping, and Colonel Pine shouting for shovels. In the end, I got down into the hole with the boy, and tried to lift him, but he turned a calm, curiously peaceful face towards me

'It's too late, mate,' he said quietly. 'I'm scuppered. It got me in the back. I can feel it.'

The firing stopped eventually and, sheltered by the rise in front of us which hid us from the Germans, the trench wall was built up again, the pit-props and sandbags replaced, the parapet strengthened once more with osier mats.

The bodies of the sentry and the lance-corporal lay on the firestep for a long time, covered with ground sheets, before they were moved, and it shocked me to see the indifference their comrades showed. I'd thought that men were mourned by their friends when they were killed, but nobody seemed to care very much. They remained unmoved by the fact that the two bundles had been men who'd joked and eaten and worked with them up to an hour or so before. All there was to show they'd ever existed, in fact, was a splash of bright blood on the duckboards. Nothing else, nothing except some new soil and some raw white splintered timber to show that a bomb had dropped there, killing two men and viciously wounding another.

As we finished working, we stood around silently for a

moment. Murray's face looked thin and Frank Mason seemed quiet and angry.

'Did you see Henry Oakley?' he said, and I nodded.

'Christ,' he said in a breathy whisper.

'When you come to think about it,' Eph said slowly, 'war comes much the same as knocking the boys about at the back of Cotterside Common, don't it?'

'For Christ's sake,' Mason said angrily. 'What do you think this is? A bloody gang-war?'

Eph turned to Frank slowly, and answered quietly and soberly. 'Look, mate,' he said equably. 'There's no need to go for me. Whatever I've been, I've tried to do me bit in this mob. *You*'ve got no complaints, 'cept for the odd bob I've took off you at cards. As for that other – well, I'm not so sure I wasn't right. It ain't all that different, when you think of it, is it? Just on a bigger scale, and no cops around taking names.'

Frank stared at him for a moment and nodded. 'Sorry, Eph,' he said at last, then he turned away and went down the trench.

While we were talking, a sergeant came along with a jar of rum. He looked tired and, as he glanced around him at the repair work we'd been doing, his expression altered slightly, but he said nothing. He'd clearly long since got used to death and no longer had any emotion to spare for it.

Eph brightened up a little at the sight of the rum. 'What-ho,' he said, his voice a little strained, as though he were trying hard but not entirely successfully to appear as normal as the sergeant. 'That's the stuff. A drop of what killed mum. I remember parties I been to after the races when the corks went like file firing.'

The man with the gravy-dipper moustache turned to Locky and me, his face in his dixie, reaching for the rum with his lips like an old horse at a trough.

'Might as well move in with me for the time being,' he said flatly. 'Plenty of room now Fred and the kid's gone.'

We stumbled after him along the trench and round a machine

gun emplacement, a semi-circular recess roofed over with sand-bags and lined with iron plates. Inside, we could see the ugly shape of a Vickers and a few mouldering pictures of half-clad long-legged Kirchner girls, torn from *La Vie Parisienne*.

'Need plenty of sandbags,' the man with the moustache pointed out, cocking a thumb at it. 'They get mortared a lot.'

He was friendly now, accepting us without question, all the hostile indifference gone suddenly. It was as though having been under fire with him, having been there when his friends had died, had made us different men.

He said his name was Bert Williamson, and that he came from Stourbridge. He introduced us to his home, a narrow cubicle with an elephant-iron roof and the sign MON REPOS over the door.

'French,' he said. 'Fred wrote that. Fred was a bit of a scholar.'

He scrambled in on his hands and knees and, stretching himself out on the earth floor, began to go through a rigmarole of tying sandbags round his feet and putting an old overcoat over his shoulders. Then he turned his face to the mud wall and began to mutter to himself.

'An' now I lay me down to sleep,'

he said

'In flippin' mud what's four foot deep,
If I'm not 'ere when you awake,
Just scrape me out wiv a garden rake.'

He finished with a fervent 'Amen' and seemed to go to sleep immediately.

Locky stared at me. I knew his mind was still on the boy we'd dug out too late.

'I feel a bit like Frank did,' he said slowly, as though making a plea for sanity. 'I feel I need help.'

259

We crept in with Bert but we found it difficult to sleep. Bert's snores were enough to wake the dead and, after a while, numb with the damp chill that struck up through the ground, we crawled out again and sat on the firestep.

Eventually, Bert reappeared, clearly refreshed, and got a fire going that wouldn't have warmed a rat. All the time he was cursing the shortage of fuel, and the company signallers who appeared with their odd-shaped leather cases and coils of coloured wire, and pushed hurriedly past him along the trench, one finger on the telephone lines, looking for breaks, disappearing round corners, intent and unspeaking until they found the damage.

As we sat down to bacon rashers and tea, another mortar bomb landed somewhere just beyond the parapet, and a shower of pulverised dirt came over on to us as we cowered down.

'Them damn' Germans'll be the death of me,' Bert muttered. 'Their sergeant must have got a liver or something this morning. They nearly put the fire out.'

He was back on the job long before we'd stopped shaking, swearing as he brushed the soil from his bread and bacon. The tea was full of pieces of dirt and bits of grass, and we examined each other's handkerchiefs to decide which was cleanest so that we could sieve it into another dixie.

'Might as well 'ave it nice and dainty,' Bert said, passing bacon round on the end of his bayonet.

Later in the day he had to take his turn as sentry, and asked us if we'd like a squint through his periscope. I'm not sure what I'd expected, but I was startled to see wide acres of fresh green, stretching away slightly uphill, and no sign of the enemy. There were a few strands of rusty barbed wire decorated with seed fluff sticking out of the lush grass, and dozens of old bully-beef tins and scraps of broken equipment just in front, which had been thrown over the parapet. It didn't seem possible that those murderous mortar bombs could have come from this direction.

Not far in front, lying across a little mound of earth, was what seemed to be a blackened skeleton in a few rags of red and blue, the weeds growing up through the cage of the ribs. There was a stiff claw-like object sticking straight up alongside it which I took to be the hand of another dead man.

'Frogs,' Bert said. 'They musta caught it in a raid some time back when the French held this sector. They've been there ever since we first came in here. There's another one just beyond, a Jerry what caught it a couple of weeks back when they tried to break in. He was there a couple of days before he died, yelling and 'owling all the time. It was enough to make you sick.'

'Didn't anybody go to him?' Locky asked.

'One of my mates wanted to, but the officer stopped him. If you look over on yer left a bit, you'll see one hanging on the wire. He's been there a lot longer. There ain't much left of him now, I reckon.'

I saw a bundle of old rags that had been blackened by the weather, supported by a few strands of wire. It looked like something the old-clothes man had thrown down, but I saw it was a man, face-down on the wire, with the same claw-like hands as the other, his clothes loose over shrivelled arms and legs.

Late in the afternoon Corker came along and sent us off to help carry wire and sandbags along the communication trench from a dump about a hundred yards back. There were no Worcesters among the party. They were obviously taking advantage of having fresh troops with them to do the work. When we'd finished, they set us digging a drainage sump in a patch of soggy ground where there were one or two bodies in rags of French uniform. We had to throw down chloride of lime to kill the smell.

Locky's face looked taut and strained and young Murray's was perceptibly green. Then someone tapped me on the shoulder and I saw it was Bold. He jerked his head and drew me on one side to where Corker was standing.

'We lost Corporal Oakley,' he said.

'Yes, I know,' I told him. 'I saw it. How is he?'

'He'll live. But he won't be playing cricket again.'

I said nothing and he looked me up and down, his eyes steely in his white, hard face.

'We've made Mason up,' he said. 'We'll need another lance-corporal now, though. I'm going to put you up.'

'Not me,' I said. 'I don't want stripes.'

Bold's brows came down and his eyes glittered. 'Why not?' he said.

'I'd rather stay with the boys.'

'You'll be with the boys, won't you? What do you think one stripe makes you? A general?'

'Give it to Murray,' I said. 'He'd love a stripe.'

'He's too young.'

'Well, Henny Cuthbert then. He's keen.'

'Cuthbert's not been in the line yet.'

'There are plenty of others.'

Bold stared at me a little longer, without speaking, then he glanced at Corker. Finally he gave me a little shove. 'Git on with your work,' he growled. 'I'll be talking to you later. There's plenty of time.'

We lived like pigs and soon began to stink like pigs. The smell I'd caught as we'd entered the trenches was around us all the time. It was compounded of turned earth, mud, latrines, the unburied or half-buried corpses beyond the parapets, rotting sandbags, stale human sweat, cordite and lyddite, with occasionally the burnt-grease smell of fried bacon or cigarette smoke to sweeten it.

We lived on bully-beef and biscuits, and Tickler's plum-and-apple jam and strong tea sickly with sugar and condensed milk, that was boiled on Tommy-cookers or issue charcoal. We played cards and slept on sandbags and ran short of tobacco so that we shared cigarettes, passing them round and allowing ourselves one suck each.

With the lack of sleep and the everlasting labour, I found myself dropping off at all sorts of odd times, and one morning I came abruptly back to life to see a big rat sitting on its haunches just in front of me, staring at me as it brushed its whiskers and pink-tipped nose with its fore-paws. As I leapt to my feet, it squealed and shot up the trench wall and out of sight over the sandbags.

Locky pushed his head out of the dugout as I yelled.

'It pinched my bacon,' I said. 'I was asleep!'

We learned to accept, if not to enjoy, the earthy dens we lived in, and the precarious candlelight with its wobbling shadows, and the dank musty air, and the lumps of chalky soil that fell from the ceiling into your food. Always, awake or asleep, you were aware of trench noises about you, the scrape and clatter of working parties and the squeak of rats, the rattle of dixies, the sound of bacon frying in the adjoining kennel and thin trembling mouth organ music coming from somewhere farther down the muddy alley.

I learned to disregard whatever noise didn't immediately concern me. The howitzer shells that sounded like express trains rushing through the air didn't concern us at all – they were heading for the rear areas – but I kept my eyes and ears well open for the local stuff – the whizzbangs which exploded again and again like a jumping cracker, and the grotesquely somersaulting *minenwerfer* bombs.

At night, we scrambled along the communication trench in parties, to bring up supplies from where they'd been hastily dumped for us in the mine-crater or from the corner of the wood where the transport mules snuffled the ground for the rapidly disappearing grass. During the day, we tried none too successfully to wash, old Corker always at our heels, chivvying us to shave. All his scrimshanking seemed to be behind him now, and his loyal old heart was squarely fixed on doing his job. There were no rations here to flog, no new recruits to swindle, and it was almost as though he were showing us what a soldier should be – crafty and cunning at home, one eye always on the main chance, using the vastness of the Army to put aside a little private loot for himself; but never, never letting the side down when we'd been reduced to the elementary necessities of active service.

'A clean soldier's a good soldier.' His harsh voice nagged us awake as we sprawled dead-beat on the firestep, trying to catch the warming sunshine. 'Come on, git on yer feet. Git yerself shaved, you lot. A good soldier can always save a drop of tea to scrape his chin with. Git yerself spruced up. And git them buttons rubbed.'

Like Bold, he was always unbelievably clean himself, his big moustaches well spiked, his bottle-nose glowing, the worst of the mud always scraped from his clothes.

I seemed to fill sandbags incessantly, learning to keep my head down instinctively at the places where the parapet was low, and not to hang around the machine gun emplacements where the mortars had a habit of dropping.

'There's one thing,' Eph said cheerfully round the corner of the firebay. 'It's a tidy way to fight a war. It keeps all the flippin' mess in one place, 'stead of strewing it all over the shop. Us on this side. The Germans on that.'

One night the Worcesters took half a dozen of us out on a raid against the German trenches. Our job was to stay in No Man's Land and cover them as they came back, and I learned the meaning of girding up my loins that night. A man's loins can get damned loose when he's scared.

'Look out for the poppies and the weeds,' they advised us. 'They grow tallest round the edges of the shell-holes and if anything happens make a dive for them. And keep that damned equipment from clinking. They'll hear it in Berlin.'

We crawled forward on our stomachs, our clothes hissing through the long damp grass, and lay sprawled in a little hollow, crouching in the cold for what seemed hours listening to the rasping cough of a German sentry just ahead of us in the darkness. Then I heard the soft thud of a heavy mallet wrapped in sacking thumping down on iron stakes, and the chink of wire.

'We're in luck,' one of the Worcesters whispered. 'They've got a wiring party out. Once the shells come down, we ought to pick up one or two.'

We waited for what seemed hours, listening to the occasional bullet whimpering by, then at last the expected shells arrived and the bombs went off and the machine guns opened up with shattering bowel-withering suddenness and all hell seemed to be let loose.

'Christ,' Mason said, hugging the earth alongside me. 'This isn't what I joined up for.'

The Worcesters got their prisoner, a scared boy with a lacerated head, and we had to dive for a shell-hole and crouch there until the hellish racket died down before we could make a final sprint for our own lines.

I almost fell into the trench and sat there panting, my head hanging, my mouth open, the breath sobbing in my throat, soaked with sweat and exhausted mentally and physically.

'Oh God! Oh Jesus Christ!' Mason was muttering aloud, abandoning himself to the first moment of panic and sheer terror now that we were safe and nerves and muscles didn't have to be kept in check any longer.

The next night, as we were preparing to leave, the Germans retaliated with an evening strafe that made my hair stand on end.

'God help the poor devils coming in,' Locky said, crouching flat against the quivering wall of the trench, his head down between his shoulders, his eyes blinking with every bang and every trickle of dust that rolled down on top of him.

A couple of mortar bombs fell in the trench away on the right and Tom Creak, in his stiff dignified foreman's way, passed the word along that we'd lost a sergeant.

'Who was it?' Locky asked.

'Don't know yet. One of t'Worcesters told me. He didn't catch t'name.'

Later on a group of stretcher-bearers went past, and I recognised pale features that belonged to a boy in A Company who'd got a splinter in the knee. The familiar faces were starting to disappear already. War seemed less a period of wild excitement than a series of small vicious shocks on the nervous system. Every time someone was hit you suffered another personal brutal blow.

I gave the boy on the stretcher a cigarette and he drew on it gratefully.

'Who else did it get?' I asked.

'Dunno. Didn't see. God, it hurts!'

'Poor, poor lad,' Tom Creak said as he was carried away.

Then Ashton and the colonel came along, followed by Bold, who called me towards them.

Pine looked tired and strained, the black eye-patch like a mark of mourning on his pale face. The wind was keening down the trench and a piece of ground sheet covering a hole under the parapet was flapping from time to time in a harassing noisy way. I saw Locky and Eph and Tom Creak staring.

'Sergeant-Major Bold says you've refused to – to take a stripe,' the colonel said brusquely, trying to quell his stammer.

I was startled and glanced at Bold, but his face was sharp and expressionless. He looked cold and bitter and hard as nails. There was a lot of blood on his sleeve and trousers, I noticed.

'Well, yes, sir,' I said. 'I suppose I did.'

Pine snorted. 'Well, you're a – fool,' he commented. 'I've b-been watching you on and off all week. You're the coolest b-beggar we've had in the line.'

'I don't feel it,' I said.

Pine frowned. 'Well, whether you like it or not,' he said, 'as of now, you're a lance-corporal.' He took an indelible pencil from his pocket and nodded to Bold, who took hold of my sleeve and spat on it. He rubbed the spittle into a damp patch with his finger and the colonel scrawled a big V on it.

He stared at me for a moment as Bold let go my arm, then without a word he turned round and marched off, poking men aside with his ash-plant as he made way for himself. I stood for a moment, squinting down at the thin blue stripe scrawled on my arm. Bold hadn't moved. He seemed to be waiting for me to make some comment.

'Sar'-Major,' I said. 'I don't want a stripe . . .'

He seemed angry and ready for trouble, as though he'd been hoping I'd object and welcomed the opportunity to snarl at me.

'Well, you've got one,' he snapped. 'The colonel's noticed you more than once. That's why Ashton told me to ask you the other day.'

'Who suggested *me*?' I asked.

'I did.'

'*You* did?'

'Yes.' He stared at me hostilely. 'Why not?'

'But I don't want a stripe!'

Bold turned and faced me, staring down at me. 'We've only been in the line nine bloody nights,' he snapped, 'and we've lost nine men, two of 'em NCOs. Oakley went first go off, didn't he, and now we've lost Sergeant Corker.'

He saw me staring and his face flushed angrily.

'Yes,' he snarled. 'Corker. An hour ago. Over there. The poor old bastard bled to death in my arms.'

He turned on his heel, as if he were on a parade ground, and marched away, still angry. The thought that old Corker was dead had taken away all the arguments I'd begun to think up. If Corker, with his South African medals and his boozy merriment, his vast experience of war and his apparent indestructibility, could be killed, what might happen to the rest of us? Henry Oakley came sneaking back again into the recesses of my mind and I suddenly felt very frail and incapable.

I caught myself looking at Locky, who seemed as full of grief and pity as I felt myself, his thin face pinched and cold-looking.

Then Eph managed a lopsided grin at me, his thick red cheeks shining as he showed his teeth. 'It's no good, Fen, old cock,' he said. 'They've caught up with you at last.'

4

We took old Corker's body with us when we marched out.

Catchpole and Murray were on the rear end of the stretcher, and Murray kept glancing down at the still figure wrapped in the ground sheet, the muddy hobnailed boots sticking out at the other end. He suddenly seemed to have left his boyhood behind him and all the eagerness had left his face. Even the rosiness had been replaced in his cheeks by the grey-whiteness of weariness.

They put the stretcher down in the little cemetery near the end of the communication trench. There was a soldier working there now, with a little pile of roughly made wooden crosses, hurriedly painted in thin white paint. On them names were pencilled and on one or two, I noticed, it said simply *An unknown British soldier*. No more. Just that, and the mouldering caps of the dead hanging on top.

Murray straightened up, staring down at the bundle on the stretcher. Corker looked so still under his blanket, I thought, so dead. He seemed like a reproach to the rest of us that we were untouched and healthy, a reminder to us of just how small and inexperienced we were in the vast sad ramifications of war.

Murray seemed to be thinking along the same lines. 'He seemed to know his way about so well,' he pointed out wearily, as though he were saying Corker's epitaph.

Eph looked up at him, lifting his head with a heavy movement. 'Poor old sod,' he said.

'Makes you think, doesn't it?' Murray went on thoughtfully, staring unseeingly in front of him. 'With all his experience, he still copped it. It makes you wonder if all that training we had was worthwhile. It's only a matter of luck, after all, isn't it?'

The sorrow about me was sharp and bitter, as though they were half ashamed to be showing their feelings.

There were two or three stretcher-bearers waiting under the trees, with half a dozen more stretchers with silent loads, and, after a while, a red-faced padre came up on a green army bicycle. He intoned a hurried service while we stood with our caps off for a minute or two, then he acknowledged Pine's salute and rode off again.

'They don't waste time putting you away, do they?' Mason said bitterly. His face looked pinched and irritable, as though he were having difficulty reconciling his beliefs and his ardour with what was reality.

Nobody mentioned Corker by name again. We were all suddenly concerned with scraping the mud off our clothes with knives, forks and entrenching tools, pretending everything was normal and that we'd never known the warm-hearted boozy old soldier with the red nose and quiff whom we'd just pushed down into the damp earth.

Bold, who was standing by the grave, signed to us to get into line. Tom Creak was the last to move and he hesitated for a second, gazing back at the little mound of newly turned earth, his square, unhandsome features sombre.

'I'm proper grieved,' he said simply.

Bold was still staring down at the grave, his bony face expressionless, the ginger moustache like a wound on his white skin. Then he seemed to snap into life and started shouting at us as though nothing had happened, as though Corker had never existed, and grief and sorrow were alien things we knew nothing about.

'All right, all right,' he said. 'Git into line, do! We ain't got all day. Don't you want your grub? Don't you want your sleep? Jump about a bit!'

We stood waiting, leg-weary, eyes closing with fatigue, while Pine's horse was brought up and he adjusted the stirrup leathers, then we shuffled across the field where we'd seen the Jack Johnson explode. The scar was still there, livid in the green turf alongside the worn, muddy path, the grass round its edges burned, the soil charred and pulverised.

We scrambled across the ditch, struggling under equipment which suddenly seemed to have grown heavier, boots clattering sharply as we climbed on to the pavé road.

There were no buses for the return journey. It was as though they'd introduced us to warfare the easy way and had decided we were now capable of managing without help. We had to march the whole ten miles back to Rippy, tramping into the drizzling rain down the wet road, furious and frustrated in our weariness at the delays caused by traffic jams, snarling at the man in front every time he stopped suddenly because the man in front of him had stopped suddenly too.

There was a lack of life about us now. Boots shuffled instead of ringing on the road, and knees and arms were slack, and there was a lot of hitching up of packs.

Only Sergeant-Major Bold walked with any erectness, in a sort of untiring lope under his equipment, and I realised that in all the time I'd known him I'd never seen him looking anything but tough, humourless, harsh and efficient, and I thought bitterly that he probably wasn't human.

As we tramped round a corner by a high brick wall, where rusty dried grass grew along the top, we bumped into a staff cavalcade – spotless-looking men on sleek horses, surrounding a car in which a general was sitting. As we passed, the general glanced round at us and jerked his hand, and one of the mounted officers whirled his horse abruptly and clattered across to Pine.

He said something sharply and Pine reined in, lifting his arm, and we halted. The staff officer was still speaking, his horse curvetting skittishly about so that the front rank had to jump clear of the flashing heels, then Pine dismounted slowly and walked across to the car.

We shuffled and fidgeted under our loads, feeling like old soldiers who'd been singled out for praise, but then I saw Pine's face was white with anger, the black eye-patch stark against his cheek. He was clearly being ticked off, and I sensed a feeling of hatred for the smooth, clean-looking unscarred staff officer flickering like lightning among the ranks behind me.

Pine was one of us. He came from the same city. He was popular. We knew he was brave and he never neglected us. He was a remote individual because of his rank, but our feelings towards him had never been without warmth, and even his stammer was regarded with affection.

'Don't know as I like that bastard there, got up to look like Vesta Tilley,' Eph growled, jerking his head at the staff officer who'd spoken to Pine.

'Can't say I'm sweet on him myself, bud,' MacKinley muttered. 'He looks a bit of an oily beggar, if you ask me.'

Pine was stepping back now, quivering with the earnestness of his salute. As he crossed the muddy road towards us again, the general nodded at the men on the horses, ignoring Pine, and the staff car roared away. The horsemen sat a moment longer, talking, then they too cantered off.

'Bastards,' Eph said, by way of farewell.

Pine halted in front of us. He was frowning, his single eye glittering in the tired hollow of his left cheek. He put one hand behind his back and with the other began to fiddle with one of his buttons as he always did when he had to address us.

272

'I've just b-been told your marching's – bad,' he said. 'Damn' bad. Well, if it is, it's – got to improve. From now. Let's see it does.'

He turned away to his horse, his eyes hot and angry, and Bold stalked slowly down the column, staring bitterly at us, as though we'd let him down. Even as we straightened up we were shocked by the injustice of the reprimand, and I could see sullen expressions around me. We'd come to France to fight, and we'd fought as well as we knew how. We'd buried men who'd been our friends and here they were, with no word of praise, not even a little sympathy, only a complaint about our marching. It was hard to understand.

'Come on,' Bold was shouting. 'You heard what the colonel said. Get them shoulders back. Let's have you looking like soldiers, even if you ain't. Get your 'eads up.'

'They say they wear their red tabs all the way down to their undervests,' Mason muttered bitterly as he hitched up his pack. 'Even tattooed on their skin so their batmen have to salute them in their bloody baths.'

Somebody sniggered and Bold told him to shut his rattle.

'Like something hanging off his boot,' Eph was grumbling in his low boozy voice. 'Did you see him? Spoke to the Old Man as if he was a scruffy little lance-jack. They want chopping off by the stocking-tops, that lot. They do straight.'

I'd listened to this kind of talk in England and believed it of the dugouts we'd had to put up with there. Out here, I hadn't expected this sort of treatment. But the old stale jokes softened the blow a little and made me feel that these smart-looking men who'd obviously never been anywhere near the trenches weren't quite real.

Locky, of course, had the last word, quoting Shakespeare in a dry precise manner that brought Eph's head up with a jerk, as it always did.

'"I remember when the fight was done,"' he said, '"when I was dry with rage and extreme toil, breathless and faint, leaning on my sword, came there a certain lord, neat and trimly dressed, fresh as a bridegroom.'"

Eph began to stare.

'"And as the soldiers bore dead bodies by, he called them untaught knaves, unmannerly, to bring a slovenly unhandsome corse betwixt the wind and his nobility."'

Eph grinned. 'What's that?' he asked.

'Sergeant Shakespeare,' Locky said. 'Hotspur. Me. You. Fen. Murray. The immortal soldier's grouse against the staff.'

We had a long way to go still, and as we neared Colinqueau Farm I was marching half-asleep, just awake enough to be aware of a vague feeling of relief and pleasure as I caught the fresh clean scent of crops and fields after the damp decay of the trenches.

As we turned into the lane that led to the farm, I saw the rest of the battalion waiting up ahead by the gate and round the corner of the field, complete with the band drawn up in a tight half-circle to welcome us in, faces smiling and eager.

Pine pulled his horse to the side of the lane and spoke to Ashton. 'For God's sake,' he said, 'let's march in like soldiers. Get 'em singing or something.'

Ashton started to whistle 'Tipperary', and when he'd been through it once there were half a dozen men singing it with him.

'Come on, you sloppy shower of old women,' Bold roared, halting at the side of the lane, ramrod-straight in the tall grass as we tramped past him. 'Get them 'eads up. Get them feet down all at once, do. Ep! Ri! Ep! Ri! It ain't the staff you're pleasing now. It's your own pals. What'll they think of their future if you come back looking like something the cat dragged in? Let's have a song.'

Tommy Mandy pulled out a mouth organ and in a few moments we were all at it, and we swung up the lane, slamming our feet down as though we didn't know the meaning of weariness.

It was a relief to shrug free of the dragging weight of my pack. Mason had flung down his equipment and was sitting on the ground in a corner of the barn, unwinding his puttees. For a second he stopped, staring in front of him, then he rubbed his hand across his face, as though he were trying to brush away a stain.

'What's up, Frank?' I asked.

He looked up, his expression strained and reproachful. 'Did *you* expect it to be like that up there?' he said abruptly in a quiet voice.

'No,' I admitted. 'Not really. I don't think I did. But it's no good brooding, Frank.'

'No, of course not.' He shook his head. 'I think a bit of me died,' he went on in a wondering voice. 'I'm sure I'll crack and go yellow, if it's all like that.'

He was still like that, dazed and bewildered, when Barraclough and Henny Cuthbert and Spring appeared, admiring and demanding to know all about it. I began to feel a bit like one of the Light Brigade back from Balaclava, and put on a bit of a swagger as I unfastened my tunic, wearing my mudstains like medals.

Then Henny mentioned old Corker and at once all the shocks I'd tried to put out of sight behind me, hurriedly stuffing them away like nightmares I didn't want to remember, came hurrying back.

'They say he's gone west,' Henny said, his long features anxious, the breeze ruffling his thin colourless hair, and it came back to me how scared I'd been and how I'd clutched at the earth with my fingers, trying to drag myself away from the noise and beyond the range of those flying pieces of steel. Death had none of the glory Murray associated with it. It was noisy, impersonal, degrading and dirty.

Henny was watching me, his eyes on my face, a little worried, eager to learn.

'Is it true?' he asked. 'About Corker, I mean.'

275

'Yes,' I said. 'It's true.'

'Poor old Corker. What happened?'

'He got hit.'

'Yes, I know, but how? They said Oakley was wounded the first day in. Where? In the arm?'

'No,' I said, remembering that gibbering blinded figure that had bounced past me. 'Not in the arm.'

'Well, come on, then, tell us all about it. You're damn' quiet, you lot.'

I pushed him away.

'I'm tired,' I said. 'That's all.'

'Oh!' Henny looked startled, his narrow face concerned and apologetic. 'Sorry. I never thought. I'll see if I can get some tea for you.'

He turned aside and began to bustle off towards the cookhouse, then he stopped and, glancing back towards me, spoke across the heads of several, sprawling weary men. 'What was it *really* like?' he asked.

I'd sat down and started to unwind my puttees, and I looked up at him. Mason was sitting sipping a mug of tea someone had given him and Henny was watching him, his face anxious and worried. I managed a reassuring grin.

'Grub's none too good,' I said. 'Otherwise pretty cushy.'

We spent the whole of one blissful day with nothing to do but scrape mud off our clothes, and while I slept Henny took away my tunic and overcoat and brought them back clean, his long face beaming.

'Thought you'd be pleased,' he said. 'There's an inspection tomorrow.'

'What sort of inspection?'

'I don't know. Some general from Querrieu. They've all gone batchy in the orderly room getting things straight. It's enough to make you feel poorly.'

I was still brooding over that stripe on my arm. I didn't want

276

the damn' thing. There was a rumour floating about that NCOs could be detached to fresh battalions to give them the benefit of experience, and I wanted to stay with my friends. I hadn't been particularly troubled about joining up with them in 1914, but now, after two years, I just couldn't imagine life without them. If I'd got to put up with a lot more of what I'd just been through, I thought, I wanted to do it with men I knew and was used to, not with a lot of strangers.

In the evening, after we'd slept and shaved, I went across to Bold's billet, which was in a little outhouse behind the farm, a drab little place smelling of age and decay.

He looked up and smiled, and I was startled to see how much it changed that rock-hard special face he always wore for us, warming it and bringing life to eyes I'd always thought could only be cold and angry. Suddenly, I realised he was a man like myself, not a great deal older even, a human being with emotions and anxieties like the rest of us, for all that aura of experience and aloofness he wrapped around himself.

'What's up, Fen?' he said, and I was surprised at the friendliness of his tone. Before I could reply, he reached over to a boxwood table for a dixie full of rum and sloshed some of it into a chipped tin mug and offered it to me. 'Sit down,' he said, pushing a box forward. 'Try the stalls.'

Suddenly, I found there was no gulf between us. There never had been with Ashton and Welch and Corker, because we seemed to have known them all our lives, but with Bold it was different. He'd been a stranger, a Londoner, and he had about him that inescapable glow of authority, the stamp of service in the Household Brigade, that made us all feel like amateurs and kept us all at a distance.

'Pity about Corker,' he said unexpectedly. 'I got on all right with Corker. A chap gets fond of another chap. Women clutter the place up. Fussy as five folk, they are. You got a girl, Fenner?'

I told him I hadn't.

'Why not?' he asked.

'I was never much good with girls.'

'Funny that,' he said thoughtfully. 'Neither was I. You got to be a bit soft, I often think, to have a way with women. P'r'aps that's why I never married. I was always shy as hell with 'em. That's why I stayed in the Army and did my time. Some bloke married a girl I was keen on because I couldn't manage to ask her meself. I'm still a bit that way, I reckon.'

I was a little surprised, but not entirely. There had to be some explanation for Bold's spartan way of life, uncluttered as it was with unnecessary comforts or emotions, as ascetic as a cleric's.

Then I realised with a start he'd been drinking, and when he asked again what I wanted I found myself hesitating before I told him of the stripe I didn't want.

He listened carefully to me while I spoke, his face expressionless, but when I'd finished he slammed down his mug, slopping rum to the table, and stared up at me angrily, all the friendliness gone from his face again at once.

'My Christ,' he said. 'You've a nerve! I was bloody *glad* to get my first stripe, I can tell you.' He stood up unsteadily, knocking over the table with the mug on it, but he didn't seem to notice it. His rage startled me.

'That's the worst of you Kitchener blokes,' he went on, his bony face jammed up close to mine. 'The way you stay such bloody amateurs is enough to drive a man absolutely fanti. You're a good lot. I've enjoyed showing you how to go on because you've learned fast. You've got a hell of a lot more guts and savvy than most. But you don't *need* promotion. That's the trouble – you're all getting your wages made up. You want to *play* at being soldiers all the time. You want to stay with your pals, just as if you was still at a tennis party or the YMCA or a girls' high school. You want to fight the Germans fairly. No kicking. No gouging. No going behind their backs. No fouls and no offside. A great big beautiful game of cricket. Well played, chaps! Jolly good show! Scrag the Hun, fellows, and hurrah for General 'Aig.'

He stared at me, breathing heavily, then he raised his arm and pointed. 'There's a bloody battery of guns down the lane there,' he went on. 'Another amateur lot. All Kitchener men. All clever book-reading sods like you lot. I 'ad a drink with 'em just before we went up the line, and do you know what they were boasting about? That they could see the Fritz postman in their forward position and could make him drop his letters. Not kill him. Not get rid of one more Fritz who might one day knock me off or you off, or who at the very least brought a little comfort to the bastards who *are* trying to knock us off. Not that. Christ, not that! Oh, no! They only want to make him drop his letters. That's all. Just a bit o' fun. Up the old school and down with war. God, what a bloody army!'

I didn't know what to say against the outburst. For a moment he stared at me, his eyes blazing, his face whiter and bonier than ever, his ginger moustache bristling along his cheeks, then he picked up the mug, sloshed some rum in it from the dixie, took a swig from it and put it down again.

'You want to remember, Mr Lance-Corporal Bloody-Reporter Fenner, that this is war,' he snapped. 'We kick and gouge and scratch and bite, and go for their ghoulies. And if we can get a bloke from behind before he sees us, then we have a go at it. In wartime people sometimes get killed and sometimes we've *got* to leave our pals. In South Africa, I once lost the whole of my section. 'Alf an hour, first to last. That's all it took, and when it was over I was the only one on me feet. Thank God I didn't stay with *my* pals. They're in 'eaven. What's the matter?' he demanded. 'Didn't the war come up to expectations?'

'I'm not grumbling, Sergeant-Major,' I said.

'I should think not, not *you* of all people. Not *you*, Fenner. Come on, I'll take you to the captain.'

Having endured his outburst, I wasn't sure that I wanted to object any more, but Bold wasn't listening to me now and there was no choice except to follow him.

He marched me in to Ashton, still white with rage, and

Ashton put on his agonised expression and polished his pince-nez and said uneasily that it was Pine's responsibility since he'd given me the stripe. He looked at Bold as though uncertain what to do and wanting to put it off till later, but Bold said bitterly that he thought the colonel ought to be able to sort it out and, in the end, the two of them marched me to Pine's room in the farmhouse.

The colonel was shaving when we arrived, standing in his shirtsleeves and braces, his feet straddling his dog which was stretched out on a blanket in front of the fire, and he started to swear at me with the shaving-brush still in his hand and the lather still on his face, his eye-patch lying on the table, his right eye milky and staring and dead.

'You d-d-damned amateurs are all the – same,' he said, taking the same line that Bold had taken, spluttering and gagging as his fury made his stammer worse. 'You won't face your bub-blasted responsibilities. We want NCOs and you're gug-going to be one. In this battalion you don't – get asked what *you* like and what you don't like. Sergeant-Major, cuc-call me the – quartermaster. He's in the office outside.'

When Twining arrived in the doorway, Pine cocked his thumb at me. 'Take this NCO away,' he said bluntly, reaching for his razor. 'And g-give him two stripes. And see they're sewn in place in time for tomorrow's inspection. If they're not, Sergeant-Major, put him on a charge.'

I marched out, blushing, with Bold grinning all over his face.

'I told you I'd make a soldier of you one day,' he crowed, his good humour suddenly restored. 'If you ain't careful you'll end up on the staff the way you're progressing. Perhaps you'll get to meet the general tomorrow, in fact. I'll send you something across to celebrate with. I expect you could do with a drink after that lot.'

They drew us all up in the field for the inspection, all polished and looking like some other battalion straight out from England.

The general was the same man who'd stopped us outside Rippy, and he was followed by the same staff officers and a group of three assorted cavalrymen with pressed uniforms and polished bandoliers, who seemed to be there solely to hold the horses whenever they dismounted to look at something.

When we got a better look at him, I saw he was a small tired-looking man with a weak mouth, who seemed as though he were plagued by having too much to attend to at once. He was on the lookout for trouble, but Pine had had no intention of being caught again. The whole day had been spent cleaning up and borrowing all the usual eyewash we needed for inspections and didn't possess. The canteen and the cookhouse were spotless, with white-garbed cooks and a daily diet sheet ready to hand, and the latrines had fly-proof lids scrounged from a howitzer battery down the lane.

The general seemed to grow more relaxed as the inspection proceeded, and, in the end, even seemed delighted to have met us. In fact he made us a little speech to tell us so.

'The hypocritical old fart,' Eph muttered from the corner of his mouth. 'Smarmy as anything now, ain't he?'

There was a faint backhander for our marching, but he went on to say he expected big things from us. We were rather an unusual unit, he pointed out, formed from men of a high degree of intelligence and integrity.

'You've never been blooded in a real battle yet,' he concluded cheerfully. 'But I can promise you it won't be very long before you will be. And, when that time comes, you'll be given a position of rare trust because of what you are.'

'It's coming,' Murray said gleefully when he'd gone. 'You heard what he said. It's coming, and we're in it.'

Certainly the portents of the approaching struggle were clearly gathering about us. Guns of every size, queer deformed monsters with villainous squat barrels and great steel mountings, in many cases of a design we'd never seen before, rumbled through Rippy at night behind clattering caterpillar tractors and were hidden in the woods and hills before dawn. New roads were being made and old ones widened. Field-gun ammunition was being taken well forward and buried, and, last but not least, bayonet-fighting practice was ordered almost every other day.

More troops appeared, newer battalions, straight out from England and rawer even than we were, slogging up through the rain that came all the time in fits and starts, dun-coloured columns sweating under their packs and glistening capes, but singing, always cheering and singing, strong, clean, cheerful men led by bright-faced young officers who still regarded the war as a bit of a lark.

Behind the trudging columns the heavy transport horses plodded through the puddles, straining at their loads in the sludgy patches, dragging GS waggons or field kitchens that were stewing their noisome mixtures of bully-beef as they rattled over the pavé, their drivers munching, smoking, grinning, yelling jibes at us as we watched them pass, staring wide-eyed, just as we had when we'd first arrived, at the little groups of German prisoners who trickled past us towards the rear.

We mended roads, jamming the holes that had been worn in the surface with broken bricks collected from the ruined cottages and farmhouses around and rolling them flat with steamrollers that came up from Amiens. We went south by lorry to where we could see the dark mass of Thiepval Wood up on a spur above us and laid part of a narrow-gauge railway track and dug ditches for telephone wire. We unloaded shells and passed them hand-over-hand through a long chain of men, to stack them in a field under tarpaulins.

'From up north,' we were told. 'They're bringing everything south for the Push.'

'Well, I hope they do some good,' I said, one eye on the rust on them. 'They look to me as though they're useless.'

'They are.' The lorry driver grinned. 'When an artillery commander's told to send twenty per cent of his ammunition somewhere else, you don't suppose he's going to send the good stuff, do you? Not likely, mate. He'll send the old stuff that might be dud and keep the good stuff for himself. You don't win medals trying to break down defences with duds.'

We erected huts for new troops, remaining ourselves in our pest-ridden barns, adjured always not to let the lice get on top of us.

'Get on top?' Eph complained. 'The sheer weight of 'em's bringing me to me knees. I don't know whether it's best to kill the old 'uns first, so you can catch the young 'uns when they come to the funeral, or go for the young 'uns first so the old 'uns die of grief.'

It might have been easier if we hadn't had so far to march for a bath. Everywhere we went seemed such a long way. We trudged for hours to find a stretch of canal for a bathe, or some half-ruined brewery where they'd rigged up a shower with a few old tubs and a drilled pipe that trickled water which always seemed to disappear finally and completely just as you'd soaped yourself all over. Even the fresh underclothing they gave us wasn't always free from lice – they naturally kept the best for themselves – and by the time we'd marched back again we were as sweaty and dirty as before.

We had to walk miles for drinking water. The nearest tap was a mere dribble, and there was always a queue of sixty or seventy men waiting. I heard they'd brought out pumps of all sorts from home to help – even fire pumps, it was said – but we never saw them near Rippy.

Once, well behind the line, we saw Haig pass by in a cavalcade of staff, lancers and Guards, a remote impersonal figure surrounded by other remote impersonal figures in pressed uniforms and boned riding-boots; inhuman unemotional creatures on magnificent horses surrounded by fluttering pennants.

They swept past us in a glittering procession that drew cheers from the labouring men by the roadside.

'That's the way to fight,' Locky commented when the cheering had died away and we were all staring down the road at the retreating cloud of dust, all feeling we'd at last seen some glimmering of the glory of battle. 'All the panoply of war.'

I was sent to a machine gun school where every kind of regiment was represented, and Catchpole disappeared to a bombing school. Ashton held lectures in our barn and tried none too successfully to pass on the information he'd picked up at similar lectures for company commanders the day before, or from the numerous pamphlets which made their appearance for the instruction of the uninitiated. Young Welch went off on some obscure course on battle behaviour at Étaples, and Milton, whose father was a director of the rolling-mills on Cotterside Common, disappeared to master the art of the Stokes mortar.

Still we dug, jeering at the newcomers who complained about the menial task and their aching muscles.

Nobody seemed to make much effort to conceal what was going on, beyond a few screens which were put up to hide the main roads that were regularly strafed by shell-fire. A new unit sprang up two fields away from Colinqueau Farm, making camouflage for the guns, huge nets hung with strips of rag and painted a dull brown and green, but their output didn't seem to be very great, and all the dumps and the hurrying troops and the great masses of machinery remained in full view of the Germans as they sat in their newly constructed redoubts on the heights to the east, watching us from their balloons and sending their aircraft over us every day to report.

As the rain stopped at last, and the better weather arrived, the roads grew choked with men. Over everything now there was a pall of dust, hiding the apparent confusion below. Guns and transport and the inevitable cavalry were everywhere, taking up every inch of grass and roadway. Vast troops of mules, staring-eyed and dirty, jostled and pushed and clattered along the Amiens road, led by turbaned Indians. Ammunition lorries averaged only a few miles an hour through the masses of animals, limbers, field kitchens, guns and ambulances.

More and more men moved up, all of them untried and eager, and Murray liked to get them on one side in the estaminets where you could buy '*bière anglaise*', vin rouge, vin blanc or grenadine; still a boy, eager, friendly, stubborn, anxious to be accepted, airing what little French he'd picked up, making a great deal of his nine nights in the line, passing on all the tips we'd been given, slightly condescending, slightly superior, pitying the newcomers for their inexperience as he'd once been pitied himself.

Inevitably, he picked on the wrong ones once in a while, and once in Rippy the jeers from a set of veterans from the Hamel area, who'd seen it all a dozen times before, brought him to his feet, tears in his eyes, so that before we knew what had happened the street was wild with scuffling men and we had to drag him away before the military police came to clear it up.

Great masses of navvies appeared in uniform, and we discovered to our disgust that these men who lived like fighting cocks and went nowhere near the front line got a princely wage in comparison with our bob a day.

We suffered under a spate of orders from divisional headquarters, one of which told us that discipline was falling off and instructed us always to address officers as 'sir'. Saluting was insisted on, and Ashton got all the NCOs on one side and informed us that we must make men stand properly to attention.

'If you think I'm going to stand to attention every time *you* open your mouth,' Murray told me without hesitation, 'you're bloody well mistaken. Some fat-bottomed little swine from Eton thought that one out. I expect he doesn't realise that if you stand to attention in some places you're in danger of getting your bloody head blown off.'

He had completely recovered his spirits now and was inclined to be boastful. He was always the most vociferous when a fat staff car rolled past us on its wired wheels, with some immaculate officer in the back berating us for slack march discipline.

He had a sharp angry old soldier's outlook on war that never dulled his ardour and his exaltation.

We went into the line again a fortnight later, this time as a battalion, absorbed once more into the huge impersonal pattern of the war, taking over a sector on the right of the Worcesters.

We'd been happy out of the line and we weren't overeager to go back. We'd had a chance to play football and a concert party had visited us, and mail had arrived regularly from home, tipped out on the grass by the post corporal who called out names and skated the letters over the heads of the straining crowd. Occasionally, I'd seen Helen's writing on letters addressed to Locky or Frank Mason, but there'd never been anything for me beyond a note from Mrs Julius to tell me she'd got married again, and would I please remove my belongings from her attic at Morrelly Street as soon as possible?

Going in a second time wasn't so difficult. It was as though I'd got myself attuned to things now and was ready for any shocks that might come along. I felt more resilient and not afraid of doing things wrong.

We took over from a battalion which didn't seem to have done much work and had left food lying about everywhere. The trenches were wide and tumbledown and far too shallow in places, with insufficient traverses which they'd done nothing to improve.

'What a bloody no-bon crowd,' Murray complained in his laconic old soldier's manner.

That they'd been regarded with the same sort of contempt by the Germans was also clear. The first night, even before we were safely established, the men opposite began to shout catcalls in English from their trenches.

'We'll wake you up,' we heard clearly in the semi-darkness. 'Just wait! What lot are you?'

'Th' Oirish Guards,' Billy Mandy shouted back in his strong Irish voice, and there was an immediate awed silence.

The trenches had been built originally by the French, who'd quitted them finally not long before. They were cut in the chalk soil in the valley near Hannay, and the first of the summer flowers were growing along the parapet. The dugouts were deeper than those we'd used before but they were lousier and there seemed to be thousands of rats about. They were like little pink monkeys and they were short of water like the rest of us. You met them in search of puddles as you went along the trench, and they were so big and desperate they wouldn't turn back, and ran up the side of the trench, squeaking crazily, and passed you head-high. Pine immediately made it a crime to leave bully-beef tins about and I found myself beginning to take a curious pride in the orderliness of my own particular strip of ditch.

They got us digging immediately, pushing out saps and new listening posts with the aid of the Engineers, building up the parapet, widening the communication trenches against the day when they'd have to feed thousands of men and munitions into the offensive, constructing new firing-bays and fresh traverses, and refuse tips and latrines. Unfortunately, the French had left indications of their indifference about in the corpses that were buried too near the surface, and we were constantly coming on dark patches of earth where we dug out blankets full of decaying tatters of blackened cloth, shin-bones still wrapped in puttees, and skulls still inside torn kepis.

We were all a little nervous at being on our own and, in our eagerness to put up a good performance, were inclined to be jumpy and over-eager. Every night there were reports from sentries of advancing parties of raiders which didn't exist, and hastily telephoned messages from Ashton's dugout asking bored artillerymen to shell what were nothing more than clumps of trees we hadn't taken proper note of in daylight.

Wiring parties went out as soon as it was dark, because the entanglement had been allowed to grow dilapidated by our predecessors, and groups of swearing men coiled wire round wooden posts, steel posts, spiral pickets and knife-rests until their clothes were torn and their hands were bleeding and the entanglement looked like a spider's web. With them went other men to cut the fast-growing summer grass that obscured the view from the machine gun emplacements.

Once I crouched in front of them, armed with bombs and rifle, listening for German patrols and trying to keep my nerves steady against the taut thread of fear.

'They say it's best to get a wound this way,' Murray whispered with unnerving enthusiasm, as we hugged the cold earth. 'When the sector's quiet there's no rush on the dressing stations, and you can expect to be taken away quickly instead of being left about. Up at Loos, during the battle, they say they had to wait for days.'

'I wish you wouldn't be so bloody cheerful,' I told him, itching for the moment when we could drag ourselves back through the grass and the remains of the old dead, shamming death ourselves as the flares went up, listening to our own rapidly beating hearts and the squeak and shuffle of rats, and wishing all the time that the wiring party behind us would make a damned sight less noise.

I came back feeling reassured of my competence and ability, and even eagerly awaiting the first streaks of dawn, in the hope that we might catch the German patrols with the light behind them. They never seemed to learn and often stayed out too late. Somehow, the darkness had not seemed so dark this time and the cold earth not quite so cold. It had seemed easier to keep jumpy nerves in check and not to panic so quickly at tree-stumps and unexpected night noises.

It wasn't so easy for everybody, though. The following night someone lost his head and started shooting, so that the wiring party had to run for their lives, bent double and swearing as the machine guns started.

'It was that big noisy bastard, Mason,' MacKinley said

288

bitterly, fighting to get breath back into his body. 'He gets so goddamned edgy out there he could bite himself.'

Fortunately, it was a quiet week. Occasionally a sniper pulled his trigger, or there was a little excitement with a machine gun, but on the whole there was silence. We'd learned very early in our career from the Worcesters that if you prevented the enemy from drawing his rations he'd prevent you from drawing yours and then both sides would have to fight on empty stomachs. Casualties were light and, what there were, were inflicted blindly.

The atmosphere was one of deadly boring stalemate that consisted chiefly of digging and fatigue parties to bring up rations and water from the waggons in a gutted village a mile or so back; and stand-to at daybreak, when the waterproof sheets which protected the machine guns from the dew were whipped off and we stood straining our eyes in the thinning darkness, trying nervously to decide what was haze and what might be the beginning of a gas attack. About nine o'clock the Germans threw over their morning strafe, which began as shrapnel over the reserve trenches, then a search among the little copses for machine guns or batteries. After that there'd be a few Black Marias into the ruins of the village and then silence, and we were left alone in the stuffy daytime trenches with clouds of noisome flies which bred in the growing warmth of approaching midsummer on the filth beyond the parapets.

Fresh bread, brought up in sandbags, was a luxury, and we lived mostly on bully-beef and biscuits. Mostly it arrived on time, but we had to be careful how we cooked because the smoke from our fires attracted *minenwerfer* bombs.

Apart from digging, the offensive seemed no nearer. Occasionally, we were disturbed by a flurry of shells as the Germans thought they saw some threatening movement, or we were chased out to assist some gunner-major looking for a forward observation post or a signals officer seeking a good dug out for his signallers, and we hurried anxiously after them

289

through the stretches of trench where the mortar gunners liked to set up their weapons and fire a few salvoes before scuttling off, ahead of the invariable response of a five-nine. Beyond that, there was no hint of the attack in the forward trenches, and all we seemed to do was wait and watch and report everything that moved in front of us.

As Murray said, it wasn't what we'd joined up for.

'I wouldn't mind if we could only advance a bit,' he mourned. 'But sitting here like this, just digging and listening, and then digging and listening some more – it's enough to drive a man stone barmy.'

He was trying to write a letter to the girl next door, one of his normal enthusiastic epistles glorifying the war, and his sheet of grubby notepaper grew grubbier all the time from contact with his grimy fingers.

'If only we could have a go at them,' he said gloomily. 'A real go, I mean. Make a bit of noise, instead of all this crawling all over No Man's Land pretending we're dead.'

We were in one of the bigger dug outs, a gloomy foetid cavern of a place, stinking of stale cigarettes and unwashed bodies, and fitted with wire-netting beds. It was lit by candles and bits of four-by-two in tins of paraffin, and by what daylight filtered down the steps. On the walls were pictures from *La Vie*, old calendars, bits of broken mirror and festoons of equipment. Outside, Catchpole had hung a sign: FOR SALE OR TO RENT. OWNER DESIROUS OF LEAVING.

Mason and Barraclough were playing cards on a blanket. MacKinley and Tim Williams were asleep. We'd all acquired the habit of falling into a deep sleep in a moment. Sleep had become the most precious thing in the world, and we could drop off at any time and in any cramped position amid the ceaseless noise and in clothes and boots that hadn't been removed for days.

Spring was sprawling on a bed among the scattered equipment, trying to dry a wet sock over a candle. He was singing gloomily with Catchpole some music-hall dirge they'd picked up from one of the Manchester battalions:

> 'We're reet down in t'cellar 'ole,
> Where t'muck splarts on t'winders,
> We've burned all our co-al up,
> We're nah burnin' cinders.
> If t'bum bailiffs come along,
> They'll never find us . . .'

Eph was busy over his monthly epistle home to his wife. All the estaminets sold sentimental cards decorated with lace, which depicted women staring into fires showing soldiers' faces that looked remarkably French in spite of the British uniforms they wore, or soldiers staring into clouds containing women's faces, but Eph stuck rigidly to the official green issue which only had to be filled in and never taxed his ingenuity.

You could hear him all round the dugout. When Eph filled in his card it was always a communal occasion, because he liked to read his answers aloud, and his rasping voice had a curious piercing quality that penetrated even the warmest desire for privacy.

'I wish you'd shut up,' Murray growled.

'What's up, kid?' Eph asked. 'You sound proper hipped. Your girl got fed up with you? You ain't 'ad many letters lately.'

'How do you know?'

'I watch out for 'em. I like to see you young lads 'appy. I wonder if we oughta cut your ear off and send it to 'er as a reminder that you're still alive. Write "Faithful unto death" or summat in blood on the box.'

He sighed. 'Pity there ain't a pub round the corner,' he said. 'Writing letters always makes me thirsty.'

As he tossed aside his pencil, boots rattled on the board treads of the steps down from the trench. He looked up quickly and Spring's song stopped abruptly.

'Now what?'

Bold's voice came down to us, sharp, high and rasping with authority. 'Corporal Fenner down there? And Corporal Mason?'

'Here, Sergeant-Major!'

'Let's have you! To the captain's dugout, quick! The rest of you stand by. I'll be needing you.'

'Here comes trouble,' Mason said, throwing down his cards and reaching for his equipment. 'Wonder what it is this time.'

'The colonel's lost his terrier,' Catchpole suggested. 'And he wants a party sent out to find it.'

Eph turned and stared at Murray accusingly. 'It's your fault,' he said. 'Last time you complained about wanting to 'ave a go at 'em, we got sent in with the Worcesters. This time it looks like we're putting on a raid. You want to keep your flippin' mouth shut.'

Company headquarters was a dark hole like our own, shored up by pit-props and nine-by-two timbers, with room for several officers and a few stores. Four or five guttering candles in tin lids threw moving shadows on the walls, and the air was foul and smoky. Only a glimmer of daylight managed to pierce the gloom.

The colonel was there, fiddling with his button as usual. His dog was on the mud floor by the telephone, its muzzle in a bully-beef tin. The adjutant stood behind him, morosely spreading Gentleman's Relish on a biscuit and looking more like his twin than his normal brother.

Sergeant Bernard and one or two other N.C.O.s were there, crowding round the table, and Pine stared at us with his one good eye and jabbed his finger at a map spread among the mugs and bottles and candles and Nestlé's milk tins.

'It appears that our predecessors have been too – gentle with the Hun opposite,' he said. 'B-Brigade say we've got to make war. We've got to start being offensive.' He took a deep breath as though to control his stammer. 'The Push's due any

292

time,' he went on, 'and we've got to k-keep him on the hop. Got it?'

We got it.

Pine stared round at us for a moment, then he stooped over the map spread across the shabby table. His brother opened a tin of cigarettes and passed them round to us all, and Ashton gave us his matches. It was as though they were trying to put us all at ease, and I sensed the unpleasant part was still to come.

At last, when he seemed almost to have forgotten us, the colonel straightened up.

'They're expecting big things of this battalion,' he said, and his hand went to the button again. 'I'd like to see that we come up to expectation. Brigade have laid on the artillery right here.' He jabbed at the map. 'And we've got to go in and find out who's opposite. That means prisoners. Understood?'

He paused and stared round at us. We exchanged glances but said nothing.

'Mr Bub-Blackett's going to take command, because he's probably had more experience of this sort of thing than anyone else. He'll tell you what he's got in mind.'

He nodded to Blackett and stepped back into the shadows, whispering to Ashton, while Blackett leaned forward into the circle of light round the map, his green eyes glowing in his ugly face, and began to talk.

He planned to use chiefly bombs and coshes. He was going to split the raiding party into three. The first group – his own – was to go in with ladders, while Welch was to wait with a second group close up to the wire with bombs and rifles to cover them as they retired with their prisoners. Sergeant Bernard was to wait behind with another party on the lookout for German patrols.

Blackett paused as he finished, and stared round at us. 'One more thing,' he said, as though it were a postscript. 'If anything goes wrong, run like 'ell. We don't want heroics.'

We paraded at dusk. Pine was there to see us off, his brother just behind him as usual, looking like his reflection in a mirror, and the little white terrier skipping about his heels. The excitement that had started when the parties had been selected had subsided to a murmur, but there were a few wry jokes being bandied about.

'Let's pick a fat one,' Eph was saying. 'Then we can cook him for supper instead of that eternal bloody bully-beef.'

The Mandy brothers had picked themselves in and lined themselves alongside Tom Creak. They were being noisily aggressive, and Frank Mason slapped their backs and teased them for their Irish tempers. There was a hint of swagger about him that didn't ring true and a trembling eagerness about Murray. Locky stood a little to one side, pale and silent, his face taut and strained.

Tommy Mandy was testing his knobkerry on the trench wall. It looked like a mace and he'd made it himself with a short pole and a length of barbed wire. The solid thump as it hit the wooden props set my nerves on edge, and I was just going to turn on him and tell him to stop it when Henny Cuthbert did it for me, sharply, his voice full of irritation. He looked nervous and ill at ease, and half-drowned under his equipment.

Men stood about, watching us curiously as we rubbed burnt cork on our faces and tightened the broad canvas belts of bombs we wore. Then we gripped our 'cosher sticks', handling them nervously, and looked round for Blackett to give the word to go.

The evening was full of yellow light as the sun disappeared and darkness began. You could hear the usual noise of carts in the distance, coming up with the rations. Occasionally, there was a bang from one of our guns in the wood behind us, and once a trench-mortar bomb burst over on the right, dull white smoke floating over darkening grass that was spotted with moonpennies and buttercups and saffron weeds. Nobody was speaking much now and there was only the clink of weapons and the thump and shuffle of boots on the duckboards. In front of us we could see the German communication trenches, like faint seams on the hill with the last of the light on them, and a demolished church, touched along its ragged edge with bronze. It seemed too peaceful to go out there and risk your neck. Then a rifle popped somewhere and there was the crash of a five-nine that broke the spell.

'Who's for a Blighty one tonight, boys?' Murray asked with a flash of white teeth.

He spoke in undertones, but excitedly. Everyone's movements were swifter than normal, hiding confidence or lack of it.

Pine appeared at last out of Ashton's dug-out, followed by his brother and Blackett and Ashton and young Welch. They were comparing watches.

'All we want is prisoners,' Pine said again. 'Not casualties. You all know what to do?'

'Yes . . .' I heard Eph's voice from just behind, nervous and faintly unhappy. 'Up, one two, point, one two, six inches of cold Sheffield is enough for anybody . . .'

With willing hands under our behinds, we were pushed up to the parapet as soon as it was dark, and we crawled through the gap in the wire and lay down to wait for the rest to catch up, feeling the long grass against our faces and the chalky stones under our hands.

After a while, Henny's voice whispered nervously by my ear. 'Fen,' he said.

'What's wrong?'

'I think I've got a stiff here next to me. We couldn't move along a bit, could we?'

'For God's sake,' I said. 'Shut up. We'll be away in a moment.'

I could hear a muttered conversation going on just behind us, then Welch appeared and we started to crawl out over the grass.

My ears tingled as I strained for the sound of men talking or working. Once a cascade of Very lights went up, and I dropped flat in the long grass with the others, my eyes looking for the enemy, the smell of damp turned earth filling my nostrils.

There was a whispered consultation between Blackett and Welch, then the party split up into the three groups, Sergeant Bernard's staying behind and Blackett's and Welch's pushing on.

After a while Welch touched my elbow. 'We've got bags of time,' he said. 'We've got a good half-hour before the barrage starts.'

While he was still whispering into my ear, I heard a distant gun go off, and the first express-train sound of a shell approaching. It grew louder and louder, until it seemed to be heading straight for us, paralysingly direct, shrieking as though it were aimed for us and us alone.

Welch turned scared eyes to me and we all hugged the earth, digging at it with fingers and toes as though we could pull ourselves closer.

The shell burst on the German parapet right in front of us, and in the glare I caught a momentary glimpse of sandbags and clods of earth flying through the air.

Welch lifted his head and stared round, then we all ducked again as more shells began to drop.

'They've started too soon,' he shouted in a frightened voice. 'What the hell do we do now?'

In that first moment of panic, I was aware of a feeling of frustration and resentment, and a deep personal secret horror that things were going wrong, and the only thing I could suggest was that we should move up quickly in case Blackett's party went in after all.

We stumbled and wriggled forward as fast as we could go in the glare of the flashes, trying to get into position, tripping over obstacles and falling into holes. A machine gun started with a vicious suddenness on our left, piercing the din with a noise like tearing cloth.

In the hurry the party became scattered, and when we flopped down again there were only six of us, Murray and MacKinley and me, and Mason, Eph and Henny Cuthbert. Everybody else seemed to have disappeared.

'They're going to get us all killed,' Henny was muttering nervously, his eyes caged and desperate in the flare of the exploding shells. 'You see, they're going to get us all killed!'

'What'll we do, Fen?' Murray demanded in a cracked excited voice. 'There's only us. Do we hook it?'

For a moment, I was consumed with a wild desire to beat it as fast as I could, full of an angry resentment that some fool had thrown the whole raid into confusion.

'Well, come on,' Eph squeaked, his voice breaking in his agitation. 'What the hell do we do? Skedaddle?'

'Better hang on,' I said. 'Stand by. See what happens.'

'Welch's gone,' Henny wailed.

'For God's sake, what if he has? There's no need for us *all* to go. He might turn up.'

I turned to Mason. 'Stay here, Frank,' I said. 'Stay here with Eph and Henny. I'll move up with the others. You let 'em have your share as we fall back.'

I knew Henny was timid and Eph a dodger; and I thought it wiser to leave them with Frank where they couldn't get into trouble.

While I was still wondering if I'd done right, the shelling stopped abruptly, and, without thinking, I nudged Murray and MacKinley and we ran forward and dropped flat again by the German wire. I distinctly heard the words '*Achtung, raus, raus, die Tommies*' shouted in a hoarse voice, and a few more frightened words that were drowned by the crash of a bomb going off behind the parapet.

The noise made me jump. The flash threw the sandbags into relief again and I heard the shuffle of boots on stones and the sound of a whistle and realised to my relief that the bombing party were going in and we hadn't done wrong.

'Blackett's going in,' I said. 'Come on! Up closer!'

There was a concentration of thudding bangs and angry

flashes as several bombs all went off together in a group. Immediately, away on our right, a flare shot up into the sky, and in its glow I could see Murray's eyes white in a black face. Then I saw shadowy figures running and heard groans and curses as another salvo of bombs burst. A few rifles went off and the machine gun started traversing again in a hammering stutter of flame and I saw sparks fly as the bullets struck against stones.

There were shouts and yells of pain and men started spilling from the German trenches in a stampeding confusion. Young Murray was quivering like an excited terrier alongside me. He half-started to his feet and I grabbed him and pulled him down.

'Wait,' I said.

In the flashes of bombs exploding just below the German parapet, I saw the figures of Blackett's men running back. I could hear someone moaning in the darkness beyond the wire, and a low wailing sound from the trench, then I saw the flashes of rifles over the parapet.

Blackett and his party were past us now, and I let go of Murray.

'Right,' I said. 'Now!'

We threw our bombs as fast as we could, and the firing stopped abruptly. I heard a shriek of pain and the harsh shouting of orders, then we were running, bent double, for our own lines, tripping and stumbling as the red and green rockets went up, sweating with fear that the machine guns would get us.

There was no sign of Mason's party where we'd left them, and MacKinley began to swear in a low vicious undertone as we flopped down again and looked round, rifles ready. There was no indication that Mason and the others were still near and, after a while, we got up again and ran for our lives.

I dropped to the earth at last by our wire, panting, sickened with fear, unable to speak, my throat dry, the sweat soaking my shirt and tunic. The machine gun was spraying the area liberally and, as we stumbled on the heels of Blackett's party, I glanced round for Murray and MacKinley and, seeing two dark shadows behind me, I dropped into the trench and was promptly knocked flying as Murray landed on top of me.

He was on his feet in an instant, grabbing me by the arm and dragging me up after him, pulling at my sleeve and twittering in a spasm of excitement and fear.

'They got Mac,' he said. 'I saw him fall.'

'Who's that then?' I indicated the shadow behind him and he burst out in a wail.

'It's one of Blackett's crowd,' he said. 'Mac's back there.'

Consumed by anger and fear, I pushed him aside.

'Why the hell didn't you say so before?' I shouted. 'I'm going back to look for him.'

The thought of going over those damned sandbags again with the machine gun chattering away appalled me, but I couldn't think of any alternative.

Murray looked at me, his jaw hanging open, his eyes big and round. He was blubbering softly but unafraid. 'I'll come,' he said. 'You'll need a hand.'

His face twisted abruptly into a rage. 'Where the hell was Mason?' he stormed. 'If he'd been covering us, we'd have got away. It's his fault.'

There was someone who looked like Frank just in front of me. I could hear him muttering softly and I thought he'd been hit. In the crowded trench I could see dark faces and white eyes staring at me in the flashing beams of torches. Someone was cursing, and down in the shadows out of sight I could hear groans.

I pushed Murray up to the parapet and, as I started to scramble out again myself, a hand grabbed my sleeve. It was Locky and he looked shocked and scared.

'For God's sake, where are you going?' he demanded.

'MacKinley's out there,' I said. 'I'm going to get him.'

'Don't be a fool!'

I shook his hand off irritably and climbed after Murray, who was waiting by the wire. 'Come on,' I said. 'We haven't all night!'

In front of us the concentration of angry flashes and thudding bangs continued, as the Germans searched in the darkness for the raiders, and bullets were cracking through the long grass on our right.

We came upon MacKinley after about half an hour. He'd rolled into a shell-hole and was lying against the scorched earth, almost upright. He'd been hit near the groin and he was moaning softly but conscious.

We put a pad on the wound and tried to pull him out, but he was a big man and it was more than we could do. The pulverised earth of the shell-hole kept giving way beneath our feet and more than once the whole lot of us slid back into the slimy mud that lay in the bottom.

'We'll have to get a rope,' I said to Murray. 'Stay with him. I'll come back.'

'Don't be long, for Christ's sake,' he said nervously. 'It'll be light soon.'

I crawled back across the broken ground towards the wire and I could just make out Mason's face above the parapet.

'Come on in,' he shouted anxiously. 'Come in, you fool!'

'For God's sake,' I told him furiously, more frightened than angry, 'stop jawing and get a rope.'

Someone found a rope and threw it up to me and I went back again towards Murray. In the darkness I lost my way and it was half an hour before I found him again.

He was peering over the edge of the shell-hole by this time, calling softly in a low voice: 'This way, Fen! This way!'

I fell into the hole beside him and we fastened the rope round MacKinley's chest. Then we climbed out and started to pull, panting and swearing and frightened to death that damned machine gun would swing round in our direction again. MacKinley groaned as the rope tightened round him.

'We'll have to stand up,' I muttered to Murray. 'We can't pull him out lying down.'

'They'll get us,' Murray moaned.

'They've got two chances,' I said. 'Either they do or they don't.'

I stood up and started heaving and Murray stood up too. The machine gun was tap-tapping away in the darkness and once I heard the zip of bullets as they parted the grass near us. Murray fell flat on his face instinctively but he scrambled up again at once.

When we'd got MacKinley out and lying on his back, we tried to lift him, but I could see we'd get nowhere that way. It only required a flare and that damn' traversing gun and we'd all be dead.

'If I get you on my back and crawl,' I said to him, 'do you think you can hang on?'

'Sure, bud, I'll hang on.'

I got down on all fours and with Murray's help we got MacKinley slung somehow across my back, and I set off across the broken ground like a donkey, with Murray fidgeting and whispering by my side.

'This is a hell of a fine position to be caught in,' I panted.

'Who's for a bullet up the tarara?' MacKinley muttered.

'For Christ's sake,' Murray groaned. 'Can't you go a bit faster?'

As we reached the parapet again, I heard the machine gun coming closer again and, in my fear of being caught by it, I almost threw MacKinley into the trench. Waiting arms caught him and I fell in after him. As I sat up, Murray came down on top of me, knocking all the breath out of my body and sending me flying.

'For God's sake, Murray,' I howled. 'That's the second time! Can't you pick some other place to land?'

He sat up and flung his arms round me, almost kissing me.

'We got the bastard,' he chirruped happily. 'We got the old

sod!' He was suffering from an overdose of excitement and his language was appalling.

Then we became aware of dazed and angry voices cursing the artillery, and climbed to our feet, our own joyous little celebration flattened by the bitterness around us. The argument about what had gone wrong with the raid was still going on.

'It was the bloody staff,' I could hear someone saying loudly. 'They laid on the artillery too soon.'

'It was the emma gee got Bernard. Poor bastard!'

'Where's Welch? He's not turned up yet.'

The raid had clearly been a fiasco. There'd been a few Germans killed, but not more than we'd lost ourselves, and there'd been no prisoners. Somebody had let us down and the bitter voices and the accounts of close shaves welled up around us.

'Standing right next to me, he was, when he got it.'

'Look, it tore my sleeve. That was a close one, if you like!'

'This sort of thing's enough to make your mouth flush out.' I heard Eph's voice quite distinctly and Murray swung round at once.

'Is that you, Ephsibiah Lott?' he demanded, fiercely indignant. 'You were supposed to be bloody well helping us.'

There was an immediate silence as Eph lay low, then the fretful questions started again.

'Where's Bernard?'

'They got him with the gun.'

'Where's Welch? He fell over me.'

As far as it was possible to make out in the confusion, Blackett had called off the raid as soon as the artillery had started, but his party had got separated from him and hadn't heard the order and some of them had gone in as instructed, so that Blackett had had to follow them to get them out again. Men had been killed and lost in the confusion and nothing had been achieved.

'They got Fred,' someone was saying in a shrill high-pitched

302

voice that was edgy with fright. 'I saw a bastard in a spiked
'at shove his rifle in his face and pull the trigger. He went 'ead-
first into the trench.'

The stretcher-bearers were bending over MacKinley now
where he was laid out on the fire step. Ashton was standing in
the background, polishing his pince-nez nervously, his face
twisted with misery, and Bold was a little apart, looking on
coldly, his face expressionless.

'What happened?' I asked him.

'The usual,' he rapped back. 'Somebody got the time wrong
at Brigade.'

He turned as he saw the colonel approaching, still followed
by his brother and his dog, poking men out of his way with
the ash-plant he always carried, and he jumped forward to
clear the trench of men.

'Come on, there,' he snapped. 'Git moving! There'd be a
nice old 'owdyedo if Fritz dropped one of his dixies in here
while you lot were all arguing, wouldn't there? Make way for
the colonel.'

Ashton turned as Pine approached. He seemed to square
himself up, looking a little like a family doctor who had bad
news to deliver, and I knew that if he soldiered for a thousand
years he'd never have Bold's professional attitude to wounds
and death.

'All in?' Pine asked.

'All who're coming in,' Ashton said.

How many have we lost?'

'More than necessary.'

There was a pause, then Pine went on slowly. 'I've been on
the b-blower to Brigade,' he said. 'They won't admit it's their
fault, of course. They're blaming us for lack of guts.'

I was touched by a feeling of misery and disappointment at
the failure. A fear for my friends in anything that might come
upon us chilled me. I knew how I could trust myself and the
men around me, but somewhere above us there were other men

303

who didn't care enough to be careful. Somebody had let us down, just when it was important for our self-esteem that we should succeed, and nobody had bothered to apologise or come up to see for himself who'd been hurt.

'They say they expect us to do b-better next time,' Pine was saying bitterly. 'I'll make sure we do.'

'That doesn't bring Bernard and the others back,' Ashton said angrily.

'Don't talk like that,' Pine snapped. 'Mistakes can always be made. Though some people can make more than others,' he added harshly.

He stared at Ashton for a second, peering at his taut reproachful face, then he tramped down the trench again towards headquarters, followed by his brother, the little dog skipping like a white shadow at his heels.

'It's all right for him,' someone growled. 'It's all right him talking. He wasn't there.'

5

The trench was still full of arguing, angry men dispersing slowly, their mouths full of resentment. I lost Murray in the confusion and when I found him he was back in the dig dugout, and he'd got Eph and Henny Cuthbert in a corner and was storming at them, his fists under their noses. Locky and Spring and the others were sitting about, their heads on their hands, wearily indifferent to his rage.

'You rotten bastards,' he was shouting. 'If it hadn't been for you, MacKinley wouldn't have been hit!'

'Mebbe he's lucky,' Eph said bluntly. 'Mebbe 'e ought to give thanks. He's got a nice Blighty one. He's well out of it.'

'That's a fine way to go about winning the war!' Murray's face was flushed and furious.

I thought he was going to hit Eph and I gave him a shove. He fell across one of the netting beds which promptly collapsed and deposited him on the muddy floor among the scraps of paper and cigarette-ends.

'Shut up, Murray,' I told him. 'You waste half your energy fighting with your own side.'

'And why not, when they're slackers like that lot?'

'For God's sake, man,' I shouted, 'you give us all the heeby-jeebies with your bloody battle-cries! Why don't you save your breath for fighting?'

'What a scrap!' Locky said wearily. 'What warriors we are!'

Murray leapt to his feet. 'You can't complain at me,' he said loudly, and I realised just how much in the past weeks his bounding enthusiasm, his noisy boyish faith, had been getting on my nerves. At best he was a little wearing and at worst he was plain irritating.

'It wasn't me who did a bunk,' he shouted. 'It's that lot!' He pointed a quivering indignant finger at Eph and Henny and finally at Mason who was standing by the steps that led up to the trench, one hand on the blanket that did duty for a gas curtain.

'Well, you heard what Blackett said!' Mason joined in on a high indignant note that somehow seemed to suggest he knew he ought to have waited. 'He said to go like hell for home.'

'Not so bloody fast as you did!'

'Dry up, Murray!' I snapped. 'You've already said enough!'

Mason had set off up the steps and he turned round now and jeered, probably more from the consciousness of guilt than from any meanness of spirit, because he'd been frightened and was tired and the last strand of control was wearing thin.

'That's it,' he said. 'Be a good boy, Murray. Do what the nice corporal tells you. He's been sucking up to Bold and the officers to find out how to do it.'

I went up the earth steps after him, in a tearing rage. 'You're a nice one to talk,' I said. 'Why the hell did you bunk?'

Frank whirled round. 'Because Blackett said to bunk.'

'He didn't say to bunk till you'd done your job!'

Frank's eyes flickered and there was a sharp look of anxiety behind them. 'It was Eph and Henny,' he said. 'They wanted to shove off when it got hot.'

'Well, why the hell didn't you stop 'em?'

'You know what they're like.'

I remembered his indecision that time at Blackmires, when we'd waited in the rain during a manœuvre that seemed now like nothing but a game of cowboys and Indians, how he'd wavered and asked the rest of us what we should do; and I could just imagine the scene out there in the darkness, with Eph and Henny nagging at him to pull back and Frank too uncertain of himself to be able to deny them.

'My God,' I said. 'What the hell do you think you've got stripes for?'

His face flushed and his anger flared up. 'That's it,' he said. 'Give me a lecture! My God, you grow more like Bold every day!'

As he stormed off, I stared after him, startled into silence.

More like Bold every day, he'd said, and God, I thought, he's right too. I *am* growing more like Bold every day. Somehow, it drained away the anger at once, because I knew I'd neither Bold's courage nor his wisdom and experience.

Locky appeared alongside me, pale still but apparently recovered now. He took the cigarette from his mouth and offered it to me.

'He said I was growing like Bold,' I said slowly.

'Well, there's nothing to be ashamed of in that.'

I looked round at him, startled, but he only smiled.

'I'm sorry about all that in there,' I said. 'I got mad.'

He shrugged. 'Just a slight show of temper,' he pointed out gently. 'It's all over now. Henny's offered Murray a cigarette and Eph gave him a light. Half an hour from now it'll be forgotten.'

The disappointment was dying in us when daylight came, and Bold appeared to tell me Ashton wanted to see me. We were all still a little numbed by the shock of failure but the resentment had faded a little. Bold's boots on the duckboards brought us out of our lethargy, and we watched him advancing on us, his pebbly eyes bright and malicious-looking.

'Corporal Fenner,' he said immediately. 'On yer feet!'

I jumped up, watched by everyone else, and he advanced on me.

'You're for the commanding officer,' he said, pointing a long white finger at me. He was watching my face as though enjoying my doubt, and he went on in portentous tones. '*Now!*' he said. 'Not tomorrow. Come on, clean yerself up a bit!'

'What's on, Sar'-Major?' I asked.

Bold's bony face was unyielding. 'We'll see,' he said. 'Come on, let's have you. And take them grins orf your faces, you lot. You'll be smiling on the other side when I'm through with you.'

As we marched off, he turned to me. 'It's a long time since you was up afore the CO, ain't it, Corporal Fenner?' he said. 'Quite like old times.'

'I suppose so,' I said, still puzzled. I followed him a little farther then I asked if Welch had turned up yet.

'Yes,' he said. 'He came in fifty yards on. He got lost and, as he ran for the trench, he tripped and went in head-first. He half-killed his silly self.'

'What happened to him?'

'He ran.'

'Did a bunk?'

Bold shook his head. 'Don't ever use that awful word,' he said. 'Better men than us 'ave done a bunk in their time. It's nothing to worry about. We all get scared now and then, and he's only a kid. He got lost and didn't know what to do. He didn't know how to be'ave in an emergency. Not many of 'em do at that age. Sheer lack of experience.'

He paused in an angle of the trench and faced me. 'At least he was honest,' he went on. 'I heard him telling the colonel just now. He didn't try to kid him along, and he took his telling-off like a man. It's the ones who tell whoppers you've got to watch.'

I was surprised at his generosity. He'd always seemed to have so little time for failure, and I'd never thought of him much as an understanding man.

He turned on his heel and set off along the trench again. 'It all comes back to what I was telling you before, see?' he was saying, and he was no longer talking to me like an escort to a prisoner, but as man to man. 'If anybody's got it in him to be a leader, well, he ought to lead. Young Welch ain't.

'He's a nice kid,' he went on. 'Friendly, not stuck up, and thinks of his lads. But he comes from generations of shopkeepers. Drapers or something. You know 'em better than me. Drapery's what's in his blood, not soldiering. Not like the youngsters *we* used to 'ave. They were a bloody snotty lot sometimes, but they'd come from a line of soldiers, father and son, father and son, all the way back to William the Whatsaname.'

He paused thoughtfully. 'It's just something that some fellers have,' he said, 'and some 'aven't. *You've* got it. I'll tell you that for nothing.'

I felt flattered by his regard and didn't know what to say and he went on cheerfully.

'It's nothing to get big-'eaded about, though,' he said. 'It's one of those things. You've either got it or you 'aven't. I dunno where it comes from. It's a sort of toughness. A streak of the old Adam, if you like. Most of the others'll stay civilians till they're pushed under the daisies. That blowhard pal of yours, Mason, for one. *He* ain't got it.

'Too fond of the girls,' he went on. 'He'll never make a soldier if he tries till the sea turns pink. I can always pick 'em out. I picked *you* out at Blackmires. You'd 'a' got promotion there if you 'adn't always been in the nick.'

He turned, staring at me cheerfully. 'You got to shepherd 'em along more – like an old 'en with 'er chicks. They don't know how to go on, see, and you've got to show 'em. You shoulda sent Mason and the others in and stayed behind yourself to see they did it right.'

'I thought they might not go up close enough,' I said.

'Well, that's true,' he admitted. 'Still, what the hell? We all make mistakes. How about young Murray? How'd he shape?'

'Murray's all right,' I said.

He grinned unexpectedly. 'He'll probably end up as the youngest colonel in the Army if he don't get hisself killed first,' he said. 'I'm thinking of putting him up for a skater. Make him a lance-corporal.'

'That'll please him. There'll be no holding him after that.'

'That's how I want him. I got to keep a lookout for these people. I got to see that Ashton picks the right sort and not the smarmy ones who're good at talking.'

He stopped outside headquarters and nodded at the bored-looking sentry.

'All right, all right,' he said to me, his voice hardening abruptly back to its normal harshness. 'Let's have you. All yer buttons done up? Boots are a bit mucky, but we'll forget that. Don't forget to salute. The captain's fussy about saluting. And rightly so.'

We stumbled down the dugout steps and Bold threw up a salute like the kick of a horse.

'Corporal Fenner,' he announced loudly.

Ashton looked up. He was standing with a mug of whisky in his hand and he seemed tired. Young Welch was just behind him, looking pale and sick and as though all the muscle had been drained out of his body. Blackett, the burnt cork still on his face, was stooping over the table with a pencil and report pad, and he didn't even bother to look up.

'I thought I told you no heroics,' Ashton said unexpectedly. He was looking at me through his pince-nez and he began to swing the whisky round in the bottom of the mug, staring at it thoughtfully, as though searching for words. For a moment he looked like a chief reporter again, trying to decide the best way to set about some job he was doing.

'We're here for the offensive that's brewing up,' he went on after a pause. 'And nothing else. That's what we've been training for two years for. Besides . . .' He paused and smiled unexpect-edly. 'Besides, now that Sergeant-Major Bold's managed at long last to get you promoted, we don't want you knocking out.'

Blackett had stopped writing now and was grinning and I saw young Welch, who was leaning on the wooden post that held up the door, manage a faint twisted smile.

'Mr Blackett told me what happened,' Ashton went on more gently. 'It's a good job you stayed behind or his party wouldn't have got away. Why *did* you stay?'

'I couldn't think of anything else to do,' I said.

Ashton laughed and Blackett looked up again.

'That's honest anyway,' he said. 'Pity there aren't a few more of 'em who can't think what to do.'

Ashton jiggled the whisky round in the mug a little more, then he stared at me.

'Well, now I've got another surprise for you,' he said. 'They got Bernard, as you know, and we're a sergeant short, and Sergeant-Major Bold tells me you're the best man for his job. So you'd better cut along to find where Bernard kept his overcoat and get his stripes off it, because you've been promoted lance-sergeant in his place.'

'Me?' I said. I was a little bewildered by the speed of my advance.

I saw Bold's eyes roll up to the roof in disgust, then Ashton thrust the mug of whisky at me. 'Here, man,' he said. 'Don't look so alarmed. You won't die of it. You'll get used to it in the end. Sergeant-Major Bold's promised you will.'

I took the whisky uncertainly. The thought that had crossed my mind immediately was that I was now entitled to regard Sergeant-Major Bold almost as an equal, and the thought of being on those terms with that magnificent, chilly, aloof man startled me more than the thought of the third stripe.

'Better drink it, Sergeant,' Ashton said, 'because I've got the colonel's permission to put you in for something else as well as an extra stripe – whatever they can spare at headquarters after they've helped themselves. There's been a big argument going on at Division about whether fetching someone in's worth a medal or not. Some of 'em don't think it is, but I'm going

311

to try. We'd like a medal in the battalion and we might as well have it in D Company.'

We went out of the line two nights later and arrived back at Colinqueau to find that everybody was due for leave. The fact that we'd got to get it in as quickly as possible indicated that the Big Push wasn't very far away.

There was an uproarious ten minutes of cheering and singing and throwing things, then we went round to the orderly room, to find they were so busy filling in their own passes they hardly had time to attend to us.

We drew lots to see who should go first, and Locky and Mason and I were among the lucky ones, and there was another explosion of riotous merriment and envious glances from people like Tim Williams and Barraclough and the Mandy brothers who'd been unlucky. Then Bold came along and told me he'd have to hold my pass back until the next batch, because there was a lot I'd got to get used to first, and I was back to my normal state of wishing I could murder him.

'Never mind, Fen,' Mason said with a trace of malice in his voice as he began to pack his kit. 'I'll give your love to Helen.'

His spirits seemed to have returned, as though, now that he was out of the line, he'd shrugged off a load he'd been carrying for a long time with aching bones, hating every minute of the toil. He was a light-hearted individual to whom the good things of life were important, and the squalid experiences in the trenches, full of nervous shocks and sudden fears, had hit him harder than most of us. But he seemed gay now, almost too gay, as though he were fleeing from reality to a little peaceful fantasia that he'd made of England.

'It's just the way it is,' he went on gaily. 'Some of us make good soldiers and get our names in the Victoria Cross department of the newspapers. The rest of us, the normal ones, find they do better at more civilised things.

'I hope you enjoy the battle,' he ended. 'With a bit of luck,

312

it'll be over by the time I get back. I'll send you a piece of cake.'

'Cake?' Locky looked up quickly.

'That's right, old fruit,' Mason grinned. 'I've arranged to lay on a special licence.'

'You getting married or something?'

'That's right.'

'Who to?'

'Helen, of course.'

'Does she know?'

'Well, I haven't asked her yet, if that's what you mean. Not in so many words.'

'Oh!' Locky turned away. 'I thought I hadn't heard.'

'I'm going to pop the question as soon as I get home.'

'I see!' Locky nodded and bent over his kit again. 'I suppose I ought to congratulate you.'

We went into Rippy to celebrate before they left, but Mason was nervous in case something went wrong before he could get away, and Locky was thoughtful and not inclined to be merry.

The reeking candle-lit room was noisy with celebrating men, and prices were ridiculous. Eph made a pass at the woman serving the drinks and, encouraged by the fact that she didn't register any objection, he pinched her bottom and got his face slapped for his trouble. The military police were fetched by Madame and we were asked to leave.

Outside, we tried to buy vin blanc at the village shop, but the proprietress pointed out the ticket attached to the bottles. '*Reservées pour les officiers*,' she said, and we left in disgust.

'This is a bloody silly war,' Murray complained. 'And if Haig allows this sort of thing, then he's no good.'

'Who said that aboot Haig?' A Scottish soldier standing with a group of friends, staring longingly into the shop window, turned round angrily.

'*I* did,' Murray said belligerently.

'Naebody says yon aboot a guid Scot.'

'*I* do,' Murray retorted with a carefree indifference, and, knowing we were in trouble already, we dragged him away.

Eph had some money with him, winnings from his crown-and-anchor board, and when we ran into Blackett, Tim Williams persuaded him with all his silky lecturer's eloquence to buy us, as an ex-ranker who understood our position, some of the wine we wanted and we retired to camp to drink it between us.

When I woke up the leave men had gone.

I found it strange to stand on the sideline with a list in my hand, ticking things off, airing my three stripes and telling other people what to do. I found it a nice change, in fact, when I got used to it, and began to wonder why I hadn't gone after them before. As a private soldier, I'd spent most of my time fighting against too much weariness, and the absence of manual labour made a great lightening of the load.

They'd marched us south to build a road to an ammunition dump, from the rubble of some old buildings that had had a direct hit, laying bricks thinly on the muddy surface of a battered cart-track.

'This ain't t'way to make a road,' Tom Creak said in his solemn foreman's manner. 'You just can't put bricks over pot-'oles. They'll all get knocked out again, just as quick.'

'Don't worry,' Murray said. 'After the first few days of the Push, we'll be using *German* roads. We shall be twenty miles away from here the week after it starts. This time, old boy, it's open country and cavalry.'

'Cavalry!' Tim Williams was sucking a split thumb he'd caught between the bricks. 'All cavalry ever do is clutter the roads up with horses and the dumps with forage.'

Nobody yet knew when the offensive was due to begin, but it was pretty obvious now it wasn't very far away and the end of the month was being freely whispered as the date. The German advance at Verdun was slowing down and the Russians were going great guns against them in Galicia, and the time seemed ripe. Even the old soldiers around us were looking forward to ending the stalemate.

A battery of howitzers appeared in the corner of the field next to ours, hugging the orchard where they might avoid being spotted by aircraft, digging their gunpits among the maimed fruit trees and making our days miserable as the crash of their firing shook the dust from the timbers of our barns and flapped the canvas of our tents.

More guns were moving into position all round us, and long-range naval guns which stood on the railway line somewhere far in the rear disturbed the night with their ragged orange flashes and the shuffling hum of their vast shells as they waddled off on their ten-mile journeys.

Trench-mortar schools were banging away all over the place, and once a bomb dump went up in a great mushroom of smoke that caught the sunshine in browns, yellows and blues. They said nine thousand tons of ammunition had vanished in the bang.

All sorts of comic units began to be seen and pigeons were issued. More navvies appeared with sanitary squads, and every tent and barn seemed to be crammed with men. Wells were dug and more railways laid. Companies were set up for the manufacture of snipers' loopholes and imitation snipers' heads to draw the German fire. More roads were screened with camouflage nets, and dumps as big as small towns grew up almost overnight, prepared to issue anything – periscopes, grenades, compasses, rations, mortar bombs, smoke helmets, tools. Casualty clearing stations and advanced dressing stations were erected and airfields were prepared for the Flying Corps.

Because we came from the north, some clown on the staff, who'd probably never been out of London, took it for granted that we were all miners and they set us to work clearing an old trench that had been used for a mass grave for a lot of

French dead. We threw chloride of lime around in bucketfuls and had to take it in short spells because of the appalling smell.

'God help the mob who jumps off from this one,' Tim Williams said. 'It'll bring things home to them a bit.' His hand was swollen now and bandaged by the stretcher-bearers, and we'd been trying for some time to persuade him to go to hospital with it.

Signs and maps sprang up, giving directions for traffic and men, all of them pointing towards the east. Ambulances appeared by the thousand. Half the British Empire seemed to be assembling on the Somme, thousands upon thousands upon thousands of splendid young men, all crammed uncomfortably together, quarrelling and fighting among themselves, nervous and edgy with anticipation, but still cheering – everything that happened seemed to produce a cheer, whether it was a rifle going off by accident or a horse getting stuck or a battalion moving up or returning. And still singing too! They weren't singing to keep their spirits up but because they were young and confident and had the utmost faith in themselves. I never heard them sing again as I did on the Somme.

There was a never-ending stream of grenades, rockets, Very lights and Stokes bombs moving up. The whole forward area was becoming a huge dump. Day and night there was always this maddening carrying, as we humped ammunition, equipment and stores and hid them in tarpaulin-covered dumps in woods and under hedges, sometimes even when the Germans had the paths taped and we were damn' glad to get away and back to greasy maconochie by the roadside that tasted like duck and green peas.

The Germans, who'd seemed indifferent up to then about the coming attack – probably they'd thought the activity was so open it couldn't be for anything but a feint move – suddenly began to wake up and dig, and everything we did began to be interrupted by shelling, which grew worse as May crept into

June. We had our share of tear gas, mustard and phosgene in the evenings; but none of it was concentrated. The brass shell-cases hanging on the trees clanged, and the klaxons roared, and you could see the gas hanging about in the folds of the low ground, moving along slowly on the wind, but it always seemed to have blown away by the next morning, leaving nothing behind except for the stink – which seemed to taint cigarettes and food – and the dozens of dead rats lying with their feet in the air.

Tim Williams went off at last to hospital with a hand the size of a football, and we lost a few men from shellfire, but not many. Barraclough was one, and it seemed a bit ironic that he of all people should have copped it before the battle, when he'd worked so hard to avoid being snatched from the battalion before we left England, spinning the tribunal who'd tried to put him on munitions some long-winded yarn about not being mechanically minded. He might just as well have saved his breath because, when he recovered, there was a good chance that munitions was where he'd end up.

His disappearance cast a blight over Murray and me for a day or two. He was the first of the group who'd joined up from the newspaper to be hurt, although Sainsbury was long since dead and Arnold Holroyd had vanished – to Mesopotamia, we'd heard from someone. Barraclough had been one of those curiously anonymous people who never impressed his personality much on you, but he'd been on the *Post* with us and was one of the platoon who'd clung together ever since the Edward Road Drill Hall days.

The farms and billets around us grew daily more dilapidated as the Germans searched out the back areas for the troops and artillery installations they knew were there. The church at the end of the street at Rippy fell to bits slowly under repeated near-misses, then it got a direct hit and collapsed like a house of cards in a rolling cloud of dust and smoke that billowed across the street, leaving the place a wilderness of broken glass and scattered bricks that was marked by one or two sprawling figures.

Why we didn't lose more men, I don't know, because the district was stiff with troops and more were being added all the time. With every new gun and every new battalion that arrived we felt better, and there was a resurgence of that old spirit we'd felt when we'd first marched off to the Town Hall to join up.

We did another spell in the line and this time things went right and we all came out as cocky as ten men with the feeling that at last we were getting the hang of it and would pull our weight when the attack started. The offensive was talked of openly now in the villages and estaminets in spite of the notices that appeared: *Mind what you say. The enemy has listening apparatus.* A few orders from headquarters couldn't hope to hold down the boiling excitement which was growing daily more intense.

There was a feeling about it all that this time we would not, we could not, be stopped. In spite of the ugly stain of Loos, and the known faults of the staff and the pettinesses that had given rise to grievances, in spite of the aspersions cast on the skill of the commanders by the old soldiers, and the trivial jealousies, and all the other things that had happened to damp the fire in the months since 1914, the first ardour was blazing up anew, fanned by optimism and the enthusiasm of the newcomers.

E Company, which had been raised at Blackmires to provide reinforcements and left behind in England, caught up with us at last. They marched in singing, like all the rest – not the straightforward old songs which were good to march to and easy to sing, but some sort of half-baked song they roared out in instalments, with one man as a pace-setter to sing the verses, a bit like the fiddlers Nelson's Navy used when they were manning the windlasses and the pumps.

I wasn't surprised to find Hardacre among them, complete

with a stripe and strangely unfamiliar in uniform, and I remembered Frank's words when he'd first tried to join up: 'We shall have music wherever we go.' It wasn't hard to see where the part-songs had sprung from.

'I got in with the West Yorks,' he said. 'But I wangled a transfer to this lot. Dicehart's here too.'

They brought with them news of a Zeppelin raid at home, where a few bombs had been dropped on Cotterside Common, and horrifying stories of the number of ships the Fleet had lost at Jutland.

I took them along to Ashton and, for old times' sake, got them into D Company. The rest of them were absorbed into the battalion but somehow they always remained slightly apart, because they hadn't belonged to the original crowd who'd fought on the Town Hall steps for the privilege of joining. They were led by a new officer as pale as the rest of them and just as nervous and anxious to please. Surrounded by the rest of us, with our brown faces and torn uniforms and battered rifles, they seemed a little bewildered and out of their depth.

'Did you see Locky?' I asked Dicehart. 'Or Mason?'

'I saw Mason going into a pub.'

'Into a pub? I thought he was getting married.'

'Perhaps he was going in for a final drink before the chopper dropped, but he looked a bit down in the mouth all the same.'

While we were talking, Murray came running up the field from battalion headquarters. He was in a tearing hurry as usual and it was clear that he was the bearer of tremendous tidings of some sort.

They were surprised to see the stripe on his arm and the obvious inner toughness of his slight frame. When they'd last met him he'd been only a chubby-faced boy, eager and keen to please, swept along by his own ardour, but still little more than the messenger he'd been at the office.

'What-ho, Hardy!' he said, panting. 'What-ho, Diccy! Fancy seeing you here. This is a bon place and you're in a bon mob.'

He dragged at his breath, trying to speak, his face flushed, his eyes bright with excitement. 'You've arrived just in time to see the balloon go up. Have you heard the news? Kitchener's dead. Some ship he was travelling in on some potty mission to Russia. It hit a mine. They got it at headquarters from the Warwicks who've just come out of the line. They saw it on a notice the Germans hoisted on their wire.'

Kitchener's death came as a shock to us all. To the K battalions he was founder, father and patron saint all in one, and it shook us to think that anyone with as much might as he had could die just like an ordinary private in one of the vast armies he'd raised. He'd long since been jostled from power by the politicians who'd undermined his reputation and authority at the War Office, and now the Germans had obligingly removed him from the scene altogether. Perhaps what his enemies said of him was true. Perhaps he *wasn't* as efficient as he seemed to be. Perhaps he *had* made mistakes. But, to me, he was rather more than some obscure field marshal I'd never clapped eyes on. Somehow, I'd always regarded him as one of us.

The news took a little of the edge off the excitement of the approaching offensive.

'They might have let the poor old sod see the lads doing their stuff,' Eph said. 'Going in and wiping up the Kaiser.'

Fortunately for our peace of mind, the leave men came back just then, and Kitchener was forgotten as the excitement started all over again. 'Leaf' for the second batch was announced and we rushed for the yellow passes and documents.

'Keep off the girls, Murray!' Spring said. 'You know what you're like, sweetheart, when you get near them.'

'Don't worry about me,' Murray said as he threw his equipment together. 'What was it like at home?'

'All right.' Spring seemed a little bewildered and suffering from a hangover. 'A bit different. Things have changed. Or *I* have. I dunno which it is. I got a bit fed up at times. All they seemed to talk about was making money. They say shipping clerks and clothing-shop assistants are getting together to form companies, there's so much to be picked up from army contracts.' He paused and shook his head. 'It seems more like home out here these days,' he concluded.

'My kid didn't know me.' Someone at the other end of the barn was making his complaint in a high indignant voice. 'He'd just got used to me when I had to come away again. I was a bit hipped, I can tell you.'

Locky seemed quieter than before, not quite the old Locky, not quite so imperturbable, and rather grave and thoughtful.

'What's happened?' he asked. 'Any news?'

'Kitchener's dead,' I said. 'We just heard it from the Warwicks.'

'I heard it on the way back. What else?'

'Catchpole said the Irish did it and collected a split lip from Tommy Mandy for his trouble. They're pals again now.'

Locky laughed. 'I mean, has anything been happening here? This damned unit grows on a chap. He finds himself getting anxious for it. Leave's a bad thing. You end up not quite knowing where your loyalties belong. Come on. What's been going on?'

'Only the Push. It gets pushier every day.'

'Is that all?'

'Tim's in hospital, with a poisoned hand. He was pleased to get away from the racket for a bit, I think. It gets worse daily and he couldn't read for it. He'll be back in time for the big shemozzle, I expect. And Barraclough. He's gone.'

'Killed?'

'No. He'll be all right. A shell splinter across the knee. We cobbled him up and sent him to a dressing station. Fritz's waking up to the fact that something's on and building roads isn't quite the sport it used to be. Cloughy was a bit late getting under cover and he got one in the leg. How did it go with you?'

He grinned and his eyes lit up. 'I was privileged to be at

home for the birth of my son,' he said. 'A fortnight after the air raid.'

'What are you calling him?'

'Lockwood. There's been a Lockwood Haddo around the city for generations. My father's name's Lockwood too.'

'Does he have *your* face or is he fortunate enough to look like Molly.'

He grinned and I paused before I went on, wondering if I could make it.

'How's Helen?' I said.

'Blooming.'

'Did you get to the wedding?'

'What wedding?'

'Frank's, of course.'

Locky looked up and gave me a slow smile. 'Frank didn't get married,' he said.

'Oh!' My heart leapt with sudden, unbelievable, wondering hope. 'Why not?'

He shrugged. 'Various reasons. I expect you'll hear them in due course. He's not saying much at the moment.'

'What about Helen?'

'She's landed some job in London.' He looked up from where he was sitting on his blanket and handed me a slip of paper, smiling, his eyes quiet and happy. 'She's been working down there on and off for some time. That'll be her address. She's sharing a flat or something. I think she might be pleased to see you.'

'Will she be there when I go on leave?'

'I wouldn't know. But you can always ask at home.'

Mason was morose and silent and not very communicative. He seemed to have put on his load again, and was already stooping under it.

'She said she didn't want to get married yet,' he told me, even before I asked him. 'She said wartime wasn't the best time for weddings.'

He looked a little beaten and downcast, not quite the old Mason I knew.

'Is that all she said?' I asked.

'Oh, she talked all round the subject. You know how women go on. I spent most of my leave trying to jolly her into it, but I couldn't.' He looked up. 'Will *you* be seeing her?'

'I don't know,' I said. It was a long time since I'd thought of Helen and I couldn't get used to the idea that she was still free. 'Locky says she's going to London.'

'That's right. She's got a job down there. Some sort of war work. She said she felt she ought to go. Fen . . .'

'Yes?'

'I suppose, if you see her, you couldn't try and talk her round, could you? They're bound to give leave again when this bloody offensive's over. Maybe I'll have better luck next time.'

'You've a hope,' I said. 'She never listened to me, even when I was trying to push my own case. Besides, has it occurred to you she might have met somebody else?'

He nodded heavily. 'Well, she might have,' he agreed. 'I don't know. I asked her, but she wouldn't say. Probably it's one of these blasted war-workers who're scrimshanking back there while we're stuck out here. They're all the same.'

'I suppose they are,' I said. 'But I didn't think Helen was.'

In spite of the approach of midsummer it was a cold morning when the second batch left Rippy, and frail metallic stars glittered overhead as Murray and Catchpole and I made our way to the railhead. Eph Lott and Henny Cuthbert and Tom Creak had all given us letters to post in England.

'If you get a chance, Fen,' Eph had said, 'nip down to the Old Light Horseman on Cotterside Common. Mabel's there. You'll find her any time. Tell her I'll be home in a couple of weeks with the next lot.'

The village street was dark, silent and deserted, but the station, a very small one with a long train waiting in it, was full of dim figures moving about the platform. Peaked caps and rifle barrels were caught in silhouette against the sky, and the murmur of many voices came from the dusk. Now and again a match flared up from one of the compartments and you could see a little group of faces. Over the whole train there was an air of expectancy that transmitted itself to us, so that the excitement that had been growing on us increased and set the pulses galloping at the thought of home.

The compartment we managed to squeeze into had hard seats and windows that wouldn't open and the train seemed to be the slowest thing that had ever been on wheels. Murray fretted all the way to the coast.

Dawn revealed the Picardy countryside, with its patches of red clover and wind-stirred corn, moving slowly past us, and it was after seven when we crawled into Amiens. We were already stiff from sitting wedged together, unable to stretch or move much, and flushed with the stuffy atmosphere and cigarette smoke.

It seemed to take hours to puff through the valleys of Normandy and it was late afternoon before we began to approach the coast. When the train pulled up at a wayside halt the word had already gone around that there'd be food, and we were hanging from the footboards long before it stopped. There was a surge of khaki towards the solitary café by the crossing; and Murray, the company's champion runner, arrived way ahead of everyone else and snatched coffee and rolls for us, while the ones behind had to gnaw at ration biscuits and fill their bottles at the water pump.

It was dark before we reached the sea. Conversation had long since ceased and only the glow of cigarettes in the stuffy compartment showed that it was occupied. Then the train started to speed up as we went downhill, and Murray opened the window and we all sat up as we caught an immediate whiff of keen salty air.

'It must be Le Havre or somewhere,' Murray said excitedly. 'Thank God for that.'

We began to pass through streets and I could see brick walls and open warehouses in the lamplight. We joggled slowly past trucks loaded with GS waggons, gun limbers and eighteen-pounder guns.

'Going up for the Push,' Murray breathed.

Ragged urchins were running beside the train now, begging in their shrill voices for 'Bullee' and 'Biscuit', and women looked up disinterestedly as they were called at from the windows. It was good to see them, after that childless, womanless land beyond Albert.

As the train stopped, men poured from it, stretching, noisy, eager to be in England. A tall red-capped MP shouted to us to follow him and turned on his heel as we streamed after him through a gate and down a cobbled street. A strong salt wind came buffeting round the angle of a shed, where I could hear a loose corrugated-iron sheet rattling just above my head, then I saw two tall black funnels and rakish masts, and the leave boat loomed up ahead.

'Home!' Murray said ecstatically. 'I can smell the sulphur fumes along Cotterside already. They come like attar of roses.'

They kept us waiting there for some time in a noisy impatient crowd, gaunt, tired men with faces shadowed heavily by the dazzle of arc-lights. Beyond the ship I could see searchlights and the glitter of red and green on dark water.

They let us board at last and we jostled our way to what we thought was a sheltered spot, but when the ship left the harbour we found we were on the windward side and we had to shiver all night through the crash of the seas and the creak of the rigging.

With daylight, I saw great white-capped waves foaming up at me and a thin squally rain beating into my face. There was no sign of land, only sea and huddled khaki-clad figures aching to be ashore and home.

Inevitably, the first sight of England was of a shining rain-wet quay with the arc-lamps still burning dully in the grey daylight.

Then Murray saw a girl standing with a tray of biscuits and chocolate in the shelter of a doorway.

'Girls,' he said. 'Real girls! Hoy, there! Cooeee! How's tricks?'

The girl looked up and waved and smiled, and Murray pretended to faint into Catchpole's arms.

'She understands English, Vicar,' he moaned deliriously. 'Now I know I'm home.'

The train north was jammed with people but we managed to crowd into a compartment with three or four stuffy middle-aged men and women. Nobody moved to make room for us and as the train left the cavernous darkness of King's Cross, and sped between the packed houses of the northern suburbs of London, we sat perched on the edge of our seats, uncomfortable, tired, glad to be home, but curiously deflated. England looked good but it seemed to have become different somehow in the months I'd been away from it. There seemed to be women everywhere now, driving cars, even driving buses, and they all seemed to have an angelic beauty, every last one of them, that I was sure I'd never noticed before. It was difficult to keep back the tears of emotion.

Nobody in the compartment made any attempt to talk to us. One of the women was telling her friend that the war was getting more difficult because she could no longer buy tea and sugar.

'It's a good job they're going to do something about it soon out there,' she said. 'Or I'd just have to give up.'

Catchpole leaned forward unexpectedly and she shied away from his burly figure in its stained uniform.

'We know exactly how you feel about it,' he went on in his best public-schoolboy-curate's voice. 'But we're doing our best to put it right. Of course, things go wrong occasionally. It takes its toll.' He indicated young Murray, who was watching him with a startled expression on his face, looking incredibly young, as though he'd left his soldier's self behind him in France with the battalion and had become a schoolboy again.

'Take *him*, for instance,' Catchpole said, and the eyes of everyone in the compartment swung round to Murray.

He blushed and his hand went to his collar in an uneasy movement.

'Me?' he said.

Catchpole leaned towards him, his face full of concern.

'How's your diphtheria now, kid?' he said. 'Any better?'

'Diphtheria? Me?' Light suddenly dawned in Murray's eyes and he grinned. 'Oh, it's not too infectious now,' he said.

Conversation had ceased and at the next stop the compartment emptied abruptly, and Catchpole stretched himself out on the seat, grinning luxuriously.

'That's better,' he said gaily. 'I discovered even when I was a schoolboy that you can always make room for yourself if you cough and spit a bit and pretend to have consumption.'

The city seemed much as it always had been. There were still advertisements for summer-holiday resorts on the station and the Oxo and Mazawattee Tea advertisements were still there, though old Kitchener's face was beginning to look a bit tatty now. He didn't seem very important any longer, I suppose, now that conscription was on its way. Like the posters, he'd served his purpose and could happily be forgotten. Like old Corker, who'd been one of his soldiers in South Africa, he'd quietly disappeared into the darkness, and even the vast memorial service which was still filling every newspaper you saw made him no better and no worse than the rest of them.

Schafers' window seemed to be whole for a change. I'd heard they'd lost two sons in France and perhaps that had managed to convince everyone at last that their hearts were in England and not in Germany, after all.

The Blueberry was full of people and the landlord looked up and promptly began to tell us about the Zeppelin raid.

'God knows what it's coming to,' he said. 'A man can't sleep peacefully in his bed at night any more.'

I persuaded him to let me use the telephone and I went to ring Helen.

Locky's wife answered, apologising because the maid had disappeared into the munitions works.

'How are you, Fen?' she asked cheerfully, and it was a pleasure to hear a sane, calm voice.

'I'm all right,' I said, and went through the usual polite rigmarole of asking about the baby.

'I expect you're looking for Helen, aren't you?' she said suddenly, stopping me in mid-sentence. She seemed to have been expecting me and I guessed that Locky had been doing a little spadework on my behalf.

'That's right,' I said. 'Is she there?'

'I'm afraid she's not. She's already left. She's in London. Do you want her address?'

'No, I've got it.'

'There's a train at midnight if you're interested,' she said. 'When were you thinking of going?'

'At midnight.'

She laughed. 'Fen . . .?'

'Yes?'

'I think she'll be pleased to see you.'

When I got back to the bar, the landlord, affable in a celluloid collar and dickey and a ready-made black bowtie, was pumping Murray and Catchpole for the date of the offensive.

'When's it going to be?' he was saying.

'When's what going to be?'

'The Big Push?'

'The Big Push?' Murray asked cagily. Just before we'd left Rippy we'd had a special lecture from Ashton and been told to say nothing to anybody. 'What Big Push?'

'The offensive on the Somme.'

'What, this offensive that's going to make the world safe for freedom and democracy?' Catchpole demanded innocently.

'Is it going to be on the Somme?' I asked.

'Didn't you know?' The landlord looked surprised. 'It's going to be the biggest battle in history! Where've you been? Everybody here knows. End of June, they say, and it won't be before time neither. There's a lot to be avenged. There's the *Lusitania* and poor old Kitchener and a few others. We're only waiting for the kick off.'

'Kick-off?' Catchpole snorted. 'It's not a game of bloody hockey.'

'Well, you know what I mean! You want to look sharp or you'll miss it.'

We didn't stay long in the Blueberry. It was pretty obvious we didn't see things the same way. The Defence of the Realm Act, brought in to stop any spread of alarm and despondency, seemed a bit unnecessary to me. I thought everybody seemed thoroughly keen.

We shook hands outside and promised to meet on the leave train going back. Then Murray took me home for a meal and his mother stuffed us full of food she must have been saving from her rations ever since he'd left home; and brought out all the family photos and Murray's *Chatterbox* annuals for me to see, talking nervously while he blushed furiously and told her to stop. 'What's the Big Push going to be like?' she asked anxiously.

'Bigger than the last one,' Murray replied with a grin.

In the evening he dragged me round to a dance at the tennis club on the corner. The place was full of young men in new uniforms who hadn't yet been out of England, and Murray, in his stained and faded khaki, soon got the girls round him. Then the girl from next door appeared and his face fell. She seemed to be a very normal girl, reasonably pretty and not very intelligent, but Murray seemed to be reduced immediately to an advanced state of nerves.

'That's her,' he said.

'She looks very nice,' I said. 'Aren't you going to speak to her?'

'Soon,' he said. 'In a minute. Give us a chance!'

The old fire-eating over-confident Murray seemed to have vanished. He was talking faster and louder already, and pretending not to look at the girl who'd just appeared. 'I've been trying to make up my mind to ask her to marry me this leave,' he said.

'Good luck,' I said.

'Only I'm not very old and her mother's not so keen.'

'It seems to me, if you're old enough to go roaring up and down France,' I said, 'risking your neck every time you go in the line, you're old enough to know your own mind about a few other things too.'

'Do you think so?'

'That's the way it occurs to me.'

'Thanks, Fen,' he said. 'That makes me feel a lot better.'

He jerked his tunic straight and pushed his shoulders back. Ten minutes later, blushing furiously and looking shy and virginal, he was deep in conversation with the girl and his evening seemed to be made.

I took the first opportunity when he wasn't paying much attention to disappear. I'd decided to go and look up Eph's Mabel for him.

The Old Light Horseman was a noisy little place, all mirrors and brown-grained paintwork, jammed to the doors with steel-workers from the mills just behind. The landlord hedged a bit when I asked for Eph's wife, and it took me some time to get out of him what was wrong.

'She's took up with another chap,' he said in the end.

I suppose Eph was no angel, and he'd probably done more than his share of cheating in his time, but somehow just then, with him still out in France and unable to get home, it seemed pretty hard luck on him. I thought she might have waited a bit.

I accepted the drink the landlord silently pushed towards me, but there didn't really seem to be much point in staying, and as soon as I'd finished it I caught a tram back towards the Blueberry.

There'd been a meeting of some sort of debating society in the billiard room upstairs and they were all in the bar now, youngish, pompous men, who looked well paid and well fed and made me feel shabby in my old uniform; and it occurred to me that while we who'd enlisted would come out of the war as poor as we went in – *if* we came out – there'd be a hell of a lot who wouldn't. Every bomb and every shell that exploded added to someone's fortune. Duty didn't seem to pay very good dividends.

There was no one about I knew. In a year everyone seemed to have changed and those who were left didn't seem to have much time for me.

They were all busy with their own affairs, with business and rationing and keeping cheerful, with being economical and yet not so economical as to precipitate industrial distress. After all, life had to go on and business had to continue. They were occupied with the fact that the city had had a few bombs dropped on it, and there was a lot of patriotic talk that was a bit nauseating. Overseas, I hadn't heard much about patriotism. Mostly a man's attitude seemed to be one of sheepish cynicism for letting himself get caught when so many had stayed behind, but we all knew it hid an immense faith that we were on the point of bringing it all to an end on the Somme. It wasn't the same sort of hilarious keenness there was here. It was a quiet certainty that at last a plan had been formed, a leader had been found, and enough munitions of war had been assembled, so that with a little luck and a little help from the Almighty we could put an end to the killing once and for all.

Here, everyone spoke of the offensive as though it were spelled in capital letters. They even talked a different language – English, while mine was a mixture of pidgin French, old soldier's Hindustani and scraps of Arabic from Suez. There seemed a weird absurdity about the normality of civilian life.

331

To shut the rest of the place out a little, I bought a late evening paper from a boy who came round, but the leader was full of bilge about 'the field of honour' and 'our noble allies', and 'We will not tolerate the cry of "Peace" until the Hun has been put where he belongs.' There were tips signed 'Little Mother' on how to give up an only son to the Army without too much heart-searching; and sentimental articles about the war from someone called *Adsum*, who most obviously hadn't had some.

Everybody who could set pen to paper seemed to be trying to make us seem smiling morons who found killing Germans a sport a bit like ratting. Nobody seemed to have the slightest conception of the degrading nature of life in the trenches. Half the Army itself didn't know it, I suppose. The cheerful rhapsodies about Tommies with the glint of battle in their eyes made me squirm.

Inevitably, a little man with a fistful of Bradburys, who said he was manager of one of the rolling-mills along Cotterside Common, spotted my stained uniform, and it pleased him to buy me a drink while he set out before me just how Haig was going to conduct the coming offensive. He seemed to know all about it and even began to work out for me how long the German reserves could last. He appeared to resent my not being there doing my bit, as though my absence might make just that fraction of difference between failure and success.

'Twenty-six divisions there are going to be,' he told me. 'Half a million men. They've massed every cavalryman in France for the breakthrough. It'll be a cakewalk – a picnic. Haig's got it taped this time all right.'

It occurred to me that if *he* knew so much about it, it would be odd if the Germans didn't too. I'd heard that some fathead in Parliament had given away the date of the offensive, in a speech to munition workers which had got into the foreign papers, and I began to wonder just how much else that had been leaked enthusiastically from one official to another over a bar had found its way to the other side of the lines.

Then I began to wonder just what our chances really were when the time came, and all the old ugly doubts that Bold had put in my mind with his talk of inexperience started again.

Were we really in the hands of competent leaders? Were we really the soldiers we thought we were or did we merely blind ourselves with excitement and grow drunk on our own patriotism and faith? I knew what Murray's answer would have been, but Murray's answer was never mine, and I began to wonder if Bold and Pine and Blackett and Appleby were the only soldiers among us, and if the rest of us were merely borne along by them, sustained by their skill and our own courage and enthusiasm, and that blind belief we had in victory.

As my attention wandered, the little man with the pound notes started waving a hand at me, anxious that I should hear him out.

'There'll be casualties all right,' he said. 'But you've got to disregard those. There's a crowd in Parliament who're all for peace, but we'll never win while people sit back and look at the Roll of Honour.'

'No, I suppose we won't,' I said.

'Plenty of soldiers. That's what we want. Conscription's a fine thing.'

'Will *you* be conscripted?' I asked.

'No. I'm reserved. But they're getting the slackers. They're going to set up tribunals to decide whether the conchies are honest or just plain yellow.'

I suddenly felt that I didn't belong there any more. This city was no longer home to me. Home had become an overcrowded village in France, with shattered houses and dusty roads full of troops and vehicles, and lined with all the litter of war.

I didn't feel much like the merry assassin my new friend seemed to want me to be, revelling with him in the joy of destroying human life. I'd gone off to war like all the rest of us, under the stress of some tremendous emotion I found hard to explain even to myself on the rare occasions when I stopped to think about it, and I suppose I was still being ruled by it. This little man with his handful of pound notes had long since given it up for some more fashionable feeling, following the lead given him by the newspapers. My background was still summer 1914. His was summer 1916. I was his ghost, the echo of all his early enthusiasm and all that half-hysterical flag-wagging everyone had indulged in as the first small bands of men went off to the war.

I was glad when it was time to head for the station.

London was full of Australians, New Zealanders, Indians, Canadians, Belgians in tall forage caps and Russians in dark blue, and even odd nationalities like Serbs, Montenegrins and Portuguese. You could buy Iron Crosses and even spiked helmets at the alley ends, and it seemed fashionable to be seen out with a wounded officer. All the smart women seemed to have one in tow, helping him in and out of taxis.

Signs were scrawled on the walls and pavements, *Strike Now in the West*, and *Save Verdun*. The truth about the Irish rebellion and the fall of Kut in Mesopotamia and the battle of Jutland seemed to be just seeping through, and the general tendency seemed to be a desire to blame it all on the troops.

There were military police everywhere, and I was itching to get away from the West End. I thought I might ring Helen up before I went to look for her, but I realised I had no telephone number and guessed that, anyway, she'd probably be at work and unavailable during the day.

For the best part of the afternoon I hung about Piccadilly, but prices were high for a mere sergeant and all the respectable places were reserved for officers and I hated the damned place. A prostitute offered to take me home, in spite of the early hour, offering me 'Oriental attractions', whatever they were, and in the end I went to a matinée of *Chu Chin Chow*.

I was looking at the pictures outside when a cavalry lieutenant offered me a couple of tickets because he'd just been given them and he'd already seen the show. I asked the first private I saw if he'd like to join me, and we went in together. He was a nice little man who'd just joined up. He was very impressed by my well-worn uniform and the fact that I'd just returned from France. He said he looked forward to 'being blooded', and the phrase sounded strange and pretentious. 'Bloodied' might have been a better word, I thought.

I tried to talk to him, but he seemed as much a stranger as all the others, and in the end we sat the show out in silence and parted afterwards with barely a nod.

By the time it had reached evening, I was debating again how I'd find Helen. Suppose she'd arranged to meet someone, I thought. Suppose there was another man? Suppose she just didn't want to see me? But Locky and his wife had both insisted that she did, and I found myself on a tram heading out towards Finchley. I'd no idea how to get to where she lived, but a friendly Bobby helped me, walking with me all the way from the tram-stop, and telling me about his son who was in the Navy and what a trial he was to his mother when he came home on leave.

The address on Locky's slip of paper turned out to be a shabby old mansion that seemed to have been divided up into flats. For a long time I stood outside staring at it, before I opened the door. I'd been travelling all night and I'd have been glad of a welcoming face.

There was a strong smell of cabbage inside and, while I was still wondering where to start, a door opened alongside me and a woman appeared with a cigarette in her mouth.

'Who're you looking for?' she asked in a rasping gin-rich voice.

'Haddo,' I said. 'Helen Haddo. She shares a flat somewhere here with a friend.'

'Haddo?' she said. 'Don't know that name,' and I was

immediately aware of a sickened feeling in my stomach. I felt sure I ought never to have come. All the way out on the tram, I'd been trying to convince myself Helen had meant what she'd always said – that she really would be pleased to see me.

I'd even wondered what Bold might have done under the same circumstances and been reassured by the knowledge that, being what he was, he'd probably have done the same thing. I found it a great comfort just then to recall that Mason had said I grew like Bold.

As I was about to turn away, the woman put a hand on my arm.

'Hold on a minute,' she said. 'Isn't she a new girl? From up north somewhere?'

My heart leapt at once.

'Small girl? Fair hair?'

'That's her,' I said. Suddenly I didn't care very much whether I was wanted or not. I just wanted to see Helen.

'Top floor, son. Straight at the top of the stairs.'

I flew up the first flight two at a time, in spite of all my kit. I'd brought everything with me, not wishing to go back north again and hoping against hope I might not have to. My rifle banged on the newel post as I swung round on the landing and the voice of the woman below came up to me, boozy but not unfriendly:

'Steady on with the paint, son!'

By the time I reached the top flight, and could see the glass-panelled door at the top, ominously dark and silent, I'd slowed down a bit. Uncertainty was creeping in again and I was doubtful of my reception once more.

My boots thumped heavily on the uncarpeted stairs and I stopped on the little landing and tapped gingerly on the glass.

For a long time there was silence, and I thought the woman below must have been wrong, then I heard a door open inside and someone singing. It wasn't possible to recognise the tune but I knew at once it was Helen and I was consumed with the desire to turn and run. If she was singing, I thought, she obviously wasn't in need of cheering up.

A key turned in the lock and the door opened.

Helen stood for a moment, staring at me, her face blank and startled, her mouth open a little, then her features seemed to crumple and I saw there were sudden tears in her eyes. The next second she was in my arms, her face against my cheek, and I knew she was crying.

'Oh, Fen,' she was saying, clinging to me with a strength that was frightening. 'It took you so long.'

For a long time we stood there, neither of us saying anything. There didn't seem to be anything to say. I knew then what a benighted bloody fool I'd been. This might have happened eighteen months before if I'd only had some sense, if only I hadn't been blind.

How long we just stood, not speaking, I don't know. Then Helen pushed me away.

'Your buckles are sticking in me a bit,' she said.

The ordinariness of the comment seemed to break the spell and we were able to laugh. She took my rifle and pulled me through the door, slamming it after me. The flat was small and seemed to consist only of a bedroom-cum-sitting-room, a kitchen and a bathroom, but it was lighter and more cheerful than I'd expected in that dingy old house, and you could see over the roofs towards a patch of green in the distance that looked like a park.

She helped me off with my pack, and we merely stood and stared at each other, both of us struck dumb and unable to stop smiling. She'd had her hair cut, I noticed, in some more modern style, and she was dressed in a white blouse and a dark skirt that showed her figure.

I'd never realised she was so lovely. She looked as though she didn't belong to my world – as, of course, she didn't. Her world was one of cleanliness and laughter and happiness, and mine was full of dirt and noise and boredom, and I realised suddenly she'd always had so much more to offer me than I'd ever known. But she looked different, somehow, more fashionable – the influence of London already, I supposed – quieter, more responsible and older, and I was scared she wasn't the same person. Then I saw her eyes flooding with tears again and she put her arms round me.

'Oh, Fen,' she said as she released me. 'Why didn't you ever come before? Why didn't you ever write to me?'

I gestured feebly, not certain myself why not, now that it seemed so clear I should have done. 'There was Frank,' I said.

Her brows came down and she became angry at once, her eyes flashing.

'Mark Fenner,' she said. 'There was *never* Frank. Frank thought there was Frank, but Frank always did, didn't he? Damn him, he always seemed to be in the way when I thought I'd got you to myself!'

I grinned. This was more like the old Helen. I hadn't made a mistake, after all. She hadn't changed inside.

'I tried to tell you in half a dozen ways that it wasn't Frank,' she said sharply. 'But it isn't the girl who has to make the running. You ought to know that. I couldn't take you on one side and knock it into your thick skull with a hammer, could I?'

I pulled her into my arms again and kissed her fiercely. She pushed me away and stared at me, her eyes on mine, large and shining.

'You've changed,' she said, smiling. 'You're more authoritative.'

'I'm a sergeant,' I said. 'Sergeants *have* to be authoritative.'

'It suits you.'

'I'll have to tell Bold you approve. I've been modelling myself on him, as the best example I could find.'

'You've lost your shyness, I think.'

'Not much chance of shyness when you're living in a barn with thirty or forty others.'

She put her head on one side and stared at me. A strand of

fair hair fell over her nose and she blew at it as she always used to, in the way that always delighted me so much.

'Remember the night of the riots after they sank the *Lusitania*?' she asked.

'Will I ever forget it?' I said. 'I ended up doing C.B. for Bold, and never saw you again properly afterwards.'

'You were like this that night too. That's how I always tried to remember you.'

'I'll keep it up. Strangely enough, I don't find it so hard these days. There must be something in what Bold's always said about me.'

She put her arms round me again and held me tight, her cheek against mine.

'Oh, Fen,' she said. 'We've been such fools.'

'Not you,' I said. 'Me. I'm the fool.'

'Molly always told me what happened to you. Locky's letters were full of you and she always passed it on. She knew, you see, like Locky did. I might have written to you but you never wrote to me and I thought there might be someone else.'

'There never was. There never will be.'

She suddenly realised we were still standing in the middle of the room, and she laughed.

'I don't know why we're standing here,' she said. 'Go and sit down. I'll get something to eat.'

I sat on the bed which had been arranged with cushions to look like a settee and she disappeared into the kitchen to put the kettle on the stove. She was a while preparing the food and the flat was warm and I promptly began to doze. We always fell asleep when we were left alone. Tim Williams always said we'd make wonderful tenants for overcrowded houses after the war. After we'd dropped off, he said, the family could stand us up in the corner and give the bed to someone else.

I dreamed of warmth and womanly sweetness, but the dream grew darker and I woke in confusion. Things were banging round me and the air seemed hot and stuffy and I thought I was in a dugout and the roof had come in on me. I started to lash out, then I saw Helen kneeling alongside me, gently holding my arms.

'Fen, Fen,' she whispered. 'Steady!'

She looked concerned and anxious for me in a way that did my heart good. All the puckish fire had gone from her and I realised she'd grown up and had her own private sorrows too.

'Is it over now?' she asked.

'Yes,' I said. 'It's finished.'

I sat up and looked round. The curtains were drawn and the lights were on in the other room. 'What's happened?' I asked.

'You fell asleep. So I let you sleep on. You looked so tired. Fen, is it really so awful out there? Tell me the truth.'

She was looking at me steadily, her eyes demanding honesty I couldn't give her. She couldn't ever have understood if I had, so I hedged a little.

'Awful?' I grinned. 'Not really. We manage. Helen, this is a hell of a way to call on a girl. I didn't sleep much last night on that damn' train and I seemed to have been travelling for days. I expect that's it.'

'Why have you come down here?' she asked.

'To find you.'

'Is that the only reason?'

'It's the best one I could think of.'

She looked up at me and managed a little twisted smile, but there were tears in her eyes.

'Fen, darling, you could always be relied upon to do the unexpected. Stay where you are. We'll eat here.'

She kissed me quickly and turned to the gas stove and fiddled with a match.

'Thank God I woke up,' I said. 'What a waste if I'd slept till it was time to go.'

She turned to face me and gave a curious little throaty laugh that didn't seem normal.

340

'There's no hurry,' she said unsteadily. 'And you don't *have* to go at all if you don't want to.'

'What about this friend of yours?' I asked. 'Won't she be in soon?'

She was looking at me with shining eyes, her face full of light, the old Helen, the old slender exciting Helen who'd always reduced me to witless stupidity every time she looked at me.

'No, Mark,' she said slowly, her voice clear and steady again. 'She's away for the week. I'm on my own. You don't have to go at all.'

What she was suggesting hit me like the blast of a bomb, and I got slowly to my feet.

'We've grown broad-minded since the war, Mark,' she went on, no trace of a tremor in her voice. 'And this is London. And there's this big battle coming soon. I may never see you again.'

She stared at me a little longer, and suddenly the spine seemed to go out of her, all the courage she'd been putting on for my benefit. Her shoulders drooped and she stood by the gas stove with the kettle still in her hand, looking smaller and strangely frail, staring at me with tears streaming down her cheeks.

'Mark,' she whispered. 'We've waited so long and there's so little time.'

6

I said goodbye to Helen at the flat. We both agreed it was best.

Victoria Station was crammed with men returning from leave, all humpbacked under their kit, all looking for seats and enviously eyeing the half-empty coach reserved for the staff, its corner seats jammed with red tabs and gold oak leaves. The platform was full of wives and mothers and sweethearts, all wearing a crucified look or pretending unconcern, some of them in black with mourning veils and crêpe on their hats. Porters stumbled over kitbags and valises and the hand-luggage trucks crowded with equipment. Serious old men with white moustaches were seeing off their sons, pink-faced subalterns obviously not long out of school. Drafts of new men were going out under officers, smart by comparison with the older soldiers who were returning from leave but bewildered by the throng and the noise, and not quite knowing where they were. There were tears, red eyes and white faces, and I was glad I'd said goodbye in private.

The crossing was easy this time and we could hear the rolling thuds of gun-fire long before we saw the French coast. The staff had a deck to themselves and the officers another. The other ranks were crammed together like cattle.

There were German prisoners working on the docks at Boulogne, whitewashing stones and carrying sacks. Huge notices were displayed everywhere. *34th Div., 31st Div., 46th Div.* An officer with a megaphone was shouting: 'Leave men to the right. Drafts to the left. 1st Army men to the end of the platform. 3rd and 4th Army men across the track. Captain Eastergate, Durham Light Infantry, report to the RTO's office at once.'

I felt at ease again to be there. I was still suffering from the confusion of joy, doubt, impatience and misery we call being in love, but, after so long, England had been like a foreign land and I felt curiously happy to be back.

Every arm of the services was represented – infantry, artillery, cavalry, engineers, signalmen, service corps, medical corps, Navy, marines, young pale-faced boys with RFC wings and hollow eyes.

Everybody seemed to be going to the 4th Army – Warwicks, Inniskillings, Gloucesters, Bedfords, Durhams, KOYLIs, the Jocks and the Buffs and the Irish. The new drafts looked as though they'd just come off parade – buttons shining, puttees exact, boots bright, peaked caps still stiffened with wire, packs mathematically correct, overcoats buttoned to the throat in spite of the weather. The leave men looked like scarecrows by comparison, in goatskins and sheepskins and overcoats which had been hacked off short with jack-knives to keep them out of the mud. Their makeshift leather equipment looked as if it had become part of them and some of them hadn't even bothered to put it together properly, wearing it as it suited them best. They greeted familiar faces with shouts and catcalls.

'I thought you were dead!'

'Enjoying the war?'

'How's Wipers?'

I saw familiar badges and faces and, as I looked round for someone from D Company, I caught sight of Murray approaching, tougher-looking, somehow, in spite of his youth, than the men in the new drafts, with a lean, curiously fine-drawn look about him, and eyes that had a faraway different stare from theirs. He looked older than they did too, young as he was, and, in his greasy-edged coat with its grimy buttons, filled with a kind of enduring energy. He was humping his equipment casually as he drew near, as though it weighed nothing, glorying in the fact that he could handle it while the new drafts obviously found it wearisome. As he greeted me, he shrugged it off and threw it down nonchalantly with his rifle.

He was cheerful and happy to be back, as though he'd known no other life. He'd spent most of his leave with the girl next door, and was still a little sentimental about it.

'Did you pop the question?' I asked.

'No.' He looked at me shyly. 'I – I thought I'd wait.'

'Why?'

'Oh . . .' He shrugged uneasily. 'The offensive coming off and all that. And she's a bit young and if anything happened to me – well, it just didn't seem fair. That's all.'

He gave me a grown-up, face-the-facts look that seemed older than his years, and tried to laugh it off.

Then Catchpole appeared from the crowd behind him, barging his way through to slap him on the back.

'Hello, Vicar!'

'Where'd you get to, boys?'

'I've been holidaying in London,' I said. 'I've just come out to spend the summer on the Somme.'

Catchpole grinned. 'Think I'll join you for the season's shooting,' he said. '"One generation passeth away. Another generation cometh." They're calling up the war-babies now, I hear.'

Farther along the dock a sergeant was chivvying men towards a train, and Murray picked up his kit.

'Have a good time?' he asked, and Catchpole grinned.

'Not half,' he said. 'My brother was home for three days.

We painted the place red. He's in the artillery. Do you know . . .' His expression changed. 'He was telling me about the high percentage of dud shells and obsolete guns they're getting. Burst in the bloody barrel, he said, or as soon as they've left it. They call the four-five batteries suicide clubs. That twister Lloyd George's doing, I suppose.'

He grinned abruptly. 'Get yourself fixed up with a girl? I did. Keen amateur. We came to a very amicable arrangement. Only she knew more about the bloody offensive than I did. Even my old man was at it, and all his Mothers' Union Knitting Circle. I'd have liked to have told 'em to send us a lot less balaclavas and a few more girls. Less wool and more whisky. Less heaven and a few more frisky harlots.'

While we were talking an RTO officer and a couple of sergeants came along, and, forming us into rough columns, marched us off through all the war-material, guns, lorries and ammunition that crowded the docks. They jammed us into the same old train with the same old slogans chalked on its battered sides, in what appeared to be the same old compartment even, with hard seats and windows that wouldn't open.

At Amiens they marched us out into the square and formed us up again in various units. We were next to a draft who were out for the first time and full of ideas of the open warfare that the papers preached so glibly. A few of them were disgruntled because their battalion had been split up and they'd been drafted to another unit, but they were all as enthusiastic for battle as only untried troops can be, a little bewildered and as amazed as we'd been once by the uncanny ability of the youngest childen to speak fluent French.

The officer in charge of them, who'd been out before, called across to me, grinning cynically.

'You got it in just in time, Sergeant,' he said. 'Have you heard? All leave's been stopped. The Push's due any day. It's a dead cert now.'

We set off by a long, slow, clanking train towards Albert,

where young Welch was waiting for us in the forecourt of the station, under the shadow of the ruined Basilica, among all the jammed waggons and guns and limbers and chalk-stained soldiers.

On the Bapaume road I noticed immediately the increased amount of air activity. A whole line of balloons had appeared in the sky to the east, yellow-bright like a lot of fat slugs, and planes seemed to be constantly buzzing overhead, whirring low over the trees to wave at us and stunting from the sheer joy of living.

'Heard about Immelmann?' Welch asked, as we tramped alongside the thickly wooded slopes of Aveluy that were throbbing with the songs of thousands of birds.

'No,' I said. 'What about him?' Immelmann was a German ace who'd been playing havoc with our flying crews.

'He's been killed.'

Somehow, the news seemed like a good omen to start the offensive with, as though Immelmann was the symbol of our success

'We've moved to Bos,' Welch went on, enjoying the high spirits of the marching men behind him. They were singing and jeering at other units as we passed, and they seemed in fine fettle and very little troubled by coming back. Nobody had overstayed his leave and, in fact, most of them seemed pleased to see their friends again.

'We had another spell in the line,' Welch said, 'then we moved farther north. We're due to take up battle positions any day now, they say.'

'When's it to be?'

'End of the month. They're feeding us like fighting cocks now.'

'Fattening us for the slaughter, eh?'

If the roads had been choked before, they were beyond description now. There were men everywhere, sitting by the roadside eating or getting their breath back, swinging along to

'Tipperary' and 'Long, Long Trail', riding on lorries and horses and gun-carriages and limbers. The chalk dust had turned everyone's boots and legs and faces to a dirty grey-white and there seemed to be millions of buzzing blowflies over the patches of horse-dung that had been flattened into the road by the solid-tyred wheels of lorries. The whole countryside seemed to be soiled by the dusty sprawling of the Army.

Querrieu seemed to be more than ever overpopulated with staff and communication-line troops, then, as we topped the rise to the north-east of the village, we swung past a great dump of shells in a field crimson with clover, and thousands and thousands of dirty-grey bell-tents belonging to a Red Cross camp, and rows of creosoted huts for hospitals and billets. Crooked chalky lines cut the green grass in the distance.

'Practice trenches,' Welch said. 'We're practising all the time now. We can do the job blindfold. Oh, by the way, you've got a mention in despatches. They wouldn't make it a medal. Ashton was a bit hipped.'

'Can't say I'm bothered,' I said. 'I've heard you have to walk all the way to Querrieu to get 'em pinned on.'

We turned north, passing Colinqueau and the old dilapidated barns we'd got to know so well. We all looked back at them, as though they were houses where we'd lived as children, then we came upon country that looked like the Sussex downs, great stretches of green grass, cut here and there with neglected growing land where the chalk came up through the surface to show grey-white against the brown. It looked a little like Newmarket at one point, and we even passed a racing stable that was the core of a sprawling cavalry camp, still with a list of winners it had trained nailed up outside. Everything was overlaid by a grey-white film of dust stirred up by wheels and hooves, and the fields around were full of watering troughs and hundreds of horses in their glossy summer coats, their tails twitching, their legs being groomed by stooping, shirt-sleeved men.

There was a heady excitement in the air, a strange intense feeling that victory was near. In every face you passed you could see a distinct expression of expectancy. Everybody was alert and cheerful and looking constantly towards the east and the open country ahead of us. The sense of impending triumph had grown stronger since I'd gone on leave and you could almost reach out and touch it, a surging new spirit that grew from the sight of this vast army hitching up its straps for a battle that now could not be more than a few days away. The sound of it all, the smell of it, the sight of it, couldn't help but stir the imagination.

'Half a million men,' Welch said. 'Just think of it. A generation, you might almost say. The best of a generation anyway. And a gun for every yard of front. It's "*finis*" for the Boche this time.'

Heavy with dust and sweat, we turned off the main road. The grass verges here were white with dust, and clamorous with old petrol and bully-beef tins and pieces of corrugated iron. Motor convoys passed us, all heading in the same direction. Then we swung down a lane and passed through a tidy-looking village and turned alongside a wood.

It was dead ground here, Welch said, and no shells had fallen to disturb the peace. I noticed mayflies in the meadows and blossom on the apple trees in the orchards that we passed, and squirrels in the copses that fringed the lane. The horse-chestnuts were in flower and there were peonies and pink roses in the neglected garden of a deserted cottage. A few isolated aspens were showing the trembling white of their leaves in the breeze that was blowing, and in the distance you could see hills and valleys hazy with the sun's rays. There were bees about and the welcome smell of bacon frying. It looked like a Sunday camp back in England.

There were no tents except for the officers, only bivouacs made out of groundsheets laced together with string and shared by two men. Sunshine filtered through the trees of a swampy woodland and at the bottom of the slope white-bodied men with brown arms and faces were splashing in the clear water of the chalky stream.

Tim Williams was back, I saw, reading inevitably, stretched out on the grass with his head on a rolled overcoat, a book of poetry in a still-bandaged fist; and Tom Creak, plodding past with a home-made fishing rod, stopped to wave as he saw us.

'T'river's full o' fish farther down,' he said. 'I've been after t'biggest carp you ever saw for four days now.'

Then I saw Locky squatting in the grass, running a thumb-nail up his shirt seam for lice, and I felt I was home.

We leapt upon each other like little boys and wrestled and scuffled until we trod on one of the bivouac tents and brought it down, and Hardacre – a strangely different and browner Hardacre already – came out cursing, and promptly joined in.

The summer evening made the war seem almost pleasant. Fires shone along the edge of the stream and the faint thin note of mouth organs came through the slow chatter of voices. A few old women in sabots shuffled across the fringe of the wood heading for Bos, carrying their long-pronged forks, a man following them with a water cart pulled by an ancient horse.

The sun dropped behind the eastern ridge and the air in the distance began to turn pearl-grey with mist. You could still hear the rumble of wheels everywhere, and somewhere out of sight the steady crunch of tramping feet. The smoke of cooking fires rose straight up into the air and you could hear the soft call of card-players.

Like Tom Creak and the Mandys, Eph had accepted the cancellation of his leave philosophically.

'Easy come. Easy go,' he said. 'That's me.'

I told him a string of lies that sounded all right to me, but I wasn't certain whether they convinced him or not. He seemed

349

puzzled, but disinclined to probe. 'Pity I shan't see her,' was all he said.

'You will,' I reassured him. 'After the offensive.'

He grinned at me, his little eyes distant. 'After the offensive,' he said, 'maybe I won't be 'ere. Maybe a lot of us won't be 'ere.'

Bold greeted me like an old friend and offered me a mug of whisky. He'd accepted the stoppage of leave without turning a hair.

'That's what we're here for,' he said bluntly. 'It's 'appened before. It'll 'appen again. Pity, though. I'd 'ave liked to 'ave seen my old ma.'

It surprised me to hear he had a mother and thought about her sometimes. I'd somehow never thought of him as a child. It had always seemed to me that he'd appeared in the world fully grown, bone-hard, ginger-haired, white-skinned, straight as a ramrod and hung about with equipment, slamming his feet down – bang-bang-bang – and shouting in his high-pitched voice; bullying, chivvying, jockeying, carrying the weaker vessels on his own strong back. I just couldn't imagine him being affectionate to a mother or making love to a wife.

'Still,' he went on, 'we didn't join the Army to stay with Mum, did we? We came out here to make war and it looks as though it won't be long before we're making it.'

He paused, toying with the bottle of whisky he'd managed to buy from the officers' mess, then he looked up at me, his eyes steady.

'Just for your information,' he said, 'you've been made strong-point NCO when the attack comes off. You know what that means, don't you?'

'Yes, Sar'-Major,' I said. 'I know.'

He grinned. 'Pat's the name,' he said. 'You'd better get used to it. If we ever have a sergeants' mess you'll be in it, Fen. You sure you know?'

'I know all right, Sar'-Major.' I felt I could never call him by his first name if I lived to be a thousand. Bold was Bold, and somehow I couldn't manage to think of him in any more affectionate terms.

'I'm not likely to forget it,' I said. 'You drummed it into me often enough.'

He grinned. 'It means wiring yourself in with a machine gun,' he said, 'and holding the flank. And staying put, right where you are, *whatever comes against you*. Ashton asked me who it should be and I told him your lot. They're all intelligent lads and they can be relied on to use their loaves in case anything happens to you. Besides, he wanted someone reliable. That's why I picked you.'

I said nothing, and he looked up, his expression faintly challenging. 'Well, that's why you got made up to sergeant,' he said. 'We'd got to make somebody up and we couldn't make up Mason, could we?'

'Mason's all right,' I said.

'Didn't say he wasn't, did I? You're *all* all right. In fact, I sometimes think you're such a lot of blinkin' nice blokes, civvies or no civvies, it's rotten 'ard luck for you to get chucked into a battle like this is going to be, knowing so little.'

I was surprised to find his face was strained and unhappy as he spoke, and I realised with a start that Bold actually *liked* us and probably even more.

He looked up and shoved across the remains of the bottle of whisky.

'Here,' he said harshly. 'Go and have a blowout! Go and celebrate the medal you didn't get! This bloody army's full of blokes who'll never get medals! It makes me feel old and fed up!'

I took the whisky and shared it with Locky. I felt we had something to celebrate together. We had some sugar and we boiled water and wet the baby's head under a tree in the darkness.

'I see you and Helen got together,' he said quietly as we smoked.

'How did you know we had?' I asked.

'It's written all over your face, man. Did you see much of her?'

I toyed with a piece of stick, poking at the grass with it before I answered. 'I stayed with her,' I said.

'In London?'

'In her flat.'

His eyebrows went up and he paused before he went on. 'Alone?' he asked, and I nodded.

He said nothing for a moment, then he looked up and smiled, imperturbable, understanding and friendly. 'You youngsters,' he said. 'The things you do get up to. Well, you're both old enough to know your own minds and, my God, it's taken you long enough to decide you need each other. If Helen's happy, it's all right with me. She knows what she's doing. In fact, dammit,' he said firmly, 'I'm glad you did. I can sit back now, can't I, and forget you both? No more matchmaking.'

He was grinning and I was thankful he was pleased.

'No more matchmaking,' I said. 'It's all right now.'

Mason seemed to guess what had happened, but all he did was grin briefly and slap my knee.

'Good old Fen,' he said. 'Always the dark horse. Did you have a wedding?'

'Not yet,' I said. 'Next time, I hope.'

'A wise man never takes a wife,' he said cheerfully. 'Only other people's.' He laughed and offered me a cigarette. 'I've got a girl in the village here,' he went on. 'Nice bit of stuff. She can't speak English, but she's all right.'

It was his way of saving face, I knew. He was disappointed, but how much I would never learn.

'My commission's through, anyway,' he continued. 'Ashton says so. They're all through – me, Spring, Catchpole – but they're being held back until after the Push, because nobody wants trained men to disappear just now. When it's over, I'll be too busy to get myself hitched up.'

He paused and went on thoughtfully. 'I'll be better off as an officer,' he said. 'If officers conk they send them home instead of just giving them a number nine and telling them to report for duty. Because I *will* crack if I have to take a lot more of it. I've decided I'm not cut out for this game, Fen. I think I'll try and get into transport where it's safer and you get more money. I might be able to make a good job of that. It's only a question of seeing this damned offensive through.'

He laughed again, pretending not to mind about Helen, and I found I liked him more than ever.

'I'm glad, Fen, old fruit,' he said. 'Honest, I am. A chap can be a bit of a conceited ass, at times. I ought to have known, I suppose. It stuck out a mile. There was only you and I who couldn't see it.'

I was glad it had worked out this way. I'd always liked Frank and been close to him, but since leaving for Egypt we'd been a bit like strangers to each other. I was pleased it was all over now, especially with what lay just ahead of us.

We went into the trenches again the next night. Before we left we drew the new steel helmets that were being issued. They were ugly things of khaki-painted manganese steel, like flat basins, and were said to be capable of keeping out the flying balls of shrapnel.

'Don't lose 'em,' Bold said in his high, cold, contemptuous voice, as though he loathed the lot of us. 'We ain't got enough to go round yet and somebody else'll want yourn when you come back. So see we get 'em returned, do. If you get yourself killed, 'and it to your pal to bring 'ome.'

They were heavy things to wear and fell off every time you bent forward. Nobody trusted them much and everybody said they'd be more useful for other things, and pretended to eat and drink out of them.

'Just do for under the bed,' Catchpole said. 'Mugs, thunder, troops for the use of.'

On the way up we picked up a lot of gas cylinders which were to be dug into the front line ready for the offensive. They were horrifying things to handle. They weighed a hundred and eighty pounds and were slung on a pole between two men. Everyone had to wear his gas-helmet all the time in case they leaked, and that meant that most of the time we were stifled and half-suffocated.

'I thought all the rest was pinpricks,' Tim Williams said. 'Now they're dealing out sword-thrusts.'

The men in charge of the gas seemed to be mostly youngsters who'd been apprenticed to chemists, or chemical plants, or worked in dyeing firms, or even were mere schoolboys good at chemistry.

They wore a red, white and green brassard which they said made them immune from being shot as deserters if they were found in the trenches after the attack had started.

'They wanted chemists,' one of them told me. 'So I looked up the formula for water and told them it was H_2O, and I was in.'

We tramped through the warm thundery summer rain, the shining wet cylinders swinging between every swearing group of men, knocking their knees and trapping their fingers.

'Doesn't it ever bloody well stop raining?' Eph mourned, his boots slipping on the mud. 'It's never seemed to 'ave give over since we arrived.'

The Germans were wide awake now to what was in the wind and had all the roads taped. As we passed through Sécourt, a battered village between Bos and the front, we were caught by a flurry of five-nines and the air was immediately full of flying tiles and whirring splinters of wood. A house went down with a roar of tumbling bricks and a bellying cloud of pink-and-grey smoke and plaster-dust.

Within a second the road was clear of struggling men as we dived for cover between the houses and into the ditches. A group of cavalrymen who'd been waiting farther up the road, the rain shining on their helmets, an extra bandolier of ammunition round their horses' necks, came clattering past, hooves rattling on the pavé. As they swung round the corner, one of the horses slipped on the cobbles and went down with a crash, and the trooper went rolling into the ditch.

'My God,' Eph said, shaking the plaster-dust from his shoulders, 'the cavalry's had a casualty at last!'

The trooper got to his feet and limped away after his horse, dragging his rifle, and as we slowly lifted our heads from the wet grass we could see nothing but the ruins of the house, a few dropped helmets, scattered bricks, tiles and glass, those damned cylinders, still fortunately intact, and three sprawling figures on the bend ahead, covered by the drifting leaves that had been stripped from the branches by the tail end of the blast.

'Fritz is getting a bit careless where he drops his coals,' Tommy Mandy said.

The cry of 'Stretcher-bearers' had gone up and the stink of lyddite drifted towards us on the heavy rain-wet air.

'Who is it?' someone demanded.

'A Company. None of our lot.'

'Ah, well,' Tom Creak said. 'Men are cheap enough.'

'So long as they're not munitions workers!'

We climbed back on to the wet road, kicking the scattered bricks aside, while the dead were buried behind the houses and the injured carted off to the nearest dressing station. Within a quarter of an hour we were formed up again, and there was no sign of what had happened, beyond a smear of blood on the pavé being washed away by the rain, and a soaked cap with a couple of holes in it lying by the splintered door of a cottage.

When we got up to the front near Serre things somehow seemed different. The communication trenches had been divided into 'up' and 'down' routes ready for the offensive, and the engineers had erected direction signs, and the military police were there to see they were strictly adhered to. Bridges had been constructed across the trenches for reserves to pass over when the offensive started, many of them wide and heavy enough to carry cavalry. The air of expectancy you could feel back at Bos had been carried right to the front line now.

As we filed into the communication trench, we passed a squad of miners coming out, plastered with chalk-white mud from the earth they'd been digging from a mine tunnel.

'Fritz's still working,' they announced, 'so it's all right. When he stops, that's the time to start worrying. His counter-mine's due to go off.'

The rain ceased at last, and it was a rich quiet evening as we dumped our gas containers. Things seemed to be more than usually quiet as we took over.

'Fritz's lying low,' they told us. 'He knows something's up.'

You could see the brown smudges of German cooking fires way ahead, rising straight up in the air, and farther along the trench I could hear a man whistling as he cleaned his rifle. The air was still and beautiful in spite of the stink of decay and the chloride of lime. Then a single gun fired and a shell whistled by overhead, roaring and clattering through the sky like an express train, and the noise startled a prowling rat which rattled the empty tins over the parapet. The first flare of evening went up, and the thudding of guns from the north started as they went at it again at Vimy.

I took over from a talkative little Glasgow schoolteacher, wearing the three stripes of a sergeant, who did his best to put the wind up me as he pointed out the strongpoints and the danger spots.

'There's a nasty open bit over there,' he said, pointing, 'wi' a machine gun on it and a sniper, and a sod of a light mortar. It dinnae pay tae sing an' play the organ much.'

He looked worn and tired as he stared through a chink in the parapet.

'They're not firing much now, though,' he said. 'They've quietened down. It's so yon RFC boys cannae spot their gun-flashes and pass their positions on tae the artillery.'

I took a look through the chink and I could see the land rising towards Serre, open ground with no sort of cover, with Gommecourt away to the north, a mound crested with feathery trees, and what looked like a château in the distance. You could see the ruins of three or four churches and, away beyond the German wire, the white lines of support trenches herring-boning the hillside.

'They're all new,' the Glasgow sergeant said. 'He's gettin' ready for us, mon.'

There was a small bird singing on the bushy stump of a tree in front of me, clear in the pale-yellow light of the evening sky, and beyond it I could see the skeleton roofs of the village over the grey-green grass and the spatter of buttercups and moonpennies and scabious. The sky was still full of larks' songs.

The Scottish sergeant looked gloomy. 'It's a hell o' a long way tae Fritz's trenches, mon,' he said. 'And there's a lot of wire on the way. You can't see it for yon grass, but it's there. There's acres of it, except where he's cut it in front o' the machine guns.'

The thought of those damned machine guns was enough to chill your heart in your breast. We all knew they were there, concealed by drainpipes, they said, to hide the flashes, and manned by expert gunners, who waited silently for us to appear, watching and listening, hiding in shell-proof dugouts when the shells came down.

'They've been puttin' raids over on oor left all week,' the Scots sergeant said. 'But Fritz is wide awake and none o' 'em got in. He even put a notice on his wire. "Why do ye no' come?" it said. "We're waitin' for you."'

I'd heard that story before and was inclined to regard it was old soldiers' hearsay, but there was certainly something in the air that was worrying. Perhaps it was the stillness. Perhaps it was the thought of Catchpole's talk at Boulogne of dud shells and obsolete artillery. Perhaps it was the rumours that had reached us occasionally, the stories of dummy trenches dug north of Gommecourt to flummox the Germans about the course of the attack, that hadn't even drawn a single contemptuous shell. Whatever it was, it gave you an uneasy fluttering in the pit of the stomach.

When the relief was completed the stillness seemed deeper, and a sense of something ominous lay like a shadow over the expectancy and the hope.

Then, as though to break the spell and set our minds at rest, we heard the Germans singing just in front of us, harmonising, out of sight in their own trenches.

'It's the "*Lorelei*",' Tim Williams said, and he began to join in.

> '*Ich weiss nicht was soll es bedeuten*
> *Dass ich so traurig bin,*
> *Ein Märchen aus alten Zeiten*
> *Das kommt mir nicht aus dem Sinn.*'

We listened for a while with pleasure, then we heard a voice that travelled clearly across the darkness and the stillness.

'Can you remember the Stoltzer choir at Ross and McCall's Empire?' it said in perfect English. 'In 1913?'

We eyed each other uneasily.

'That's a fine thing,' Mason breathed. 'The bastards have rumbled who we are.'

'Let's get someone to call up the artillery,' Murray said immediately. 'That ought to shut 'em up.'

'Dry up,' Mason snapped. 'Yes,' he shouted, 'we can remember.'

'That's us,' came the voice again, thick and guttural, but quite distinct. 'How's FitzHerbert Square? How's the Lord

Mayor? When we come over there we'll string him up from one of the gaslamps outside the Corn Exchange.'

There were a few more catcalls back and forth.

'What's it like over there?'

'Bloody wet.'

'How do you fancy it on the Somme?'

'All right, but for you lot.'

Murray was itching to send over a trench-mortar bomb, but no one did.

On the third day in, a raid was laid on to snatch a prisoner. A bangalore torpedo was discharged under the German wire and twenty of us, armed with coshes and bombs, plunged unwillingly into the usual berserk scuffle in the dark before we got back minus two men and plus a whimpering unwilling boy, his head bloodied from a clout from a potato-masher, who was far more afraid of the barrage his pals were putting up than he was of us.

The following morning there was a piece of corrugated iron propped up against the outside of our wire, covered with crude letters painted with whitewash. It wasn't easy to read at first, and Welch and I tried for a long time before we finally made it out.

Thanks for the raid, it said. *When you come over, we'll be waiting. We'll crucify the first City Battalion man we capture.*

Welch looked round at me, trying a little smile that was lopsided and twisted.

'They're only trying to frighten us,' he said. 'There's nothing to worry about. Nothing can go wrong when it starts. They'd never risk the K. armies. They'd never dare. Kitchener must have laid down some conditions to make sure of that.'

Probably he had, I thought, but Kitchener was dead now, drowned off the Orkneys, and in his death lingered the first hint that these mighty armies of his weren't immortal. In spite of the singing and the patriotism that hadn't yet been dimmed, there was somehow in Kitchener's end the knowledge that perhaps *we* were pretty frail too, and that life was a tenuous thread that could be snapped in a second.

We all of us had the wind up a little that week, I think.

We were glad to get back to Bos. The rain had come down steadily all the time and we'd never seemed to be dry. Even the rats had been growing bolder and Murray had amused himself by sticking a piece of cheese on the end of his bayonet and sitting with his finger on the trigger waiting for a chance to blow one of them to perdition.

We'd spent the whole time digging, cutting lanes in our wire for infantry to pass through when the time came, pushing saps and jumping-off trenches forward and covering them with wire netting and grass to make them invisible from the air, working at night while cartloads of empty biscuit tins were driven up and down just behind the line to drown the noise. Twice a German aeroplane came over, followed by puffs of smoke where shrapnel burst around it, hurting the ears with the noise and making us duck as the bits of old iron came whizzing down. He dropped a few small bombs, but the second time an English aeroplane chased him away and, after that, buzzed over us every morning to make sure he hadn't come back, sometimes low enough to wave to us.

As we tramped homewards to Bos, we passed huge compounds, acres wide, with rows of strong wire wound round thick stakes.

'What the hell are those for?' Murray demanded. 'Cattle?'

'Prisoners, man,' Bold snapped. 'Prisoners of war. Thousands of 'em.'

The sides of the nearby hillocks had been dug out for casualty clearing stations, and lorry-loads of stretchers had been dumped there. A party of West Yorkshires were digging great pits.

'What's all that for?' Mason asked. 'Gun positions?'

'Graves,' Bold announced laconically. His eyes were fixed

ahead as he marched alongside us, his expression disapproving, as though these preparations were a grave contravention of the old soldier's unwritten law that death was never spoken of in camp or barracks.

Mason's face had grown hard and pale, and I could see Henny Cuthbert's had become thoughtful. Catchpole jerked his hand towards the digging men.

'There's your spot, Eph,' he called. 'In the corner. I'll arrange for Hardacre to be next to you so he can sing you all the way to the Happy Hunting Grounds.'

'Shut your rattle,' Bold snapped. 'You won't think it so bloody funny when it comes.'

As we neared Bos, the last columns were moving up, thinner now and led by harassed officers anxious not to miss the battle, the last few guns jolting and rattling eastwards into position, men sitting stiffly on weary horses, waggons, field kitchens and limbers, the last mobile Red Cross unit, the last few infantrymen. Once we passed a hole blown in the road and a brand new unit who hadn't been quick enough off the mark when they'd been caught by shrapnel; and we had to stop to clear up the mess. A splinter had taken the chin off a driver and another had opened the skull of one of their officers, and with all the wounded lying about they were still a little shocked and scared.

Farther back there were streams of civilians moving to the rear, with handcarts laden with bedding and belongings, mostly black-garbed old women and a few weary children. Even Madame at the farm where we had our bivouacs, who'd been there since 1914, was packing as we arrived, staggering in and out of the door with mattresses and family portraits and kitchenware.

'We've been warned to go,' she said. 'They say it'll not be possible next week. There may be shelling.'

We gave her a hand to tie her things together and she trudged off, pushing a laden pram, picking up what fell off every time the wheel bounced in a rut.

'Well, that's it,' Mason said bitterly. 'If they didn't know before when we're coming, they're bound to know now. It's only a question of, "Which day is it going to be?"'

The staff welcomed us back with open arms. We were immediately given back the steel helmets we'd handed in and marched to a valley beyond the railway track at Meycourt for a final rehearsal, eight hundred bored men in full kit and gas masks learning the art of passing through another battalion of eight hundred bored men in full kit and gas masks.

The hillside had been lined with shallow trenches dug by the Pioneer Corps and as we filed into position we were watched by bitter French farmers who'd had to give up their crops, and by magnificent red-tabbed men on well-fed horses who glanced superciliously at Pine's sorry mount as we passed.

They deployed us along the whole side of the valley, all sweaty and damp from the thundery rain that kept falling, all patient, fuming and not very interested.

'Bear in mind,' Ashton told us, 'that the men with the flags in front of you are representing the barrage as it moves across the Serre Road. Watch them carefully and keep your distance from them. You'll be a hundred yards behind the first wave. When the flags disappear, that'll be the moment when the barrage lifts and moves on to the second line of trenches.'

He paused to consult one of the bulky sheaves of orders he carried, then went on with an anxious frown as though he were having trouble remembering everything.

'Try to imagine you're carrying your full kit,' he went on. 'Together with the extra equipment you'll have. You'll all be carrying something – barbed wire, pigeon baskets, signalling gear, drums of telephone wire, water cans, bombs, et cetera – and, if you remember that, you'll have an idea of the speed you're expected to move at. On no account must we move too fast.'

'Christ,' Eph muttered, 'with that lot, we'll be lucky to move at all!'

362

The engineers, pioneers, gunners, signallers and staff waited just to the rear of the massed troops, then someone started a battery of smoke pots so that a thick white cloud began to drift across the valley. A rocket flared into the sky on our right, ending in a red star, and we began to advance down into the young wheatfields of the valley and up the other side. As soon as the first wave had advanced a hundred yards, the second was sent after it, and then the third at the same distance, and then the fourth, until we were all moving down the valley together, mounted officers cantering about between the lines shouting instructions.

'Keep your distances,' they called importantly. 'Not so damn' fast, there! Hold on to your men, Colonel! They're getting out of hand!'

'Into the valley of death strolled the six hundred,' Tim Williams quoted.

'I'll bet them queens on 'orseback won't be out in front there when the real thing starts,' Eph grunted.

It was a tremendous sight to see all those men moving forward together, shoulder to shoulder, waving to each other and laughing as they went. Once we set up a hare and someone threw his cap at it to the accompaniment of cheers.

As we reached the other side, panting and cheering. I saw a staff officer gallop up to the brigadier who sent an officer off to Pine. Eventually the order found its way down to us, and we were faced about ready to march back.

'For God's sake,' Ashton said, tramping up to us, as hot as we were, his face martyred. 'Keep your faces straight this time. They say it wasn't taken seriously enough.'

'I think it's a lot of bloody nonsense,' Mason complained when he'd gone. '"Take your time." "Don't hurry." Just as if we were on parade. Why don't they just blow a whistle and let us go full belt. I thought surprise and speed were important. The *Infantry Training Manual* says so, anyway.'

Only Murray's faith seemed undimmed. 'Good Lor',' he said.

'What a lot you are! Haig and Co. have been doing this all their lives, haven't they? They know what they're up to.'

'I'm not so sure,' Mason said darkly. 'That lot at GHQ are just a lot of amateurs who preferred playing polo to learning their jobs.'

We tried it again, less enthusiastically.

'I hope they let us go faster than this when it actually starts,' Spring said. 'At this speed we'll be sitting ducks.'

Three times a day for three days we crossed that blasted valley, while the staff treated it as a field day, galloping about with stopwatches, saluting each other and sitting in groups over packed lunches and wine.

'Down with the staff!' Catchpole shouted in disgust, bull-sensitive to red tabs. 'They only do it so that if anything goes wrong they can say it wasn't their fault.'

Some of the resentment must have found its way upwards because, when it was all over, they lined us up on the slope below the road and a general appeared above us and went out of his way to tell us what a fine lot of men we were, as though someone had decided spirits were sinking under the weight of boredom and needed a little boosting up.

He was a tall man with a clean pink face and a small bristly grey moustache. He was strung about with equipment, field glasses, map-cases and revolver, and he seemed so different from the smooth-faced men who'd been harassing us that I felt that at last the office generals were being pulled back and the fighting generals were coming to the front for the battle.

Behind him there was a padre with a colonel's rank badges, and a staff-captain with a starched collar that picked up the sunshine, and the usual cavalrymen to hold their horses.

The general read some fatuous order of the day from the divisional commander, then dismissed it with a wave of his hand as though we were all pals together and he didn't think much of it, either. Then, in a hearty man-to-man way, he went on to say we'd made a jolly good job of the rehearsal, so that we all began to feel better, but that rehearsals were now a thing of the past and the next time we lined up it would be to face the Germans.

That bucked us up immediately and we began to listen to him for the first time with interest.

His instructions seemed clear enough and he put them across in his clean, crisp, businesslike way, so that I felt encouraged by the thought that we were in safe hands after all.

'Men are strictly forbidden to stop for the purpose of assisting the wounded,' he said firmly. 'You must be prepared for casualties. Your generation was born to suffer in this war, but it's got to be won whoever falls, and we rely on you. Never mind your pals. Just keep going. And remember, there must be no looting. You're British soldiers and you've learned the meaning of fair play. Prisoners are to be sent back at once, preferably in the charge of the lightly wounded. We *must* have them back for the information they can give us. But, remember, white flags must not be regarded as a sign of surrender. If you come across white flags, just let us know about them and *we*'ll decide what to do.'

It sounded easy, but we'd just spent hours sweating up and down those blasted hills to verify the fact that semaphore would be as useless in battle, with all the smoke and old iron flying about, as pigeons and wireless and the rockets which nobody would see for all the other flashes that would be going off. In the end, we'd had to compromise with triangles of tin sewn to our packs in the hope that aircraft might spot them shining in the sun and know where we were.

Obviously the general hadn't thought of that, or, if he had, it had slipped his mind. He went on to tell us that Englishmen were always better than Germans, even when the odds were heavily against them, but that now the boot was on the other foot, so it should be easy.

He paused, ruffling through his notes, and when he looked up again he was smiling and enthusiastically matey.

'There may be one or two minor hold-ups,' he went on,

'but you've got to treat 'em as if they didn't exist. Once we start, it's up to us to keep on going until the final objectives are reached. Rip up the duckboards of any trench you capture and lay them across the top for the following troops to use. You'll have plenty of time. You won't find a German in those trenches opposite you when you arrive. All they want is to be off.'

He went on to recall the reputation of the division and the high position it held in the eyes of the army commander, and reminded us of the German treatment of the occupied countries, of the violation and the rape and the bestiality, until it appeared to be our sacred duty to die fighting in such a cause as we had.

'We've got him by the short hairs,' he concluded, 'and by the grace of God we'll give him such a hell on earth he'll wish he'd never created such misery. In three days we'll be in open country and you'll see the beginning of the great pursuit to the Rhine. The cavalry's waiting,' he pointed out, 'and we know where all the enemy's batteries and machine guns are. We've just got to kill as many of the swine as we can. That's all. Good luck to you all. God be with you.'

He stepped back and gave us a tremendous salute, as though he'd been proud to meet us, and it made us feel good and important. Then the padre with the colonel's badges stepped forward and conducted a short service and we all sang the old faithful, 'Fight the Good Fight'.

We gave three cheers and, as we were dismissed, I turned away, optimism sweeping through me, touched by what the general had said and by the surging enthusiasm I could feel in the men around me. The feeling of being caught up in a crusade reached out to me again.

Then, as I began to walk off after the others, I heard Blackett turn to Appleby and make a rude noise with his mouth.

'They told us all that eyewash at Loos,' he said.

*

366

The general was certainly right in one thing. Parades stopped at once and we were told to enjoy ourselves.

We played football, wrote letters home, or lay on the grass in the fields and orchards, half-dressed, watching the aeroplanes that buzzed overhead; talking about the Trades Union bosses who were making sure, in their efforts to release men for the front, that they were never included themselves, about Bottomley's hysterical latest in *John Bull* – '*What a German Officer Said*' and '*Lies, All Lies*' – and about the Dublin rebellion which was reputed to be causing the Irish troops farther south a considerable degree of heart-searching.

The newspapers were full of the offensive and said we were going to go over the top shouting 'Remember Kitchener' and 'Remember the *Lusitania*'.

'More likely, "Where's the bloody artillery got to?",' Eph suggested.

Someone had decided that music might rouse a proper martial spirit and the band began to play incessantly. In every valley behind the line, between the brown-green banks that hid a million men and a million horses, there was always some group of instrumentalists playing 'The Broken Doll', or 'They'll Never Believe Me'.

The inevitable morbid rumours flew around. The Germans knew we were coming and they were ready for us. They'd captured a prisoner who'd talked, and they had listening posts that could pick up all our staff messages. It was certainly true that junior officers had been forbidden to use the telephone and that everything that was going on could be clearly seen from the German positions on the high ground. Even the mines that were being pushed forward couldn't be properly concealed because it was impossible to hide the tons of chalky soil that were dug out.

Nerves grew edgy with waiting and there were a few fights, and people answered NCOs back. Someone punched a sergeant in A Company on the nose and someone else put a bayonet through his own shoulder as he larked about with his rifle, demonstrating what he'd do to the Germans when we went over, and a few angry slogans were chalked on walls.

Tom Creak and the Mandys redoubled their efforts to catch the fabulous carp in the stream at the bottom of the field, and a few men took advantage of the opportunity to go by lorry into Albert for a meal or a drink, and even – if they could summon up the energy to walk to the railhead – by train to Amiens for a meal of fried eggs, potatoes and wine.

Murray went once and got himself into a fight with some French soldier, not much older than himself but bearded like a pard and probably in and out of the trenches since 1914, who called him a 'Bwa Skoo'. At first Murray thought it was a compliment, then it dawned on him that this was the French pronunciation of 'Boy Scout' and he felt called upon to show he wasn't anything of the sort.

The only work we had to do was sew on the divisional signs that were introduced, pieces of coloured cloth for our collars and ribbons for our shoulder straps, to identify various parties quickly in the expected confusion of the attack.

Sheets of notices and orders bombarded the camp. THE STRICTEST ATTENTION MUST CONTINUE TO BE PAID TO THE CULTIVATION OF THE POWER OF COMMAND IN NCOS one went with heavy authority, I remember. NO OPPORTUNITY MUST BE LOST TO INCULCATE DISCI- PLINE WHETHER IN THE TRENCHES, ON THE MARCH, OR IN BILLETS. THINGS WHICH MAY APPEAR TRIVIAL TO THOSE WHO HAVE ONLY LATELY JOINED THE ARMY ARE REALLY OF THE GREATEST IMPOR- TANCE – SUCH AS SALUTING, CLEANLINESS, TIDINESS IN DRESS, MANNER WHEN SPEAKING TO SUPERIORS.

Lately joined the Army. That was us; but it took more than a notice from headquarters to change lifelong friends to superior officers, and we went on much as before.

As we reached the last days of June, we were plunged into a riot of activity and speculation. The newspapers were eagerly read for some hint of the date, and we started trying to assess from the reputations and prowess of the regiments around us just what was going to happen and where.

'The Royal Welch are here,' you'd hear someone say.

'And the Ulsters. There'll be some fun where they've stuck the Ulsters.'

'The Durhams,' you heard. 'The Jocks. The York and Lancs. It won't be long now.'

All the complicated processes of war were carrying us nearer to battle. Folders were being taken out of files down at Querrieu and quick sums totted up by clerks. People with big buff envelopes kept arriving at the colonel's billet and from time to time some middle-aged brigadier would appear with a whole sheaf of orders under his arm.

'It'll be the end of the month, you see.' Men were discussing the date now with easy abandon, knowing the secret couldn't possibly be kept much longer, if indeed there'd ever been any secret from the beginning, and you could hear them at nights in the barns and tents, their voices low and muffled, coming from the humped shapes under the blankets and round the circles of glowing cigarette ends.

We were told to get rid of all unfit horses and mules and to draw special carts for transporting the Lewis-guns to the jump-off points, and there was a vast sick parade to find the fittest men. Only the strongest were to take part. All others were to be ammunition carriers or were to stay behind with the clerks and the cooks and transport men, to form a new unit in case of disaster.

Nobody wanted to be left behind now and a lot of lies were told.

'How are you sleeping?' Eph was asked.

'Like a log,' he said. 'Takes me all me time to stay awake, sir.'

'Cheerful enough?'

'Not a smile in me, sir,' Eph grinned.

'Looking forward to going over?'

'No, sir.'

'Why not?'

'Scared stiff, sir.'

'What about? Machine guns?'

'No, sir. That somebody'll pinch me crown-and-anchor pitch.'

Sick men proclaimed themselves fit and they had to scrape up the cadres from the doubters and the faint-hearts. We'd been together for so long it seemed a shameful thing to back out now. We were all volunteers, and we took a suicidal pride in being front line troops. It was impossible to stand aside at this late hour.

The notice outside company headquarters, *The following officers and men have been carefully selected to participate* . . . resulted in a riot of backslapping and cheers. Only Tim Williams from our platoon was found to have been left out, because of his hand which was still not completely healed.

At first light the next morning, a despatch rider arrived at headquarters, and we all knew what that meant. Soon afterwards the company commanders were called to the colonel's billet, then Bold appeared to summon all the NCOs to Ashton's tent, and, as we assembled in a self-conscious little group outside, Ashton told us we were to go in opposite Serre.

'That's nice,' Bold commented in a flat expressionless voice. 'Serre's supposed to be a hard nut to crack.'

Ashton nodded. 'Perhaps that's why they chose *us* for the job,' he said with a hint of pride in his voice. 'We shall be going forward on a three-hundred-yard front. We're to form up on tapes that will have been laid for us in No Man's Land.'

He indicated a map spread out on the grass and poked at it with his stick.

'The code name for the battalion is Beer. The battalion on our right is Gin. The one on our left is Rum. We're to attack and capture the trenches marked on the map with the names Tom, Dick and Harry. We're to form up with C Company in this trench here – code name, Cheerio. A and B will be just in front in China trench. Better have a good look at the map before you leave. We shall go over in the four waves as practised, the first wave – that'll include A and B companies – to clear any wire or other obstacles. They'll carry ladders. The bombardment will intensify from six-thirty ack-emma onwards and the first wave will move forward at seven-thirty.'

Bold looked up sharply. 'Seven-thirty?' he said. 'That's late, isn't it, sir? The sun'll be up. We'll be going up'ill right into it. We shan't see a thing.'

'Something to do with the French, I believe,' Ashton said easily, dismissing it. '*They* want it that way. But there's no need to worry. We've only to walk across and take over what's left after the bombardment. The French can't give us a lot of help because of Verdun, but this time I'm not sure we need it. It's *our* show and we've got to prove to 'em what we can do.'

Bold still looked dubious and Ashton laughed. 'Good heavens, Sergeant-Major,' he said. 'There are only about twenty enemy battalions along the whole front. We know that for certain. We can muster nearly that many divisions. He hasn't a cat in hell's chance.'

'He's got machine guns,' Bold said.

'They're all taped. We have nothing to fear from them. The gunners are looking after them.'

As he spoke, there was a tremendous crash of artillery and a suggestion of back blast that flapped the tent canvas and made us all glance round. Ashton began to smile.

'That's the beginning,' he announced, gesturing with his papers. 'That's the beginning of the bombardment. Today's the first day and it's to go on all week. Listen to it. Surely that ought to convince you all how little we have to fear?'

The noise increased, and began to ripple and roll all the way along the front from north to south. You could pick out the individual guns as they went off – the earsplitting bark of the eighteen-pounders, the cough of the howitzers, and the reverberating crash of the heavy guns away in the rear.

It started with the one tremendous bang that had startled us, then settled down to a jerky roar that was flung from horizon to horizon like thunder rolling across mountains.

We moved away from the map and stared silently towards the east. Shirt-sleeved men were standing in groups in the field below us and you could see rolling clouds beyond the curve of the hill, green and yellow smoke that reminded you of the Cotterside steelworks.

I could see young Murray capering among his friends. 'They've hit a dump!' he was yelling gleefully. 'They've hit a dump!'

All the doubts and fears which had been forming in my mind after Bold's question dropped away again under that rolling iron-throated thunder. Down below in the field high-spirited figures were cheering and singing and leaping about, and you could see that all the old soldier's cynicism that they'd acquired in spite of themselves had fallen away as the offensive was set in motion.

There were so many guns going off all round us Ashton had to continue in a shout.

'Well,' he said, 'you can hear it now. The light stuff's on his front line. The medium's on his artillery. The heavies are on his communications so he can't bring up reinforcements to hinder us. We've got fifteen hundred guns. One to every few yards. The front's stiff with artillery. We'll be home by Christmas.'

Through the din I heard names like Montauban, Contalmaison, Pozieres, the Miraumont Spur, Hannescamps and Maricourt.

'That's twenty-odd miles from north to south,' I said, startled. 'Is it going to cover the lot?'

'This is the biggest thing that's ever been put on,' Ashton pointed out. 'Ever in the history of war. We can't fail.'

A whole set of instructions followed, which Ashton read from a sheaf of cyclostyled papers in his hand, enlarging on every point as he went along.

'We've got the times of the artillery lifts,' he said, 'and we're not to get in front of them and we're not to lag too far behind.'

'What happens if we stick?' Bold asked disconcertingly.

Ashton laughed. 'Stick?' he said. 'Listen to the racket. Nothing can exist after *that*. Do *you* think we'll stick?'

He stared at Bold for a moment, waiting for a question, but Bold said nothing, and Ashton began to read again from his instruction sheets.

'It's impressed on us that we hold on to every yard of ground we gain,' he said. 'We must be ready in case he tries to push us out. But, as all the enemy's balloons have been destroyed, his counter-attacks can only be shots in the dark.'

He paused and took a breath. 'Every man will wear a steel helmet,' he continued, 'and will carry an entrenching tool, a rolled groundsheet, a water bottle, a haversack containing shaving gear and extra socks, the unconsumed portion of the day's rations and extra cheese, a preserved ration, an iron ration, two gas-helmets, tear goggles, wire-cutters, a field dressing and iodine. In addition, there'll be flares to carry, and bandoliers of extra ammunition, wire, sandbags, Mills bombs, picks and shovels, water, pigeons and other things. I'll let you have a list of those last items section by section.'

'What happens if we have to go in with the bayonet with that lot?' Bold's question was harsh and angry and lacking in respect. It was quite unlike his normal manner, and Ashton took off his spectacles and polished them, peering at him, mournfully and a little owlishly, as he always did when he was uncertain, as though disapproving but unable to make up his mind how to reply.

'Doubtless that's all been worked out too,' he said sharply.

'It's to be hoped so,' Bold growled, and I saw Ashton look at him with an annoyed expression on his face. For a moment he stood fiddling with his sheets, staring at Bold, then he seemed to shrug off the distraction. When he went on he seemed a little irritated and nervous, as though things had been pointed out to him that he hadn't considered and the thought worried him because he *ought* to have considered them.

'The men will pile their personal belongings and greatcoats near the waggons for storage,' he went on, his voice a little higher and firmer, as though by that means he hoped to prevent further interruptions. 'One man will be detailed to remain on guard over them until after the offensive. Blankets will be handed in at once and the men are to start immediately getting their kits ready. We shall be moving up at any time.'

Bold didn't seem any too happy as we walked away.

'The plan's too rigid,' he said angrily. 'It don't allow for anything going wrong. And that bloody list of things we've got to carry! – it's obviously been got out by some fat little donkey who's never lifted anything heavier than a ceremonial sword. The lads'll not be able to lie down or get up even.'

He turned and looked keenly at me. 'Me and you are going to be busy, young Fen,' he said. 'Looking after this other lot who don't know how to go on. We're going to have our hands full, me and you and a few others who know how many beans make five. Believe me, there's precious few of us, and *I* shall be busy looking after Ashton. I like Ashton. He's all right, in spite of that gloomy look he gets on his old mug from time to time. Game as a pebble, he is, and he never loses his temper when he's tired, but he'll always be a better penpusher than a soldier, and he needs somebody to keep him straight.'

There was a lot of laughter as we put our kits together. It was a bit like preparing for the summer holidays as we stuffed in the few extraneous things we considered necessary or rejected the things we didn't want. I had three hundred cigarettes spare and I put them all in, thinking we might be glad of a few extra if we were cut off for a while.

The air seemed supercharged with emotion that evening, and as the sun started to edge towards the hills, and the first owls came out, you could hear groups of men singing all the old sentimental songs in soft, surprisingly sweet voices that left a bewildering sense of loneliness. Hardacre's choir started up and

I was surprised to find out just how good they were; and before anyone quite realised what was happening an impromptu concert was in full swing, and even the officers left their tents and came down the slope of the field to join us round the fires.

Hardacre sang 'Bright Stars of Italy' to Tommy Mandy's mouth-organ, and 'The Road to Mandalay', and Spring, in a plummy pompous voice, started a poem which began '*We take to fighting as a game, and do no talking through our hat . . .*' then, when the boos and catcalls started, he grinned slyly and announced instead a ditty entitled, 'Fred Fernackerpan, or the Hero Who Made Victoria Cross'.

There was a storm of cheering and laughter that increased as he unrolled a bawdy ballad, then Catchpole and Henny Cuthbert appeared in a rough-and-ready sketch about capturing Germans with a string of sausages and a bottle of lager beer. It wasn't really very funny, but we all laughed a lot and I saw the colonel almost weeping as he rolled about in his chair. We were all ready to see the lighter side of anything just then. It stopped you thinking and, in that heightened atmosphere of excitement and dread, it was easy to think too much.

All around us, in every field and orchard, in every village and by every roadside, the final preparations were taking place. Thousands of other men had put their kits together too, and hundreds of harassed officers had checked their lists for the last time. The final loads of ammunition had arrived and the last few men and horses. The last few batteries had rattled into position, digging their pits hurriedly and searching out their observation posts.

It was here. The end of all our training, the moment to which we'd all dedicated our lives for the past two years, the end of all frustrations, doubts and sorrows. Battle. The Big Push.

Beyond the hills, the bombardment was still continuing, rattling and muttering over the valleys like the flutterings of gigantic wings, like some iron monster that would soon snatch all these thousands of well-trained men – the heroes, the

375

cowards, the fainthearts and the strong together – all the guns, all the animals, all the machinery, and fling them into the final holocaust that would end the war.

The offensive seemed to have rolled itself together like some tremendous beast about to spring.

The concert ended on an emotional note. Inevitably the famous speech from *Richard II* had to be quoted and inevitably it had to be Murray who chose to do it.

There was a storm of cheers and jeers when he announced his intention but, as he plodded solemnly through it, the shouting died.

'This royal throne of kings, this sceptred isle,
This earth of majesty, this seat of Mars,
This other Eden, demi-paradise . . .
. . . this blessed plot, this earth, this realm, this England.'

His firm, sincere young voice carried clearly in the still air and the laughter had gone completely from the faces of his audience by the time he finished.

Without any suggestion from anyone we started to sing '*God Save the King*', and I remembered that other occasion I'd sung it like this, on the night before I joined up. It seemed a lifetime away now, but the rough, strong voices in the open air had the same overwhelming effect on me, and I felt proud and sad, and glad I was there.

Death wasn't very far away over the hill that night and the savour of life seemed twice as powerful. Emotion was strong in all of us as we were confronted with the substance of life and the pre-eminence of death. We were the chosen people, poised on a lofty height, and the tendency to be tolerant with the sentimental, even with the would-be heroic, was strong.

Every man I saw seemed to be concerned with his neighbour and there was a strange gentleness about them all; and underneath the air of excitement, an extraordinary politeness. The normality that had disappeared in the two years we'd been in uniform had returned, as though in this moment of emotion we'd become sane thinking men again, thoughtful of others, forgetting all the brutality they'd taught us and concerned only with trying to do our best. Selfishness had suddenly been left behind.

Part Three

I find a hundred thousand sorrows touching my heart and there is ringing in my ears like an admonition eternal an insistent call, 'It must not be again.'

WARREN G. HARDING

1

Well, we knew now. We knew when it was coming and where it was coming and what we were expected to do. We had everything on our sheaves of orders and in our notebooks and in our heads. We knew what was happening up ahead and what had been happening during all the past weeks, where all the frustrations and hard labour and waiting had been leading to. It made it easier to face up to it and we all felt better for it. Perhaps it was the definiteness of it, the certainty that now there was no backing down, no escaping. It was much as it had been when war had been declared. It had been hanging over us for weeks, but, now it had arrived, the feeling of 'Oh, well, now we can get on with it' came as a relief rather than as a nightmare.

It began to rain, pouring down out of a leaden sky, and as the little camp in Bos Wood became a quagmire, the flights of aircraft we had seen so much of disappeared. The RFC couldn't see anything and flying had become pointless.

The intense excitement faded a little when no orders to move up came through. We changed into our best khaki and spent the days sitting about out of the rain, crouching in the little bivouacs, cleaning our rifles again and again, going over and over in our minds with a nagging monotony the things we were supposed to do and supposed not to do, pestering for information the cooks who always knew long before the orderly room when there was a move on foot. There was a lot of horseplay that sprang from overexcitement and nervousness, and a lot of sentimental letters were written, in which things were said that somehow had never managed to reach daylight before.

Near the farmhouse the orderly-room staff were stowing typewriters and deed boxes and burning old documents in a puther of blue-grey smoke and flying scraps of charred paper. During the morning, a big grey staff car came churning up the muddy lane, sliding wildly from side to side, and a staff officer got out at the farm door and went to see Colonel Pine. Immediately he'd gone, there was a conference for the officers, and when it was over, the NCOs were all called to Ashton's tent again to go through the plan once more.

As I came away, I saw Henny Cuthbert sitting alone under the two groundsheets he shared with Spring, cleaning his rifle with a slow faraway thoughtfulness. He looked depressed and in no mood for battle. I squatted down alongside him, and he pushed the weapon out of sight behind him.

'What's wrong, Henny?' I asked.

'Wind-up, I suppose,' he said.

'We've all got that,' I pointed out. 'I expect most of us are sick with funk if the truth were known.'

He ran his fingers through his thin colourless hair. 'I know that,' he said. 'As a matter of fact, it probably isn't wind-up. It is in a way, and yet it isn't. It's hard to explain. I've just – well, I've just been thinking a lot about all the things I'd like to do and probably won't ever have a chance to do now. I suppose we've all got a good chance of getting knocked out when the balloon goes up, and I'd got around to thinking that I wouldn't like to die without trying some of the things I've never sampled. Fen, do you know – I've never been drunk. Never in my whole life.'

'You can soon rectify that,' I said.

'It's not just that.' He gave me quick nervous smile. 'I've never – I've never been with a girl. I was always what my mother called "well brought up" and went to chapel and that sort of thing and – well, we were taught never to think about that. It seems silly now to have worried about what was right and what was wrong. It probably won't make any difference either way twenty-four hours from now.' He looked up and went on with a flash of anger, 'It seems a bit bloody hard, though, doesn't it, to go and get knocked out without getting round to experiencing some of the things a man ought to know about.'

'Who says you're going to get knocked out?'

'Oh, nobody,' he agreed dully. 'But you've got to admit the chances are pretty good. I started thinking how I'd spent all my life working – all hours, I worked – then just when I was getting old enough and making enough money to enjoy myself the war came along. That's why I thought . . .'

'You were going to have a hell of a time, weren't you?' I said.

He managed to laugh. 'Yes,' he admitted. 'I suppose I was. I was going to spend my leave in London. They tell me that sort of thing's easier there.' He sighed and his smile faded. 'Still,' he ended, 'perhaps I'd never have got around to it, after all. I can't somehow imagine it really. I'm a bit on the shy side.'

He managed another smile and reached behind him under the shallow shelter of the laced groundsheets for his rifle. As he began to clean it again, a thin forlorn figure, I thought of Helen. I'd come back from leave feeling I had something strong and tender and delicate that couldn't ever be destroyed in the battle ahead of us, but as I watched Henny turn away from me, seeking privacy where there was no privacy and comfort where there was no comfort, I thought of his lack of love, and of Murray with his first love and Mason with his lost love; of Eph with his faithless Mabel and Locky with his newborn son; all of them thinking that they too had something to sustain them through the future, a sort of talisman that gave them the right to return, when by all the laws of average some of us inevitably wouldn't survive to see the fulfilment of our hopes.

I found Henny had made me feel depressed and I went in search of company. The platoon had taken shelter in a barn and were playing cards in the straw, Murray as usual holding forth on his faith, which he wore always like a suit of shining armour.

'Intelligence says Fritz has no idea when we're coming,' he was saying, aggressively and indignantly,' and I guessed someone had been baiting him.

'Intelligence underrates friend Fritz a bit,' Mason retorted. His face seemed taut and there was only a thin veneer of cheerfulness over a nervous irritation. 'When the Bantams went in, they shouted "Cockadoodledoo" at them. They called the Royal Welch "Bloody Welsh Murderers". You heard what they shouted at us. Fritz isn't as daft as they'd like us to believe.' He cocked a thumb at the heavy sky. 'He's only got to look up there and count the observation balloons to see how many divisions we're going to use. He even knows how many of us there are.'

He threw down his cards and lay back in the straw, his eyes far away. 'I think I've had enough cards for a bit,' he said.

Nobody else seemed to want to play either and Catchpole began to collect up the money. For a moment he stared at it, then he took off his cap and threw it inside. 'Why not pool all our spare cash?' he said. 'We can hand it over to somebody who's staying behind – somebody like Bickerstaff. He's staying with D Company's cadre.'

'What the hell for?' Spring asked.

Catchpole put the cap down on the straw. 'Well,' he said. 'Whoever's left after it's all over can share it out. It's not much use to us if we're dead or back in hospital with a Blighty one, but it'll be a nice consolation prize for anyone who has to stay out here.'

They all looked at each other for a moment, thinking over the implications, then Eph dug out a handful of crumpled five-franc notes and threw them into the cap. ''Ere y'are,' he said. 'I'm game. All me winnings for three months. That cleans me out. Me conscience is clear now. I've 'anded me swindles to one of the cooks and one of the orderly-room boys has got me watch. Now you've got me cash, Vicar, so I've nothing to lose now but me life.'

While they were all digging in their pockets, Ashton appeared in the doorway, the rain dripping off his cap, and called me out. There was a group of men behind him, an officer, a sergeant and about ten men who looked as though they'd come straight out from England. There was something vaguely familiar about the officer and when I looked again I saw it was Arnold Holroyd.

'Hello, Fen,' he grinned. 'I made it. I got back just in time.'

Locky and Mason and Murray and the others were on their feet at once, and the air was full of questions.

'They posted me up from Gibraltar,' Holroyd explained. 'They split up my unit. Some of 'em went to Mesopotamia and some of us came to France. I was due to go to the East Surreys, but I heard of someone who'd been posted here and I managed a swop.'

Ashton interrupted. 'You'll be in charge of the strongpoint party,' he said. 'You two had better get your heads together. Better check kits.'

'Well, it's up to you,' I said when Ashton had gone. 'Just tell us what to do.'

Holroyd grinned shyly. 'Not me, Fen,' he said. 'I've been away too long. I've not even been in the line yet. I'll do what *you* suggest.'

I indicated the sergeant. 'What about him?' I asked. 'Perhaps he's senior to me.'

'He probably is,' he said. 'But he's not been out before. He'll do as I do. Don't worry.'

That afternoon we erected a final colony of tents in the next field for an emergency casualty clearing station, and at tea time there was another kit inspection. Eph still had his crown-and-anchor board in his pack.

'Kit only, Eph,' I said.

'It *is* kit,' he grinned. 'You never know, we might find time for a game with the Germans.'

After we'd finished, we were paraded on the slope of the field and Pine appeared in front of us, his cap rakish over his eye-patch, fiddling incessantly with that button of his, his other hand full of papers, his dog at his heels. His brother was behind him, holding more papers, and Ashton, and Blackett and Arnold Holroyd and all the other officers, standing in a group.

Pine told us again what was expected of us and where we were to jump off from. We listened restlessly. The repetition was becoming irritating and all we wanted to do was go. We were sick of talking and practising and only wanted to get on with the job and finish it.

'There won't b-be much in front of us, I'm told,' he announced. 'He's only got low-category troops left after Verdun. And his batteries and machine guns have all been pinpointed and they're all to – be knocked out at the last minute so he won't have time to replace them. We've only to get across there at the right time.'

Somehow the field with its little colony of brown bivouacs and its brown-clad men, and the brown ruins of the farm behind, seemed to stand out more clearly just then than I'd ever noticed before. There were clouds like hewn marble picking up the sunshine, their lower skirts full of rain; and buttercups, dandelions, poppies, cowslips and moonpennies about my feet, and mustard and thistle and convolvulus in the hedgerows with the last of the day's butterflies. Above the thud and rumble of the bombardment, you could hear cuckoos and linnets in the wood down the lane and the pipe and whistle of water-birds drowning the croak of frogs among the bulrushes and tufted weeds and poplar stems by the cool grey pools, and the last of the skylarks falling out of the sky for their evening's rest. The voices of the cooks cursing the flies round the field kitchens came up to us quite clearly from the hollow. It was the full heat of the summer now, despite the rain, and the flies, breeding on the unburied dead in front of the wire, had been making eating a misery for a long time as they poised determinedly over the food, sickening you with the knowledge of where they'd come from.

Thursday was to be Zero Day, the colonel concluded, and we were to parade in battle order the following morning and be ready to move off at daybreak.

There was a strange kind of excitement about the camp as we were dismissed. Even those of us who were afraid put on a show of bravery and went in for laughter to hide their fears, seeking courage from the rumbling of the guns and the red pricks of light that speckled the heights in front of us in clusters, as the nine-point-twos dropped behind the German trenches, wallowing down from the top of their curves to explode on reserves and communications.

That evening thousands of little fires burned in the darkness in the hollows where the Germans couldn't see them, twinkling back at the stars that pricked the sky. Groups of men were singing softly and nostalgically to the nasal chant of mouth organs, and as the fires burned low in the damp evening air the water-birds called from the marshes, and the nightingales in Bos Wood seemed louder than ever.

'Them bloody sparrers,' Eph called them, turning over restlessly as he tried to sleep.

Sleep didn't come easily, though. A few men still played cards and someone was reading the war news aloud from the *Daily Mail*. Tom Creak and the Mandy brothers didn't even pretend to try, and in the dusk at the bottom of the field they were making one last effort among the yellow irises in the pools to catch the carp that had eluded them for days.

All around me, men were resting against the trees. Scraps of paper, many of them letters from home, were scattered about the grass, giving the place a forlorn look. I could see Ashton eating sandwiches with Blackett and young Welch and Arnold Holroyd and Appleby. Sheridan was up ahead somewhere arranging for our arrival.

The smell of mown grass was strong in the air, with the musty dead smell of old leafy gardens. Somewhere in the distance I could hear the sound of a train coming through the continuous croaking of frogs from the marshy bottom ground.

I sought out Locky, feeling I needed someone to talk to, and found him writing a letter to his wife.

'Well,' I said. 'How do you feel?'

He looked up. 'All right, I suppose,' he said. 'Hoping to see the downfall of the wicked and to share in the kudos therefrom.' He grinned. 'A little concerned, nevertheless,' he went on gravely, 'that the paths of glory have a habit of leading but to the grave.'

I laughed and squatted beside him. 'I'm trying not to think of it,' I said.

'You're all right,' he said. 'You'll come out of it trailing clouds of glory and drunk on victory.'

'You sound more lyrical than normal,' I said. 'Been at the rum?'

His smile faded. 'I wish I had,' he said. 'I wish I were like Murray. Weariness and scepticism haven't touched him. Death in battle still manages to be glorious. He's fighting for right and the honour of his country. He's full of England, my England, the precious stone set in a silver sea. I feel like dropping maudlin tears on him. This time tomorrow night it may be earth that I'm dropping on him.'

He handed me a cigarette, and paused with the match flame in his cupped hands lighting the curves of his features.

'I always think they managed it better in other times,' he said. 'There ought to have been a ball somewhere last night with us all called out in whispers from the ballroom. There ought to have been a few tearful goodbye kisses in the corners, then the clattering of hooves as we cantered off to war. A few swirling capes and rattling scabbards and jiggling plumes. The fun's gone out of fighting.'

'You're sure you're not drunk?' I asked.

He gave me a grin, the old imperturbable grin that I loved so much. 'No,' he said. 'Just a touch of the hump. I'm trying to live up to being honourable and noble and all the rest of it, and finding it a bit harder than I thought. It's all right for you, you blasted militarist. You're tougher morally and physically than all the rest of us put together.'

'That's what you think.'

He grinned again but his smile faded quickly. 'I don't fancy it, Fen, that's all,' he said. 'It's as simple as that. If you want the bitter, old and wrinkled truth, the old Adam's getting awkward about the possibility of getting hurt.'

'You'll be all right.'

He shrugged. 'It doesn't help a child with toothache to tell it it'll be all right,' he said. 'I'm not all right. I'm scared I'll let you down. In spite of all this paraphernalia they drape about me and all the swearing of strange military oaths, I still keep remembering Molly and the child. I belong to quiet streets and noisy offices, making money and doing a little gardening and playing lawn tennis at the weekend, pushing the baby and going to church. I was born to get married and stay married to some woman for fifty years and tell whoppers about my past to my kids.'

'We'll tell some whoppers after this lot.'

'I suppose we shall. Twenty years from now we'll be ageing windbags who can't forget we were once in battle. The kids'll sneer at us and the youngsters'll dodge us whenever we appear.'

'Can't say I'll mind, so long as I'm still around.'

'No, I suppose not.' He laughed. 'I've begun to take a new view of bores. I'll welcome them after this lot. Come and bore me. Fill me with dusty valour. I wouldn't mind boring people myself. Am I boring you?'

'Yes.'

He leaned back and laughed. 'Thank God for Fenner,' he said. 'You're worth a guinea a box. There's always been more to you than met the eye. Helen wouldn't have got it so bad otherwise. She always felt the same about you. As long as I can remember. Did you know?'

'I do now.'

'She's a discerning child and I hope you have lots of kids, with legs and arms and real eyes and teeth. Between you, you ought to make a good job of bringing up a family.'

'Give us a chance. We're not even married yet.'

'You'll be more married than I'll ever be.' He gave me a warm friendly glance. 'Go away now, Sergeant Fenner. I want to be alone without my military superiors standing over me. What are you doing? Visiting the nervous cases: "Sleep no more, MacFen?" or "a little touch of Fenner in the night"?'

'Neither. It's just that talking to people stops me thinking.'

He grinned. 'I hope you come out of it with a very small wound that looks very heroic and a very large medal on your chest.'

I was a little uneasy as I left him. He hadn't sounded much like Locky somehow. He'd seemed a little shrill and tired.

As I went back to where I'd left my equipment, I saw that Henny was asleep. At least, he seemed at peace. I was glad, and settled down myself, but I wasn't as lucky as Henny, though most of the men around me were fast asleep by now. Young Murray was lying on his side, his face curiously boyish. He seemed untroubled by what lay ahead of him and quite sure

390

of himself. He'd spent half the day debating the efficiency of knuckle dusters in close combat with Eph, who he felt was some authority on the subject.

'The cops always used to think they were nice and handy,' Eph had said dryly, and Murray had seemed satisfied.

Over the horizon the bombardment thumped and thudded and grumbled, and the flashes lit up the sky. You could hear the neighing of horses from the nearby artillery lines down the lane and someone was playing a mouth organ dreamily in the darkness so that the haunting music came thinly through the night.

> 'There's a long, long night of waiting,
> Until my dreams all come true . . .'

The words went round in my head long after the mouth organ had stopped and I found I couldn't get Helen out of my mind. I was in no mood for battle and, as I thought about the future with her, I couldn't help wondering again and again if there were to *be* any future.

I sat up and smoked a cigarette, thinking it was better to do that than struggle with sleep that wouldn't come.

All around me equipment and arms were piled and nearby were the carts with the Lewis-guns on them, covered with ground sheets against the rain and the dew. I found myself thinking of old Corker and wondering if, in his search for a cushy billet, he'd have dodged the battle. I decided in the end he wouldn't, in spite of what he'd always said. Then I thought of Henry Oakley and Barraclough and that corporal from Loos who'd died in my arms the first day we'd been in the trenches, and I found that certainty of survival wasn't very strong. There was an uncomfortable beating in my chest and I felt angry with myself for being afraid, but there was nothing to do to take my mind off the battle and scourge me of its dread. I had no doubts about the attack succeeding, but I had grave doubts about my own fate. Then, somehow, I thought of Bold and decided, with a warm flooding affection I'd never been aware of before, that he'd pull us through somehow. Whatever happened, Bold wouldn't let us down.

In the end, I threw away the cigarette and tried to write a letter with the aid of a candle-end, but it was pretty hopeless.

I tried to tell Helen what I felt and that I wasn't afraid. But I *was* afraid and the letter seemed to show it.

After a while, I heard a boot brush through the grass alongside me. It was Ashton.

'Keep your light down, Fen,' he said. 'There are staff wallahs about, and we're not supposed to show lights.'

'I'll fix something over it,' I said.

'How do the lads feel? How're they taking it?'

'They're all right. I think a few of 'em feel they've been kidding along a bit. After all, most of 'em are pretty intelligent chaps. There are four degrees in this company alone and dozens of university men who'd have got commissions easy in any other outfit. They work things out for themselves.'

He nodded. 'That's right enough,' he said. 'I hope *I* haven't tried to kid them. It's a funny thing, isn't it, to think of all the men around us, asleep or trying to sleep, and that in a very short time we're all going to get up and try to kill each other. Nothing can stop it now. They've even got the graves ready for the dead. When you think about it, it seems incredibly cruel, doesn't it?' He paused. 'How do you feel about it?' he asked.

'All right,' I said. 'How about you?'

'Frightened.'

'So am I really.'

'It's a big thing to be facing, isn't it?' he went on, and I knew he was feeling far more like a chief reporter and a friend at that moment than a captain in the Army.

'Yes,' I said. 'I suppose it is.'

'It's what we're trained for,' he went on, 'but I sometimes wonder if I'm good enough as an officer.'

'Of course you are.'

'Brave men are entitled to good leaders and, when I think of it, I realise I don't know very much.'

'None of us do, really.'

'I hope everything goes all right. There'll be a grievous shortage of good men at home if it doesn't.'

'Of course it'll go all right.'

He nodded and crouched down alongside me on the grass.

'We're pretty raw,' he said. 'It's only when you think about it that you realise just how raw we really are. They've taught us how to salute and when to use the bayonet, but we've not been told much about mopping up and we've not got much experience except for what Bold and Blackett and a few others have passed on.'

'Nobody seems to be afraid,' I said, not very truthfully.

'Courage's no substitute for skill,' he said soberly. 'I keep thinking about my wife. Have you got a girl, Fen?'

'Yes,' I said. 'I've got a girl. I'm going to marry her if I come out of this lot alive.'

He paused for a while, then he went on thoughtfully. 'I wonder how many of us will march back here to Bos,' he said.

'All of us, I hope.'

'That's too much to hope for. But I hope they don't hurt us too much. I don't think I could face up to it, if we lost too many.'

'We'll be all right,' I said.

He sat silently for a moment.

'Sixty-six pounds of kit's a lot for a man to lug about,' he went on. 'Sergeant-Major Bold was right to question it. But there's nothing *I* can do.'

'I know what I shall do,' I said. 'If it comes to a pinch, I shall chuck mine off and chance it.'

'I wish they'd let us go in at first light.'

'We'll be all right,' I said. 'It's just that none of us has been in a battle before and it gives us all the wind-up. We're all worried we won't do our jobs properly. But we shall. If it goes wrong it won't be through lack of trying.'

'I expect you're right,' he said. He climbed to his feet again. 'I'm just going to look up Locky and Mason and a few of the others – anybody who's awake and feels like talking. It seems the least I can do. There'll be a post first thing in the morning.'

I nodded, but I fell asleep before I finished the letter.

I woke up dreaming that someone was hammering on a door by my ear but it was shell-fire dropping on the road ahead, and I sat up and listened to it for a while, wondering who was copping it at that moment.

The candle had burned itself out and the letter ended in a scrawl. I finished it quickly with the first of the light, and signed it, then I stuck it in an envelope and went to find the postbag.

The birds had already started to sing and I could see a pale yellow streak in the east. The guns had stopped firing abruptly and there wasn't another sound just then. You could have heard a pin drop. Then I heard voices, and saw the cooks starting their fires. They gave us hot sweet tea and rashers of bacon and fried bread that tasted like heaven in the thin dawn air.

Here and there, men had slipped down to the stream and were shaving. The padre was holding a communion service in one of the barns, and I went up with a lot of other communicants, but all the time through the muttered prayers you could hear the clicking of rifle bolts outside and the shouts of the cooks and the sudden bursts of laughter.

The last of the bivouacs had disappeared by the time I came out, leaving pale yellow squares on the grass that gave the place a curious dead look, an air of finality that was a little worrying.

When the whistles blew, the laughter and the shouting stopped at once as though it hadn't been quite genuine and everybody had only been acting a part to hide the fact that they were waiting. I saw Eph sigh as he picked up his rifle, but I knew it wasn't a sigh of fear, but because the moment had arrived when we had to face ourselves and discover whether we had courage, whether we had strength or whether we were weaker than other men.

Everybody seemed to be quiet, alert and quick to obey, though occasionally you could hear the harsh impatience of some over-driven officer across the subdued commotion of men getting into their kit. There was no lust for battle, just early morning snappishness, and nervousness mixed with eagerness.

Bold went along the ranks checking gas masks, iron rations, ammunition and field dressings and examining water bottles to see if they were full.

'You horrid little man,' he said to Eph when he found he'd forgotten to fill his bottle. 'It's men like you that get whole nations defeated. Just because you forgot to fill your silly little bottle. Go and fill it and get back 'ere, double quick.'

When the inspection was over, the officers disappeared and we still waited in ranks. There was a little high-pitched laughter and an occasional explosion of anger that spoke of nerves. There was a hint of something ominous and urgent in the faces around me, which were quiet for the most part and grave under the tension.

'"Oh, my, I don't want to die,"' some wag in the back row began to sing, but he was immediately shut up.

We were called to attention at last and Colonel Pine came along the ranks, followed by his brother and his dog, and Ashton. They'd all discarded the tailored tunics and knee-breeches, that made them so distinguishable at a distance, for the issue trousers, puttees and jackets of the other ranks.

I noticed Pine looked as tired and taut as everybody else. He stopped and spoke to one or two of us and I noticed he particularly singled out a few like Henny who'd been a little nervous.

'How do you feel?' he asked me as he passed.

'All right, sir,' I said.

'Good.' He nodded slowly. 'We're relying on your p-party, Sergeant, to look after the flank.'

When the inspection was over, we were told to stand easy again and waited yawning, stretching and fidgeting. Then Pine found himself a spot on a hummock in the field above us and made us a little speech, standing up there small and pale and eye-patched, much as Nelson must have looked on the morning of Trafalgar.

'I've got a special order of the day from the brig-brigadier-general,' he said. 'It's just come up – but I'm not going to read it. It only says the usual stuff. Something about us each being worth ten of them.'

There was a muffled cheer from Murray's direction and Pine managed a smile. 'However,' he went on, 'I might as well b-be honest with you. It's not going to be easy up there in front. But you must stick it. You'll just – *have* to stick it.'

The words had a sinister ring, and Pine probably noticed it himself and tried to make it right.

'We none of us know what's ahead of us,' he finished. 'But you can rest assured that everything p-possible's been thought of – by me, at least. It's up to us now. We can only do our best.'

The padre conducted a short service and we all spoke the Lord's Prayer.

'"Our Father, Which Art in Heaven, Hallowed be Thy name, Thy Kingdom come, Thy will be done . . ."'

The prayer came out as a long rumbling murmur in which the words were hardly distinguishable, and when it was finished we all stood there in the road, swaying under our packs, our helmets in our hands, busy with our thoughts. Then there was a rush from the men who were to stay behind, and final hand-shakes and backslapping and grins.

'So long,' Tim Williams said. 'Look after yourself. Fen.'

396

We gave three cheers and the band started up with 'The Girl I Left Behind Me'.

The voices of the company commanders rang out one after the other and there was a quick stamping shuffle of feet as we turned right, and a ripple of movement that ran through the company.

The details and the orderly-room staff and the cook-house men who were to stay behind drew back in a long line on the bank above the road. I could still see Tim Williams, and Twining, the quartermaster, and Bickerstaff and the colonel's brother, his hand full of papers – and as we set off they gave us three cheers.

A and B Companies had moved off first, each platoon pulling its little cart containing its Lewis-gun and ammunition, and they were waiting just along the road. We joined on behind, marching at ease. The few villagers who had refused to leave their homes in spite of official encouragement were watching us, standing at their doors, their faces expressionless. The curé stood by the iron calvary at the end of the village, sombre in his black soutane and shovel hat, and as we tramped past him he raised his hand in blessing. '*Il vous faut détruire les sales Boches,*' he said, as though that excused us everything.

The night-time colours had faded from the earth now and the light had flooded over the contours, bringing out the shadowy woods and downs. As the stars faded, the sky lost its dawn luminosity and changed to blue.

Somebody started whistling, and Tommy Mandy dragged out his mouth organ and the usual banal tune was roared out:

'Never mind the weather, now then, altogether –
Are we downhearted? – NO! – have a banana . . .'

The singing swelled up as we reached the main road. There were other troops there, and bands seemed to be going all over the place. A bunch of Jocks were waiting for us to pass them and we all put on a swagger for their special benefit. A few more villagers appeared at their doors, old and tired-looking, and their pitying expressions, which showed they knew where we were going, struck at us more harshly than the thought of battle itself, and we sang louder than ever as we tramped along the unyielding pavé between the sycamores and poplars that had never been close enough to give us shelter either from the rain or the sun. The trees all seemed to have been bashed and splintered at wheel-hub height, where lorries and caterpillar-drawn guns had struck them.

A mile from the front, we began to file past various dumps, picking up picks and shovels, and wire and corkscrew stakes and sandbags for my party.

I soon began to feel like a packhorse, and every time I leaned forward to adjust a strap my helmet almost fell off. By this time I was loaded down with wire-cutters, a bandolier of extra ammunition, and extra bombs. In addition, I had a sausage hanging at my side. The colonel had found them somewhere and had had them issued to parties like mine, who might become isolated. The bombers carried red and blue flags to help aircraft flying low over the battle to identify us, and a few others had noticeboards which were to be erected on the parapet, facing backwards for artillery spotters to see. There were also baskets of pigeons and, in one or two cases like Murray, home-made banners with slogans on them. Murray's said, *Look out, Kaiser Bill! Here I come!*

The larks had got up now and were rejoicing in the early-morning air, and the poppies – clusters of them, blood-red against grass that was still grey-green with dew – threw up bright spots of colour against the dun landscape of uniforms.

The whole front seemed to be on the move now, horse-drawn waggons and caterpillar tractors, the occasional gun still, ambulances and steam engines, everything that would move, all going in the same direction, the leaders always dead slow because of the crush, the tail-end, by some curious alchemy, always hurrying to catch up. Tremendous columns of men were tramping forward, flowing towards the sun, singing as they went, excited, scared, or thoughtful, but all touched with the same bright faith in victory. There was something splendid about all those young men, all of them the pick of their towns and villages, all of them the first to volunteer, not a conscript among them, all of them inspired by love of country and a widespread conviction that human freedom was challenged by military tyranny. They didn't grudge the sacrifice or shrink from the ordeal, and as they marched forward to fulfil the high purpose of duty with which they were imbued I felt a lump come into my throat at the thought of how many of them might soon be dead. Their courage touched me and I had a curious feeling of being caught by the light of glory.

My kit soon began to feel like a ton weight and the leather straps began to bite into my shoulders. From time to time the column ahead of us halted, and we shuffled to a stop behind them, fidgeting under our loads. The singing had died away at last and I was only aware of the grey-white road and the heavy tramping of feet, and the indistinct shadows of trees that grew blurred as the sun disappeared.

After a couple of hours, my left boot went slack and I saw a lace had broken. I fell out to make repairs and had to run to catch them up again, but the damned lace started to nag at me. Would it give way when we went in, I found myself thinking. Would it let me down at the last moment? I couldn't get the thing out of my mind.

The villages we passed through now were deserted and empty. Troops had obviously been quartered in them and I saw walls daubed with divisional signs and scrawled with slogans. *Now for Berlin*, they said and, *Look out, Little Willie*. Outside the cottages, the torn letters fluttered.

We seemed to have been on the move for hours, but the delays were so great on the crowded road we made very poor progress. Murray started to get anxious in case he missed the fun, but they still kept halting us and pulling us on to the grass verge every time a convoy of lorries went past, or for a battery of field guns to move by at full speed to get into the attack before it was too late, swerving off the road to the crack of whips, wheels gouging great ruts in the damp earth. We passed a Welsh regiment, inevitably singing a hymn, and a crowd of Newcastle men singing 'The Blaydon Races' with appropriate rude words and gestures.

The air was full of petrol fumes and the smell of warm oil, and a sickly sweet scent that I thought at first came from the abundant yellow weeds, but turned out to be the lingering aroma of gas shells. The tramp of boots and the grinding of wheels were interrupted constantly by the clatter of hooves as columns of mules went by, pushing and shoving, loaded with boxes of ammunition, or clouds of lancers with their fluttering pennants, jeered at and catcalled by the long-suffering infantry.

About midday it started to rain in torrents. It came on so suddenly we were drenched before we could get our ground-sheets out. They pulled us off the road and we covered our packs and rifles, so that we looked like a lot of curiously shaped camels, shuffling slowly forward on the jammed road, the water dripping off the shining rubber sheets and from the brims of our helmets on to our noses and down our necks. The surface of the road changed to mud that splashed everything with a whitish paste.

'My God, what a war!' Mason moaned. 'This is the giddy limit!'

During the afternoon the rain stopped again, and we moved through a howitzer battery where men were washing clothes and cooking, and clearing away the litter of empty shell-cases, then they turned us off the road and at the edge of a village they fell us out in a field full of sodden calf-high grass. They posted air-raid sentries with whistles and told us we were to remain there for the night. There was no indication of what had happened or why we weren't to go into battle the following morning as arranged. There were no tents and we had to do the best we could with groundsheets.

Everybody was angry and bewildered, wondering what had gone wrong, and anxious too, because our orders had stated quite clearly that we were to go in with the second wave within a few minutes of the battle opening.

There were other units around us, all equally puzzled and worried. I could see Ashton in conference with the colonel, and Murray, still clutching his home-made flag and looking like a little boy who'd lost the party he was going to.

'Lie down,' I advised him. 'You'll probably be glad of the chance before long.'

Bold came up to me and offered me a flask of rum.

'Well,' he said. 'How're you feeling?'

'All right,' I said. 'At this rate, though, everybody'll be whacked before it starts.'

'You can't get a hundred thousand men into position,' he pointed out philosophically, 'without a bit of a scuffle.'

Despatch riders were roaring up and down the road alongside us, bumping round the potholes and shouting what news they had to the men in the ditches and fields and crouching under the trees. One of them brought his Douglas to a skidding halt, sending the mud and water flying, shouting as he paddled his machine round a shell-hole.

'It's off!' we heard him yell. 'It's been put off!'

Bold was on the alert at once. 'Put off?' he snapped. 'What the hell do they think they're playing at?'

He stuffed his flask away and tramped off through the rain towards the road.

'It's true,' he said as he came back. 'It's been put off all right.'

Everybody had seen him go and they crowded round to hear the news.

'Rain's stopped play,' Eph shouted. 'We're all dressed up and nowhere to go!'

After a while, Ashton came along, splashing through the puddles, and stopped before Bold.

'It's been put off,' he said.

'I 'eard so, sir,' Bold said, giving him a salute like the kick of a horse, as though he felt that no amount of rain and confusion was going to stop him being a good soldier. 'I 'ope it's not for good.'

Ashton gave us a shaky smile. 'Not on your life,' he said. 'It's only for forty-eight hours. Everything's temporarily in abeyance. The weather's so bad the RFC boys haven't been able to do any spotting for the guns and they're extending the bombardment for another two days. We go in on July first.'

Bold grinned, his ginger moustache lifting as his teeth flashed – healthy white teeth as strong as he was himself.

'Nice clean-sounding date,' he said. 'Sounds like a good omen, as though an attack's just the thing to start a new month with.'

We stayed there for the forty-eight hours, listening to the unbroken murmur of the rain and the trickle and rush of water in the gutters and the strenuous firing of batteries all around. A few of the more enterprising managed to find shelter in the barns and the ruined houses of the village; but it wasn't easy, after keying ourselves up, to relax and start all over again with the same old repetition of orders, the same nervous checking of equipment. News kept filtering back as various people – Pine or Ashton or one of the other company commanders – went forward to find out what was happening.

'The wire's been cut,' Ashton told us in the evening, coming upon Bold and me as we crouched under a cart out of the rain. 'And there's been no sound all day from the Hun, so it looks as though we've plastered him into the ground.'

'Nice to know,' Bold said, trying hard to look respectful with the rain lashing into his face. 'It's always a help to have that kind of information.'

'They're putting on a raid now in front of Serre to find out,' Ashton went on, 'and the colonel would like you to go up with Mr Welch, Sergeant-Major, to find out what happens. He'd like to know what we're up against.'

I watched with Locky from inside the barn as the guns opened up, drowning the cries of the waterfowl in the linked pools along the Ancre. The flashes lit up the broken houses and the bare rafters of the ruined barns. Even from where we were, we could hear the spreading crackle of musketry and the racket of gunfire.

'That's machine guns,' Murray said, his head on one side, listening.

'There's more than one by the sound of it, too,' Mason commented. 'Business seems a bit brisk.'

'That's handy, troops! That's jolly handy!'

We stared at each other silently, listening to the din, trying to ignore what it meant to us, while the howitzers down the road stopped all time with gigantic orange flashes like bats' wings that sent the vast shells up into the sky with a high diminishing rush.

At first light the next morning, ambulances came through the village, carrying black-faced men who'd been in the raid, bandaged and wounded and crying out with pain, but the police kept them moving and nobody could ask questions. When Bold returned, he looked strained, and his face seemed harder and stiffer than ever.

'What's it like?' I asked him.

'The 'ole bloody front opened up,' he said. 'They lost eight men and got stopped before they even got to his wire. They said you could 'ear Fritz shouting: "Come on, come on. We're waiting." If the staff think there's nothing there, they've got another bloody think coming. It was stiff with 'Uns.'

He was in a tearing rage, and the words tumbled over

403

themselves, but when Ashton appeared, he pulled himself bolt upright and gave his report calmly and factually, and with no trace of anger.

'The trenches was fully manned, sir,' he said. 'They was jammed with Huns, as far as I could make out. I counted four machine guns meself. The raiding party said the wire hadn't been touched. I understand Mr Welch's reported it to the colonel, who's got on to Brigade.'

During the morning, Pine, worried about what was in front of us, sent Welch down to brigade headquarters, but they knew already. Battalions, it seemed, had been reporting the same thing all along the line. Even Brigade was worried. But Division, it seemed, safely back from the line, merely shrugged it off with the suggestion that the K. battalions had got the wind-up. The raids, they claimed, were all completely successful, and there was nothing to fear.

They even sent an official report of the shooting of a man who'd been found guilty of desertion up in the Ypres Salient – to discourage others, it was said. We were supposed to have been assembled to hear it, but Pine ignored it and we only learned of it through one of his runners.

The news spread quickly and a howl of indignation went up.

'We don't desert in this mob,' Catchpole said angrily.

'Who do they think's scared?' Murray demanded. 'I'm not, anyway. But I wouldn't mind taking some of those fat little rotters from the staff in with us, all the same.'

'They ain't got much idea,' was all Bold said, but it was clear from his expression that he wasn't very impressed by the psychology of the staff.

We were all a little quieter during the day as the weather slowly improved, all a little subdued by the news of the machine guns. If that tremendous barrage wasn't blotting out the Germans, after all, I thought, there was going to be an inevitable and terrible slaughter when we went over.

During the day, a drying breeze sprang up and we began to

see aircraft buzzing about over us again. Murray and a few others took off their clothes and hoisted them on rafters and on bayonets stuck into the plaster walls of barns and houses to dry. The break in the weather cheered us all up and the first gleams of sunshine came like repudiations of all those scares about machine guns.

The whistles went after dark and we fell in again in the village street. Voices seemed to be pitched lower as the companies numbered off, and orders were given quietly, as though the darkness gave the operation an air of stealth. There was no band to see us off this time, only the shuffling crunch of hundreds of boots, and the quiet grim jokes of men strained to a pitch of nervousness by waiting.

After a while, we turned off the main road, on to an ash track through a wood where there was an iron calvary among the trees that fringed the fields. The sound of big shells ahead quickened the apprehension and I could hear nervous laughter around me. A star shell rose up ahead, gleaming on the bunched helmets, wavered and hung in the air and, by its light, I caught the quick glimpse of a melancholy landscape and a few shattered tree trunks, petrified like lunatic arms lifted in agony. On the right, there was a smashed farmhouse that gave off a momentary gleam of yellow through a sacking-covered window where some company had its headquarters or some dressing station had been established.

I could still hear the crunch-crunch of boots on the road behind me as more troops moved into position further south, and the grind of wheels, and the higher distant clatter of led pack mules and horses bringing up more shells for the batteries of field guns hidden in farmyards and orchards and copses and behind hedgerows all the way along the front.

There was a mist hanging about in the hollows that made the knuckly hills stand out like islands in a pearly sea, and it swirled around me as I moved, clutching at me with ghostly fingers, dripping off my helmet, clinging to my eyelashes and the down at the top of my cheeks. Its dampness was chilling and seemed to get through to the bones.

There was a momentary halt to pick up more picks and shovels and sandbags and coils of wire and the path became alive with the firefly glow of cigarettes, then we moved off again and into a communication trench where a sign, *Chaffinch Trench*, was illuminated by a lantern. The trees here were growing alongside and over the trench, and their roots projected from the earth walls and snagged on equipment with a wearying regularity. Above us the branches were thick with foliage, with here and there a gap and splintered fallen branches where a shell had carved its way through.

The nightingales were singing again all round us with rich nostalgic notes as we moved off once more. The trench, which started behind the broken farmhouse, descended quickly, and the bottom was full of water and wet clinging mud that made it difficult to stand up. There was a sickly sweet smell in the angles that I recognised as gas.

Battle equipment seemed to have been stacked in every corner, and the walls were festooned with dozens of wires that the signallers had slung from every possible projection. At every yard someone seemed to get tangled up in it.

The machine-gunners in the strongpoint party were wearying of carrying the gun now. They'd dragged the carts all the way to the ash path and had left them behind as we'd entered the wood, and they were complaining loudly now about the delay and the ache in their arms. But the shuffling file of men came to a halt again, knee-deep in water. We were all already plastered by the mud we'd picked up from stumbling against the trench walls.

'This is war, if you like,' Catchpole said. 'Wire, ire, mire and fire.'

He laughed and started singing a hymn that sounded like a dirge, and a few others joined in.

'Come on, Vicar, how about a prayer?' Eph called, and Catchpole obliged with a sacrilegious mockery of a psalm.

Sick of the mud, I climbed out of the trench in the dark and sat on the parapet, deciding to chance it.

'You'll get knocked off, Sarge,' Tom Creak warned me.

'I'll chance it,' I said. 'Might as well be now as later.'

Somehow the waiting and all this maddening carting of equipment didn't seem quite what any of us had expected. There was no excitement now, no half-hearted cheering, not even any movement. We all supposed the battle would start some time, but getting into position seemed to involve more effort than the actual fighting. We were in a black mood just then and if we'd met any Germans it would have been God help them.

I didn't know it, but at that point the trench was passing through a battery of eighteen-pounders hidden among the shattered trees, and, while I was sitting there on the parapet, I heard an officer's voice call out in the darkness.

'One-three-five, fire!'

There was a roar and a flare of flame as the battery fired in a piercing stab that was scorching and white, and seemed to fossilise the trees and the sprawled dead mules and the leaping camouflage netting around it. Fragments of cordite bags dropped out of the brown acrid smoke whisping away in the oven-hot air that followed the three buffeting cracks.

The blast blew my helmet off and very nearly my head, and I fell into the trench and staggered about, slipping in the mud and holding my ringing ears.

'Bull's-eye,' someone shouted.

'What did I tell you, Sarge?' Tom Creak said seriously, his voice full of concern as he handed me my helmet. 'It's a mercy you weren't killed.'

Everybody seemed to be laughing suddenly and the incident seemed to have done them a lot of good and cheered them up.

Eventually we moved off once more, boots shuffling on

duckboards that wobbled in the gluey bottom of the trench, forced to stop again and again as some more urgent party had to pass up or down. As we got further forward, we moved through squads of military police who'd been posted to deal with prisoners or deserters or men who might hang back when the attack started.

We were growing weary now and we eyed the policemen with dislike.

'Scabs,' someone said bitterly.

'Come and join us,'

Catchpole started to sing.

'Come and join us,
Come and join our happy throng.'

Everybody took up the words, staring pointedly at the military police, each deriving some satisfaction from his own derision and scorn, then we moved off again and the song stopped.

Here and there in the moonless summer night, we came across shaded hurricane lamps that gave us our directions, but at one point a shell had destroyed them and we lost our way in the maze or tapes and signs, and stood in a confused mass, complaining and swearing as they tried to turn us about. An officer with an armband kept appearing to ask who we were, pushing past us to the rear, cursing, thrusting among us, nervous and anxious and worried.

'Where the hell have you lot come from?' he demanded. 'Who are you, anyway?'

'Fred Karno's Army,' Eph muttered, and there was a muffled snigger of laughter.

The officer looked at the glowing face of his wristwatch, swore and disappeared again, vanishing into a dugout where we could see a candle burning, and someone shouted, cheerfully and without anger, 'Put that bloody light out.'

'He looks a bit hipped, poor feller,' Tom Creak said heavily.

Then the officer came back, holding a sheet of paper, and began to push at us.

'Keep going,' he snarled, edgy with weariness and anxiety. 'Keep going. Along Charley Trench. You're behind schedule. You must stick to the schedule.'

Once, we had to crowd against the wall as bangalore torpedoes were brought past us in a last attempt to blow more holes in the German wire.

'The bloody artillery's let us down again,' one of the raiders was grumbling as they shuffled past. 'As usual, the poor bloody infantryman has to do everybody else's job.'

We heard the explosive hissing chatter of machine guns and the flurry of shelling as the raiders went over the parapet, then there was silence again, a sudden silence that seemed sinister. Someone coughed and a bullet whined overhead in a melancholy hum, and the silence came again, deep and limitless.

Bold looked at me, his face a blur in the darkness, but he said nothing. We heard later that nothing came of the attempt. No one was able to get forward for the shell-fire.

Then Murray dropped the Lewis-gun into the mud and water in the bottom of the trench and, in his disgust and weariness, threatened to stamp it out of sight.

'Pick it up, you bloody fool,' I said, as tired and angry as he was.

'What's the good?' he stormed. 'Those staff bastards'll never get us there in time.' Savagely he kicked at the slurry, and I gave him a shove.

'Pick it up, blast it,' I told him again, and he stooped wearily. His helmet fell off at once and filled with water and thin liquid mud. He stared at it, almost weeping with exhaustion.

'Oh Christ,' he mourned. He slammed the helmet back on

his head, indifferent to the mud and water that ran across his features, and leaned on the trench wall.

'You'll have to clean the gun as soon as it's daylight,' I said.

'Have a heart, Fen,' he begged.

'I haven't got a heart. I've got a swinging brick.'

'My God,' he said bitterly. 'Bloody jumped-up NCOs!'

He picked up the gun again and stood holding it in a martyred way, his head up, his helmet lopsided on his head, and started to sing softly:

> 'Oh, my, I don't want to die.
> I want to go home.'

And thankfully we all started laughing again.

The flares in front were lighting up in black silhouette the uneven edge of the trench and putting pale outlines round the men in front of me. Shells kept dropping to right and left of us, far enough away for safety, but near enough to make us duck and flinch and move restlessly as showers of mud and stones came into the trench. Once we heard screams in the darkness and shouts for the stretcher-bearers, and once or twice there was a flurry of gunfire in front and to the south which swelled into a tremendous racket.

'Raids,' Spring said. 'They're trying to break into Jerry's trench.'

We began to shuffle forward again, struggling to keep up to that all-important schedule, passing through a trench which led to a dressing station, and we saw we'd been waiting for a group of wounded to be brought up.

'It's started already,' Mason growled.

There were a lot of men sitting about the trench, victims of the German retaliatory fire, clutching their injuries and moaning, some of them mere heaps of twisting rags, muttering and groaning with pain, with here and there groups of dead men, lying or sitting in curious stiffened attitudes.

As we took up our positions, we stumbled over blackened butchered bodies that hadn't been moved and lay about on the firestep and on the duckboards and among the boxes of smoke bombs, most of them uncovered. Their faces were pearl-coloured in the torchlight, the blood on them startlingly vivid. There was one corpse on the firestep with its arms out, its fingers clenched as though in the act of holding a rifle. It had an unnerving effect when you first saw it, but Billy Mandy, a miner well used to death in normal life, shook hands with it.

'So long, mate,' he said. 'I'll give your love to the Kaiser.'

Mason was glancing about him nervously, his eyes a little wild, his nostrils flared like a young colt's.

'If this is what it's like before it starts,' he said in a high-pitched voice, 'what's it going to be like before it finishes?'

'Dry up,' I said angrily. 'Don't take any notice.'

He turned and managed a twisted smile.

'Don't worry, Fen,' he said. 'I'm all right. Just the old bull smelling blood.'

The bodies had an unsteadying effect on us all and I got everybody who had a hand to spare to lift them on to the parados and roll them out of sight. We began to feel better then, but the trench walls were splashed with blood and I got them all to dump their equipment and widen the trench to give us more room, cleaning the place up as much as possible with shovels, covering the blackened gobbets of flesh that lay under the duckboards, and burying other remains in sandbags in the trench walls.

All the time as we worked, there was a steady stream of wounded coming up from the first wave in front of us where A and B companies were, all of them complaining that the Germans had been able to enfilade them as they waited. One company quartermaster-sergeant who'd been trying a last-minute exchange of footwear, said that as fast as he put the old boots on the parapets the Germans shot them off again.

Beyond the valley in front of us and to north and south the noise was growing now, as though some vast symphony was swelling to its climax. Big shells were falling away to the east and they'd set fire to a village just behind the German lines that was sending up a thick column of smoke into the sky. You could see it all the time in the flickering light of shell-fire. All along the eastward horizon behind us, you could see the flashes of field guns and hear the rumble of their thunder that was drowned from time to time by a tremendous crash as the giants to the rear added their terrible voices like the bass of some plutonic orchestra.

2

We were finally settled in just before daylight, in a reserve trench marked with the grimly light-hearted name, Cheerio Crescent. Up in front, the bombardment had wakened up and was screeching through the air. The Germans weren't asleep either and were thickly plastering with shells the ground behind us where the reserves were.

The place was hopelessly congested with exhausted exasperated men and it wasn't possible to sit in comfort. Murray had finally set about cleaning the Lewis-gun with a sullen look on his face, and occasional bitter glances in my direction.

There was still a lot of water in the bottom of the trench, seeping through puttees and turning the soil into clinging mud which stuck to the boots in great stiff blocks that felt like ton weights.

The second and third waves were crowded together and there was hardly room to move, only to sit still and brood on the blood-stained future. But after a while a group of engineers who'd been occupying a hole cut in the trench wall moved away and I curled up in the hole out of the congestion and tried to sleep. Young Welch came along after a while, also looking for somewhere to rest, but I pretended not to see him and stayed put, and he moved morosely off.

Then Locky put his head round the corner and I made room for him and he curled up alongside me, strung about with equipment like a Christmas tree.

'How do you feel now?' I asked.

His face was pinched and grey-looking as he spoke to me.

'I think I'm going to die,' he said.

The words shocked me and I didn't know what to say.

'Come off it, Locky,' I said after a pause. 'You'll still be around when it's over. So shall I.'

'Do you think so?'

I paused, considering it. All we had behind us were a few weeks in France and even less in the trenches. It wasn't a great deal in all conscience, but it was still vastly more than many of the thousands of men about us had. It didn't amount to much when counted against the experience of the Germans we were to meet, the finest army in the world probably, and one that had twice been through France in forty-five years, but I couldn't somehow manage to face up to the likelihood of not being alive when it was all over and the guns had stopped.

'Yes,' I said. 'I think I shall. And so will you.'

He shook his head. 'I'm not so sure,' he said thoughtfully. 'Did you know I considered dodging this damned business? I thought of telling the doc I'd got neuralgia – or something else nice and handy that you can't see.'

It surprised me. I'd never thought Locky was the kind of man who'd consider dodging what he'd already conceived to be his duty.

'Why didn't you?' I asked.

He shrugged. 'I've told you before,' he said. 'This damned unit gets into a man's blood. You get scared of letting your friends down.' He paused then went on, as though he were putting into words thoughts he was vaguely ashamed of. 'But then you start thinking you're letting your wife and family

414

down more,' he said. 'What's the good of comradeship to *them*, if you're under the daisies with the worms doing eyes-right and fours-about between your ribs? I thought of saying I was ill. I was going to, right up to the minute when I faced the doc, and then I found I couldn't. I think I must have been barmy not to.'

I didn't know what to say. He was so obviously sincere and I knew he wasn't a coward.

'Molly would never have known,' he said. 'Come to that, neither would anyone else. There are plenty of dodges to beat the doctors. Chew cordite or eat soap. Eph knows them all.'

'Eph's still here in spite of that,' I pointed out.

He nodded and managed a smile. 'Yes, he agreed. 'Eph's still here. But if he'd used one of his dodges, if I'd used one, even if everyone had guessed I'd used one, it wouldn't have mattered much. No one'll be able to distinguish the heroes from the cowards when it's all over, or the ones who dodged from the ones who didn't. And when I died at a ripe old age, surrounded by sorrowing grandchildren, they'd have remembered me with respect, knowing nothing of what I'd done on the eve of the greatest battle the world's ever seen. They'd never have known I wasn't man enough to face it, and the grass would grow just as green over my grave as it will if I'm killed.'

'I wish you wouldn't talk like that,' I said.

'Oh, it's nothing to worry about.' He put his hand on my arm. 'I think it was that damned rehearsal that set me thinking. Lines must be straight. Backs must be straight. Rifles must be straight and held neatly across the chest, so that bayonets catch the morning sun. Shoulder to shoulder, just like that kid from Loos told us. No talking. No smiling. No joking. No eating. No sleeping. No hawkers. No German bands. Clean, bright and lightly oiled. This is how they advance down the Horse Guards on the King's Birthday. This is the way they charged the guns at Balaklava. This is the way they charge the guns in France. Damn it, Fen, it didn't seem very realistic to me. *C'est*

415

magnifique mais ce n'est pas la guerre. I'm not in the mood today for the cavalry-and-cricket minds of the generals. I'd rather go home. I've listened to Tim Williams too much, with all his talk about defence always being superior to attack. I wish I were like Murray.'

He paused and gave me a playful punch on the shoulder.

'And yet,' he said thoughtfully, 'I think I'm glad I'm here, all the same. There's something about it. There's something about all these chaps. There's something in the air, Mark, this morning, and I suppose we're blessed among men to have experienced it.'

None of us slept, and the likelihood of death was with us all. But we were tired with the move-up and hadn't the energy to do much else but think.

I sat down on the firestep. I wasn't looking forward to what awaited me on the other side of the parapet, but I knew I'd be glad to have it all over and done with. The chance of wounds and death wasn't easy to thrust out of my mind, but at least, I felt, it was worthwhile, to bring to an end all this miserable waiting, all this wretched humping of loads.

I longed to be home, holding Helen to me again. Before I knew where I was, I had us married with a couple of kids. All round me other men were sprawling in ungainly attitudes also trying vainly to sleep, still clutching their burdens, the weapons, the wire, the cans of water, the pigeon baskets, their tin hats shadowing their faces; their boots, their puttees just as plastered with mud as mine, their faces blank with weariness to the point of indifference, their eyes faraway as their minds wrestled with the same uneasy thoughts and the same aching longings.

We'd all attached our entrenching tools in front of us instead of behind, in the hope that they might stop a bullet, and sitting down was uncomfortable, and we shuffled and moved restlessly, wishing the moments would pass, and in the same eternity of time praying that they'd stand still and the future would never come. We were alive now and anything, even this misery of waiting, was better than the other.

Nobody talked much in the charged atmosphere, but I could see eyes moving under helmets, and everyone seemed to be listening intently. Everybody's hands seemed to be gripping something, a rifle, a strap, a piece of timber, anything, so that none of them looked relaxed, and their expressions showed they knew, just as I did, the exact time, every passing second of it.

I kept thinking of all those waves of men moving forward at the rehearsal beyond the railway at Meycourt, strong upstanding young men laughing and smoking and trying to keep their faces straight because the staff had thought we weren't taking it seriously enough, and like Locky I uneasily began to remember the words of the boy from Loos. 'Shoulder to shoulder, they came,' he'd said. 'You couldn't miss.'

We couldn't write letters, but someone managed to bring mail up from Bos Wood and it was passed round. There were two for me from Helen, and Mason gave me a wry grin as he saw them. 'I used to get those,' he said. 'Now the boot's on the other foot.'

Eph fished out his crown-and-anchor board and tried to spread it on the firestep. ''Oo's for a game?' he said. ''Oo's for a tanner on the old mud-'ook?'

But there wasn't room and no one had any money anyway, and Eph stared round him silently for a moment.

'Oh Christ,' he said. 'What's the bloody use?' He screwed up the square of canvas with a twist of his fat red hands and tossed it over the parados.

Hardacre and a few of the men around him were singing softly, but they were all tired and when Hardacre tried to start them on part songs, they started arguing and eventually quarrelling and finally someone told Hardacre to shut up, for God's sake.

I was surprised to see it was Tim Williams, dressed and

equipped like the rest of us, his hand still bandaged and smelling of iodine but daubed with mud.

'What the hell are you doing here?' I asked. 'I thought you were out of it.'

He smiled, his thin sensitive scholar's face grey with fatigue. 'Well, now I'm in again,' he said.

'Who said so?'

'Me. I followed you up.'

'Get the hell out of it,' I said. 'While you've got the chance.'

'Not likely.' He grinned. 'I'm going over the plonk with my friends. It'll be a change to make history instead of always reading it. The colonel's brother was coming up and wanted a runner. I thought if he can, I can, so here I am. I came up with him, but then I very obligingly lost him. I don't suppose he's worried. He's no intention of going back either.'

'You're both barmy,' I said.

He grinned. '"We owe God a death,"' he quoted. '"Let it go which way it will. He that dies this year is quit for the next."'

German shells were banging away now at the front line which, we'd been told, was being held only by a few men with trench mortars to save casualties among the attacking force, and more shells were dropping round the first reserve line. I could see smoking clods of earth and showers of stones flying through the air and shrapnel bursting with high jetting trails of swift sparks and twists of smoke.

Occasionally there was a ribald shout of 'Foul' or 'No ball' or 'Fault', but they were all a little forced and not very funny.

'Now's the time to go in,' I heard Mason say.

''Oo says?' Eph asked disconcertingly as he always did.

'This is always the best time to go in, before the light's any good.'

'Been 'aving lessons, 'ave you, from General 'Aig?'

'No, fathead,' Mason snapped. 'But this is obviously the time – before Fritz can see properly, before the sun gets into the valley. Perhaps they've changed the plan.'

'Not them, mate,' Eph said. 'It'll upset breakfast at 'Eadquarters.'

I found myself hoping Mason was right, but the time passed and I knew it had only been a forlorn hope at the best.

Just before dawn, we were told to push to our left a little to make more room, and we found ourselves in a length of badly sited trench that had been hit several times during the night by counter-fire.

It was a litter of ruined ramparts with smashed timbers, twisted wattle-work and old iron. We were treading on the dead left behind by the previous occupants and the flies were appalling. Even the rats seemed to be leaving and we saw them run up the side of the trench from time to time and disappear into the long grass behind us, fat old-stagers who looked as though they'd been there since 1914.

'They can wait,' Eph said grimly. 'They can afford to. There'll be plenty of grub about later. 'Ow wide's No Man's Land just 'ere?'

'Too wide,' Mason growled, 'with this bloody weight we've got to carry.'

The Germans were still dropping their shells into the forward trenches and we could see men climbing out and lying in the grass behind them.

'He must be making a rare old mess down there,' Eph said.

Pine pushed his way among us, throwing us all off-balance, and barged his way towards Ashton and Welch, followed by his brother. I noticed that damned dog was still with him. Neither of them wore steel helmets and both seemed unconcerned about the firing. The colonel stared over the parapet for a while at the shelling ahead.

'He's got 'em d-damn' well registered,' I heard him say.

A few injured men began to make their way back through us from the front line and we had to crouch against the trench walls as stretchers came past. None of the wounded seemed sorry to be out of it and I found I could hardly blame them.

Pine watched them go, his face grave and strained. While he

was standing there, the brigadier-general came along the trench, a tall handsome man with a worried expression, and they all started to synchronise their watches as they stood near me, comparing closely typed sheets of orders.

'8th Div. had a go at breaking in just south of here,' the brigadier said to Pine. 'They didn't get within yards of his front trench. It was stiff with troops. It is all the way along. The London Div. caught it in the assembly trenches at Gommecourt, they say.' He paused, then went on quickly. 'I've been told I've got to be willing to sacrifice the brigade to capture Serre,' he said.

'What's the wire like?' Pine asked.

'Uncut,' the brigadier rapped back.

'Uncut?' Pine looked startled, then his brows came down and he looked serious.

'Not touched,' the brigadier went on. 'Shall we say there's an odd gap here and there, but that's all.'

'What about machine guns?'

'They're all there. They know we're coming all right. But I'll try to get the gunners to put an extra strafe on before zero hour. That ought to settle their hash.'

He went away and we all waited for the strafe to begin, but it never did. I'm sure he tried, but I expect somebody at head-quarters decided it would interfere with his artillery schedule and nothing was done. In any case, by this time there was so much noise and so many shell-bursts ahead it was hard to tell just what *was* happening. We were all numbed by the noise now and you could see the sign *Cheerio Crescent*, black letters on mud-spattered cheap white paint, quivering with every thump and crash and every shower of stones and dirt.

I was crouching on the firestep, hugging the basketed revetting, when daylight arrived. There was no sign of movement ahead of us. Through the periscopes you could see long waving grass and poppies and charlock and scabious and clover. Apart from a few stakes and strands of rusty wire, it looked like a meadow back home in England, full of bees and insects and warmth. All you could see of the Germans was a low broken ridge of sandbags and a little more wire, and white reserve trenches herring-boning the hillsides.

The daylight increased and soup miraculously appeared. We could see the sun touching the hilltops clearly now and the outline of the trees along the horizon to the east. The rain had stopped completely by this time and the sky was growing lighter, and clear with a jade green luminosity that spoke of a perfect summer day.

There was a mist in the hollows in front of us, lying in white rolls in the folds of the ground, and the larks got up one after another and you could hear the sky full of them. The notes seemed to fall in cascades. One or two birds had got into the trench somehow and were fluttering about as though dazed by the gunfire. They were perching on the bodies trussed in ground sheets that had been there when we arrived, or fluttering against the trench walls, as though they couldn't find their way out.

Spring managed to catch one and for a second he stood holding it, stroking its quivering body with his finger tip, then he released it and watched it fly away.

'"Hail to thee, blithe spirit,"' he said. '"Bird thou never wert."'

I saw him staring after it as it soared away into the cloudless sky, and his eyes were full of a remoteness and longing that seemed strange in Spring.

Then he turned round and saw me looking at him.

'Nice day for a fight,' he said with a grin.

'It's not the day for dying,' Mason said snappishly.

He was sitting reading letters on the firestep, though I could see his mind wasn't on them. Most of the time his eyes rested enviously on young Murray who'd been busy since daylight with the Lewis and his home-made flag and his home-made weapons. He'd finally decided he hadn't enough hands for all the things he'd proposed to carry in addition to his kit and he'd solemnly offered his coshes and knuckle-dusters to the Mandy brothers. His bounding good humour seemed unchanged and he'd got over his surliness, so that he didn't seem very different now from the boy he'd been on the *Post*.

Locky was smoking a pipe and talking to Tom Creak, and Hardacre was cleaning his rifle, his cadaverous face serious, wiping the mud away from the bolt with a look of too-deep concentration that indicated his mind was elsewhere.

Catchpole was sitting in silence, and I was surprised to see he had a small khaki-coloured prayer book on his knees. Henny Cuthbert was forcing himself to whistle but he wasn't making a very good job of it and his long sad face made him look more like a horse than ever. Eph was sitting with his back to the trench wall, his little eyes distant, his pudgy body hunched, his red face expressionless, lost in illimitable isolation, and I wondered what a man like Eph might be thinking at a time like this – of death, of victory, of Mabel? Or merely perhaps that his feet were hurting him and the straps of his equipment were chafing?

Tommy Mandy had his harmonica in his mouth and was playing it softly, not to please others for once, but because it seemed to soothe his own uneasy spirit. Tim Williams was reading what looked like a pocket book of verse and Murray had started arguing with Dicehart and Billy Mandy. In a sudden lull I heard his voice.

'Two goals down in the first ten minutes,' he was saying. 'No wonder they lost the cup.'

I could see Bold standing farther down the trench, his face expressionless, a pipe in his mouth, tall, straight-backed, unflinching, a sullen streak of a man, the man of Fontenoy and Quatre Bras and the Peninsula. Men like Bold had stood exactly as he stood now thousands of times before in every corner of the world, apparently unconcerned, considering it unmanly to show the slightest emotion, upright, honest, gentle for all their harsh speech, considerate of other men's weaknesses, the immortal soldier.

Welch was near us, sitting on a rum jar, smoking a new pipe he'd affected since his leave. He'd started to grow a moustache and the little fuzz of yellow hair on his upper lip caught the sun. He looked like a schoolboy.

Sheridan, the stockbroker, was talking to Appleby who was sitting studying his sheets of orders, his lips moving as he tried to commit them to memory. Ashton looked worried as he stared over the parapet with a periscope.

Every man about me was isolated in his own little oasis of loneliness, each man waiting with a different set of fears and hopes for the sun to come up. It seemed important to me just then to set my mind in order, in the same way that we had all set our affairs in order. It seemed important, if I were to remain untouched by the fears that lurked in the shadows at the back of my mind, that I should know how I felt about God. I seemed to be looking directly into His face just then, yet I was still uncertain of my feelings. It was a hard thing, to believe in God, when I knew that many of us might be dead before the day was out, but it still seemed necessary to reconcile myself to His existence. Strangely though, I found I couldn't, not then, with my mind so full of so many other disturbing and distracting thoughts, and I remember a sense of panic that nothing would come straight in my head when it seemed so important that it should.

My stomach was twisted with apprehension and my throat dry with a salty sickness and, to take my mind off it, I forced myself to think of Helen and found that her image came to my mind with a painful intensity in this surrounding of ugliness and utility, and all the angularity of warfare; and I thought of home and the sun falling in the parks and dusting with gold the drab little houses on Cotterside Common.

The sky was brilliant now and it was suddenly warm. The

sun's rays had edged over the hills at last and were finding their way into the valleys and lining with gold the edges of the trees behind us.

Unexpectedly, Catchpole began to read aloud from his prayer book, in a low voice as though he was trying to commit it to memory, and I realised it was the 23rd Psalm which I'd learned in Sunday School: '"Yea, though I walk through the valley of the shadow of death, I will fear no evil; for Thou art with me; Thy rod and Thy staff comfort me. Thou shalt prepare a table before me against them that troubleth me; Thou hast anointed my head with oil, and my cup shall be full. But Thy loving kindness and mercy shall follow me all the days of my life; and I will dwell in the house of the Lord for ever . . ."'

Everyone stopped talking as he read, and he looked up to find himself being watched by a dozen pairs of eyes.

'My father gave it to me.' He indicated the prayer book. 'I don't think I've ever looked at it before.'

'Go it, Vicar,' Eph said.

Catchpole shrugged his big shoulders. 'A lot of men are going to die today,' he observed simply, as though that explained everything.

'Sure.' Eph seemed a little embarrassed. 'I don't mind. It sounds nice.'

Arnold Holroyd grinned at me. 'How d'you feel, Fen?' he said. He was nervous and anxious to talk to someone.

'Awful,' I said. 'As if I'd just gone to have a tooth out.'

'I remember feeling like this once when I fell off a wall and knocked all the breath out of my body. Just think, if it hadn't been for the war, I'd still have been subbing church and chapel paragraphs for the *Post*. But I wouldn't have missed it for anything,' he said hurriedly. 'Wouldn't old Corker have liked to have been here today?'

He listened to the firing for a while then he went on in a strained breathless manner.

'Fritz hasn't retaliated much up to now,' he said. 'Looks as though he's copped it and there isn't much opposition. I've heard he's asking for an armistice already.'

'I hope so,' I said.

'Mind you, I hear things aren't so good up at Gommecourt. They've not broken into his trenches there.'

'They haven't here.'

'They'll have fixed that now. Gommecourt's only a subsidiary. This is the main attack.' He paused, then went on quickly. 'Just think,' he said, 'half a million men just waiting to go. I'm going to rush for it. Blackett says it's best. The Hun always sights his machine guns low, he says, so if you don't crouch you can only get it in the legs. If you can just get clear of the bags you're all right. I hope I don't let you chaps down. You've all got so much more experience than I have.'

I began to wish he'd shut up, but he was a bit scared and was trying to convince himself everything was going to be all right. So I kept on talking to him, and after a while he quietened down, and I went round reminding the others what they'd got to do.

'Leave me alone,' Mason snapped. 'I know. You've told me twice already.'

He was edgy with nervousness and kept looking at his watch. 'Six-twenty,' he said. 'Any moment now the guns'll start.'

Even as he spoke the guns opened. There was one solitary crack behind us somewhere and we heard the shell hurrying over, rattling through the air like a railway waggon on bad rails, then, before it burst, the whole front seemed to open up. The din was terrific, and you could see the drying earth walls of the trench shuddering and sending little cascades of dirt down on to the duckboards.

The sun was well up now and was beginning to fall on the trenches which, crowded as they were, began to grow stuffy and hot so that we started to sweat under our equipment as we jostled and pushed for a chance to see what was happening in front of us.

'What a lovely sound,' Eph crowed, listening to the barrage. 'Shove over, Murray. I'd like to see the 'Un going through it for a change.'

But it wasn't easy to see anything. Up ahead, the dust rose in tremendous clouds and began to drift across our front, obscuring the view we'd had like great evil birds.

The noise seemed to grow in intensity until it began to throb in the mind and the body and the veins, and set our helmets jigging on our heads. It seemed less a succession of explosions than one continuous roar. The air seemed to be full of a tremendous agonised violence, bursting first into groans and sighs, then into shrieks and whimperings, and then shaking the earth with terrible blows, and hanging over us as though someone were playing some fantastic symphony on guns of different sizes. It was like the cracking of unearthly whips. It seemed to be supernatural, and it didn't pass one way or the other. It didn't begin, intensify, decline and end, but just hung in the air above us, a stationary arc of sound over our heads, as though it were part of the atmosphere and not a thing of human creation. They said afterwards that even the worms were dead in the ground of the shock.

The air rocked and quivered and when I tried to light a cigarette I saw the flame staggering crazily. The trench seemed to heave and shudder and we stumbled drunkenly as though the noise was beating us into the earth.

I felt at times that if I lifted my eyes I'd see vast gigantic armies writhing in torment above me. It seemed that we were all in danger of being snatched up into it, like fragments in some gigantic whirlpool. It was awe-inspiring; yet, because it was so vast, it filled you with exultation and courage, as though the noise gave you strength at the knowledge that all those tremendous forces passing overhead were there to help us. We began to shout as we cleaned our rifles, adjusted the leather straps we wore, and paid the last little attention to equipment and compared watches, gripping the sandbags, the iron sheets, the billhooks, the wire and all the rest of the rubbish they'd given us to carry.

I suddenly remembered that broken lace, but just then I felt I didn't care. With that din above me, I felt I could have run barefoot all the way to Serre. Someone started to cheer, his voice thin in the racket, and one or two men lifted their helmets on their rifles and yelled and laughed.

'Fancy getting that lot on your breakfast plate,' Eph shouted, cupping his hands to speak. 'I bet it's hell's delight over there.'

Murray was fiddling with the Lewis-gun again, but enthusiastically now, and I could see him laughing and shouting eagerly as he worked. Catchpole had put aside his prayer book and his eyes were bright and clear. Locky had tucked his pipe away and I could see him standing beside Tom Creak, his mouth hanging open with excitement, his fears forgotten. Tom Creak was arguing with the Mandy brothers and it seemed almost as though he were giving them a final ticking off, telling them where to go and what to do when the time came, as he'd been doing ever since we'd arrived in France. Mason's face was shocked, as though the noise were too much for him, but there was a smile playing round his lips, as if he drew reassurance from the din. Spring was putting on an act and pretending to be drunk on the noise, and Henny Cuthbert and Ashton and Appleby were laughing at him as he danced a cumbersome jig. Bold still stood motionless, withdrawn and apart, his head up, his body erect, his face still expressionless, still waiting.

I was cleaning the dirt from my rifle, trying to hold myself to the earth, when all the time that colossal din seemed on the point of snatching me up into the air. Then, suddenly, when we felt we'd reached the very limit of all sound, the guns seemed to open their lungs and we began to laugh with the exhilaration of it all. This was our voice we were hearing, the voice of the whole British Empire at war. They claimed later that they heard the guns in England.

Someone said a mine went up to the south – they said they

427

could see pink smoke and clouds of dust – but I couldn't see it and I didn't hear. In front of us the German line seemed to have been blotted out by curling smoke in white and green and orange, rolling and twisting and blotting everything from sight. Then another salvo of shells fell into it and it was shredded into wreaths that were disintegrated again and again by blast.

'They can't live through that lot,' Murray was shouting gleefully. 'There'll be nothing left when we get across there.'

Suddenly a scarlet star-shell burst in the air above the German line and curled over us, slowly falling.

'He's calling up his artillery,' Appleby said abruptly. 'It'll be our turn in a minute. Take your partners for a waltz.'

Machine guns started firing and we heard shells begin to bang in front of us. The noise seemed to increase and they brought a lot of gas casualties along the trench from the front line towards the dressing station, yellow-faced men coughing their lungs up, their buttons tarnished as though with lyddite. Most of them were wearing the red, white and green brassards of the gas units attached to the engineers. The German shells had thrown the gas pipes back into the trench and smashed the gas cylinders that had been dug into the parapet. Instead of gassing the Germans they'd gassed themselves. They'd lost fifty-eight men out of sixty-four.

'Us next,' Eph said with a growl.

The banging of shells came closer and bits of stone and clods of earth came bouncing over the top of the sandbags into the trench, and dropped among us with the showers of dirt that pattered on our helmets.

'They're searching us out,' Holroyd said. 'We're going to get an awful slating in a minute.'

The peppery reek of high explosive drifting back from the shelling on the first-line trenches seemed to dry my tongue and make me thirsty. Then Henny Cuthbert, whose eyes were white now and his lower lip trembling, let off his rifle by mistake.

428

At the bang, everyone ducked and there was a nervous cheer as the bullet whined away into the air.

'What goes up must come down,' Catchpole said, and there was a little nervous laughter.

Then the shells came down on us and we all flung ourselves into the bottom of the trench, cowering awkwardly under the weight of equipment, as we heard them screaming and whimpering and whining and shrieking towards us.

'The bastard's got a bracket on us properly,' Eph shouted. 'Tell him not to waste ammunition.'

The drumming increased as the shells drew nearer. A gale seemed to howl overhead, piling up great barriers of sound. Something rushed at me with a scream of exultation and I found myself holding my breath, empty and tired and cold, shot through with a shrill core of terror, as though my inside had dropped out. It came down just behind the trench with a solid *crump* and clods of earth and bits of rubbish fell on top of me. Eph cried out as he was hit by a flying stone, but I heard him say: 'I'm all right. Only a cut, mates.'

Then there was a wild eruption of mud and the singing cries of flying shards of steel. The trench side bulged with a tremendous grunt and I was covered with a shower of pulverised dirt.

Someone started shouting in a high-pitched scared voice and I saw that one of C Company, who were mixed up with us, had been buried up to his neck in loose soil. The pressure of men increased as someone went barging past, causing the crowd to surge and stumble off-balance as we grabbed for shovels and entrenching tools and started to dig out the buried man. It wasn't easy to work because of the crowd but we got him out in the end and sat him on the firestep. He was covered with dirt and sobbing for his mother. His face was clay-white and his eyes were rolling wildly, his hair matted with mud, his hands fluttering feebly. When we tried to stand him on his feet, his legs simply buckled under him and he flopped down in the mud on the bottom of the trench. We picked him up again and sat him on the firestep, watched by huddled, crouching figures, all flinching and ducking every time a shell cracked nearby, while he gibbered and moaned and muttered.

'For God's sake,' someone growled uneasily. 'Put a sock in it! Fetch him one, somebody!'

'He's not in a fit state to go over,' Welch shouted in my ear.

'Well, he can't stay here,' I shouted back. 'They'll pick him up as a deserter if we leave him behind.'

'But the man's shell-shocked!'

'They don't know the meaning of the bloody word! We'll have to get his pals to shove him up and let him take his chance.'

'It's murder!'

'Better than being picked up by battle police and shot.'

'Here!' Welch fished in his pocket and produced a flask of brandy. 'There's something here I'd saved for myself. He can have it. Shove it into him.'

We forced his jaws open with fingers in his mouth and poured the lot into him. He sat back, gagging and gasping for breath, his face flushed. But he seemed quieter, and his friends offered to see that he went over.

'If he only goes over,' I shouted, 'it'll be all right. But he hasn't a chance if he stays here.'

Five-nine shells were still dropping round the trench, banging away just beyond the parapet. I saw Locky blinking at every bang and Mason with a haggard flinching face and chattering teeth, sobbing and gasping for breath as though each crunching crash was a blow on his own body. Henny Cuthbert was breathing unevenly and licking his lips.

'Scared?' Murray cupped his hands and shouted in his ear, and he nodded and immediately seemed to be better, as though facing the fact had made him feel stronger.

'Stick it, Henny,' Murray yelled. 'It can't go on long now. Then it's our turn. It'll be a picnic.'

The din was appalling and my head was ringing. It was only

possible to speak in a shout. I saw Henny swallowing quickly and Spring moaning softly to himself, as though borne down by an intolerable burden. He met my eyes and we both turned away, both of us refusing to admit the question in the other's face.

There was a smell of mouldering rottenness in the air, as though all the stale earth of the trench had been upturned by the shells that were landing alongside it, picking up the foetid odour of sweaty clothes and the veils of mist that seemed to hang over us, the relic of all the rain.

Murray miraculously began to sing and I blessed him for his courage, then Catchpole looked up and grinned, staring along the battered trench, with its tumbled sandbags and splintered wood and the landslide of earth where it had fallen in.

'*Ne pas cracher dans les corrideurs,*' he said, and Spring gave a harsh cackle of laughter that relieved the tension.

The shells moved on at last, probing out the reserve trenches, and we all drew a deep breath of relief. The peace seemed unbelievable after the din and the fear.

'That's better,' Eph observed. 'I always said I wanted to die in one lump.'

Bold came shoving along the trench, bone-white and hard as ever, a spattering of blood across his cheek.

'Your lads 'olding on all right?' he asked.

'They're all right,' I told him. 'No damage done.'

'Bit of a fuss back there,' he said. 'One dropped in the trench. Knocked off eleven men in one pop. Unsteadied 'em for a bit. Better get some rum into the lads. They'll probably need it.'

I was glad of something to do and sought out young Welch. Taking the earthenware rum jar, I sloshed half a mugful into the tin cup he held out.

'Nasty ten minutes,' he said shakily.

I went along the trench, filling dixies. 'Between three men,' I pointed out. 'And don't spill it. There's no more.'

431

It seemed to cheer everybody up and put life into them.

'Here come the loaves and little fishes,' Catchpole shouted. 'Here comes Sergeant Fenner to feed the multitudes.'

When the rum was drunk, we all felt better and even a little proud to be there. Scared as he might be, being in at the making of history has a profound effect on a man, and we knew we were part of history that day. I knew I would remember it for the rest of my life and I found myself quoting *Henry V* to myself for the first time in years:

> 'This day is called the feast of Crispian:
> He that outlives this day, and comes safe home,
> Will stand a-tiptoe when this day is named,
> And rouse him at the name of Crispian.'

The words wouldn't leave my head, and went round and round like a broken gramophone record.

Just ahead of us the ground sloped upwards slightly, then dipped towards the German trenches and I could see the big shells that were heading for the back areas parting the rich long grass as they whistled over our heads.

Above us, the sun was now burning bright, laying a line of gold along the top of the parapet where you could see the heads of poppies and marigolds among the withered stubble of the two-year-old corn. A flight of aircraft went over, picking up the sun in flashes of gold, then a machine gun somewhere ahead of us began to tap and rattle and I was startled to see poppy heads fly off, and the sandbags above my head disintegrate into feathery rags of bleached grey hessian. My stomach and limbs seemed to dissolve and liquefy with fear and I hoped no one else had seen. But they had, and I could see Henny's eyes fixed hypnotically on the gashed and ripped material and the soil dribbling down the osier mats from the holes.

'Ten minutes to go!' Ashton came along the trench, shoving his way through the crowded men with difficulty, and I saw the sun glitter on lines of bayonets as they were dragged out and fixed. The sight of them threw me into an uneasy sweat at the fear of mortal combat.

The clods and pieces of stone were dropping into the trench again and Eph called out, "Oo wants sugar in 'is tea?' and there was a ripple of lunatic mirth, then everybody started wishing each other luck. I saw Tom Creak shaking hands solemnly with the Mandys. Bold hitched at his straps and looked round.

'Best of luck,' I said to him.

'Same to you,' he said unemotionally.

All time seemed to have stopped in an icy pause. The bombardment roared over our heads still, but somehow I seemed to be in an oasis of silence.

I caught Locky's eyes on mine and he raised his hand briefly, then I heard once more the rattle of the machine gun ahead of us, penetrating the din. The bullets began to splash and chatter among the sandbags above our heads again, cutting the grass and sending little glissades of dirt into the trench.

Henny was still staring at them fixedly.

'Don't take any notice,' I said. 'We'll pick the moment when he's at the end of his traverse and we'll be on to him before he can come back.'

Then the bombardment lifted, and we stared at each other in dazed relief at the cessation of all din. For a few seconds, the whole front seemed to be silent, then the German shells came down again on the forward assault trenches, and I saw Pine tramping towards us, armed only with a walking stick and followed by his brother. There was a trickle of blood on his cheek, and his eye-patch was lopsided.

'Out!' he was shouting. 'Get out! Get up in front and lie down on the tapes! His next salvo's going to drop in here or damn' near! Get out!'

We all scrambled to our feet and I saw Bold reach towards the parapet and pull himself up.

433

The shells that were dropping in front of the trench came closer, and Ashton came along, forcing his way through the surging crowd of men.

'Come on!' he was shouting. 'Out! Out!'

Locky looked round at me and gave me a push up towards the parapet.

'"For what we are about to receive,"' I could hear him saying, '"may the Lord make us truly thankful."'

3

The German counter-bombardment was cracking and banging away all round us as we scrambled up the ladders and the earth steps that had been cut in the parapet.

My heart was hammering a mad tattoo in my throat, but as I got clear of the trench I slipped on a patch of muddy ground and went down under my load with a crash that knocked all the fear out of me. That's a bloody fine start to a battle, I thought viciously as I scrambled up.

As I got to my feet, I saw a ruined church far in front and was aware of the heat of the brilliant sun that was climbing well beyond the slopes in front by this time. The mist in the hollows in front of us was masking the German lines now and the ground was white with chalk dust that had been thrown up by explosions and now lay on the grass like snow.

There seemed to be flowers everywhere, even more than I'd thought, and with the gay little pennants the bombers were carrying, it seemed absurd to think of death. At that moment, back in England people were sitting down to their breakfast of bacon and eggs and enjoying the summer sunshine, unaware that the greatest battle the world had ever seen had just begun.

I must have been one of the first out and, as I stood there, heaving the others up one after the other with their loads, I felt exposed and lonely in the flying dirt and smoke, but I was overjoyed to find I wasn't afraid any more.

'Lie down on the tapes,' Ashton was shouting, but the tapes seemed to have disappeared and, judging by the number of shell-holes and the amount of scorched grass about, they must have been blown to blazes during the night.

We ran forward, each watching the man on his right for dressing, and tried to get into the two lines of artillery formation.

'This way to eternity,' Murray shouted. 'Who's for a soldier's grave?' He was still carrying his home-made flag with its slogan, *Look out, Kaiser Bill!* and waving it crazily.

'Lie down! Lie down!' I saw Bold standing as erect as a sign-post, shouting, and we all got down, awkward and off-balance under that awful weight we carried on our backs; and we lay on our faces in the long coarse grass that was still grey-wet with dew.

I had time now to look in front of me, but there was no sign of the first wave. There seemed to be no one else in that world of noise just then but us.

I thought I saw Serre just above the smoke which was rolling in the hollow in front, but where before there'd been thick trees and hedges, now they all stood bare and leafless, empty trunks and shattered branches with all the foliage blasted off them.

Then I saw red rockets fly into the air from the German lines in front of us and the shells came droning down on us again with a triumphant whooping fury, seeming to tear the earth apart in a vast black savagery. I was consumed with dread again, and tormented with a sudden envy of those luckier men who weren't there with me, men who were at home with their families, eating their breakfasts or reading their papers. All standards of sanity seemed to vanish in the din.

A line of shells burst in front of me and I saw clods, earth

436

and stones flung whining up into the air, and the smoke puffs that looked for all the world like a clump of trees suddenly sprouting from the earth.

Why was the damned artillery so useless, I kept thinking. Why didn't they silence the German batteries? Why didn't someone do something?

The fog shook and twitched with the shelling, and the world seemed to dance and flicker in front of me as flying fragments whirred and shrieked down around us. Every gun in Germany seemed to be pointed at us just then.

'Spread out! Spread out! Don't bunch!' Ashton was standing wide-legged, shouting, pointing to offending groups of men with the ash-plant he carried.

The air rocked and trembled with the concussion and the hard high-pitched detonations hammered on my eardrums, and I caught the acrid smell of explosive. From horizon to horizon the earth seemed to be spouting dirt and stones, and the air was full of drifting smoke, snow-white, venomous green and woolly impenetrable black. My brain felt numbed with the sound, and my helmet rang with whirring stones.

Then I heard the swish of bullets going through the grass with a strange chipping whistle, and I heard someone yelp. As I turned, I saw a man dragging himself to the rear, his right leg covered with blood.

'Lucky bastard,' Billy Mandy called after him. 'You're well out of it, mate!'

We were still lying down and men kept running forward to join us, climbing out of the confusion of smoke where the shells were tearing the trench to pieces behind us. Ashton was still standing up in front of us, shouting to us not to bunch, and as I watched him I saw his left hand jerk, and a spatter of blood leapt from his finger-ends. He looked down at it, startled, but he went on standing there, flinching but upright, his hand limp by his side.

I heard a bang behind me and, looking round, I saw Spring

with his face to the ground. I knew it was Spring because his helmet had fallen off and I could see his fair wavy hair. I knew he was dead. Alongside him another man was rolling about with his hands to his face, and I saw his fingers were red with bright blood. As he yelled and whimpered with pain, I realised it was Henny Cuthbert, who'd gone down on the tram that day with me two years before to enlist.

I caught a glimpse of a few scared faces – Mason, Locky, Murray, Eph Lott, Arnold Holroyd and Catchpole – then I saw Ashton look at his watch. He seemed to move slowly and with deliberate care. The sun beat on my shoulders and legs like the blast from an oven.

'How much longer?' I was saying to myself. 'For God's sake, how much longer?'

'One minute to go!' I couldn't hear Ashton's words and only saw them form on his lips. One-handed, he'd tied an orange handkerchief on the end of his ash-plant and was waving it.

'Keep your eyes on this, lads,' he was shouting. 'Where this is, you'll find me!' He tucked his stick under his arm and, stooping, picked one of the enormous moonpennies that grew around his feet and stuck it with a self-conscious gesture in his buttonhole.

Then I saw Arnold Holroyd had a sandbag with him and he fished a football out of it.

'How about a goal for the Rovers?' he said.

Ashton's whistle went just as he shoved it into my hand. It seemed a pointless gesture, but I scrambled to my feet, full of a wild senseless hope that, after all, it might be easier than I'd expected. I was aware of other men heaving themselves up with difficulty out of the grass on either side of me, and I gave the ball a tremendous kick and started to walk forward after it as it went bouncing into the grass.

What happened to the wave ahead of me, I don't know. I never saw anything of them but for a few still khaki figures lying in

438

the front trench as we clumped over a narrow bridge made out of planks. The trench looked as though it was pretty badly smashed up, and the sandbags were all lying in heaps in the bottom, among the bodies and the splintered timbers and the charred holes where the shells had landed.

There was another long row of figures just in front of the sandbags, the remains of the first wave lying where they'd been caught in the open by the machine guns and the slicing splinters of the barrage. I found it hard to believe there could be so many of them, for they were lying in a thick swathe, almost like corn cut down by a scythe, huddled all ways, some of them in shell-holes with their feet sticking out, looking like fish in a basket. Most of them were still, but a few of them moved awkwardly, with the clumsy horrifying slowness of crushed beetles, trying to get up, or turn over, or drag themselves on their elbows or hands and knees back to the safety of the trench.

There was one of them who was shot through the loins, and as I stooped over him, he only grunted and stared at me with hatred, as though he loathed me for being still unhurt and able to move.

I could hear Ashton shouting: 'Keep your extension! Don't bunch! Keep up on the left!' and all the time my mind was ticking over like a clock. 'Suppose the next one's me!' it kept repeating. 'Suppose the next one's me!'

Figures flickered around me, curiously unreal in the excitement, silhouetted by the sun on the haze of dirt and smoke. Shell-fragments were smashing into the ground and great clods of earth were thumping down on us and rolling end-over-end through the grass.

In front of us, there was a slight slope and we went up it in perfect alignment, masked for a moment by the crest.

'If it's all like this,' Murray shouted, 'it's a cakewalk!'

The smoke and whiffs of lyddite fumes swam past me and everything started to become confused. Nothing after that seemed to follow rationally on anything that had happened before. It was as though a series of violent isolated pictures were flung briefly on a screen and I caught only glimpses of what was happening.

A group of men came pushing back between us, most of them wounded and bloody, and a fight nearly developed as they got in our way. The men going back were hurt and frightened and the men going forward were caught by the intoxication of the attack, their minds focused only on getting forward and down into the earth again, and I saw the wounded men brushed aside impatiently by others who thought of them only as an obstacle in their path.

I knew already that the barrage had moved too quickly for us and, with a sick feeling of horror, I guessed that things were beginning to go wrong. I felt a tremendous urge to turn round and run, abject and fearful, while I still could, for the shelter of the trenches, but everyone else was going forward and I stayed with them and just in front. Doubtless they were thinking the same way as I was, some of them probably even thinking they must do as I did.

We came up against a patch of wire that had been erected in the middle of No Man's Land, half-hidden in the long grass, and we swung to the right to avoid it, and I remember thinking it had probably been put there to funnel us on to the machine guns.

As we closed up, breasting the crest, I saw men stumbling forward, heads down, backs bent under their packs, with the slow, steady, beast-of-burden stride that was so familiar in the trenches, rifles at the port, bayonets catching the sunshine, just as Locky had said they would. Then there was a sound like escaping steam all round me and little spurts of dirt began to leap from the ground. I saw men stagger and roll forward, still holding their rifles, sinking slowly to their knees and sagging forward until their heads touched the ground, and it startled me to realise they could die so quickly.

'Don't bunch!' I turned and shouted to the men behind me.

440

Young Murray was still there, I noticed, carrying the Lewis now, his flag gone, his helmet missing, a smear of blood on his face, and Eph Lott and a few more I recognised. Bold had disappeared, and so had Locky.

Then Arnold Holroyd seemed to lose his head. He was running about, waving his revolver, and shouting to the men behind me.

'Come on, you bastards!' he was yelling. 'Or I'll shoot the lot of you!'

He pointed the revolver at a man who was kneeling with his head down.

'Get up!' he shouted. 'Or I'll let you have it!'

I knocked the weapon out of his hand so that it swung on the end of its lanyard. 'He's dead,' I shouted, and he looked stupidly at me.

'What about all that lot?' he shouted hysterically, pointing back to a row of men all crouching in the grass, their heads half-hidden.

'They're dead too,' I said.

Murray had disappeared now, I noticed, somewhere among the drifting smoke and crashing shell-fire, but Ashton was still there ahead of me, still waving his little flag, and there was no wavering, no attempt by anybody to turn back.

As we approached the main German wire, great looping tangles of thick rusty ungalvanised stuff that my wire cutters would never have touched, I could see a few stakes had been uprooted, but it had been cut only in places and there were bodies lying in heaps in the openings. They looked like a lot of skittles knocked over in some giant game, whole rows of them, lying dead where they'd fallen, and whole masses more heaped up against the outside fringe of the wire, scarecrows with their arms spreadeagled, caught there in a moment of time.

Inevitably, we drew together at the gaps and it was there those patterned criss-cross streams of bullets caught us again.

Men began to crumple and disappear out of sight, and the

line of bobbing helmets I'd had in the corner of my eyes all the time seemed to thin away to nothing as the gaps widened in the scattered ranks.

I saw the spurts of dirt move towards me, the ground jumping and stirring in all directions, and I remember I was horrified to realise the bullets were coming from the flanks as well as from the front, then they changed direction at the end of a traverse and moved away again, ploughing little furrows in the earth. Men were running backwards and forwards trying to find an opening in the wire, and all order seemed to have gone out of the attack. Figures were stumbling about in the haze as though bewildered. The ground seemed to be littered with dud shells, I noticed.

Ashton appeared through the smoke. He'd been wounded in the head now, I saw. His helmet had gone and there was a lot of blood on his face, but he still held that little orange flag of his. He was gesturing frantically to his right and I joined him and we got going again. I saw Catchpole and the Mandersons and Tom Creak, still sticking together, and Mason and Bold, who'd turned up again. Locky had vanished completely and I wondered briefly where he was, when I saw a crowd of men bunching behind me and I waved to them to spread out.

'Come on,' Bold was shouting, magnificently erect. 'The beggars can't shoot for toffee! Look 'ow they're missing us!'

Up ahead I could see a group of Germans dragging a heavy machine gun up on to the parapet. I noticed they wore no equipment and moved easily, and still struggling under that cursed weight on my back, I envied them their freedom.

'Come on,' I shouted. 'Before they start firing!'

But we were too late and the bullets caught us like a hail of sleet once more, and I saw the whole line go down round me, some dead, some wounded, some in an instinctive dive for the earth. There seemed to be only half a dozen left when I turned round, half a dozen unwounded men looking to Ashton for orders, and in a rage at that stupid load on my back that was impeding my movements, I undid the buckles and left it where it fell.

The machine gun swung away from us and we scrambled to our feet again, but it came back at once. I saw Mason's head go up and he took two or three steps forward with his head in the air, his rifle dropping from his outstretched hands. Then he stopped dead and began to stagger backwards and fell. The wire caught him and seemed to bounce him half-upright again, his arms stretched out wide as though in appeal, and I saw him moving them feebly as he tried to free his clothes from the barbs.

'No!' I heard him screaming, his face twisted in an agonised expression of horror. 'No! No! No!' Then his cries were sliced in half by a spurt of bullets and his head fell back and his body sagged inside his clothes.

I plunged on, my head bowed as though against the weather. More men fell about me but, just then, I was conscious only of a desire to get out of that appalling storm of flying steel and dirt and stones. I saw more wire and it tripped me and I almost fell.

Then I saw a battered stretch of trench with dazzle-painted sandbags and stumbled towards it, but a strand of wire caught my trousers and pulled me to a stop with a loud twang. For a second, I saw myself caught up and crucified like Frank, then I wrenched myself free, my trousers torn, my flesh scarred by the barbs. Bombs were being flung from the trench and someone was flinging more bombs back. The machine gun seemed to be jammed and I could see a big German crouching over it shouting and hammering at it with his fist. There were more Germans just behind him, scared and grimacing, and I realised they were as frightened as we were. I caught a momentary glimpse of Bold away on my right, his arm drawn back with a bomb in it, then there was a brilliant flash in front of my eyes and I saw the gun and all the men round it topple over backwards and disappear.

I smashed desperately through the last few strands of wire, and went forward in a final tempestuous rush. A falling body crashed against me as I reached the parapet and knocked me forward so that I slid into the trench on my face. Someone fell on top of me, and we sprawled on the duckboards, both of us yelling with rage and fear.

I felt as if I'd run a five-mile race, and the breath was tearing at my lungs. When I sat up, I saw I was in a flattened ditch full of splintered boards and wreckage that looked like nothing I'd ever seen on maps or on exercises and I decided it couldn't be the front line. But then I saw two or three Germans lying in stupid attitudes, their faces the colour of old bone and marked with dribbles of brilliantly coloured blood, and I realised it must be.

As I stumbled to my feet among the litter of burst sandbags and scraps of equipment and humanity that had been pounded into the chalky tangle, I noticed there appeared to be others with me, and I looked round quickly to see if Locky had turned up. But there only seemed to be Tom Creak whom I knew. His eyes were wild and frightened and he seemed to have been hit in the hand. As I looked at him, he shook his arm and a couple of fingers fell off. He stared at the mutilated limb for a moment then sagged weakly against the trench wall, his mouth hanging open.

Even as we fought for breath, grey-uniformed figures with dirt-stained faces and earth-matted hair seemed to emerge from under the broken baulks of timber and out of what I'd thought were mere holes in the earth. They had grimy bloodless faces and glaring eyes, but they had weapons in their hands. In a moment I seemed to be lost in a heaving, scuffling mass of men, kicking and cursing, striving to get my bayonet up and finding it impossible because of the crowd, and using my fist instead because it seemed easier. I fired without raising my rifle, then someone staggered against me and knocked me down and I couldn't get up again for the number of men about me, and I was terrified someone would kill me before I could defend myself. All round me I could hear the grunting, gasping, breathless striving of men, and groans and sobs and shouts of pain and the crack of bursting bombs. Everybody seemed to be yelling at once, praying and using every kind of filthy word I ever heard. I saw Tom Creak with his bayonet in a screaming German who was struggling to pull it out with crimson clutching hands, and someone else with bloodshot eyes shouting, 'Kill the swine, kill the bastards!'

Then suddenly I had room to move, and everyone round me seemed to have red-tipped bayonets and sweating faces. We stumbled about, tripped by strands of wire that had been blown into the trench, slipping in the muddy puddles and stumbling over squirming bodies. We all seemed drunk, demoralised, and staggering with incomprehending terror, but we seemed to have control of that unspeakable ditch at last.

We were all covered with dirt, and blood seemed to have been scattered about as though it had been thrown from a bucket. It splashed the sides of the trench and lay in puddles on the floor, and was smeared on hands and faces, and on the lolling bodies under our feet.

There was a dying German drumming his heels on the duckboards and moaning, '*Wir sind Kameräden, wir sind Kameräden,*' and two prisoners, both wounded, who seemed to find it difficult to stand up, either through fear or because of their injuries.

Now that the fighting had stopped, we became aware of the bullets, which seemed to be plucking at the parapet from both sides now, and we had to keep our heads down, our equipment bumping and catching against the projections of the trench. Tom Creak was leaning against the trench wall again, his face white and sick, his hand a bloody mess of mangled fingers.

'Any chance for us, Fen?' he said. We were huddled together like a lot of sheep, and they were all looking at me for a lead, all except one who was bending over a man shot through the chest who sat clutching his knees, rocking to and fro in the bottom of the trench.

'The rest'll be up in a few minutes,' I said.

Tom shook his head. 'They won't find nothing but stiffs,' he said.

In the distance on my right I saw a wave of men going forward up the slope. It was almost as though they were flights of partridges being driven towards waiting guns and as I stared I saw the whole line crumble and begin to fall. A few isolated figures swept on, no more, leaving whole rows on the ground behind them. I could hear a bugle and drums somewhere and once the skirl of bagpipes carried to us by some trick of the atmosphere, then a thin cheer as the last fragments of the wave swept towards the German parapet.

Tom Creak started to shout and point.

''Ere they come!' he yelled. ''Ere they are! Right on time! We're all right now!'

I swung round and saw the third wave coming up behind us, the sun gleaming on their helmets as they emerged from the sunlit smoke that lay in front of our trenches, in a perfect line, each man a yard or so from the next, their backs bent, struggling under that idiotic load they were carrying, their rifles across their chests, their bayonets catching the light.

We picked up our rifles and prepared to join them, crouching against the trench wall with the heat on our backs.

'Don't bunch!' I screamed, but I heard the hidden machine guns begin to fire again and I saw the whole line stagger as they were caught in the criss-cross streams of bullets. Mason's body, still hanging on the wire, supported inside its clothing, began to do a crazy dance as the bullets ripped at it, and whole bunches of the advancing men fell. The rest kept on coming forward, but their legs seemed to have turned to jelly, and they stumbled on splayed feet, their knees sagging, almost like Charlie Chaplin in the pictures I'd seen, then the whole line seemed to vanish into the grass until there were only one or two isolated figures left, standing almost stupidly, like calves smelling blood, their eyes dazed.

As I watched them, my eyes burning themselves out in my head, there was an awful crash behind me and we all went down under a shower of stones and flying dirt and shards of steel. A man had flung himself down across me, and when I pushed him off blood welled across my trousers and I saw there was a hole in his temple and his skull was shattered at the back.

When I'd recovered my wits, I saw the fourth line coming forward just as the others had done, like a human wave against an iron shore, but they were moving faster now, running at a stumbling trot.

Oh, God, I thought. Not another lot!

Tom Creak was beside me, fuming.

'Where the 'ell's t'barrage?' he was saying, his eyes glittering with a sort of drunken hatred. 'Why don't them bloody staff bastards bring it back?'

The Germans seemed to have recovered a lot, now that the bombardment had moved on to the rear, and I saw the advancing line disappear just as the previous one had, staggering in groups as though they'd been caught by a high wind, and falling in heaps among the other dead. I don't think a single man even reached the wire.

There was a cheer from the German trenches, then they swung their machine guns round, and the blast of bullets made us all duck. One man was a little slow and he slid to the bottom of the trench, staring stupidly, his bright blue eyes wide, his mouth lolling open.

Tom Creak stared at him, then at me, then the bullets came popping into the side of the trench again, sending the dirt flying, and we all huddled there, not certain what to do. The attack seemed to have sunk into the ground.

*   *   *

447

For a while, I stared at the dirt wall of the trench and the crouching stupefied figures among the burst and tumbled sand-bags, then I forced myself to try and take stock of things.

There seemed to be only half a dozen of us – Tom Creak, and a few others I didn't recognise from the first wave, and a few wounded – all of us with clothes, hands and faces besmeared with blood. I couldn't see where I was because the smoke, which was charged with fumes, was opaque and coppery in colour.

Murray and Locky and the Lewis-gun seemed to have vanished, and we had no wire with us. But there appeared to be no shells falling near us just then and we seemed safe if we kept our heads down.

I wondered what had happened to Bold and wished he'd appear as he always seemed to do at times of stress, with his strong upright figure and that harsh nagging voice that always seemed so confident.

'We've got to look after 'em,' he'd always said. 'There's precious few of us know how to.' The memory of it seemed to snap through my stupefaction and I forced myself to make decisions.

Tom was leaning against the trench wall, hugging his maimed hand to him, his face white and taut with pain.

'You all right?' I asked, shouting to make myself heard above the din.

'I'm not 'urt,' he said. 'Well – not much. But t'place's a bit of a mess, ain't it?'

He seemed to stagger and his face became empty and expressionless.

'Steady on,' I said. 'Where are the Mandys?'

'I dunno. I lost 'em out there.' He gestured with his rifle towards the open grassland we'd just crossed. 'They just disappeared.'

'We'll find 'em eventually, I suppose,' I said. 'For the time being, get that bloody load off your back. You'll move easier.'

He looked at me and saw I'd got rid of my equipment and he shrugged out of his own pack and dropped it to the trench bottom.

The others started to do the same, then someone indicated the two gibbering Germans who still crouched together, their eyes rolling, their hands wavering above their heads. 'What the hell are we going to do with them two?' he asked.

Someone said he'd heard that prisoners were shooting their captors in the back and Tom shoved himself upright, his face bitter and savage.

'Send 'em back,' he shouted. 'Send 'em back through t'bloody barrage, like we 'ad to go, and all them lads lying out there!'

Before I could stop him, he started buffeting the two wretched men one-handed with his rifle, and they scrambled out of the trench and started back the way we'd come, their hands in the air. They didn't seem to have gone far when they were caught by one of their own machine guns, and they rolled sideways, lolling spinelessly, and fell out of sight.

'Well, that's that,' Tom said flatly.

I felt I ought to have stopped him, but there didn't seem to be much point in worrying about that now and I tried to concentrate on the problem of saving ourselves.

I scrambled to where the German machine gun was lying on its side, half-covered with earth and debris, the bodies of the gunners draped across it, their blood soaking the chalky soil.

'Let's try and get it going,' I said.

We dug out the gun, but it was choked with earth and the man who was crouching over it, trying to make it work, looked up at me with stupefied eyes.

'Keep at it,' I said. 'I'll see what I can find farther on.'

At the back of my mind was the certainty that I should come across Locky somewhere along the trench, crowded in with other missing men. I felt sure I'd see Tim Williams and Murray as well, and all the others who'd disappeared. It was as though the mind rejected the possibility of them not being there.

I knew we were still a long way from our final objectives and I wondered if I ought to try and press on. But the few men I had with me wouldn't have lasted two seconds in the sleet of bullets that was flying overhead, and I decided instead to see if I could find anyone else before making a move. The biggest problem was the confusion. I didn't know where anyone was or even if there *were* anyone. We had no weapons beyond our rifles and no means of getting in touch with the reserves.

I left the others struggling with the gun and, scrambling over the bodies that choked the angle of trench, half-fell into the next bay.

As I straightened up, a grey-uniformed figure lurched blindly round the corner right into me. Without thinking, I lashed out and he went flying on to the tumbled sandbags and I realised I'd still got an entrenching tool in my hand.

'God, sorry!' I turned to the German who was lying on his side moaning, his face covered with blood, and I realised how absurd it was to be apologising.

The blade of the entrenching tool had carved a hideous wound in his shoulder right by the neck. He was obviously dying, and I stumbled away again over the rubbish. There were a lot more bodies lying about in the wreckage, both German and English, but there was no one I knew. I tried to avoid treading on them, but it was difficult because there were so many, and I was terrified of hanging about. I'd seen rockets poised in the air above me and guessed it was the Germans appealing for artillery support.

As I reached the next deep stretch of trench, a shell burst on the parapet and I was covered with a shower of fine earth and small stones. When I looked up, I saw Ashton in front of me. His hand was roughly bandaged but he seemed to have been wounded again in the chest and his tunic and shirt were open, as though someone had tried to get at his wound to attend to it. He'd lost all his equipment except his little orange flag – even his pince-nez, so that his eyes had a curious peering look about them.

'We must get on,' he said immediately. 'Get the men together.'

'There aren't any men,' I said. 'There's nobody left.'

He nodded dully and sat down, not far from fainting. 'Yes,' he said. 'I know. Those machine guns. We're wiped out.'

Catchpole was with him, crouched against the sandbags, scared-looking, his jaw hanging open. He managed a weak grin and the three of us huddled together while the shells banged and cracked just above us, throwing us against the trench wall again and again with the concussion.

'Is there anybody else?' I asked, cupping my hands and yelling into his ear.

'I think they're all dead,' Catchpole said, his eyes blinking at every explosion.

'Well, we'd better see if we can find someone. There's nobody on the left except Tom Creak and a few more. I've just come from there. Stay here and I'll go and look.'

I scrambled farther along the trench, feeling better now I'd got my breath back. Down there in the trench I felt fairly safe.

Farther along, I found three or four more men from the third wave, all of them unwounded, but no more. I took a chance and stuck my head over the parapet and saw in the distance tiny figures running forward.

'It must be the York and Lancs,' one of the men I'd found said. 'There aren't many of them.'

I didn't know what to do. There weren't enough of us to be of much use, but the Germans seemed to have abandoned the trench we were in and I thought we'd better stay where we were and see what we could do about holding it.

'He'll be counter-attacking soon,' one of the men with me said. He looked dazed and his eyes were full of tears. 'If he does,' he went on. 'I'll give myself up.'

'You bloody well won't,' I told him.

'Well,' he said hysterically, 'we can't stop 'em if they come!'

'We'll be all right when the reinforcements arrive!' Ashton said when we got back to him. 'They'll be here soon.'

I didn't believe him. The Germans seemed to be in complete control of that strip of open ground behind us, and I couldn't imagine anyone getting anywhere near us.

Then, startlingly close, a machine gun opened up, stopped and started again, and we all stared round at each other.

'They're coming,' Catchpole shouted.

As he spoke, a figure appeared round the corner of the trench and I was just on the point of throwing a bomb when I saw it was Bold. He had a head wound and his hair was dusty, his face ashen, but I could have hugged him. We'll be all right now, I thought immediately. Bold will know what to do.

He grinned as he saw me and I felt it was wonderful just to have him near.

'How many have we got?' he asked Ashton, who merely leaned against the trench wall and shook his head, too far gone to know.

'Just what you can see,' I said, and Bold stared round us. 'Christ,' he said. 'Is this all? I've got another dozen round the next corner, and that's the lot. None of our mob. We'd better try and form that there strongpoint. Got any guns?'

'Not any more. I've got a couple of the lads trying to get a German job going.'

'Good lad! We'll have to do the best we can.'

He disappeared round the corner again and came back with a few men, all of them blank-faced and dazed-looking, all covered with dirt and blood, until there were about three dozen of us crouching in the trench, staring back the way we'd come, in the hope of help. The German gun had a smashed breech, we found, and it was impossible to repair it.

I could see Germans on our left only a hundred yards away, standing on their parapet and shooting at anyone near their wire who tried to move. One group had even dragged a machine gun into the open and were traversing over the open field, the bullets slapping along the ground, ripping and tearing at the bodies of the already dead. The men in the trench with me crouched together, almost as though they drew courage from each other. They all looked shocked. They'd seen a thousand men die before their eyes in a matter of minutes. Ashton's face had gone inhumanly white now, but he still clutched that silly little flag of his. Tom Creak's face was like stone and Catchpole's raffish good looks were marred by a stare of stupid bewilderment. Only Bold seemed unmoved.

'We've got to get forward,' Ashton kept repeating.

He clearly didn't know what he was doing, only what his orders were. But there was no sense in trying to obey. There weren't enough of us.

An aeroplane flew over us, a small yellow machine, and I remember looking up and thinking how clean it must be up there away from all the filth and foulness below. It turned beyond us and swung back, the sun glinting on its varnished wing surfaces, then the pilot waved and I heard its klaxon horn droning.

As it came over us again, an object like a truncheon trailing coloured streamers dropped from it. But it fell short and disappeared into the trench near the German machine-gunners and we could do nothing about it.

In the end, Bold told me to send a runner back, and I hadn't the courage to send Tom Creak or Catchpole and I picked one of the strangers.

He stared for a second, his face suddenly empty, then he nodded and scrambled out of the trench without a word.

'He's hit,' someone shouted almost immediately, and I turned away with a feeling of guilt and looked at Bold.

'Not worth trying another,' he said. 'He'll only cop it too.'

The shells were still droning overhead like a million birds in flight. There seemed to be noise everywhere, above us, to right and left, almost coming out of the ground underneath our feet.

The whole world was full of noise, and not much else, except flattened figures sprawled like sagging khaki bags on the torn chalky grassland and among the black tangled wire.

Bold crawled towards me, flinching at every bang, pulling himself over the dead, the wounded and the living. He looked like a man who'd been buried and dug up again. His face was stained and grimy and his hands looked like great lumps of mud. He glanced quickly at the pathetic little wire barricade we'd thrown up around us, made of scraps of timber and wire that we'd pulled out of the debris of the trench. It was useless for the purpose of stopping anything, but it gave us a measure of confidence and made us feel that we were doing what we'd come for.

His face twisted as though in a spasm of pain and disgust, then he swung round to me again.

'It's a wash-out!' he said viciously. 'We're finished! All them fine lads!' He seemed to choke over the words, then he pulled himself together. 'We'd better just 'ang on,' he said calmly. 'The reserves ought to be over soon.'

As he spoke, an officer came along the trench in a scrambling, crouching run. He stopped dead when he saw us, his face startled. He was only a boy and he looked frightened.

'Christ,' he said, 'I didn't think there was anyone else left alive! Were you with us, or in front?'

'Second and first waves,' Bold said. 'This is all that's left.'

'Well played, chaps,' the officer said. 'You're a bloody fine lot . . .' His voice trailed off unsteadily and he looked around him, his eyes staring.

'I've got nobody . . .' He paused and gulped, looking like a lost child. '. . . I've lost all my chaps. Every bloody one of them. They're all out there.'

Tears started into his eyes, then he seemed to pull himself together. 'We ought to try and do something,' he said. 'What do you think, Sergeant-Major?'

'We ought to 'ang on, sir. We've been told to 'ang on.'

'There's not much to hang on to,' the officer said. 'But perhaps you're right. What do you suggest?'

'We can try and build the parapet up a bit more,' Bold suggested. 'Reverse the trench. Give ourselves room to move. We might get a gun eventually. There ain't much else we can do.'

'All right. Let's get going.'

We tried to clear the trench, hastily shoving the dead to one side, but it wasn't deep enough to stand upright and the Germans were watching and kept turning their machine guns on us. Behind us, the battlefield seemed to have emptied of men and they were able to direct their attention to the portions of their own line that had fallen into our hands.

Gradually we cleared the debris, summoning up a few last dregs of strength for the effort, digging and swearing and panting, trying to carve out a new firestep. We lowered the trench bottom and filled sandbags with what we dug out, and raised the parapet with them and with the German dead, and crowned it with a jumble of wire we dragged up from farther along the trench, pulling out broken stakes and twisted iron rods to support it. Then we collected the water bottles and the cigarettes and the iron rations from the corpses, and huddled together in what was still not much more than a hole in the ground, dead, wounded and living together, hugging the earth, unable to do anything but wait.

The officer glanced at his watch. 'The reserves ought to be up now,' he said. 'God, they should have been sent forward half an hour ago!'

As the Germans started to bombard their own trenches, the shells began to clump down around us again, and we gripped the quivering dirt closer, clawing at it with grimy fingers, stupefied by the heat and the blind terror and the noise, and by the shock and tragedy of the battle. I was blown off my feet and when I picked myself up I realised the party had dwindled to about a dozen unwounded men. By this time I was terrified of being hit, and even more terrified that Bold would realise it.

Nobody suggested going back, though hanging on in that quivering little hole grew more and more senseless. I saw the sun rise higher and the heat in that filthy ditch seemed to grow unbearable. There was no sign of any reserves coming forward to help us. The attack in front of Serre had died away in slaughter and utter defeat.

The Germans were probing all the little pockets of resistance in their front line now. Out in front of us were the remains of those four vast waves of the attack, and Mason still there on the wire, in a hideously alive attitude, his head back, his eyes wide open and staring. Occasionally, an arm or a leg moved among the heaped bodies but for the most part the battlefield was curiously still.

'This is bloody silly,' the officer said in a shrill nervous voice. 'They've obviously called the attack off. We'd better get back.'

Bold stared at me, then he nodded. As the shelling lifted, we scrambled out of the trench. The officer waited on top for us and then began to lead the way back. I pushed Ashton after the others, and when I left there was only Bold behind me, scrambling about the trench, pawing at the bodies to see if there was anyone left alive. I reached back to give him a hand up, but, as he grasped my fingers, a machine gun started again from somewhere and he went limp, half in and half out of the trench, and slid back. For a second he tottered on his long legs, as though trying to hold himself upright, then he sat down abruptly, his back against the sandbags, his feet out in front of him, his boots among the rubble and the scattered cartridge cases.

I saw there were small red patches on his uniform across his chest and stomach, and there was a trickle of blood at the corner of his mouth.

'Oh God,' I said. 'Not you!'

I fell into the trench again beside him, sliding down the loose dirt across the sandbags, but he shook his head from side to side, lolling limply against the trench wall.

'Git going,' he said. 'I'm done for.'

'Don't talk barmy!' I shouted, almost sobbing with misery, 'I can carry you.'

He brushed my hands away angrily. 'I'm done for,' he said. 'I know when I'm done for.' His head lifted and he snarled at me. 'Git going,' he said. 'What 'ave I always told you? Don't behave like a bloody amateur! I thought I taught you better'n that.'

I stared at him sitting there, his eyes turned up to me, unemotional, expressionless, waiting for death like the soldier he'd always been, and I felt as though something had been carved out of me, inside. My eyes were full of tears.

'So long, Pat,' I said. 'So long!'

I caught up with the others as they huddled in the sunshine in a little hollow just beyond the wire. The dead lay thickly just there and we found one or two desperately wounded men, waiting for help, grey-faced, their teeth exposed in haggard painful grins that sent a chill through you.

We tried to make them comfortable and picked up those who might survive and carried them tenderly to the top of the hollow. I could hear rifle-fire and bombing, but I couldn't see much fighting now, though the British front and reserve trenches were being shelled to blazes.

Someone started to rush over the lip of the slope and a heavy machine gun started rattling at once from the direction of Serre and I saw several men fall as the bullets started cutting the grass and sending chips of earth and stone flying.

Suddenly there seemed to be only Ashton, Catchpole and Tom Creak left with me, and we were running now, crouched low and stumbling, frightened and wanting to survive. I saw Tom Creak go flying as a shell blew us both over, and I caught a glimpse of his helmet as it went sailing through the air, end over end, twenty feet up, the strap whipping as it turned. As I got up, I was raving a little, swearing and praying and cursing to myself.

Ashton was still on his legs, still weakly waving that damned orange handkerchief on his stick, but even as I looked at him, I saw him spin round as a blast of bullets caught him and lifted him off his feet. As he disappeared, I saw a hand come up out of the grass, still holding the ash-plant – the handkerchief was wet and shining now in the sun with the blood on it – then it slowly sagged and vanished from sight.

There seemed to be nobody left now but me, out in front of the German trenches on my own. There were great piles of dead in front of me and just behind, and more of them hanging on the wire, sprawling against the looping strands like a lot of scarecrows. There was no one else on his feet beyond a few scattered figures in the distance running in and out of the heaps of dead like frightened rabbits, trying to seek shelter from that awful fire.

Shrapnel was bursting over us in little puff balls and I saw more of the running figures go down, then something hit my helmet and knocked it over my eyes. The chin-strap tore my ears and made me bite my tongue. Lights flashed in front of me and I tasted blood, and I remember the grass coming up to meet me as I fell over.

The crash as my head hit the ground knocked me silly. My helmet fell off and rolled away and I was certain I was dead or dying.

4

When I came round I was lying on my back in the grass, staring up at the blue sky and the brilliant sunshine, and the first thing I heard was someone crying out in a long dying shout of pain, fear and incredulous disbelief.

A machine gun was firing over the top of me, and I wanted the ground to open up and swallow me every time the traverse brought the bullets hissing into the ground near me. I could hear them cracking as they went over me, kicking up the dust and chinking as they hit the stones among the grass.

My head was splitting but I couldn't feel any serious pain, and, squirming round in the grass, I felt myself all over. But there appeared to be no fresh blood anywhere and I realised I was unhurt.

For a long time I lay there, trying to decide which way was safety, staring up at the sun which was beating down now out of a brassy sky, then I realised I was lying with my head towards our own trenches.

I'd lost my rifle and I'd no idea where the Lewis-gun had gone. There seemed to be no one left of my section and no sign of the rest of the battalion. I'd seen many of them go down – Ashton, Mason, Henny, Spring and Bold.

At the thought of Bold dead, I almost sat upright. Of all the men I'd seen fall, I felt Bold's loss most keenly. Without my being aware of it, friendship had grown up between us, unnoticed almost, and never mentioned because Bold wasn't the man to show friendship and I'd been too stupid to realise just how much I'd admired him. From an inauspicious start when I'd hated him, I'd grown closer to Bold than to anyone else, save perhaps Locky, and I was consumed with misery that I'd realised it too late to be able to show it to him. At the thought of him sitting in that tumbled trench, not knowing how much I'd liked him, his back to the sandbags, his rifle still in his hand, his head still up, unafraid of death, the tears flooded into my eyes and I started to sob.

I lay there, among all the scattered equipment, the punctured water-cans, the pigeon baskets, the rolls of wire, and the dead men, still staring upwards, my fingers clutching at the grass in paroxysms of misery, then after a while, when it grew easier to think about it, I turned on my face. I knew what Bold would have said: 'It's up to you. You've got to survive for next time.' And as the machine gun bullets passed beyond me, I scrambled to my feet and went in a flat diving run for the nearest shell-hole. The grass was fairly long and partly hid me.

There were several men in the shell-hole. I saw Catchpole among them and I felt like hugging him.

It was impossible to get to the front for the crowd, and I cowered on the edge of the huddle of bodies that seemed to shudder every time a shell cracked nearby.

'Think we pulled it off?' Catchpole shouted.

'Not here, we didn't,' I said.

'Where's our barrage?'

'Up ahead. Miles away, I expect.'

Catchpole started to beat at the earth wall of the shell-hole in a bitter frustrated way.

'It was a bloody brainless plan,' he snarled. 'But for all that bloody equipment and trying to walk instead of running, the first wave would have got in before they got the machine guns going, and then we'd *all* have got in.'

We were all a little shocked. We'd been spurred along by the thought of the heroic in war and we'd been suddenly initiated into all that was terrible about it. We'd come to the harsh realisation that the price of all the hardships we'd paid and the long period of waiting had been wasted on a result that never had a chance of being attained. Where we could go from here, I couldn't think. I could only foresee years more of pain and darkness.

'I suppose the bloody papers'll say a strong party penetrated into the German trenches,' Catchpole went on in a low angry snarl. 'I suppose there'll be speeches in the House and the flags'll be run up.'

'Shut up, Vicar,' I said. 'It doesn't help much.'

'I saw Mason get it,' he said heavily. 'And poor old Spring. He was the first to go.'

He pointed to a line of men lying on their faces on our right. 'Why don't those bloody fools get under cover?' he asked irrationally.

'They don't need cover now,' I said. 'They're dead.'

An aeroplane came over us, buzzing along about fifty feet up. The pilot seemed to be waving to us, either to encourage us to go forward or to stay where we were. It was impossible to tell which.

'"Varus, give me back my legions,"' Catchpole said, and it sounded odd to hear him quoting anything but the sacrilegious prayers he'd liked to give us. 'Not much chance of that now. They're all dead. Thousands of 'em. The whole bloody army's dead!'

Somewhere under the pile of bodies, a man was weeping hysterically and I could hear someone praying in a flat shocked tone.

'"Almighty God, Father of our Lord, Jesus Christ, Maker of all things, Judge of all men . . ."'

A shell cracked nearby and as the shower of dirt came down and the pieces of earth and fragments of metal hit the rear side of the hole, the prayer stopped abruptly. I decided it was too dangerous to stay there, and pulled at Catchpole's sleeve.

'I'm moving,' I said. 'Come on.'

'All right,' Catchpole said. 'I'm coming.'

I scrambled out and dived for the next hole, but as I went I heard a machine gun start rattling again and Catchpole ducked back again until it stopped.

It was only as I slithered into the next hole that I realised it was an old one and half-full of slimy water. I scrambled to my feet, spluttering and gasping, and hugged the side. I was dying for a cigarette, but I'd left them all in my pack – three hundred of them – somewhere out there in front of me.

'Try the next one, Vicar,' I shouted. 'This one's full of water!'

But even as I put my head up to direct him, I saw a shell drop in the hole I'd just left and the whole lot – Catchpole and everyone – went up in a flurry of stones and smoke and fragments of shattered bodies, and I buried my face in the earth. Now even Catchpole had gone and there was no one left. I just wanted to cry at the uselessness of it all.

The battlefield seemed to have emptied of human beings now and, as the smoke drifted away, I could see the ridges and folds of ground quite clearly, all covered with bodies, as thick as sleepers in a London park on a summer afternoon.

Where the Germans were shelling their own trenches, I saw a few scattered figures climb out as we had and start running back, some of them without helmets, some without packs, some without rifles. But they were caught by an enfilading machine gun as we'd been caught and they all disappeared into the grass, dead, wounded or hiding, and there were only the grey-clad figures standing on the parapet fifty yards away, jeering at them.

A shell dropped just in front of me and as it shoved earth into the shell-hole, it pushed me out. I lay dazed for a while, then I got up and ran in a scrambling run for another hole. I was frightened. I'd survived that first awful slaughter and I was terrified now that I'd be hit as I found shelter. I still couldn't believe I was unhurt and alive. I knew Bold and Mason and Catchpole and Ashton and one or two others were dead because I'd seen them die with my own eyes. Tom Creak was certainly hit, and Murray, Tim Williams and Locky seemed to have vanished from the face of the earth, lost somewhere in that vast golgotha of a battlefield.

There was still no sign of the reserves, and it looked as though they'd stopped them – perhaps to end the slaughter, for the German wire seemed to be hardly touched and, although his trenches were a tumbled mass of sandbags, they seemed to be still full of men.

I remembered the rumours I'd heard about deep dugouts big enough to house whole companies in safety. Obviously, that was what had happened. They'd stayed down there, snug and safe during the bombardment, and it was only our slow advance and that awful weight we'd carried that had stopped us. If it hadn't been for that, we'd have been among them before they could get to the parapet. We'd failed by minutes.

I lay staring with burning eyes over the scorched lip of the shell-crater. In front of me, I saw a man raise himself on his hands, then his strength seemed to give out and he fell on his face and rolled over, and I saw one hand come slowly upwards and claw the air. It stayed there, like a plea for mercy, and I saw there were a couple of shrapnel bullets embedded in the fingers, like two black balls.

Suddenly the banging of shells seemed to have fallen off and the smoke began to clear and I noticed there were a couple of larks singing above me. There didn't appear to be much point in staying where I was, and I made up my mind to get back, in short rushes so that snipers wouldn't have time to shoot at me.

In the next shell-hole, though, Eph Lott was lying. He'd been hit in the head and his left arm was gone. I could see the smashed bone and pearly ligaments of his shoulder, and his face was pitted with dull grey little holes as though some explosion had driven stones and dirt into his flesh.

The bloody fingers of his right hand clutched a rifle and I bent over him to take it away. Just then it seemed more than likely that the Germans might counter-attack and throw us all back while the confusion was at its height and I thought it unwise for a wounded man to hold his rifle like that.

'I should get rid of that, Eph,' I said gently. 'If they come and find you with it, they'll shoot you.'

He stared at me with dazed stupid eyes that were milky with pain and quite uncomprehending. He never moved as I took the rifle off him.

Then I saw it had an orthoptic sight. I don't know where Eph had picked it up, because none of our section had had one and Eph had been empty-handed when I'd last seen him. I'd fired with an orthoptic sight once or twice and, as it occurred to me that I hadn't done much so far towards winning the battle, I swung round with the rifle and flung myself down, bitter and savage.

Everybody seemed to be dead or dying around me. Corpses were lying all over the place and I could still see that clawing hand with the two shrapnel balls in it, clutching at the air. It was the stillness of the dead that seemed so awful. Even their boots didn't seem to lie on the earth like those of living men. They rested on the ground with such an appalling unnatural limpness.

There was a big German who looked like an officer, standing on the parapet, waving and cheering. He had a spiked helmet on the end of a rifle and he was laughing at other men who were climbing out to join him, triumphant in their victory, certain that there was nothing we could do to them.

I pulled the trigger and he disappeared backwards into the

464

trench and the other Germans dived out of sight after him. Then I remembered I still had my bombs with me and, in a rage, not so much at the Germans but at the people who'd caused the disaster, I flung them towards the trench. I was too far away to do much damage and, with a feeling of frustration and futility, I saw them burst just in front of the parapet. The Germans who'd stuck their heads up again to see where my shot had come from vanished once more, abruptly, like a lot of Aunt Sallys at a fairground shy.

There were still a lot of them visible on my right, certain they were safe, but there didn't seem much point in shooting any more. So I turned round and tried to bandage Eph as best I could.

An officer was lying on the rear edge of the shell-hole. He was on his back and his face and hands were white as marble. He'd been hit several times in the chest and his shattered ribs were sticking in red and white splinters through the blood-soaked tatters of his tunic. He lungs were labouring like broken bellows, and although he was still alive his soul had already gone from him. When I turned him over, I saw it was Arnold Holroyd.

I tried to find the morphia tablets I knew he should be carrying, but I couldn't, and had to give up, so I did the best I could without them. Eph didn't seem to be in pain, just stupefied. I expect it was the head injury. His brains were bulging out behind his ear and I didn't know how to push them back. In the end I took my jack-knife out and used the flat of the blade.

It seemed strange to see Eph like that. He'd been a cheerful soul and, in spite of his reputation, he'd never given any trouble. I couldn't move him and I decided in the end to stay with him, and I lay in that hole all day, waiting for the reserves to come up and drive the Germans away.

There were other men out in front – from time to time I saw them wave to one another or heard them shout. After a while, one of them got up and ran towards me, dragging an injured leg, and fell in beside me. He'd been shot through the knee and I tried to make him comfortable.

It was breathlessly hot now and he began to gasp for water. But I hadn't any and Eph's bottle was empty, punctured by a bullet. He'd drunk all his own and I was just debating whether to risk going out to find a full bottle on one of the corpses when shrapnel shells started to bang around us again and we crouched back to back in the sparse shelter of the shell-hole to dodge the flying metal. When it had stopped I sat up and discovered the other man was dead. He'd been hit by a shrapnel bullet as he lay there and I was covered with his blood.

Eph hadn't moved and was still staring fixedly at me. The wounded began to cry dreadfully in the heat now, and one of them shouted for water until his voice grew thick and finally faded away. Behind me, another man was screaming in a harsh way which tore at the nerves, shouting that his head hurt, so that I realised I hadn't got a helmet and I put the dead man's on.

The sun rose higher and it became witheringly hot and in the lull I felt unutterably lonely. Eph's eyes seemed to grow more opaque and dead-looking, though he was still alive, his gaze fixed on me in a terrible stare, his chest heaving steadily and slowly, almost as though his breathing were normal. Then, not far in front of me, I saw a man lying on his back, moaning for help, and after a while I couldn't stand it any more and went out to him, turning over every body I came to on the way, certain a dozen times that I'd found Locky. When I got to him, I saw it was Tommy Mandy. A shell must have burst near him – probably the same one that had caught Eph – for there were several other men lying nearby, all burnt and torn.

The blast had blown off his puttees and scorched his trousers. Both legs were bloodily smashed and drenched with blood, and the thigh bones were exposed. There was a splinter stuck in his cheek like a dart and he was moaning softly and didn't recognise me, so I tried to put on a tourniquet with a strap and an entrenching tool, and started to drag him to where Eph was lying. As soon as I moved him he started to scream.

'Kill me,' he begged. 'For God's sake, kill me!'

I didn't know what to do about it. Crouching in the grass, I got the iodine out of his field dressing and poured it on the wounds and he promptly fainted, so I finished dragging him back towards Eph. I knew it wouldn't do his legs much good, but lying there he'd have got shot eventually, because I'd seen the Germans firing at anything that moved.

Later in the day, when things were quieter, I saw another man trying to crawl towards us and I went out to him. When I got closer, I saw it was Billy Mandy. He'd been hit in the chest and his face had turned a grey putty colour. The whole front of his uniform was soaked with blood and the ground underneath him was brown with it. His hands were full of grass, as though he'd tried to drag himself along by it.

He was quite conscious and he recognised me at once.

''Ello, Fen,' he said. 'Are you all right?'

'I think so,' I said. 'Hang on. I'll get you in.'

'You're wasting your time,' he said.

He was right. I got him into the hole in the end but he died like his brother.

It was about this time that Eph suddenly seemed to recover consciousness. He didn't move and that awful fixed stare in his eyes didn't waver, but his breathing seemed to quicken and he began to mutter.

''Oo's that?' he said after a while, as though he could hear but not see, and I scrambled across to him.

'It's me, Eph,' I said. 'Fenner.'

'I'm done for,' he muttered. 'Say us a prayer, Fen.'

I recited the Lord's Prayer but he seemed to have lapsed back into his coma and showed no sign of whether he'd heard, or even whether he was still aware that I was there.

One or two other men had crawled in from the tangle of corpses by this time and rolled into the hole. By midday, there were about nine of us in there, all of them wounded except me. I'd brought three in myself because I couldn't bear their crying.

The Germans were standing on their parapet again now, in groups, indifferent to us, and whenever anyone moved they sniped at him or turned their machine guns on him. Once or twice I saw odd men get up and run to the rear, singly or in little bunches, but they all seemed to be bowled over, going down like shot rabbits in a tangle of arms and legs.

Just after midday, over on the right, there seemed to be an informal truce and I could see stretcher-bearers moving about. But it didn't seem to happen where we were and eventually the machine gun fire started again and the stretcher-bearers all disappeared.

Eph died during the afternoon and by evening the Germans had climbed down into their trenches again, though we could hear them from time to time, jeering at the men who crouched in holes in front of their wire. The guns were still firing sporadically and the shells were still going over, but there was nothing near us. The barrage had swept miles away to the rear, searching out the second-line and third-line trenches. Down to the south you could hear the rumble of fierce fighting, but just round me the battle seemed to have died away of inanition.

5

I shall never forget that day. It was a day of birdsong and intense midsummer beauty that was made all the more heartbreaking by contrast with the carnage around me. It burned its agonising way past midday and into the afternoon as we prayed for dark and tried to tell the time by the shadows.

The sunlight in the blue arc of the sky became harsh and sizzling in its heat, so that the earth seemed to glow and shimmer around us. No Man's Land still seemed like a summer field, for the long grass and the flowers hid the dead except on the slopes where you could see them lying in heaps.

Eph's face turned to the colour of old bone, dead white and stiff-looking, and someone took off his jacket and put it over the staring eyes.

There seemed to be no indication that further attacks were coming, though we could still see the smoke drifting in pink and blue clouds to the south. It seemed incredible that all those vast singing armies we'd seen such a short time before could have sunk into the earth within a few short minutes. There was no longer any sign of the iron strength we'd felt in the morning. The wave of emotional excitement had passed in the tragedy, and the frenzy was spent. We were only derelicts now in a ruined world.

As we crouched there, all the spine blasted out of us, I saw the obscene flies descend in their thousands on to the disfigured dead, grim bloated carrion-eaters darkening the bloody wounds and crawling in blue-black hundreds over the stiff lips and yellowing eyes. There were rats, too, scuttling up from the old shell-holes and through the morbid patches of poppies that grew along their white lips, to explore the heaps of dead. But the larks were singing, too, as though they'd recovered from their early fright, and they were filling the air again with cascades of glowing notes. With my face on the edge of the shell-hole, I could see flowers everywhere, unreal among the carnage – scabious, poppies, marigolds, yellow weeds shaking in the breeze – and thousands of insects, bees, grasshoppers and beetles, trudging round the scattered packs and rifles and bayonets and helmets and scabbards and cartridges and bodies, indifferent to the sickly scent of death, as though nothing had happened, as though whole armies hadn't died in the hours between dawn and midday.

All the time in my mind was the chorus – I must get back, I must get back; I shall die if I stay here. Sooner or later, the Germans are bound to attack, I thought, and I'm no damn' good to Helen dead. Mason was already dead, crucified on the wire, bringing to an end all the jealousy and unhappiness that had passed between us. It seemed odd that it should be Mason and not me, because once he'd always seemed so lucky and untouchable. But now the flies were on him and I was still alive and hardly hurt.

I started wondering if I'd done my duty as I ought. I'd seen Ashton and men like him give everything of courage, patriotism and self-sacrifice, trying to press on when it was clearly hopeless to press on, because they'd been told to capture certain objectives and because they felt it was their duty to try to the limit of their strength and courage. Hundreds must have died

470

in those few hours between seven-thirty and midday solely because their courage led them to go on trying when there was no longer any hope.

Then I began to wonder why it was that I'd been picked out to remain alive. Why not Mason or Bold or Catchpole or Ashton? Why me? Why was I so favoured? We were all the same shape, wore the same clothes, suffered much the same hopes and fears, yet I'd been left alive when all the others were dead. I didn't know whether to be overjoyed or saddened. Mostly, I just wanted to cry.

It didn't start to grow dark until nearly ten o'clock. It had been a glorious summer day and the light hung on and hung on. About ten o'clock the dusk set in with a bloody smear of sunset and we decided to try and make it to our own lines. As we scrambled and pulled each other out of the shell-hole, I saw the whole of No Man's Land had come to life, with wounded men rising like ghosts, silently and slowly crawling out of the dips and hollows and making their painful way back.

The Germans started firing flares and there was still the rattle of machine guns and the tap of rifles, but the place was shadowy now and it was difficult to see much at a distance. I set off with two men hanging on to me. I still had Eph's rifle, because I'd heard somewhere they could charge you with cowardice if you came out of it unhurt without your weapons, and it kept getting between my legs and tripping me up.

We seemed to stumble around in the dark for hours, then we saw a trench in front of us. We weren't certain whether it was ours or the Germans', so I put the other men down and scrambled forward. When I reached the parapet, I hung over it, head down, ready to slip back again if it proved to be the wrong one. Dead men were lying anyhow inside it but it was too dark to see what uniform they wore. Then I heard an English voice and saw lights and by them, stretcher-bearers moving along, trying to clear away the wounded. I brought the two men in and lowered them down. Someone handed me a mess-tin full of tea and rum and it tasted like heaven, and I sat with my head flung back against the earth wall, my eyes closed, frowning, perplexed, unable to believe I was still sane.

After a while I felt better and went back to see if I could find any more wounded, and when I returned the second time, I saw Appleby standing in the trench. There was a light from a dugout shining on him and I was startled at his appearance. His arm was in a bloodstained sling and he was plastered with mud, his hair spiky with matted dirt. I must have looked much the same, I suppose.

'Fenner!' he said. 'You all right?'

'I'm all right. How many are there left?'

'I don't know,' he said. 'I think I'm the only one on his feet. Me and you. The colonel's down. I saw him go. And Blackett. They brought Mr Sheridan in. He must have been caught by shrapnel. They said he'd got about fifteen holes in him.'

'Ashton's dead,' I said, and I felt again as though I wanted to cry. 'I saw him. And Bold. And Holroyd.'

'We ought to try and get the lads together,' he said brokenly. 'That's why I'm hanging on here. This has been a bad day for us. A damned bad day. They've been trying to send me back for a couple of hours now but I can't go without seeing everybody's all right. I'm just waiting for the lads to come in.'

All that night – and under the red sickle of the midsummer moon and the inaccessible peace of the stars it was only half-dark most of the time – the unhurt and the wounded kept coming in. No Man's Land was teeming with them now, and all the time the reserves waiting in the front line, nervous of the German counter-attack that was expected hourly, were challenging everyone who came near.

But the Germans never came. In spite of what he'd done to us, we must have hurt him too. He could have walked in if he'd wanted, and in the confusion that existed we could never have stopped him. But he never came.

Men were stumbling in all night, calling out the names of their units and asking if anyone had seen their friends. Nobody ever had. Tired men staggered in, and wounded crawled in, faces smashed, arms and legs broken, crying for help or stubbornly brushing aside assistance and saying, 'I'll manage.'

Men were sitting on the broken firestep weeping, and there was a padre, bare-headed, his face martyred, bending over the dying. All night we went backwards and forwards over the parapet. There were stretcher-bearers everywhere, calling out softly in the darkness. From time to time, you heard whispered answering cries and, following them, you found someone making his painful way back, dragging his lacerated, punctured body on hands and knees, or little groups of wounded men in the hollows as though they'd crept together for comfort, sagging men with every bone in their bodies broken but still managing to give out inarticulate little cries.

In other hollows were the dead and wounded who'd found momentary shelter and hadn't been able to withstand the pain and the thirst. And all around us were those pathetic mounds of men – four foot high in places they were, crouching in huddles – and still more, lying in rows like sheaves of corn after the reaper's been past, thick as flies on fly-paper, with the noticeboards and pennants, and the pathetic-looking home-made flags that proclaimed their enthusiasm and their faith and their exaltation, still grasped in dead hands. They'd died crawling, stiffening as they moved, or bandaging each other's wounds.

I'd no idea who was alive and who was dead but, no matter how much we searched, there were always more alive and just alive to bring in. I seemed to have lost touch with our own people for I saw no one I knew.

Once, in the wan daylight, just as dawn was breaking, I saw a colonel and a brigadier lying together, both unarmed except for walking sticks, face down in the grass, their arms outstretched towards the German trenches as though they were still trying to point the way to the legions of dead behind them. The flayed earth around them seemed to be covered with scrap-iron, shards of old shell-cases, spent bullets, bomb splinters and shrapnel balls, and it amazed me to realise that men had got as far as they had through all that sleet of flying metal.

As the light increased, I stumbled back into the trench for the umpteenth time and saw young Murray coming towards me. His face was foul with dirt and his clothes were torn and covered with blood. He looked dazed and older and grimmer but he didn't appear to be hurt. He was licking his lips and his tongue seemed strangely pink and clean in the squalor of his blackened face.

He appeared to be drunk and I saw he was carrying a rum jar. 'Found it out there,' he said. 'Have a swig!'

He was laughing in a way that was nearer to crying, and as he passed the jar round, he jerked a thumb. 'I got up to their bloody wire,' he said. 'Then we stuck. A shell bowled me over and Tim Williams took the gun. God knows what happened to him. When I got my breath back he'd gone and it was too late to do anything then. If only we'd not had those bloody packs we'd have made it. They're all out there, Fen. They're all out there in front. Every last one of 'em. I saw Tom Creak just now. He'd crawled in with a smashed thigh. He said he saw Locky. He said he was hit but still alive. There's nobody else though. Only me and you.'

I thanked God Locky was alive, and thought it odd that it should be Murray and me who were still on our feet, after what Bold had always said of us. We seemed to have an instinct for survival.

'They got Bold,' I said. 'I was with him.'

'Poor bloody old Bold,' Murray said sombrely. 'He wasn't a bad bastard, you know, as far as bastards go.'

We decided to go out to look for Locky, but we were forbidden to try because it was now daylight. But as soon as the sun got up again we saw there was a white flag flying from the German parapet and there were Germans among their own wire attending to the British wounded. They were moving among the piles of dead, pulling living men from among the heaps of corpses.

'Let's chance it,' Murray said, and we scrambled out in broad daylight.

No one fired at us and more men began to scramble after us until No Man's Land seemed to be dotted with men in khaki and grey. It developed into an informal truce and the Germans didn't seem to object so long as we went nowhere near their wire. I saw Red Cross flags and ceremonial saluting and even friendly handshakes which seemed to make the whole thing even more futile and heartbreaking, with the wounded crawling back around us and the dead lying in heaps.

The humiliation of knowing we were there only because the Germans allowed us to be there never occurred to me. All I wanted was to put an end to the sound of crying. They said later, that all the time, even while we couldn't move for the dead and the wounded, headquarters were urging harassed brigadiers to push on with more attacks.

We found the battalion dead in rows where they'd fallen, many of them hit not once but half a dozen times. There seemed to be none of the living left by this time and they lay there, mostly huddled forward on their faces, weighted down by those dreadful loads, their rifles, their loads of sandbags and wire, and all the other equipment that had been piled on to them, dusty and utterly without dignity, their features pressed into the grass, stiffening fingers clutching at their wounds.

There was Hardacre, the flies about his mouth, grit on his staring eyes, and no living hand moving up to brush it away. We saw nine men in a row in the sunshine with no sign of injury on them, victims somehow of blast, and the colonel way out in front with the adjutant, his brother, who shouldn't have been there at all – lying on his back, his eye-patch blown away somehow, one eye closed and the other, the blind one, staring in a mad milky fashion at the sun.

The little terrier was still with him, draped across his chest, its head on its forepaws, whining. We tried to take it away with us but when Murray picked it up, it wriggled out of his arms and went back to the body and squatted down again in the same position.

'Leave it,' I said. 'It'll only find its way back here if you take it.'

Murray nodded and let it go, a taut distressed expression on his face, and we moved on among the dead, taking their pay-books but leaving their identity discs for whoever had to bury them. These were the cleanly dead, the dead of the machine gun bullets, stitched across by that murderous fire, but there were others lying in the shell-holes and round their lips in groups of stark, mangled, half-naked bodies that looked as though they belonged more properly in a slaughterhouse, ghastly pieces of scorched and blackened flesh and bone and blood that were unrecognisable as men.

Finally I found my own platoon, Spring still where I'd seen him hit, and all the others, one just in front of another in a diagonal line as the bullets had caught them at the top of the crest. Then Ashton, huddled alone on his side, still clutching his home-made orange flag, the moonpenny wilting in his buttonhole, and Eph and the Mandys all together in the same shell-hole.

Locky was lying a little apart in a hollow that stunk of acid fumes and the smell of corruption. There were other men in there, more dead than living, and one or two old bodies I noticed, mere skeletons in rags of French uniform. One of them had bones the colour of the musty edges of a century-old volume piercing the blue and red cloth, a skull with black matted hair, looking like a mushroom in the grass, and teeth that gleamed in the sunshine. They seemed to belong to another war from ours, another age.

Locky was lying on his back, and you could see the crushed grass and the trail of blood flecks on the flowers where he'd dragged himself along.

'Molly,' he was moaning softly to himself. 'Molly!'

He'd been hit twice in the chest and looked in a bad way. When we turned him over, we found he had a hole in his back you could get both your fists into. We got his shirt off and went among the dead for bandages.

In the end we got him into a blanket and carried him back like that, Murray and I and two other men, stumbling and tripping over the scattered equipment and abandoned weapons and the dead.

Back in the trench we handed him over to the stretcher-bearers. They examined him briefly, then gave me a quick stare that told me he was slipping between our fingers even as we watched, to some realm where he was no longer approachable, no longer able to restore sanity with his calm imperturbability, where it was all cold and comfortless and dark, and for a while I felt bereft of reason and certain I couldn't stand any more.

Somehow, going round in my head was the knowledge that his son was alive and bore his name, and I was glad there was another Lockwood Haddo to carry on his name, his sanity, his sense. Just then it seemed important that there should be.

I watched them carry him away and Murray slapped my shoulder.

'He'll be all right now,' he said loudly, but I knew he was as well aware as I was that we'd never see Locky again.

I turned round and stumbled away, numbed, stupefied, and devoid of emotion. I felt as if tears were falling on to my heart – slowly, one by one. I moved and performed actions, but my heart was still inside me. There was no agony, just an icy living death. If only I could have talked to him, I thought, if only we could have had a few minutes together. I felt I'd never get used to the fact that he was gone.

There was a stink of rum in the trench but we never found

out where it came from. I could have done with some more rum just then, for the place seemed to be littered with corpses. There was one man just on top of the parapet, sitting down, bolt upright, looking as though he were quite comfortable, supported by the bodies of his comrades, gazing back into the trench, his blue eyes wide open, a fine-looking man. He sat there, staring, until the doctor, giving anti-tetanus injections to the wounded by a first-aid post that was recognisable among the rubble only by its Red Cross flag and the smell of carbolic, ether and chloroform, looked up and noticed him.

'For God's sake,' he said irritably. 'Put a sandbag over that man's face, someone!'

After a while, the truce seemed to stop and everybody came in. What happened to those we missed I don't know. We hung about in the front trench, counting noses, but of our company there seemed to be only Murray and me left.

Already the ugly name of Gommecourt was filtering through. They said that up there the troops had been wiped clean off the face of the earth, though God knows what they thought had happened to our brigade. Someone said the York and Lancs had got into Serre village only to be destroyed from behind by Germans coming up out of deep shelters. The attack at Fricourt was a failure too and the West Yorks had been swept away before they'd gone a hundred yards. Their second wave didn't even manage to reach the starting tapes.

The Irish had smashed through four sets of trenches at Thiepval but there'd been no reserves left to follow them up and they were still there, cut off and isolated, being shelled to blazes. Down in the south by the river and in the French sector, there'd been some success, and someone said the cavalry had got through, because dead men and horses had been seen, but it turned out they were artillerymen.

All at our end was failure. The Newfoundlanders had been wiped out against Hamel and the South Wales Borderers at

Beaumont. The Durhams had been decimated at Ovillers and the Green Howards at Fricourt. Whole battalions, thousands on thousands on thousands of men, had been swept away in an unbelievable butchery in the first five or ten minutes after seven-thirty.

Prisoners had been shot in the berserk excitement. Signalling had broken down and runners had failed to get through; and the barrage had gone gaily on, though some of the artillery commanders, ignoring orders, had brought the shells back on their own initiative to help the stranded infantry. But by then it had been too late. The attack had failed. The men were dead. The battalions had vanished.

There was a Jock piper in the trench, miles from where he should have been, a little drunk or a little shocked or both, marching up and down, sweating in the sunshine, playing a pibroch and swearing at anyone who tried to stop him.

'Where's the bloody cavalry?' someone was shouting. 'Where did they get to?'

'You should have seen it, bhoy,' a wounded man wearing the Bloody Hand badge of the Ulsters was saying. 'Real soda-water we found in thim trenches. And cigars as long as your arm.'

'The bastards used flame-throwers on us,' another man said. 'Where I was, they'd chained their men to the machine guns.'

A gunner officer, swinging a German helmet in his hand, stalked past, his clothes torn and scorched, his eyes bewildered. 'Hamel's full of dead,' he was saying in shocked tones. 'Full of dead!'

Someone started singing in a drunken hysterical voice:

> 'Après la guerre fini
> Tous les soldats partis
> Mademoiselle avec piccaninny
> Souvenir des bloody Angl'is.'

'Shut your row, Joe,' he was told. 'I've got a splittin' headache!'

'That's all right.' The singing stopped, and a merry voice, full of rum, was raised. 'Tell Sir Douglas 'Aig that Private 'Obbins of the York and Lancs congratulates him and hopes 'e'll be made a dook for this day's work.'

The whole area stunk of gas fumes and lyddite. Men of the decimated battalions were trying to find their way back to their units through the uncontrollable stream of wounded and the support troops who were still trying to move forward for follow-up attacks which had long since been cancelled. There wasn't a single telephone line still intact to stop the reserves moving forward, and with them came the Pioneer Corps who were supposed to repair the German trenches when they'd been captured, but were set to work instead to bury the dead.

They lay about everywhere still, like pieces of wreckage, their faces senseless and grey, and the salvage parties were busy collecting the bombs and the rifles off them. A harassed sergeant-major was trying to organise stretcher-bearers.

'For God's sake, get me out of here,' I heard one wounded man say, and the sergeant-major, driven to the point of exhaustion, turned on him brutally.

'Shut your mouth,' he said. 'I'm coming to you.'

Men were bringing up little stretchers on wheels, bumping them over the rough ground, and we began to lift the wounded on to them, bandaging knees that were bloody with crawling. Beef tea miraculously appeared in basins. A doctor in a blood-soaked apron, crouching over a hideously wounded man in a hacked-out hollow of the trench side, was staring at a blunted needle.

'This damn' thing's inhuman,' he said to an orderly. 'Take it away.'

As we helped to carry the wounded back, I saw artillerymen and engineers, all roped in to help the ambulance men, and hundreds of cavalrymen, those wonderful cavalrymen who were going to break through and turn the Germans' flank. Here they were, shifting the wounded and burying the dead, handing stretchers over the parapet where the trench was too narrow. Old Corker hadn't been far wrong.

There was a curious absence of prisoners, just indignant men shouting they'd been let down, and stretcher-bearers, and harassed military police trying to restore order among the shocked, dazed and angry men who were slowly recovering their wits, and the bewildered support troops still trying to fight their way forward.

'We got in and nobody came to help us,' someone was shouting furiously.

'Lloyd George said this was a fight to the finish,' he was answered. 'The bastard wants to come and finish it!'

I saw an officer with a bandaged head trying to muster a pathetically small group of men. He was swaying with fatigue. None of us seemed to have eaten or slept for days. I was beaten to the wide, light-headed, almost exalted. Somewhere eventually, I knew, I would sleep, and I cared little where we went. The world seemed to have emptied of men I'd known and lived with, and there was only young Murray and one or two others who'd struggled in. Appleby had disappeared at last.

My throat was dry and my water-bottle empty. Searching for food and drink, I found my way with my little party into a big dugout, groping past the musty folds of a blanket and a piece of Wilson canvas. We lit a candle-end stuck in its own grease in a tin lid and sat staring at it, spent and broken, a greyness in our hearts. The air was thick with smoke and the reek of the dying candle. The faces about me were brooding and enigmatic, and curiously old, mouths munching pieces of bread and cheese or pursed round Woodbine stumps. Murray's features wore a yellowish pallor and his eyes were red-rimmed with sleeplessness. His hands were trembling, and his voice had an echo of overexcitement in it.

'We could have got in,' he kept saying, repeating it like a prayer, 'if we hadn't had those bloody packs.'

'Don't talk wet,' someone answered. 'We never had a chance.

Never! Never in a thousand years! The bloody staff have done it again. The bastards think a battle's only a matter of a few sums on a piece of paper.'

After a while, an officer called us out and we got up slowly, glad to have our actions determined for us, all of us still half-stunned by emotions that weren't under control, all our uniforms torn by bullets and shrapnel.

''E was still trying to get 'old of 'is rifle,' one man was saying. 'And 'e'd got no bloody 'ands. I told 'im, "Fred, lie still," and 'e tried, but then 'e died.'

The tears were running down his unshaven face as he spoke. There was no quaver in his voice, only a high abnormal note as bitterness and grief swept over him.

'I'll have to find Catchpole's kit when we get back,' Murray said heavily, picking up his rifle and buckling his belt. 'He'd got some letters and some smutty photos he asked me to chuck away.'

His face was expressionless and uninterested, and he moved about like a man condemned. 'Wonder if they'll keep us here in support,' he muttered.

As we crept out into the sunlight, a staff captain with a startlingly red-and-white bandage over a grimy face came up to me and asked me where our officers were. I said we didn't appear to have any, so he told me in a cracked voice that wasn't quite under control to collect what remained of the battalion and get them the hell out of the way.

I managed to raise about twenty-eight and we stumbled off. As we left the trenches, I noticed a loud wailing sound like huge wet fingers being dragged across an enormous glass pane. It rose and fell, interminable, unbearable, and as we turned an angle of the trench I saw where it came from. All along a muddy sunken roadway they lay, hundreds of wounded, brown blanket shapes, some shouting, some moaning, some singing in delirium.

The anaesthesia of shock had worn off now and the pain

and thirst were setting in among the torn bodies and ownerless arms and legs and equipment. The sound of their cries had a uniform level of muted anguish and despair. During the night, they'd became little boys again and were crying in the heat for their mothers, for help, for water, for death, for God, in a vast and terrible monotone, while an elderly staff officer moved about them, trying to tell them it was worth it as we'd won. We'd thrown the Germans back and victory was within our grasp.

They gazed at us with piteous eyes and called out to us as we moved past them.

'For God's sake, come 'ere, mate!'

'Lift this man off me, Sarge, please! He's snuffed it.'

'No, leave me,' one man said. 'Go to that poor sod from the York and Lancs. He's in dreadful pain. I might even manage to walk if you can 'elp me up.'

We passed through the little wood with its calvary and I noticed there were a lot of new graves about, with the caps of the dead askew on them. Except where the path had been cleared, the wood was a dreadful tangle of trees now, the ground criss-crossed with broken bullet-clipped branches and splintered timber. The Germans had been dropping shells on it for two days now and it was just a mass of shell-holes, abandoned equipment, smashed guns, splintered SAA boxes and undergrowth.

Every tree seemed to have been broken off at the top or bottom to add to the impenetrable tangle that sliced the sun into broken dusty beams. They were burned and scorched till they looked like the blasted heath from *Macbeth*, their uplifted arms twisted as though begging for mercy. On the fringe, some attempt had been made to set the graves in order and there was a red-faced padre there with lines of new crosses. With all those shattered trees about, it was like being in the graveyard of civilisation. Dead horses and mules lay about, still in their harness, hideously smashed. Some had obviously kicked each other to ribbons trying to get free, and others lay, with their legs starkly in the air, among the smashed waggons and limbers and scattered shells and the incredibly broken guns that showed where the German artillery had done its deadly work. A few morose men were trying to drag them off the road with a tractor and ropes. It was like a Gustave Doré etching of Purgatory.

Watched over by Indian cavalry sitting their nervous horses, their headdresses the only colour in that grim landscape, the dead lay in untidy groups, their life staining the chalky puddles, their crimson fingers in bloodstained bunches. Battle equipment lay everywhere, trampled into the mud with shreds of clothing, riddled boots and broken rifles. The birds seemed to have vanished from that awful charnel house, and the dead looked as though they'd been dropped in giant handfuls from the sky, with their clutching fingers and liquid eyes staring at the sun.

There were bodies in all the ditches, and I saw a little machine-gunner, scarcely more than a child, kneeling by the grass verge, his head hanging forward as though he were crying, and an elderly man with grey hair and groping hands. Bodies and still more bodies, most of them brought back from the trenches to give the living room to move, some of them fallen where the shells had caught them on their way up, were packed close together among the dead horses and wreckage, in every kind of grotesque attitude, their uniforms filthy with mud and blood, some of them strangely contorted as though they'd died in agony. One of them had his arms outstretched as though he were playing a violin, and others were flung down shapelessly like clothes without bodies in them. Most of their equipment had already been salvaged and their pockets had been slit for cigarettes and iron rations. Letters and photographs lay scattered about, trampled into the mud by passing boots.

From the bent iron calvary nearby, Jesus Christ stared down on them with iron unfeeling eyes and iron cheeks. They lay on their backs, their arms crossed, their faces dirty and aghast, their mouths open and their jaws askew in dreadful grins, their eyes closed, their convict-shaven skulls broken. One man had put his elbows on the edge of the ditch to die and was staring with horrible eyes, and I saw another man coming through that army of dead, stumbling to the rear, groping at a lacerated wound in his chest, staggering from one side to the other, one arm feeling into space for support, the blood trickling through the torn hole in his flesh.

Unwounded men and walking wounded, half-asleep on their feet, passed him unconcernedly or drank tea and slept indifferently among the shambles, exhausted, their faces grimy, their hair matted with mud. Only his friend walked alongside him, begging him to sit down.

But he kept plodding on. 'Don't touch me,' he kept saying. 'Leave me alone. If I sit down I'll get trodden on.'

And he went staggering on until I saw him stiffen as he walked and fall like a log in the middle of the road, where he lay, forcing a passage through the advancing living until someone dragged him to the side of the road and threw a torn groundsheet over him. All around him men sat indifferently in attitudes of shock, wearing turbans and white body-belts of bandages, absorbed with trying to stanch wounds, going through the dumb, stupefied, mechanical actions of exhaustion, packed on the handcarts that had brought the Lewis-guns up, on chance stretchers, or even on the ladders on which they'd been carried from the trenches.

A doctor halted us there to help and we seemed to work for hours, sweating, praying, cursing, as we shifted the stark and mangled bodies, dead fists swinging in heavy blows against our legs as we turned the bodies over, spreadeagled and stiff so that we had to stand on them to force them into blankets.

While we worked, the same harassed staff officer who'd sent us out of the trenches came up to us and stormed at me because we hadn't made ourselves scarce.

'There's no room here for scattered groups of men,' he said.

'There can be no co-ordination when the place's full of stragglers. For God's sake, Sergeant, get your men away! I'll warn your people you're coming.'

When we reached the road, we were told to wait because the Germans had got it thoroughly taped and were stopping traffic all the way along. Every now and then, a clump of shells set us swaying as they stirred the air, but I was indifferent to danger now, just conscious of little things like tilting duckboards or barbed wire catching at my clothes and bringing me to a paroxysm of exhausted fury. Young Murray had fallen asleep where he sat, his head cradled in his arms, lost in an anguish of memories, and he was twitching in fretful uneasy movements, his lips parted, his teeth grinding, his jaws working, whimpering and giving little sobs, long quivering moans and half-incoherent obscenities. Just above him in the sunshine on a fragment of broken wall, a lizard poised, warming itself.

Somehow, in spite of weariness, I couldn't sleep and I started thinking of what we'd just come through. It didn't seem possible that it had happened to me. I still couldn't believe Locky was gone, and Bold and all the others. I'd wake up soon, I kept thinking, I remember, and I'd find myself back at Bos and hear Locky's dry humour or Bold's harsh shout. Then I realised that it *had* happened and the pain started all over again through the numbness.

We got word to move on again at last, and I tried to wake Murray up. I shook him and shouted in his ear but he didn't move. Then, as I started swearing at him, frustrated and angry, he gave a quick convulsive jump and came to wakefulness again with his disordered nerves seeking to readjust themselves. He sat up with a start, still half-asleep, giving a reluctant cry of pain as though I'd touched an exposed nerve, then he reached out wearily and picked up his rifle.

'We can go now,' I told him.

'All right,' he said. 'I'm ready.'

Along the road, there were hundreds of fresh soldiers moving up, men who were clean and unstained with blood, probably straight from the Bull Ring at Rouen. They stared at us curiously as we passed them, their faces bearing surprisingly little sign of emotion, and I felt them patting me on the back.

'Well played, chaps,' someone said.

Some of them were still cheering and singing, and I envied them that they were untouched by disaster. The man in front of me, a youngster from A Company who couldn't have been much more than nineteen, was strung up to breaking point and kept shuddering.

'They might have given us a rest,' I heard him saying.

As I stood at the side of the trench, watching them file past me, one of the incoming officers took the cigarette from his mouth and offered it to me.

'Cigarette, Sergeant?' he said unemotionally, and I took it and forgot to thank him.

'What was it like.' he asked.

'Like a butcher's shop,' I said.

'Lose many officers?'

'We lost the lot,' I said, and somehow drew an immense bitter satisfaction from the shocked look on his clean, well-shaven face.

We reached a village that seemed nothing but a grey-and-red ruin of charred ribs and broken walls, a skeleton blasted by counter-fire, just a huddle of shell-perforated bullet-spattered walls and splintered beams. Everywhere, there was the same appalling desolation, with the muddy street empty except for us. Shutters hung limply, and doors and windows gaped in utter despair over a brick-strewn road littered with scraps of paper. Here and there, a dead man sprawled like a flattened bag. An ancient French peasant was slumped against a wall, his face angry, as though he'd died hating, and there was a woman lying on her back, half inside a doorway. A British soldier lay twisted on a mattress that had been dragged out for him to breathe his last on, his head back, his face plastered with blood and mud around the mouth and chin, his glazing eyes groping up at the sky. In one or two of the houses, out of reach of shell-splinters, beds had been shoved to one side and graves had been dug and crosses erected. There were more dead horses in muddy clotted heaps.

Beyond the village, we joined the mainstream of traffic, where artillerymen sat stiffly on tired mounts by the long steel guns, and limping weary infantrymen trudged rearwards in little groups like our own that seemed no bigger than a company or a platoon, heads heavy under helmets, out of step, unspeaking except for an occasional muttered curse, so tired they stumbled straight on into the ditch when the road turned. Mounted officers were asleep on jaded horses, and men drooped over gun limbers, still hanging on while sound asleep. The chink of equipment or the tap of a bayonet against a petrol tin half full of water seemed to be the only sounds over the shuffle of boots.

On either side of us, there were barley fields and the rich beauty of the countryside with its glowing glistening wheat wreathed in the haze of dust that lay over everything.

A Ford ambulance jolted past, acridly stinking of disinfectant, and I heard the men inside, roughly wrapped in blankets, calling piteously. 'Go steady,' they were saying. 'For Christ's sake, go steady!'

How long we were getting back to Bos Wood I don't know. I was so tired that, after a while, all I noticed was the steel helmets of the men in front of me and the eyes in the blank drawn faces of the men behind.

As we reached Bos, I remember seeing a little orchard with blossom still out, looking awkward and frail, and I wanted to cry at the sight of it.

The camp details had been told to expect us and they were ready for us. They'd laid out mugs and plates, and food seemed to be everywhere. There seemed to be a hell of a lot of it for so few men, I thought.

There were about forty-five of us now. We'd picked up a few

more, all of them like ourselves, aged and grown shabby in battle, daubed with chalk dirt and the blood of their friends, their faces and hands brown-grey with mud, their hair tangled under dead men's helmets, their faces unshaven, one or two with bandages over trivial wounds, bowed under shock and exhaustion, their clothes mere rags.

As we turned into the lane, I heard someone shout, 'They're here,' and I heard the band strike up.

'Johnny's a-walking. Oompa, oompa.
Johnny's a-walking home.'

They were gathered in groups, some with cameras, to watch us come in, standing about in the sunshine in shirtsleeves. As we shuffled into the orchard, the cooks, the unfit, and the headquarters details surged forward cheering. There seemed to be a tremendous gulf between them and us. They looked clean and rested and we were just sweating wretches half asleep on our feet, unmoved by the welcome, all the grief and pity gone out of us, broken-hearted, broken-spirited, with no tears left to shed.

'Any souvenirs?' somebody called. Nobody replied, and the voice asked again more quietly, 'What was it like?'

'Don't ask me,' the shuddering boy in front of me said. 'It was terrible!'

I saw the camp details staring down the lane as though they expected more of us to follow, then they saw there weren't any more and thankfully the damned band had the sense to stop and the cameras were shoved out of sight.

The major, who'd stayed behind in command, had been called to Brigade, it seemed, and it was Bickerstaff who came towards me, squinting against the sun. He looked scared, as though he didn't know what to say, and I saw the brigadier behind him, prompting him, his face drawn and tired. He looked about twenty years older.

'Is this A or B Company, Sergeant?' Bickerstaff asked.

'It's A and B and C and D,' I said. 'This is the lot. All of us. The whole battalion.'

'All?'

'All I know about.'

'Good God!'

'Just because some bastard on the staff preferred playing polo to learning his bloody job!' Murray shouted bitterly.

I saw the brigadier turn away. 'It's butchers they want, not brigadiers,' he muttered.

He gestured at the cooks and I noticed them begin to whip away mugs and dixies of food that weren't going to be used. Then the brigadier turned round again, his mouth working.

'I expect some more will be coming in soon,' he said. 'I – I . . .' He hesitated, searching for words, then he burst out, 'If it's any consolation, and I don't suppose it is, I'm proud to have had you chaps under me.'

'We'll go in again, sir,' young Murray shouted.

'Thanks, lads.'

'How did we do?'

'All right, my boy.'

'Did we save Verdun?'

The brigadier lifted his head slowly. 'I think so,' he said. 'I suppose so.'

'How many prisoners did we get, sir?'

The brigadier paused and his reply was only a whisper. 'Three,' he said.

'What? The whole division, sir?'

'The whole division.'

There was a long silence, then I heard a man sob, and Murray started to laugh in a high-pitched note that came from tiredness and shock and hysteria.

'Three? All those bloody great cages, and only *three*?'

The brigadier turned away abruptly, stumbling a little, and we went on just standing there while he spoke to Bickerstaff.

I wasn't angry. Just bewildered, and suffering from a sense of waste that was as bitter as gall.

The quartermaster sergeant-major stepped forward and saluted. 'Sir, do you think I ought to call the rolls or leave them till later?'

'Better do it now,' the brigadier said. 'The way they look they might not remember later.'

Twining began to call the roll, starting with D Company because I was in charge, but there weren't enough of us left to know what had happened to the others. A lot had to be put down as missing but we knew there weren't any prisoners, and anybody who wasn't there was either wounded or dead.

'Ashton,' Twining called. 'Where's Mr Ashton?'

'Dead,' I said. 'He was hit about four times altogether. He got into the trench with us. He was killed coming back.'

'Are you certain?' Twining's face looked anxious and concerned and incredibly clean.

'I saw him,' I said.

Twining made a note on a sheet of paper and looked up again. 'Appleby? Mr Appleby?'

'Wounded,' Murray said. 'He's all right, I think.'

'Mr Blackett?'

'Dead.' The shout came from somewhere along the line. 'I saw him go down.'

'Mr Welch?'

There was silence. No one knew what had happened to Welch. One minute he'd been there, the next he'd vanished.

And so it went on.

'Sergeant-Major Bold?'

I found I couldn't answer at first for the lump in my throat.

'He's dead,' I said in the end. 'He got in. Naturally.'

'Catchpole? Is he here? He's been told to report back with Spring and Mason. Their commissions are through.'

'They're dead,' I said bitterly. 'The lot of them. The whole bloody lot.'

'What happened?'

'The usual. Spring was the first to go. Catchpole was hit by a shell.'

'What about Mason?'

'They crucified him,' I said.

Twining stared at me, as though he were wondering what to say, then he sighed and went on:

'Cuthbert?'

Name after name was called. In some cases, no particulars were available. No one knew what had happened to Tim Williams. After all the effort he'd made to keep up with us, he seemed to have disappeared off the face of the earth, like Dicehart and young Welch. Then some name came up that belonged to someone whose disappearance could be vouched for, and heads craned to see the speaker, sympathy focusing on one spot as the meagre details were given, though in truth they were impressive enough in most cases.

'I saw him, sir! The poor bastard was blown to bits. There were about four of them caught by the same shell.'

Everybody seemed anxious to restrain their feelings and show no sign of sorrow. Everybody seemed to be gentle just then, keeping their feelings to themselves as though by some tacit understanding they might help in this way. The camp details stood around, clean, respectable men, staring with awe at the huddle of savages that we'd become with our haggard filthy appearance and our bitter pitiless faces.

'Haddo?' Twining went on.

'Wounded,' I said, choking over the word. 'We brought him in.'

'Badly? Will he live?'

I don't know what was in my face, but Twining took one look at me and didn't press the question.

'Hardacre?' he said hurriedly.

'Dead.'

'Lott?'

'Dead.'

'Manderson, T.?'

'Dead.'

'Manderson, W.?'

'Dead.'

It went on like that until Twining gave it up. He turned to Bickerstaff and the brigadier, his eyes appealing, and the brigadier signed to him to stop.

Then I noticed that some of the men with me had sunk to the ground and were already asleep. I found myself leaning on Eph's rifle, staring stupidly at the men who slept around me, my eyelids drooping with maddening insistence.

It didn't occur to me to lie down until someone pushed me into a bed of fern. There were flowers among the fern and my last thought was a dull wonder that there could still be beauty in the world.

6

More than five hundred thousand of Kitchener's men fell in the unspeakable agony of the Somme before the battle finally withered and died in the winter mud. Five hundred thousand – fourteen thousand that first morning in front of Serre alone, where the casualties were the heaviest of the whole day.

The Germans lost another five hundred thousand. A million men altogether. A generation of children without fathers. A generation of women without husbands. A quarter of a century of fumbling politics that let Hitler start it all again twenty years later because all that was finest in physique and intelligence and courage, the finest in any army we'd ever put into the field, died there on the Somme. The *In Memoriam* notices started at once in the newspapers and went on for a quarter of a century and even after another war had swept across the world.

Lloyd George called it 'a disastrous loss of the finest manhood in the United Kingdom', and he should have known. And just for a few miles of tortured ground that was no good to anybody. We never did get Serre, and by Christmas the mud was so deep we couldn't have advanced if we'd wanted to and neither side bothered to put up wire because we knew nobody could move for the bog.

Battalions, brigades, divisions went into the fight, were worn down swiftly and soaked into the ground. Growing older and tougher and cannier, we shivered in those trenches we captured one at a time, throughout the whole winter. The papers told us we'd won a major victory, and we stared open-mouthed and laughed out loud. They even tried to tell us July 1st was a victory.

It was the graveyard of Kitchener's Army. It was probably the biggest disaster to British arms since Hastings. Nearly sixty thousand men fell on that day alone and still lay there in their rows when winter came. More young men from our city died on July 1st, 1916, than on any other day before or since, and the regimental history contained a virtual blank because there weren't enough of us left to piece anything coherent together. Bold had been wrong. We'd been good enough all right in spite of our inexperience. But we couldn't cope with the futile staff work that never gave anybody a chance to show anything but courage. A vast wonder of valour was wasted because there wasn't a hope right from the beginning, and the only excuse they could think of was to blame it on our lack of know-how and to try to make out we'd had a jolly successful day.

It wasn't a rout or a retreat, and our losses didn't include prisoners. The sixty thousand we lost on July 1st were almost all dead or wounded, and they nearly all fell in the first few minutes, for an unrealistic plan that, in the light of later years, never had a chance of succeeding. It took seven days for the last of the wounded and the stragglers to come in, but even then there weren't enough of us left to re-form the battalion and it just ceased to exist. They offered most of the survivors commissions and drafted us to other battalions, assuming, I suppose, that we'd learned something about war after July 1st.

More and more men came up and the guns never stopped firing. The skeletons of the dead lay in rows, huddled in the hollows and heaped against the wire until the Germans retreated the following spring. All through the autumn, the fighting went on and it never seemed to be anybody's concern to bury them. The generals were always too busy with new plans, never losing heart as they looked for fresh places to butt their heads against.

Never for a moment, night or day, until the end of the year, in rain, frost, sleet or sun, did the artillery cease to thunder or the machine gun bullets stop along the broken trenches and in the ruined fields and villages, with their scattered graves marked by rusting helmets, wooden crosses or bayoneted rifles.

They say we smashed the old German Army there on the Somme, but we smashed something else too. The faith we'd had found its grave there in the knuckly hills and valleys round the Ancre. The men who followed us into the long arc of wretchedness until 1918 grew younger and older all the time as conscription caught up with them, none of them half the men they were on July 1st. Never again was the spirit or the quality so high. After the Somme, the French sneered at the British, and the British at the French, and the Australians and Americans at both. Last sons were called up and the conscripts went forward like driven sheep. I never heard them singing again as I heard them that summer of 1916.

There was never an enquiry into the Somme. Nobody seemed to mind that all the fine prophecies of the generals were wrong. After Gallipoli, many people got the sack, many of them people who'd had no share of the blame. But after the Somme, it went on just as it had gone on before.

God knows who had to answer for Serre and Gommecourt, but I noticed nobody seemed to get the push.

I never fancied going back, in spite of the 'Tours of the Battlefields' that they organised in the 'twenties. I felt I'd left a bit of me behind, there in front of Serre. Everything that seemed to belong to my youth was there.

I met the few who were left from time to time, growing a little older every year: Oakley, blind and helpless and unable to the end of his life to do much for himself; Barraclough, limping and one-legged; Appleby; Murray, as mad-headed as ever and never changing; Tom Creak; and Henny Cuthbert, his face twisted by a scar that never seemed to grow less livid.

I'd probably never have gone back, except that years later I chanced to pass through Amiens by car on the way to Calais and was persuaded at last to pay a visit.

At the Hotel Centrale-Anzac near the Place Gambetta, I found an Australian who'd fought at Villers-Bretonneux near the river and had finally married a Belgian girl he'd met. He'd never been home and when he was asked he'd show people the way around. He lent me a map with all the regiments marked on it and all the cemeteries. Fricourt, Mametz, Contalmaison, Serre, Hamel, Thiepval. The words come out of the lines and patches of colour on the old linen-backed paper as if all other names were trivial by comparison.

The little graveyards lie by the roadside all the way from Gommecourt to Maricourt and beyond, British and French and German, one after the other, in neat little plots full of shrubs and flowers that are curiously not saddening because they're so quiet and the Somme these days doesn't see much traffic. The trees have grown again round Serre and Gommecourt, and Delville Wood's come up again and the copses are back once more round Beaumont Hamel and Thiepval, full of ghosts and the hint of those old nostalgic songs. The Golden Virgin on the top of the Basilica in Albert is holding her Child up to the sky again and the place looks as dull as it must have done before.

The countryside hasn't altered much. The water-carts and the flies still hang round the water-taps in Bos and Rippy, and the women are still the same sturdy shrewd peasant stock who lead those great plodding Percherons because they still haven't got around to using tractors much. The white chalk dust still lays over the grass verges and among the moonpennies and poppies along the Serre Road, and the smell's still the smell of horse dung and burning vegetation. There are the same lush hedgerows and nettles in the deep damp fields down by the Ancre, and the same big double row of poplars stands on either side of the road just outside Aveluy, backed up by buttercups and dandelions and clover and the long, long grass among the pollards and willows.

I drove up the Serre Road and found the City Battalion memorial. You can see from the position of the little cemeteries the route we took and how far we got.

I stood on the green slope of a field where a row of Picard men and women were hoeing and realised it must have been somewhere near that tangled front trench of the Germans that we reached. Somewhere here, I thought, must have been where Bold fell, and even across the years I could still see him sitting there, unafraid, his eyes undismayed, as he waited for death to come to him. Somewhere near here, I kept thinking, was where we found Locky, and somewhere near here the shell-hole where I crouched with Catchpole, and the spot where I stayed all day in the sunshine with the bodies of Eph and the Mandys.

Down in that little hollow just behind the crest where the machine guns caught us, I found a small cemetery and saw all their names again on the neat headstones – Colonel Pine and his brother, Ashton, Blackett, Mason, the Mandersons and Eph Lott, and Hardacre and Locky and Arnold Holroyd. Some of them, like Spring and Tim Williams and Dicehart and Welch and Catchpole, were missing and I suppose they lay in those little plots that were marked simply *An Unknown British Soldier*. They wore their names instead on that red brick and stone monstrosity, like a cross between Waterloo Bridge and the Albert Memorial, that they erected on Thiepval Ridge, the memorial to the seventy-four thousand who fell on the Somme and have no known grave. It was there I found that fine, quiet, brave man's, Patrick Bold's.

As I stood and looked along the rows of silent graves, I found that memory was being kind as usual. I could only remember the laughter and the singing, and the immense pride we had in ourselves, and things like Ashton's sad face and gentle courage, and the colonel with his stammer and his eye-patch, giving me three stripes I didn't want; and Catchpole, and that service he held at Blackmires that had brought us round when we'd been in the depths of despair; and Mason's gaiety, and Locky's dry, never-failing humour; and Eph's riotous raucousness; and the harsh, unswerving honour of Bold.

The memory was poignant, a memory of trial and sacrifice, but somehow one of great beauty, a memory of the agonies and rejoicings of hearts caught by a sense of sacrifice. Nothing that they'd done, neither extravagance nor meanness nor selfishness, nothing could touch that frail immortal glory.

Including those like Tim Williams and the adjutant who'd sneaked up to join the battalion, seven hundred and ninety-five men from the battalion went into action that hot July morning and, out of them, seventy-eight – two sergeants among them and not a single officer – finally found their way unwounded to the orchard at Bos. Seven hundred and seventeen we lost in those three or four hours between seven-thirty and midday when the field finally emptied of human life, and of these most vanished from the earth in the first ten minutes of the battle.

That was what we joined up for. That was why we endured that bleak winter at Blackmires and the heat of Egypt, why we ate that awful food they served us and went through all those exercises again and again and again until we hated them, why we sang and sang and still went on singing, why the bands played and we cheered on the slightest excuse, why we endured and kept faith and never lost our first impassioned belief in victory, why we went on until the clamour of battle obscured the sky and destroyed the thousands of separate existences in a mere matter of minutes. Two years in the making. Ten minutes in the destroying. That was our history.

Historical Note

Introduction

Although a work of fiction, John Harris's book could just as easily be factual, relating the story of a recruit into the Sheffield City Battalion – the 'Sheffield Pals' – and reaching its climax with the 1st July attack on Serre.

In common with other industrial towns in the north of England, Sheffield was quick to form its own 'Pals' battalion in the early weeks of the First World War. On 1st July 1916, the Sheffield City Battalion fought alongside the Accrington Pals in the heroic but hopeless attempt to capture the heavily fortified village of Serre. In the memorable words of John Harris: 'Two years in the making. Ten minutes in the destroying. That was our history.'

The Making
Within a month of Britain's declaration of war against Germany on 4th August 1914, the Duke of Norfolk and Sir George Franklin presented themselves at the War Office to propose the formation of a Sheffield battalion recruited from both university

and commercial men. The proposal was readily accepted and on 10th September enlistment began at the Corn Exchange for the Sheffield City Battalion, the 12th (Service) Battalion York & Lancaster Regiment.

The heady atmosphere of the time was caught in placards reading TO BERLIN – VIA CORN EXCHANGE. It took little time for the battalion to reach its full complement, with between 900 and 1000 men being recruited in just two days. The recruits came from all walks of life; in *History of the 12th (Service) Battalion, York & Lancaster Regiment* (1920), Richard Sparling recalled there being '£500-a-year business men, stockbrokers, engineers, chemists, metallurgical experts, university and public school men, medical students, journalists, schoolmasters, craftsmen, shop assistants, secretaries, and all sorts of clerks'.

The battalion's early instructions in drill took place at Bramhall Lane, the famous home of Sheffield United Cricket and Football Club. Other grounds had to be found before long, as the Club's directors took exception to the loss of grass! On Saturday 5th December – a miserably cold and wet day – the battalion of 1,131 officers and men left Sheffield for Redmires Camp, a windswept camping ground a few miles west of the city. The battalion trained at Redmires for just over five months, a period which saw it placed in the 94th Brigade (31st Division) alongside the 13th and 14th York & Lancasters (1st and 2nd Barnsley Pals) and the 11th East Lancashires (Accrington Pals).

Preparation for active service continued throughout 1915 with spells at Penkridge Bank Camp near Rugeley, Ripon – where training in small arms fire began in earnest – and Hurdcott Camp near Salisbury. On 28 September, Lt. Col. J. A. Crosthwaite, formerly of the Durham Light Infantry, assumed command. On 20 December 1915, the battalion embarked on HMT Nestor at Devonport for Alexandria.

The 31st Division had been assigned to Egypt to defend the Suez Canal against the threat of an attack by the Turkish Army. In the event, the threat of attack soon evaporated and the 31st was reassigned to take part in the planned summer offensive on the Somme. On 10th March 1916, the Sheffield battalion embarked on HMT Briton at Port Said for the five-day voyage to the French port of Marseilles. Eighteen days after arriving in France, the battalion took over a stretch of the front line opposite the fortified hilltop village of Serre.

The Destroying

The weeks preceding the offensive were by no means quiet. The battalion suffered its first fatal casualty as soon as 4th April when Pte. Alexander McKenzie was killed by a rifle grenade. On the night of 15/16 May, fifteen were killed and forty-five wounded as the Germans mounted a trench raid under cover of an artillery bombardment of such an intensity that in places the front line was practically levelled. Meanwhile, preparations for the offensive continued and by early June the battalions of 94th Brigade were practising the attack on Serre. The Sheffield City Battalion would have the dubious honour of being at the extreme left of the fifteen-mile British offensive front that stretched south from Serre to Maricourt.

On Saturday 24th June, the British artillery opened a bombardment that over a five-day period was intended to destroy the German defenses completely. Each night the battalion sent out raiding and wire-examining parties; ominously, the German wire was found to be incompletely cut. On 28th June, word was received that the attack would be postponed for two days because of the poor weather. The new time for the start of the offensive was 7.30am on Saturday 1st July.

The day before the offensive began badly with the news that Lt-Col. Crosthwaite was seriously ill, necessitating his hurried replacement by Major Plackett. At 3.45am on 1st July, the battalion was in position in the assembly trenches, finding them already in an atrocious condition from German shellfire. Patrols from the 4th and 7th Companies of the 169th (8th Baden) Infantry Regiment defending Serre noted the build-up. With the appearance of daylight at 4.05am, German artillery began to shell the British front line.

At 7.20am the first wave of the battalion moved a hundred yards into No Man's Land and lay flat on the ground as the brigade mortar battery and divisional artillery placed a final hurricane bombardment over the German front line. A few minutes later – with the British front line coming under an intense counter-barrage – the second wave took up position thirty yards behind the first.

At 7.30am the bombardment lifted from the German front line. All four waves rose, took a moment to align themselves, then advanced steadily towards the German lines into a devastating hail of machine gun bullets and shellfire. An ineffective smoke screen exposed the battalion to machine gun fire from the left as well as from ahead. The third and fourth waves, caught on the opposite side of the valley, were reduced to half strength before even reaching No Man's Land. On the left of the battalion front, long stretches of barbed wire had been left uncut. Men brought to a halt in front of the inpenetrable entanglements were reduced to firing vainly through the wire to the German lines beyond. Only on the right of the attack were a few men somehow able to force their way into the German trenches. Some found themselves alone and managed to return to the British lines. Others were never heard of again.

Within minutes it was as if the battalion had been wiped off the face of the earth. Cpl. Signaller Outram recalled that as far as the eye could see, the last two men left standing on the battlefield were himself and another signaller, A. Brammer. They signalled to each other. Outram turned his head for a moment, and when he looked back Brammer had gone.

On the right of the Sheffield City Battalion, the Accrington Pals made greater inroads into the German trenches but were unable to hold on to the hard-won gains. The battle for Serre was lost.

The Aftermath

The remnants of the battalion were taken out of the line in the evening of 3rd July, having lost 513 officers and men killed, wounded or missing; a further seventy-five were slightly wounded.

Throughout the long months of the Battle of the Somme, Serre remained uncaptured, falling into British hands only after the German withdrawal to the Hindenburg Line in February 1917.

Although the battalion was gradually returned to strength, the 'Pals' character was unrecoverable. During the harsh winter months of 1916-17, an almost unbelievable 887 officers and men of the battalion were evacuated to hospital. For two spells in May 1917 at Arras, the battalion defended the vital Windmill spur in the Gavrelle sector, suffering 143 casualties, before playing a successful part in the attack at Oppy-Gavrelle on 28th June. The battalion was again to suffer in German gas attacks at Vimy Ridge in August and September 1917. Finally, in the early weeks of 1918, the weakened battalion was forced to disband.

After the war, Sheffield placed a memorial in the village of Serre to the men of the City Battalion who had fallen in the attack of 1st July 1916. In 1936, the Sheffield Memorial Park was opened on the site of the British lines below Serre. Sheffield had served the memory of its boys well.

Andrew Jackson is the author of Accrington's Pals: The Full Story *(Pen & Sword, 2013).*